THE QUEEN OF SUGAR HILL

ALSO BY ReSHONDA TATE

Miss Pearly's Girls
A Little Bit of Karma
The Stolen Daughter
The Book in Room 316
Seeking Sarah
The Perfect Mistress
Mama's Boy
Finding Amos (with Bernice L. McFadden and J. D. Mason)
What's Done in the Dark
A Family Affair
The Secret She Kept
Say Amen, Again
A Good Man Is Hard to Find
Holy Rollers
The Devil Is a Lie
Can I Get a Witness?
The Pastor's Wife
Everybody Say Amen
I Know I've Been Changed
Let the Church Say Amen
My Brother's Keeper

WITH VICTORIA CHRISTOPHER MURRAY

Saints & Sinners
Friends & Foes
Fortune & Fame
Pay Day
It Should've Been Me
A Blessing & a Curse
If Only for One Night

ANTHOLOGIES

The Motherhood Diaries 2
The Motherhood Diaries
Have a Little Faith
Four Degrees of Heat
Proverbs for the People

NONFICTION

Help! I've Turned into My Mother

POETRY

Something to Say

TEEN FICTION

Eye Candy
Boy Trouble
Truth or Dare
Real As It Gets
You Don't Know Me Like That
Rumor Central
Drama Queens
Caught Up in the Drama
Friends 'Til the End
Fair-Weather Friends
Getting Even
With Friends Like These
Blessings in Disguise
Nothing But Drama

A Novel of
HATTIE
McDANIEL

THE QUEEN OF SUGAR HILL

ReSHONDA TATE

wm
WILLIAM MORROW
An Imprint of HarperCollins*Publishers*

This book is a work of fiction. References to real people, events, establishments, organizations, or locales are intended only to provide a sense of authenticity, and are used fictitiously. All other characters, and all incidents and dialogue, are drawn from the author's imagination and are not to be construed as real.

HarperCollins books may be purchased for educational, business, or sales promotional use. For information, please email the Special Markets Department at SPsales@harpercollins.com.

FIRST EDITION

Designed by Leah Carlson-Stanisic

Library of Congress Cataloging-in-Publication Data has been applied for.

ISBN 978-0-06-329107-2

23 24 25 26 27 LBC 5 4 3 2 1

For my grandmother, Pearley,
who introduced me to Hattie and dared me to dream like her

What dreams we have and how they fly
Like rosy clouds across the sky;
Of wealth, of fame, of sure success,
Of love that comes to cheer and bless;
And how they wither, how they fade,
The waning wealth, the jilting jade—
The fame that for a moment gleams,
Then flies forever,—dreams, ah—dreams!

—PAUL LAURENCE DUNBAR

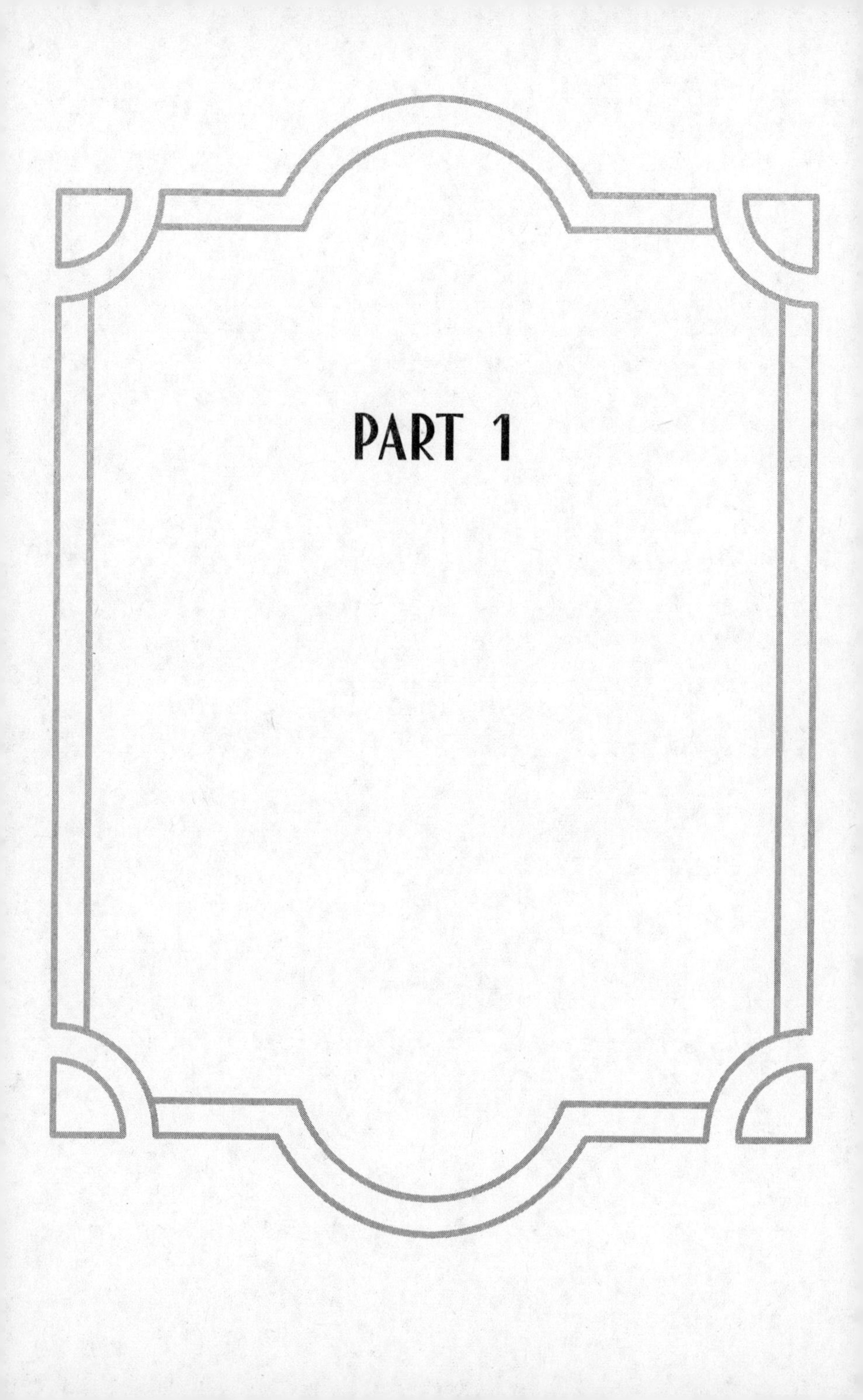

PART 1

HEDDA HOPPER'S HOLLYWOOD

February 29, 1940

"Hello, everybody, Hedda Hopper reporting to you from Hollywood, that fabulous place where everyone wants to live but seldom does. Everybody, look over my shoulder as I write my column. We'll have news about famous people. Okay? Let's go.

"It's Academy Awards time. Some of the greats are vying for that coveted statue . . . from Hollywood heartthrob Clark Gable . . . to Judy Garland to Robert Donat. But all eyes are on Hattie McDaniel. Miss McDaniel, a Negress, is up for best supporting actress, the first member of her race to be so honored. I was on the scene as Miss McDaniel, full of smiles and gardenias and bosom, trundled into the venue.

"I believe everyone is delighted that Miss McDaniel, who gave such a superb performance as Mammy in Gone with the Wind, *is up for an Academy Award. Will she or won't she make history tonight? The world is watching . . ."*

CHAPTER 1

February 1940

If my mama could see me now . . .

I was a long way from the one-room, wood-frame shack in Wichita, Kansas, where I was always singing a spin on a Negro spiritual or dancing the cakewalk with my three siblings. That's what we used to do to take our minds off the rumblings in our stomachs. Gone was the indescribable hunger I had back then, when I lived in a home haunted by my parents' memories of how they'd escaped slavery and their never-ending quest to give us a better life. I'd come into the world malnourished and destitute and now—forty-six years later—my story was about to be rewritten.

I pushed aside thoughts of where I'd been—and focused on where I now was, inside the sprawling ballroom of the Cocoanut Grove club, basking in the atmosphere of the black tie Academy Awards dinner. I was overwhelmed by the smell of rose, jasmine, and most of all vanilla Chanel No. 5, the perfume every glamour girl in the room was wearing.

The large ballroom was flanked by massive columns ornamented with white lilies cascading from the top. Gauzy beige curtains draped from the ceiling. Negro waiters in white jackets flowed back and forth with bottles of Lanson champagne and silver service trays perched over their shoulders. They twisted and turned like Busby Berkeley dancers through the crowded tables filled with Hollywood royalty—twelve hundred movers and shakers and their guests. All white. I was the only colored actor in the room.

I strained to get a glimpse of my costars from *Gone with the Wind*.

We were up for eleven awards, so they had prime seating near the stage. Their tables were round and held anywhere from ten to twenty-four people. I'd been led to the very back of the room, just outside the double doors leading to the kitchen. There was seating only for three here. A grudging, mean little message meant just for me: *Don't be too full of yourself. Never ever take up too much space.*

"Why is she here?" someone muttered from the table across from me. I recognized the woman as a character actress from a silent movie. I wanted to shout, *I deserve to be here!* but I nodded pleasantly at her.

Even those who tossed passive smiles my way didn't want me here. It was one thing to share a scene with them. There, I was subservient. But here, I was on their level—even if I was seated at the very back of the room.

The sounds of the orchestra filled the club. The saxophones were playing, the show was beginning. Young Bob Hope was a good choice as host; he easily bantered and wisecracked his way through the program. Now it was eleven thirty and with all the bubbly and cigarette smoke in the air, my heart was pounding. But then it turned into a full-on race when Fay Bainter walked to the podium.

She'd won best supporting actress for her performance as Aunt Belle Massey in *Jezebel* last year and was therefore presenting this year. And since that was the category I was nominated in, I strained to commit every word she uttered to memory.

"I'm really especially happy that I'm chosen to present this particular plaque," Fay began. I could hear the smile in her voice even if she was so far away I couldn't clearly see her expression.

"To me, it seems more than just a plaque of gold," Fay continued. "It opens the doors of this room, moves back the walls, and enables us to embrace the whole of America, an America that we love . . ."

I scooted to the edge of my seat as her next words tumbled out.

". . . I present the Academy Award for the Best Performance of an Actress in a Supporting Role during 1939 to Hattie McDaniel."

I'd won! I'd known I won, but hearing it made it real.

Ferdinando, my very suitable date for the night, squeezed my hand and reached to help me slip off my white cropped ermine jacket. He was impeccably dressed, with an ankle-length black coat, slacks, and a white silk pocket square. As handsome as Ferdinando was, he was just a friend who often escorted me to events.

My agent, Mr. Meiklejohn, was clapping as if his name had just been called; there was no doubt he understood the magnitude of this moment. He'd given up his seat in the front to sit with me. He'd always looked me right in the eye and treated me with respect. He was one of the only white agents to represent colored studio actors in Hollywood. In fact, I was his sole colored actor. Now he was smiling at me with joy.

I stood as applause filled the room inside the Ambassador Hotel. As I stepped away from the table, I gave silent thanks to Ruby Berkley Goodwin. Not only was Ruby my dearest friend, a wickedly funny, smart-wise woman who knew how to cut me down to size, she was the perfect secretary. She'd talked me into this designer crepe turquoise gown and then efficiently had it customized for me. This dress, with its long sleeves, cropped jacket, tailored bodice, and cummerbund, was the perfect selection to make history in.

I adjusted the gardenias and headband sitting atop my head, lifted my dress, and walked around the table next to me that was storing all the Oscar statues. I couldn't help but notice that the applause was tepid when Fay first announced my name, though it got louder as I approached the stage. I'm sure most people expected my fellow actress in *Gone with the Wind* Olivia de Havilland to win. Her performance as Melanie Hamilton, the sad, strong, loving wife of the rather drippy Ashley Wilkes, had been heralded in all the movie magazines as groundbreaking and heartwarming.

We'd both been nominated for best supporting actress, but my nomination as Mammy was the first time a colored woman had ever been nominated for this prestigious award.

That's why no one expected me to win—except me.

I knew long before the *Los Angeles Times* leaked the list of winners just before the ceremony. I knew I'd delivered a stellar performance in the role I'd fought so hard to get. As Mammy, I'd squealed and yanked on Vivien Leigh's corset so hard that she and I both nearly vomited. I knew the previous director, George Cukor, didn't want me because he thought I "lacked dignity," so I had something to prove. I channeled my thirty-one years of stage and theater experience to deliver a solid, lovable performance.

Since the awards part of the event started at eleven P.M., after the banquet dinner, the academy gave the winners to the newspapers so they could get the papers out on the street by midnight. But the *LA Times* broke the embargo and published the names of most of the winners in an early edition before the banquet began. So almost everyone arriving at the Cocoanut Grove, which was the popular nightclub nestled inside the Ambassador Hotel, already knew *Gone with the Wind* would sweep the awards. Vivien would pick up the Oscar for her portrayal of Scarlett O'Hara and I won for Mammy. Though we had the list of winners, everyone was reserved until the winners were actually announced—just in case. But with or without the *Times*, my heart knew the truth. I had won.

And now that it was official, I wasn't about to let anyone, or anything, steal my joy.

I held my head high and quickened my pace since it seemed like the entire room was waiting on me as I maneuvered my five-foot-two frame down the narrow aisles and through the maze of tables covered with white linen. The Who's Who of Hollywood was here, dressed in the finest formal wear—floor-length colorful satin gowns with long Vs in front and tuxedos with tapered collars and custom cuts. I nodded at Olivia, who looked like she was fighting back tears, yet still tepidly clapping. We'd been cordial with each other on set, but this was her first nomination and, history be damned, I knew she wanted to win.

I smiled at Vivien in her stunning white Irene Lentz fitted dress and white headwrap, her cigarette dangling from her hand. She returned my smile, though it never quite reached her eyes as she was close to Olivia and I'm sure she had been hoping for her friend to win. The two men sitting beside Vivien, Laurence Olivier and some man I didn't know, didn't bother with pretenses as they sat stoically without clapping.

I gave my friend Clark Gable a special smile and a nod. Outside of my girlfriends, Clark was my dearest friend, and the only white man with such a distinction. He was the only white person who knew me behind the smile.

Tonight, Clark was dapper in a midnight-blue shawl-collared tuxedo jacket and boutonniere. His tapered mustache hugged his upper lip. His wife, Carole, was grinning like a seven-year-old who had just been given a puppy, and in her stunning purple silk gown, she glowed with celebration. Carole and Clark were in sync with their excitement. Really, they were in sync with everything. It was a miracle they'd found this kind of happiness in a town notorious for dismantling marriages.

On the other side of Clark, my producer David O. Selznick sat grinning hard. My win was a win for him as well. Though it had taken some convincing to get him to nominate me, his expression said he was glad that he had. As one of the top producers in Hollywood, he usually got what he wanted without effort, but he'd had to pull strings to get me into the Ambassador since the hotel had a no-coloreds policy. My win made his fight worthwhile.

I felt beads of moisture dampen my forehead as I marched toward the stage. Was it the journey across the room or my jubilant nerves?

I ignored the sour expressions to my right, refused to be bothered by the people on my left who wouldn't make eye contact with me, and strutted with my head held high. Negro actors had been invited into the Hollywood room—as servants and slaves, but as my friend

Langston Hughes always said, we were never given a seat at the table. Tonight, I was claiming my seat.

The applause was still going as I neared the stage and had audibly picked up, then suddenly, the music stopped. In the three minutes it had taken me to walk from my seat at the back of the room, the orchestra music had ended.

But that wasn't going to steal my joy either.

I had been banned from the film's Atlanta premiere just this past December, where more than a million people lined the streets of downtown Atlanta to celebrate *Gone with the Wind*'s release. So this was redemption. This was validation of my more than thirty years of blood, sweat, and entertaining—the triumph that made my tragedies worthwhile. All the rejections because I was too dark, too fat, too whatever. All the chances I was never given meant nothing tonight. I'd accomplished something 90 percent of the people in this room could only dream of—I'd won an Academy Award.

From the first time I'd ever won an award, back in the sixth grade at 24th Street School in Denver, I'd been treated as less than. Back then, despite being the best performer, I couldn't be recognized along with my friends because of the color of my skin. Now, not only was I on equal footing, dare I say, I was leaps and bounds ahead of my counterparts.

The NAACP protestors outside the hotel, the incorrigible security at the front who hesitated before letting me into the Cocoanut Grove tonight, the attendees who held their noses up in an air of superiority, insulted that they had to share a space with me. None of that was going to steal my joy either.

I made my way up the steps. It wasn't lost on me that the usher didn't extend his hand to help me up the stairs like he did the other winners. But at this moment, my eyes were focused on the small gold award Fay was extending toward me. I wrapped my hand around it, my heart swelling with pride. Yet, as proud as I was of this achievement, this was too big a moment for my personal backslapping. I wanted this occasion to inspire Negro youth for many years to come.

I took my spot in front of the podium, then reached in my pocket for the acceptance speech that Mr. Selznick and his team had crafted for me. But just as my fingertips touched the piece of paper, I froze. I knew the marketing team had put much time and thought into my speech, but at this moment, I wanted to speak from the heart.

"Academy of Motion Picture Arts and Sciences," I began as I pulled my empty hand back, "fellow members of the motion picture industry, and honored guests. This is one of the happiest moments of my life, and I want to thank each one of you who had a part in selecting me for one of the awards, for your kindness. It has made me feel very, very humble; and I shall always hold it as a beacon for anything that I may be able to do in the future." I paused as tears filled my eyes. I inhaled, then continued. "I sincerely hope I shall always be a credit to my race and to the motion picture industry. My heart is too full to tell you just how I feel, and may I say thank you."

This occasion was momentous, but I did not want to look like a blubbering fool. I was representing my race and I needed to do so with dignity. So I simply dabbed my eyes and added, "And God bless you," before exiting the stage.

I was so overcome with emotion that I forgot to thank Mr. Selznick, the director, my costars, and everyone else. Well, at least I'd left everyone out, I consoled myself. No one's feelings would be hurt.

When I reached the bottom of the stairs, I encountered the brightest grin, eyes filled with genuine happiness, and the loudest applause in the room.

"I told you that you were a shoo-in!" Clark whispered as I approached his table. He had stood to applaud me as I exited the podium.

I wanted more than anything to throw my arms around my friend's neck and tell him he was right. Let him know that it was his faith, his encouragement, and his support that had led me here today. But knowing that all eyes were on me, I did the only proper thing.

"You sure did, Mr. Gable," I said with a slight nod of the head.

His smile faded slightly. Clark hated when I called him Mr. Gable. And generally, I didn't. But my spirits were too high to mess it up by creating conflict because I called my dear friend by his first name in mixed company.

However, whatever apprehensions I was feeling, Clark was not. He reached out and pulled me into a big bear hug, and I swear, the gasps were audible. First Lady Eleanor Roosevelt and civil rights leader and educator Mary McLeod Bethune had shocked the world a few years ago with the first public display of interracial affection when they shook hands, but that was still frowned upon, especially in Hollywood. But as usual, Clark didn't care. He'd solidified his place as the King of Hollywood and that's why it shouldn't have surprised me when he said, "If I want to celebrate my friend, then I'm going to celebrate my friend."

I fought the urge to hug him back—and kept my arms by my sides, though I rejoiced inside.

As he released me, I swallowed the lump in my throat, ignored the shocked stares, and then returned to my seat as the program continued.

I hugged my award tightly and wiped the tear trickling down my cheek. After years of struggling to make it, this was the beginning of something new.

CHAPTER 2

February 1940

The entire *Gone with the Wind* cast was ready to celebrate this phenomenal night. We'd left the Cocoanut Grove via a motorcade of limos and were dropped off in front of Ciro's, a new nightclub that had just opened on Sunset Boulevard. We'd won a total of eight Academy Awards. And we all knew that history had been made by this movie, which had been the talk of Tinseltown since we started filming in December of 1938. Clark had lost his best actor nod to Robert Donat, who starred in *Goodbye, Mr. Chips*, a move that had shocked all of Hollywood. But Clark was still a good sport and came out to celebrate.

Ferdinando had retired for the evening as he was a schoolteacher and had to work in the morning. Though he enjoyed accompanying me on dates, I think the pomp and circumstance of celebrity life was a bit intimidating tonight. I wished that he had his arm around my shoulders now, however; it had been a long time since I'd had the support of a good man. Everyone else was here with their significant others—Vivien was with Laurence Olivier, Clark was with Carole, Olivia with Jock Whitney, and the director, Victor Fleming, was with his wife, Lucille. Mr. Selznick and his wife, Irene, had gone home as she was very upset. She'd missed the first part of the ceremony because he'd forgotten her at home when he and his guests climbed into the limo after the pre-Oscar dinner at his house. I hoped for Mr. Selznick's sake that Irene would forgive him.

The night breeze sent a slight shiver up my arms and I pulled my coat closed as I watched the photographer corral everyone for photos. Everyone except me, of course.

"Miss Leigh, look this way, please," the photographer said to Vivien. She was truly the star of the century. With her incandescent blue eyes, her flirtatious manner, and her many long-term love affairs, there was no one who had generated more publicity than this woman. She'd made her mark on the stage, but her command of the camera was why so many movie execs overlooked what they called her boorish behavior.

Mr. Selznick had ginned up her reputation even higher by daringly casting her as Scarlett O'Hara. Yes, the most Southern and American of roles went to a British actress. But there was no denying Vivien *was* Scarlett. At twenty-six years old she knew exactly how to manipulate a man just the way Scarlett had in the *Gone with the Wind* novel. And it was obvious by the way she was giggling as Laurence, a commanding, strikingly handsome British actor, whispered in her ear. They both were married to other people but clearly had no qualms feeding into the rumors that they were dating.

All the winners were clustered together in a beaming pack, posing with their awards—and I stood off to the side watching.

I was here. I had won. But I was no fool. If I had been photographed with the rest of the cast out partying, there would have been trouble. The photographer had even made it clear when he whispered, "This is for the mainstream papers, so . . ."

I'd nodded my understanding of the unspoken completion of his sentence and stepped back.

"Fabulous, Miss Olivia, just gorgeous," the photographer sang as he snapped away.

Images of the printed program for the movie premiere flashed through my mind. When *Gone with the Wind* opened in Atlanta, I was not only forbidden from attending the premiere, but my photo was even removed from the programs distributed there.

Watching my costars being photographed again, without me, brought that painful memory roaring back.

A part of me was praying that someone—anyone—would motion for me to join them in the picture. I was used to being excluded, but I was supposed to be a part of this moment. I had earned it. I locked eyes with Clark, and I could tell he wanted to say something. But I immediately shook my head.

"Okay, that's enough," Clark said, walking away before the photographer could protest. "Let's get inside and celebrate."

He grabbed Carole's hand and headed toward the walkway. Vivien and Laurence followed.

"Hattie, would you come on? She won an Oscar and now is making everyone wait for her," Olivia joked when I didn't move. Or at least I thought she was joking. Olivia had made no secret how bad she wanted to win, so I couldn't be sure if her comment was veiled in envy.

All of us were carrying our Oscars. I thought it was rather presumptuous of us to take our awards into the club, but I didn't want to be the outlier of the group.

"She's simply beside herself with her little plaque," Jock said.

"There's nothing *little* about that award. How many do you have?" Clark said, coming to my defense.

I could tell by the way Olivia's lips tightened; his words didn't sit well with her. Especially since neither she nor Jock had ever won an Oscar.

"Now, now, you know Clark is sensitive about his Hattie," Vivien said. She draped her arm through Laurence's and bounced toward the front door. Clark flashed a smile at me. Since we'd met in 1935 on the set of *China Seas*, Clark had been my biggest cheerleader. Of course, he was starring and I was once again uncredited, but we'd immediately clicked. He was a practical joker and I appreciated his sense of humor, so despite our differences, we'd become instant friends.

"Come on, we're not letting anything spoil our night," he said, leading our group forward.

I quickly jumped behind my friends as we headed toward the club's entrance, where the line to get in snaked out the door and down the walkway. But we were not only Hollywood stars. Tonight we were Oscar winners, so we glided toward the front, still floating from our historic win.

I clutched the plaque to my chest, repeated a quick prayer of thanks, and followed my friends toward the door.

"Mr. Gable, such a pleasure," said the burly, brown-haired man in a three-piece suit at the front door. His grin was wide as he enthusiastically shook Clark's hand. "I'm a big fan."

"Why, thank you . . ."

"Burke. I'm the manager here." Given his three-hundred-pound frame, I definitely thought he would've been security.

"Burke," Clark replied. "We're excited to celebrate at your fine establishment. We want a table in your VIP section, of course."

Burke shifted his weight from one foot to the other, his smile slightly fading as his eyes swept over Clark's shoulder to me. He glanced at me as most white men did, like I shouldn't be allowed to breathe the same air that they did. "Um, I'm sorry, sir. Everyone can come in, uh . . ." He looked away, then lowered his voice. "Except her."

Clark glanced over at me, his brow furrowed in confusion. "Who, Hattie?"

"Yes, sir."

I pulled my fur jacket tighter as if a chill had swept through the air.

"Are you serious?" Clark said. "She just won an Academy Award."

To me, Burke said, "Congratulations." He turned back to Clark. "But she still can't come in." He jutted his chin to the Whites Only sign that hung above the entrance.

"That is ridiculous," Clark said.

Burke shrugged. "Maybe so, but it's our rules."

My fellow actors looked from me to Clark. Their reactions were mixed—some were appalled like Clark, and others were ready to leave me where I stood. I, meanwhile, was humiliated to my core.

"Mr. Gable, many of your fans are inside waiting to see you," Burke continued. "Now, I loved the movie." He looked at me again. "And you did a mighty fine job, Mammy."

"Hattie. Her name is Hattie," Clark snapped.

Clark's defensive demeanor did nothing to change Burke's stance. "Bottom line is, I must look out for my patrons and they are not keen on partying . . ." Burke glanced around at the crowd. "With a ni— with a colored woman." He stood erect, his body language putting a period on this discussion.

As progressive as Hollywood was, this place was still like the South in many ways.

"It's okay," I said, finally pulling my voice out from under the mound of humiliation. "Go on and have fun. I'm . . . I'm a little tired anyway."

"No, this is insane," Clark huffed.

Olivia leaned in, her lips grazing Clark's ear. "Clark, people are watching," she whispered. "Tonight is about celebrating our movie, not changing the world."

There had to be sixty people in line, dressed in the finest party attire. Some bounced anxiously, ready to get in. Others seemed pacified for the moment to get a glimpse of celebrities. And still others looked like they were ready to gulp down some Tinseltown drama. Clark was always toasted as the consummate gentleman. Anything he did out of character could easily backfire and affect his career.

He inhaled. I put a hand on his arm, but then quickly removed it. "No, really, it's okay," I told him.

Clark looked to Carole, who said, "We can leave if you'd like."

Before he could answer, I said, "I'm fine. Really."

"Excuse me, sweetheart," Clark said to his wife before pulling me off to the side of the building, next to the shoe-shine man, who busied himself sifting through his shoe-shine box.

"Are you sure about leaving, Hattie?" Clark said, his tone hushed. "This doesn't feel right celebrating without you."

I feigned a smile. "We are not about to have a repeat of Atlanta." Clark had ruffled feathers when he threatened to boycott the Atlanta premiere of *Gone with the Wind* because they wouldn't allow me to attend. I'd had to talk him out of it then and was definitely going to talk him out of it now.

I gave him a look to let him know this wasn't open for discussion. "Butterfly, Eddie, and several other Negro actors from the movie went to the Dunbar to celebrate. Louis Armstrong is supposed to be throwing a party there. I'll head over there to meet up with them," I said.

"Are you sure?" he repeated.

"Positive." I nodded, even though there was no such party. I just knew Clark would never be satisfied if he believed I was simply going home in shame.

Clark paused, hesitation across his face. He leaned in like he wanted to hug me. But we both knew better. He might've been able to get away with that inside the Cocoanut Grove, but here, crossing the line of public display, especially with all the eyes watching us, could be detrimental for both of our careers.

As Clark returned to the other cast members, I turned in time to see the shoe-shine man and two colored women wearing aprons standing about six feet away, chuckling. They looked like they were on a break and since they had a direct view of the scene that unfolded, I'm sure it wasn't hard to deduce what had happened.

"Don't she know the help doesn't get invited to the party?" one of the women said. She was thin and looked as if she'd been through some hard times. Her arms were folded and a cigarette dangled from her fingers. "I guess she thought that award was gonna make her one of them."

"It's a shame they even chose a club with a no-coloreds policy," the other woman said, her plump cheeks filling with disgust. "Show you how much they think about her."

The women didn't bother trying to lower their voices.

The first woman shook her head in repulsion as she took a long drag on her cigarette. She exhaled tiny plumes of smoke. "White people hate being forced to acknowledge a colored person's success. She is and always will be Mammy to those white folks."

I swallowed the lump in my throat and scurried down the sidewalk to the limo Mr. Selznick had secured for me.

"I'd like to go home," I told the driver, who had jumped from the car to greet me.

"Yes, ma'am," he said, opening the back door. I was grateful that he didn't ask any questions. I climbed into the back seat and closed my eyes. The taste of humiliation stung as it slid down my throat. What a way to end the greatest night of my life.

CHAPTER 3

February 1940

The pain of the night rattled around inside my heart as I made my way up the sidewalk toward my apartment. Though it was two in the morning, the bright lights of Central Avenue illuminated my walkway.

I'd moved into my apartment nine years ago, shortly after arriving in Los Angeles. I loved this area. That's why I'd just bought a modest home nearby, on West Thirty-First, which I was slated to move into at the end of the month. It wasn't my dream neighborhood—that was the posh West Adams district, an exclusive area of some of the grandest homes I'd ever seen—but it would do for now.

The light was on inside my apartment, which meant Ruby must still be there. After getting me dressed for the ceremony, she'd waved me off, saying she was going to straighten up and do some work.

I eased the front door open, preparing to see Ruby asleep on the sofa, but instead, the sounds of Glenn Miller's "In the Mood" poured out from the living room. A mountain of flowers lined the foyer hallway. There had to be at least twenty-five different bouquets: gardenias, roses, and tulips in an array of colors. I lowered my nose to the first bouquet of white gardenias, just like the ones I had in my hair. I inhaled the fresh aroma, then retrieved the note: *To our Academy Award–winning friend. Sorry we couldn't support you in person, but we were there in spirit. We love you and are so proud of you! Love, Ruby, Louise, and Lillian.*

My heart fluttered in gratitude. All three women had wished me good luck earlier today, but I thought it would be days before I saw Louise and Lillian again since both of them were in the middle of filming. But they made time to do this for me. That thought filled me with joy as I continued down the foyer and into the living room.

A wide smile filled my face as Ruby Berkley Goodwin, Lillian Randolph, and Louise Beavers danced around my living room like they were at the Cotton Club. Warmth washed over me as I watched my three closest friends dance like no one was watching. They were swinging their wings, whipping their hips, and tossing their torsos so hard they didn't even hear me come in. Ruby, who was usually reserved, was jitterbugging across the carpet. Lillian's signature high-pitched laugh filled the room as she and Louise clapped their hands and twist-walked around the room.

I removed my jacket, set my purse down, and just watched. This had to be Ruby's doing—gathering everyone to party even though she wasn't the partying type. I'd met Ruby when I got to LA in 1931. She was a local newspaper reporter, and even though I wasn't well-known in Los Angeles, she was well-versed on my blues career and followed me back when I was making music on the radio in Denver. She interviewed me for a story and that one interview led to her becoming my personal secretary and assistant and turned into a friendship that was approaching ten years.

I depended on each of my friends for different reasons.

Louise, despite her ability to have a rosy outlook on everything, was the worrier. She always got worked up at the smallest thing. If I chastised a member of the colored press, she worried about them writing more bad stories. If they wrote disparaging stories, she fretted over how it would affect our careers. In her many roles, her character was always a nurturer, so it was no surprise that Louise protected me like she was my big sister, even though I was seven years older.

Lillian was the calm to my storm. With her smooth sandpaper-colored skin and bright eyes, she had a pleasing personality that brightened my day almost every time I saw her. She would often try to find the bright side of every situation, and she was the friend who I lamented my love life with because she loved having a handsome man on her arm as much as I did. Right now, though, she was enamored with her new beau, boxer Isaiah James Chase. I was hoping this relationship would work out, but Lillian had been married three times already and her taste in men was as bad as mine.

Ruby was, in many ways, the dearest of all my friends. She not only kept my schedule, but she kept me in line and never hesitated to be my voice of reason. She was the one who could simmer my rage over my constant mistreatment in the media and was the consummate friend who never hesitated to speak her mind, like when she shot down the original red dress I wanted to wear to the Academy Awards because it was "too worldly." Maybe it was the fact that she wasn't an actress, so she didn't get caught up in Tinseltown drama. Or maybe it was because she lived in a house with her husband and children and didn't seem to want anything from me. Or maybe it was just that her voice was so kind that when she offered a comment, it felt like a balm and not a wound, but Ruby would forever have a place in my heart. In actuality, I was grateful for all three of these women.

Finally, Ruby noticed me, and her eyes danced with excitement.

"Hattie!" she sang.

Both Louise and Lillian slowed their dancing and turned to me.

"We didn't even hear you come in," Ruby said, grabbing my arm and pulling me out to join her in the jitterbug. So that's exactly what I did—swishing my hips just like my friends, then switching to fancy footwork and doing the Charleston.

"Let's do the Lindy Hop," Lillian said, grabbing my hand.

"And who's flipping who over?" I said, causing us all to pause, look around at each of our ample hips, and burst out laughing.

The laughter gave us a reprieve to catch our breath, and Louise turned down the music.

"So you all are having an entire party in here without me," I said, gathering myself from this dance fest that had exerted more energy than I had left.

"We're celebrating our Academy Award–winning friend!" Ruby exclaimed, hugging me tightly. "I'm so glad we got to listen." This was the first time the Oscars had been broadcast on the radio, so my friends had been able to hear everything.

"We're so proud of you," Lillian said.

"Thank you so much." I took a seat, exhaustion from the night finally settling in. "But you all really didn't have to do all of this."

"I know you said you were going out with the cast after the ceremony, but we wanted to be here when you returned," Ruby said.

"We thought it would be close to dawn before you got back," Louise said. "Though I'm happy because you know it's way past my bedtime."

That made me chuckle. Louise was right about that. We always teased her because she was in a deep sleep by ten o'clock on most nights.

"We just wanted you to feel the love from your friends," Lillian said.

"I started to have everyone come over, but I wasn't sure how long you would be," Ruby added.

A mist instantly covered my eyes. This was where I should've been in the first place—with the people who wanted to celebrate *with* me. With the people who loved me.

"Long story," I said. Their eyes were questioning, so I just added, "The cast went to a whites-only club, and of course, they wouldn't let me in." As the music appropriately switched from a big band song to the blues song "Step It Up and Go" by Blind Boy Fuller, I filled them in on the joy and humiliation of the night.

Thankfully, my friends didn't assail me with "I told you so" (which was classic Lillian) or "Well, it's probably best that you didn't go in" (which was classic Louise).

I only got "Well, you're right where God intended you to be" (which was classic Ruby).

"And the night is young," Ruby added, grabbing my hand and pulling me up and back into the center of the living room. "Turn off that sad blues music and come on, baby, let's bop!"

I switched the music to Cab Calloway's "Jumping Jive," ignored the exhaustion permeating my body, and once again joined my friends in dancing like everyone was watching!

• • •

When I first moved to Los Angeles, my sister Etta and brother Sam had laughed at all my lofty dreams. It had taken me nine years of struggling, taking small, often uncredited roles on one film after another, while working side jobs as a maid just to make ends meet. I received a little notoriety when Sam got me a spot on his radio show, *The Optimistic Do-Nuts*, where I performed as "Hi-Hat Hattie," a bossy maid who often "forgets her place." It had taken some time, but I'd been able to save up enough money to get an apartment right in the heart of Central Avenue. Though I could see the hustle and bustle of the neighborhood from my living room window, I loved strolling down the street—as I was doing now—to catch fresh air and take in the sights. I could spend hours watching patrons going in and out of Club Alabam, The Last Word, or The Showboat, which was run out of the Dunbar by the former heavyweight champion Jack Johnson. My apartment was only four blocks from the Tivoli, the Gayety, and the Rosebud theaters, all of which played Hollywood's most popular studio releases.

On any given night, a clientele of a mix of races filled the sidewalks, strolling past the crowded movie houses, going into theaters hosting Negro vaudeville and musical comedies, and dipping into cabarets featuring the best in entertainment. Just last weekend, Duke Ellington had been here. Louis Armstrong was coming next week.

All that action was why they called it Brown Broadway. All that action was why this was everything I dreamed of. I was only moving because I needed a bigger space and could now afford it.

A white couple in derby attire rushed by, pulling me from my thoughts. I'm sure they were heading to the Kentucky Club down the street. It was almost noon and the Kentucky Club had one of the best brunches in town.

I don't know what made me kneel and pick up a handful of dirt. I sifted it around in my hand. The soil here in Los Angeles felt different, magical. I thought of how my friends back in Denver were probably drowning in three feet of snow and shivering in ten-degree temperatures and I inhaled the sixty-degree air and smiled in satisfaction. If dreams had a smell, this would be it. It was such a noticeable change from all the other places I'd lived. Denver with its smog. Milwaukee with its factory-contaminated air. Chicago with its growing population and dirty coal fumes polluting the atmosphere. This place smelled fresh. Like new beginnings.

I let the handful of dirt I had picked up sift through my fingers and onto the ground. Then I brushed my hands off on my dress and headed back up the sidewalk and into my place. Before I closed the door, I turned and looked up at the large sign directly across the street, blaring the words "Florence Mills Theatre." It was named in honor of one of the nation's most celebrated Negro female stage stars of the 1920s, who died at a tragically young age. She was known for creating an all-Negro musical revue. I gave her special place a nod of acknowledgment.

When I'd first moved here, I'd promised myself that this was the restart my career needed. I'd moved to Los Angeles after the club I'd been performing in in Wisconsin abruptly shut down, never quite recovering from the Depression. I'd made a name for myself in music, in vaudeville, and onstage in several cities. But when I arrived in LA, I might as well have been a novice because no one knew—or cared—about Hattie McDaniel.

But that was then. It was a different story now.

Inside, I positioned some of the flowers around the small golden plaque I'd set on my mantel (supporting actors got a nonpersonalized plaque as opposed to a statuette). My self-congratulatory hymns were interrupted by a knock on the door. I opened the door to find the postmaster standing there with a gigantic box.

"Good afternoon, Mr. Stanley. What in tarnation do you have there?" I asked, peering to get a better look at the box, which towered over his five-foot-eight frame.

His grin was wide like this was a personal gift from him. "Telegram. For you. It was sent over from your studio, I think."

I stepped aside and motioned for him to bring the box inside. He did and leaned it against the wall in my living room. "That's a mighty big telegram," I said, removing the brown paper it was wrapped in. It was addressed to me in care of Metro-Goldwyn-Mayer Studios, Culver City, Hollywood, California.

Mr. Stanley must've wanted to see the oversized telegram himself because he didn't move as I unwrapped the paper.

It wasn't an actual box; rather, a giant Styrofoam telegram.

"I'll be," I said, taking in the massive display. I began reading. "'Your Washington admirers take this opportunity to compliment you on your brilliant work in *Gone with the Wind*. Your unforgettable portrayal is a monument to which we pay homage. We predict it will go down as one of the great roles of all time.'"

I teared up with pride. Finally, I had a role that impacted people all over the country. Finally, I'd been recognized far and wide for my talent. And this was just the beginning.

"Guess you got a lot of fans." Mr. Stanley pulled a newspaper out of his bag. "Including my wife. I hope this isn't uncouth of me, but would you mind signing my *LA Sentinel*?"

He opened the newspaper to the front page, where my picture

covered half the top fold. And above my photograph was one word: "Winner."

My heart swelled. "I'd be honored," I said, grabbing a pen and scribbling my name.

I'd just bid the postmaster farewell, when my agent strolled up the walkway.

"If it isn't my Academy Award–winning client," Mr. Meiklejohn said, his face lighting up as if he were greeting an old friend. His broad shoulders, strong jawline, and slicked-back hair made him look more like a football player than a top Hollywood agent. Hiring William Meiklejohn had been one of the best decisions I'd ever made. He repped everyone from Mickey Rooney to Judy Garland to Ronald Reagan, who he brought to Hollywood from a radio station in Des Moines, Iowa. I considered myself blessed because most white agents didn't take Negro clients. When I'd approached him about representation, he'd been genuine when he said, "You know I've never had a colored client before?"

I'd retorted, "And I've never had a white agent, so we're perfect for one another." He'd laughed and we'd had a great relationship ever since.

I extended my hand for the customary squeeze Mr. Meiklejohn always gave upon greeting me.

"Good day, Mr. Meiklejohn. To what do I owe this pleasure?"

"I understand you're probably still floating from Saturday, but I wish to speak to you about business," he said.

"Of course," I said, motioning for him to enter.

"Can I get you anything?" I said, moving the telegram against the wall in the dining area.

"Tea would be fine." He began examining the telegram. "Did this just come?"

"It did."

"Amazing," he said, leaning in and running his eyes up and down the rows of names. "There has to be at least five hundred signatures here."

"Yes, it is wonderful. Excuse me while I get us something to drink." I made my way into the kitchen and commenced making tea.

"Here you are," I said upon my return. I handed him the small China-imported Damascus teacup.

"And all the flowers?" he said, motioning around the room.

"From my friends."

"You have great friends."

"That I do." I sat down across from him, then said, "So, what business is of such an urgent nature that you can't even take today off to celebrate our monumental achievement?"

Mr. Meiklejohn sat down on the sofa, lifted the teacup to his lips, and sipped. He closed his eyes as if appreciating the minty taste. Finally, he opened his eyes, set the teacup on the table, and folded his hands in his lap.

"Well, I didn't want to waste any time. I wanted to meet with you to suggest that we promptly begin negotiations for a higher salary," he said.

My eyes widened. Mr. Selznick had paid me over seven thousand dollars for my role as Mammy. Colored folks rarely saw money like that. "Are you serious?" I asked.

"Yes. You don't agree?"

I didn't. I believed if it wasn't broke, don't break it.

"Mr. Meiklejohn, a post-Oscar raise does not necessarily translate into more earnings," I told him.

He scooted to the edge of his seat. "Now is the time for us to capitalize on your win," he argued.

I stood and began pacing across the living room. This conversation was making me nervous. I was in a good place, on the cusp of great things happening in my career. I did not need to be ruffling feathers.

"Other actresses have gotten raises only to be laid off," I said, turning to face him. "It's more important to remain before the public eye. Big salaries and little work don't interest me. I don't want more money. I want more work." I'd done seventy films since I'd moved to Los Angeles. But only four had been speaking roles and only two were main characters.

"Hattie, I really—"

"It's not open for discussion," I said, cutting him off.

Mr. Meiklejohn looked at me in shock. But if there's one thing he knew about me, it was that I was headstrong, so there really was no use in arguing with me. Yes, he was an adviser to my career, but I didn't think he realized the rules were different for colored folks.

"Okay, Hattie," he said, standing. His disposition belied his disappointment. "I hope you know what you're doing."

I nodded. "I do. Trust me. This Oscar win is about to open a number of doors."

I didn't know why he wore such an ominous expression, like he knew something that I did not.

"Let's hope and pray," he said.

"That's already done," I said with a confident smile.

"Well, I have to head out of town for a shoot with Judy next week," he said. "But when I get back, we need to be strategic in mapping out your future."

I agreed. I guess it was his job to worry. But I'd had obstacles thrown in my path all my life. And I always found a way to overcome them. I didn't want to block my blessings by being greedy.

I saw Mr. Meiklejohn out, then returned to my seat and sipped my tea as I thought about all the blessings that were on the way.

CHAPTER 4

March 1940

The fact that my best friend was back on my doorstep—at ten in the morning, with a newspaper in one hand and a bottle of rye whiskey in the other—was not a good sign. The expression on her face confirmed it.

"I guess the chance that you come bearing good news is slim," I said, stepping aside and motioning for Louise to come in.

"You guessed right. Lillian is on her way too," Louise said. She brushed past me, through my foyer, and into my living room. "Have you seen this?" Louise spun around, holding up the newspaper. Her plump cheeks puffed with exasperation.

"Seen what?" I asked, following her inside. She held out the *Pittsburgh Courier*, one of the most respected colored newspapers in the country.

"Look at the article on the front page," Louise said, plopping her hefty frame down on my sofa.

"What in the world are you talking about?"

"Just read."

I read the headline. "Uncle Thomasina: Hattie McDaniel and *Gone with the Wind*."

I took a deep breath, then read and reread the words that I knew were about to ignite my rage.

"'We feel proud over the fact that Hattie McDaniel won the coveted role of Mammy,'" I read aloud. "'It means about two thousand dollars for Miss McDaniel in individual advancement . . . [and] nothing in racial advancement.'"

I silently scanned the rest of the article, too furious to utter these ugly words out loud. The *Courier* had been fighting against this film since word of its production first began because it was based on the novel by Margaret Mitchell, which had been controversial since it was first published in 1936 and won the Pulitzer Prize for fiction in 1937.

The *Courier* motion picture editor, Earl Morris, had written an extensive article that not only sullied my name but said that *Gone with the Wind* was worse than *Birth of a Nation*, the pre–Civil War film that had polarized the nation only two years prior. In the article, Mr. Morris had blamed derogatory images and the use of the word "nigger" in the movie to explain why he despised it. He even threatened a letter-writing offensive and boycott of the finished picture. Mr. Morris had no idea how hard I'd fought to keep that horrid word out of the film, and was even promised by Mr. Selznick that it would be removed.

"'Negro movie audiences now have the best opportunity to fight against such pictures. Negroes in Hollywood need to reject any further roles in such films and put an end to these economic slaves like Hattie McDaniel, whose participation in the film amounts to racial suicide,'" I continued reading.

Slave? My daddy was a slave and I used to sit at his feet and hear stories of how he picked cotton, had his relatives sold off, and worked from sunup to sundown for free. I was anything but a slave! I was working my behind off to open the doors of opportunity for other young Negro actors.

And if this article wasn't bad enough, right next to it was a photo of the man who had been a thorn in my side since we began filming *Gone with the Wind*: NAACP president Walter White.

"Can you believe what Walter White said?" I resumed reading out loud. "'McDaniel had the audacity to tell us not to worry, that there was nothing in this picture that will injure colored people. If there was, she wouldn't be in it. Nothing could be further from the truth.'"

Walter White had been on a one-man mission to change Hollywood's portrayal of Negroes. He was already fighting segregation in education, housing, and the military, so he used his connections as a prominent civil rights leader to pressure Hollywood to portray Negroes in all kinds of roles, not just menial ones. That was a noble cause. But me and my contemporaries were his sacrificial scapegoats.

This article was so disheartening. It made it seem like I was a lone colored actor, dismissing my colleagues in pursuit of the almighty dollar. Second, there was no mention of Mr. White and other Negro leaders' many meetings with Mr. Selznick, which had gone on for months; they had even signed off on the production after receiving reassurances that it would be done with care.

"I'm going to the restroom. That garbage done got my bladder worked up," Louise said, shaking her head as she stood, then left me alone in the living room.

I knew Louise was angered because this attack was about me today, but it could be her tomorrow.

Louise had been my best friend in Hollywood ever since I moved here. She, Lillian, and I were always at the same auditions. All three of us had auditioned for *Imitation of Life* and *Gone with the Wind*. We'd bonded over our disdain for our limited options, the controversies we were forever embroiled in, and how we were constantly defending our work.

At first we would make jokes because everyone from press to producers would get us mixed up, especially Louise and me. One producer had even callously said, "Doesn't matter which one we hire—if you seen one fat colored woman, you've seen them all."

That had crushed Louise, probably because she was the heaviest of the three of us. But it didn't bother me none. I'd been heavy my whole life and had long ago learned to embrace it. What I didn't care for was them trying to encourage me to put on weight because as one producer told me, it would make me "doughier and more lovable." Lillian, who was the sensitive one out of the three of us, responded to the crass comment by dropping twenty pounds and focusing on being the best-dressed Negro woman in Hollywood.

I dropped down on the sofa as my thoughts returned to the article before me. I scanned it again. I didn't fight for my people? That was laughable. Then, suddenly, a flash as I remembered a time when I didn't. It was on the set of *Gone with the Wind*. We'd been at it for a hundred days and my friend Butterfly McQueen, who played Prissy, was furious that Mr. Selznick had changed her character to be what she deemed "demeaning." Butterfly lost her marbles when she saw the scene where Scarlett O'Hara was supposed to slap Prissy.

"It's bad enough they have me playing such a dim-witted girl, but now I'm supposed to endure physical abuse too?" Butterfly's high-octave voice grew even louder as her hands moved wildly (which was how she got the nickname Butterfly). "It's just not right how they're doing us, Hattie!"

Butterfly was fifteen years younger than me and she could be a pistol. What was so ironic was the character Prissy was the complete opposite of who Butterfly was as a person. Prissy masked her aggression behind a false veneer of passivity and helplessness impenetrable enough to escape the notice of her oppressors. Butterfly would burn a plantation down at a moment's notice.

But like me, Butterfly was a Negro actor who wanted to work. So like me, she took the roles she was given.

She'd been furious at me for not coming to her defense over that scene, especially when she'd later jumped in Vivien Leigh's face, accusing her of slapping her hard on purpose. It had been such a mess and that little stunt had gotten Butterfly blacklisted, which meant producers had spread word that she was difficult to work with. That just proved my point that Negro actors had to go along if they wanted to work.

My relationship with Butterfly was rocky after that. She'd lost respect for me, though for the life of me, I didn't understand why she thought I could have made a difference. Everyone in Hollywood was replaceable—especially a Negro woman. I wondered if I would ever be able to have Butterfly's spunk. I shook away that thought. I didn't get where I was by being combative. I chose to fight my battles a different way, from the inside. Didn't do nobody any good if me and my convictions were sitting at home unemployed.

While on set, the colored crew members mostly got through those grueling production days by cheering each other on. We would applaud after key scenes wrapped. But after that scene with Butterfly, things were never the same between the two of us.

"You're lost in thought. Where did you go?" Louise asked, returning to her seat.

I shrugged, shook away the memory, and turned my attention back to the newspaper. "I just can't believe this article. I have half a mind to give an open-letter response."

Louise dismissed that idea and the article with a wave of a hand. "You're a key player in Hollywood now so people are going to come after you," she said, removing her shoes and massaging her feet like she'd run over here and now her feet were tired. "That Walter man couldn't have a more appropriate last name. Him and his blue eyes and blond hair and one-eighth-colored-blood self. Ninety-five percent of that man's ancestry is white, but he's holding on to that colored five percent like some kind of badge that gives him carte blanche to crucify us," she said.

"Listen to this," I said, reading another paragraph. "'It is crucial that the NAACP rail against the demeaning, stereotypical roles of actors like Hattie McDaniel, Lincoln Perry (also known as "Stepin Fetchit"), and Louise Beavers, from *Imitation of Life*. *Gone with the Wind* celebrates the slave system and condemns the forces that destroyed it.

We call on these Uncle Toms to stop mugging and playing the clown before the camera.'"

"I read that drivel." Louise rolled her eyes, her nostrils flaring in anger.

"Walter White is trying to take food right out of my mouth!" This was a constant source of frustration for me. I just didn't get why Negroes didn't understand that my actions were necessary to support myself and my family. Not to mention how I'd paved the way for future performers.

Louise leaned up and reached for the paper. "Hattie, I didn't want you getting all worked up. I just wanted you to be aware. We know this is what they do to us."

I was about to continue my rant when a light tapping on my back door stopped me. Louise stood and headed to answer.

"That's Lillian," Louise said. "I told her to meet us."

Lillian would calm us down. We each made our friendship a priority, no matter how busy we got. And right now, Lillian was the busiest of us all. She'd done something few colored women had: she'd crossed over to animation and was the voice of Mammy Two Shoes in the *Tom and Jerry* cartoon. She also played Madame Queen on the *Amos 'n' Andy* radio show.

The three of us played the same kind of characters in film—maids, servants, and slaves, often uncredited. But we'd made the roles our own. Acting was hard work, long hours, and sweltering lights, but every day I'd been dropped off on the MGM lot, I took a moment where I pushed aside all the wrongs in my life and savored my blessings.

Though many applauded our performances, they'd been met with mixed reviews. The first time I'd been crucified in the press was in 1935, when I starred in *The Little Colonel* with Shirley Temple. The *Chicago Defender* had called me a "happy Southern servant" who was perpetuating negative stereotypes. The *Houston Defender* had called me an embarrassment to my ancestors.

"This article is trash," Lillian said, tossing the newspaper on the table. I hadn't even realized that she'd started reading it.

"Right," I said. "What do they want me to do? Play a glamour girl and sit on Clark Gable's knee? When they ask me not to play the parts, what are they offering in return?" I snapped.

"We're in complete agreement," Louise said.

"So what are we going to do about this?" Lillian asked, pointing to the newspaper.

"We can't let the Walter Whites of the world's voices be louder than ours," I said.

"What can we do?" Louise asked.

"The problem is the roles we're given, right?" I said.

"Yes, we play what we can," Lillian said.

"Well, I'm hoping this"—I pointed to the plaque sitting on my mantel—"award can make Hollywood take us seriously. I'm praying it opens the door to more substantial roles for all of us."

"I wouldn't hold my breath," Louise said. She was the most skeptical of the group. I think it was because she'd poured her heart and soul into playing Delilah Johnson in *Imitation of Life*. Even though she played her usual—a sad, downtrodden maid—she stole the show from the white lead, Claudette Colbert, and white folks hated her for that. And Negroes despised her for playing a maid. Nobody got mad at the woman who played her daughter, Fredi Washington, for her character trying to pass for white, but they persecuted Louise every chance they got. She'd been dejected for months after that film.

"Hattie, honestly, if anyone is in a position to demand change, you are," Lillian said.

I sighed. I just wanted to make movies, be respected for my craft, and make a difference for future generations. I would've loved to take up the mantle of equal rights, but that role couldn't exist in the same universe as Mammy.

"My agent wants me to use this opportunity to get more money," I admitted. "But I want to use it to get better roles."

"I'm with you," Louise said.

"Well, just do something. And don't take too long. Act now," Lillian interjected. "Your star is shining, Hattie McDaniel. If ever there was a time to strike the match of change, this is it."

The words of my friends swirled around in my head, settling like a bird into its nest. They were right. I wasn't going to sit back and wait for change. I was going to go out, grab it by the reins, and guide it in the direction I wanted it to go.

CHAPTER 5

April 1940

I marched across the lot of Selznick International Pictures, my steps fueled by determination. I was not slowed by the usual chorus of "hellos," though I did acknowledge the array of "congratulations" for my Oscar win; I was on a mission.

My friends had been right about one thing—now was the time to capitalize on my accolades. Now was the time to demand better, more meaningful roles. I wanted to show the world that Negro actors could be more than servants and slaves. I'd already let a month pass and I couldn't afford to waste another day.

I made my way into Mr. Selznick's office building, taking the elevator up to his fourth-floor office. I hadn't been here since this past January, when I'd shown up with a stack of newspaper clippings from all over the country, praising my performance as Mammy, along with letters from supporters urging my nomination for an Academy Award. I'd wanted Mr. Selznick to see that the pressure to nominate me was not confined to the Negro community. I knew he'd been inundated with backlash for the movie but he needed to see all of the positive press as well.

My move had paid off. Mr. Selznick had been thrilled at the response and secured a spot on the ballot for me for best supporting actress—despite the fact that he'd already nominated Olivia de Havilland in that same category. Some people might have thought I was too bold with such a request, but I didn't care. I'd been audacious already when it came to securing the role of Mammy. That had been the biggest audition of my life. Every colored actress wanted the role of Mammy in *Gone with the Wind*, from Madame Sul-Te-Wan to Georgette Harvey, in addition to Lillian and Louise. Even the First Lady of the United States, Eleanor Roosevelt, had called Mr. Selznick, demanding that her maid Elizabeth McDuffie (who had no acting experience) be given the part.

I'd gotten an audition at the behest of the actor Bing Crosby, who knew of my work through my brother Sam. I wanted this role very much. So much that I left my job working as a maid for a wealthy Beverly Hills couple and came right to the audition in my black-and-white maid's uniform.

I knew that I brought authenticity to the role since not only were my parents former slaves but my grandmother had worked on a plantation not unlike Tara, the plantation in *Gone with the Wind*. So as far as I was concerned, I *was* Mammy. I had told myself on the bus ride to the audition that I would not return to the Pattersons', where I'd been working as a maid/cook for three months. Those months had been some of my hardest. When I'd taken the job, I'd been toiling as an uncredited actor for seven years. Yet I still had to subject myself to the unreasonable and degrading demands of Mrs. Patterson and her spoiled twin teenage girls. So this role of Mammy was my lifeline. That's why when I walked into that office to audition, I wanted there to be no question that my feisty and sassy attitude would make the perfect Mammy.

Since Mammy was the last role to be filled, along with that of Scarlett O'Hara, they'd had me and Vivien audition together, in a scene where I had to convince her to eat before attending a barbecue. The chemistry was instant, as was the job offer.

In addition to Butterfly playing Prissy, there were other Negro actors in big roles: Oscar Polk, who had signed on to play Pork, and my friend Eddie Anderson, who worked on radio as Jack Benny's manservant, Rochester. He was cast as Uncle Peter, a personal slave and coachman. My brother even had a small role, as did tons of other colored performers.

I stepped off the elevator and into the receptionist's area, which displayed opulent décor that Mr. Selznick proudly boasted came from the richest parts of the world, including mythological sculptures and a sparkling chandelier in the center of the waiting area. Strategically placed lamps and sconces cast shadows on the marble flooring.

I smiled at Mr. Selznick's secretary as I approached her large mahogany desk. "Hi, Marcella. I'm here to see Mr. Selznick."

She greeted me over her cat-eye glasses. "Hello, Miss McDaniel. Mr. Selznick is in a meeting. You can have a seat and I'll let him know you're waiting." Marcella motioned toward the brown leather couch that sat against the wall outside Mr. Selznick's office.

I nodded and took a seat under a row of framed black-and-white eight-by-ten photos of all MGM's biggest stars. Of course, I noted how my photo was not on the wall. Neither was I on the covers of any of the ten or so trade magazines fanned across the oak coffee table in front of the couch.

Mr. Selznick's door was open and I could see he was talking to the famed Negro casting director Charles Butler. It had been years since I had seen Mr. Butler, who was the reason the world even knew of Hattie McDaniel. People always told me about the "lucky break" I got in pictures. I didn't take the trouble to tell them of all the years I sang in choruses, worked in mob scenes, thankful for the smallest thing.

There had been about sixty people waiting in his office when I first went to meet Mr. Butler. Their faces reeked of desperation, and after ten minutes there, I knew why. Anyone who had any hope of working in Hollywood had to be anointed by Charles Butler.

"Well, if it isn't the Academy Award–winning Hattie McDaniel."

I smiled as Mr. Butler's voice snapped me from my thoughts.

"Mr. Butler," I said, standing to greet him. He hadn't aged a bit since the day he sent me out on my first assignment.

Ever the gentleman, he took my hand and kissed it. "Super proud of your win. It couldn't come to a more deserving individual," he said.

"You know me. If Lady Luck won't pay me a visit, I'll go grab her by the neck."

He laughed. "That I do know." He placed his wide-brim hat back atop his head. "Looking forward to more great things from you, Miss McDaniel. Good day."

After he left, I waited for another fifteen minutes and had just stood up to go back over to Marcella's desk when she said, "Hattie, Mr. Selznick will see you now." She flashed a warm smile as she extended her arm, giving me permission to enter the office lots of us joked was sacred ground.

Mr. Selznick was on the telephone, but motioned for me to take a seat in the chair in front of his desk.

"I want it done yesterday," he said into the phone. "There's nothing attractive about 'Phyllis Walker.' Get her a new name. Nothing too fancy. And I would like to get at least a first name that isn't also carried by a dozen other girls in Hollywood. Something like 'Jennifer Jones.'"

I watched him mark up a script with intensity with one hand as he held the receiver to his ear with the other. No wonder this man was one of the most respected in Hollywood. Power seemed to seep from his pores.

Images of the last time I'd sat in this chair filled my head. When I'd petitioned for the Oscar nomination, I'd stood the whole time. The last time I'd sat here, we'd gotten into a raging debate over Mr. Selznick's use of the dreadful word "nigger" in the *Gone with the Wind* script. I didn't cause a ruckus for much, but when I'd read the line where they'd had Mammy use it deridingly against Atlanta colored tramps, I had stomped right over to Mr. Selznick's office and complained.

He hadn't wanted to change it, telling me, "We won't offend any Negroes if we use the word with care."

I respectfully explained to him that there was no such way to use that word with care. What was disheartening was that I think, from the bottom of his heart, he believed what he'd said. But I'd insisted that there was no way I would say it, so he'd told me they would remove it. However, on the day of filming, it was still in the script. So when it had come time for me to say it, I just didn't.

". . . I don't care how special her name is to her," Mr. Selznick shouted, jolting me from my thoughts. "It's boring. Change it." Then he hung up the phone without saying good-bye. His eyes brightened as his hearty voice greeted me. "Hattie McDaniel! Are you here to strong-arm me for more money now that you're an Academy Award winner?" he asked with a wide grin.

"Good afternoon, Mr. Selznick," I said, returning his smile. "It is not more money that I seek," I told him, diving right into the reason for my visit. "I want more roles. I want to play more modern parts, perhaps something like a courageous, lovable Negro mother."

His grin faded just a bit, then expanded again. "Well, Hattie, you know I want that for you as well. When you do well in this industry, we all do well."

I relaxed a bit because that was exactly what I wanted to hear.

"Thank you, Mr. Selznick. So where do we begin in searching for those roles? Perhaps we could enlist our own writers to create those stories." I leaned forward in my chair. "I was thinking . . ."

He held up his hands to cut me off. "Whoa, whoa. You get paid mighty nicely to *act*, not *think*." The way my body stiffened was not lost on him, because he quickly added, "But let's take a minute and slow down. We have to be strategic in our approach. I've been thinking and meeting with my team about this very topic. The first thing I'm working on is a sequel to *Gone with the Wind* and you, or rather,

Mammy, would be the focus. I've already requested that the author write a sequel. I want to call it *The Daughter of Scarlett O'Hara*."

I didn't know who Mr. Selznick thought he was fooling. I'd already heard that rumor, just as I'd heard that Margaret Mitchell had balked at that plan and refused to sell any rights to a sequel to Mr. Selznick or anyone else. I'd even heard that he'd had folks writing their own sequels.

"Well, that would take some time," I told him. "So I would suggest that we find something else for me to do in the interim.

"Mr. Selznick," I continued, inhaling the strength to make yet another case to this powerful man, "other actresses that win Academy Awards go on to big things. I'd like to do that too."

"Well, I was thinking of loaning you out. Someone else should get the benefit of the sensational services of Mammy." He clapped his hands together like he was applauding his own brilliant idea. "That's the route we need to take. I've even put feelers out, asking for a starting price for your services of two thousand dollars a week. Isn't that wonderful?"

No, it sounded like a high-dollar form of slavery, especially since I knew no matter what he got another studio to pay, my contract stipulated that I would be paid the same regardless. But I kept quiet as he continued.

"You would receive expenses and perhaps a guaranteed minimum of thirty weeks of work at five hundred dollars each, with rights or privileges to rent you out to radio and personals." He leaned in. "I'm even in talks to have you be the official Aunt Jemima." He leaned back, satisfied as if I'd agreed to his plan. In reality, my insides were coiling in anger. He continued, "In the meantime, I'm also working on a radio show for you. We'll call it *Mammy*. I'm getting some pushback from advertisers because they don't want to make a colored character too dominant in a show but I think Southerners, colored and white, would welcome a colored-dominated program as long as the Negro stayed in her place and did not mix socially with whites."

He was enthralled with his own suggestions, which appeared to have been well-thought-out. It actually made me sad because Mr. Selznick was one of the good guys, at least in terms of giving colored actors an opportunity. But like so many in the world, he was just ignorant to how misguided his thought process was.

"Think about it, Hattie," he exclaimed. "You would be received like a visiting monarch. Negroes would storm the theaters to see you. You might even get some honorary degrees from colored colleges in the cities that you visit. We could appoint a Negro tour manager, maybe an educator or newspaperman to be your adviser. You can go on tours through each city's colored district, give talks to neighborhood meetings, present awards to children and parents for some meritorious services they might have performed, and make commercial tie-ins with Negro businessmen."

His words poured out like he was filling a pitcher of sweet tea. "Now, just a minute," I said, holding up my hand to stop his barrage of ideas. "I don't want to go on the road. I want to do films with meaningful breakout roles."

"You don't think Mammy is meaningful?" A look of shock crossed his face.

"Of course I do. But . . ."

"Then there are no buts. Personal appearances are the benchmark of making the big time. That's where we need to start. We've received an avalanche of requests for personal appearances," he said.

"Well, that's good news," I said, wondering why he hadn't passed those requests on to me or my agent.

"Not quite," Mr. Selznick replied. "That's why I didn't let William know about them. I've had to nix those requests because they required a lot of money upfront and often tender unpredictable returns."

"Well, what are you suggesting?" This conversation was tiring and not going at all as I had hoped. I wished I had waited on Mr. Meiklejohn.

He clapped his hands together like he'd just come up with another great idea.

"I think we should send you to colored movie houses in the meantime. You could do one of your shows with that dancing and singing."

I inhaled a sharp breath. "Mr. Selznick, I don't mind playing colored houses, but I prefer playing white houses first."

If I must tour, I was determined to become one of the first Negro actresses to embark on a major tour of the prominent movie palaces. Louise and Fredi Washington were the only colored actors sent out on such tours and they booked colored and white venues.

"Book me in the same theater as any other best supporting actress honoree," I continued. I was not going to let them Jim Crow me by segregating me to colored theaters only.

Mr. Selznick picked up a fountain pen and began scribbling on a piece of paper. "I will pay you a $125-a-week bonus while on tour, and I'll pay for a maid and cover travel expenses," he said as if he hadn't heard a word I'd just said.

"Mr. Selznick . . ."

He sighed and looked up at me, exasperation covering his face, warning me that I was venturing into "difficult Negro" territory. "Hattie, you're a good employee. I love working with you, not only because you're talented but because you truly understand what it takes to make it in this business." He inhaled. Why did his words feel like they had a threatening undertone? "Tell you what, let's compromise. You will play mostly white theaters but also make appearances at two colored venues on the East Coast. Do this for me, sign on for this radio show, and we'll make sure you can tour how you want later on."

"While we look for more meaningful roles?" I found myself adding.

Without hesitation he added, "While we look for more meaningful roles."

I studied him for a moment. He was right. I knew the rules if I wanted to play the game. Fighting the powers that be and making waves would have me at home like Butterfly praying for my phone to ring with a job offer. There were thousands of Negro actors who would love to be in my shoes. I released a long sigh, then finally nodded in agreement.

"Fine. When do I hit the road?"

CHAPTER 6

April 1940

I didn't know whether to be happy or sad about my meeting with Mr. Selznick. Clark had insisted that it was all good news and all of it deserved celebrating. That's why we were now at his twenty-acre ranch, preparing to do just that.

It shouldn't have surprised me that Clark would want to celebrate my historic win. Part of me wondered if it was his way of making up for the night at the club. But my heart knew that it was more than that.

My five-year friendship with Clark had proven to be one of the most solid relationships in my life. When we met, he was unhappy in his marriage to his second wife, Ria Langham. She was a wealthy socialite who was seventeen years older than him and though she was a sweet woman, they had nothing in common. For some reason, Clark felt comfortable opening up about that relationship to me when the two of them separated while we were filming *China Seas*.

Clark had been raised by his father after his mother died of epilepsy when he was a toddler. He dropped out of school at sixteen to pursue acting. From the moment we met, I could tell the confident, dapper Clark Gable was much more than his macho persona. His electric smile and playful winks rendered him a charming rogue who failed to take himself too seriously. I was able to see that underneath the facade, Clark was still the insecure boy with oversized ears who used self-deprecation to cope with stardom. I think my ability to appreciate the flawed Clark endeared me to him.

And when it came to lamenting my stature in Hollywood, Clark was a masterful listener and adviser. In fact, he had been the main one rooting for me to get the role of Mammy.

When he met Carole Lombard, I had encouraged him not to pursue her until his divorce was final. Of course, he didn't listen since Ria was dragging out the divorce. Clark was her third marriage and she had no desire to split from him; she felt like she'd had a hand in making him a heartthrob since she'd invested in his acting lessons and wardrobe. I didn't initially approve of Clark and Carole's relationship when they started dating in 1936 because he was still married, but I supported my friend—even if I didn't like his decisions.

Eventually, like everyone who met Carole, I came to love her. Unlike Ria, she was personable and lively, and her foul mouth was endearing to all who met her. Maybe it was because she was younger, but she made Clark feel alive. I'd been there when they finally married in 1939 and had even been there the day they moved into this nine-room house the previous year.

The redbrick terrace home was stately, but hardly extravagant. Carole had renovated it the year before and made it into a place where they could enjoy unspoiled country living and raise her beloved farm animals far from the tour buses that prowled the streets of Beverly Hills, yet close to the studios.

This was going to be some celebration. Just glancing at the sleek cars—everything from convertible Cadillacs to silver Thunderbolts to shiny Mercedes Benzes parked in the long driveway—I knew an array of Hollywood luminaries were in attendance.

I brushed down the skirt on my purple Monastic dress, which was a good measure of fancy and elegant, just perfect for this kind of a soiree, then made my way inside.

At first glance, I estimated that there had to be 150 people packed in the living room with its canary-yellow carpeting and white-painted pine paneling. Guests stood in small groups, and all of them smiled at me as I entered. I spoke to blues singer Billie Holiday, who introduced me to her protégé, an accomplished jazz pianist named Hazel Scott.

"She was a child prodigy. Remember her name," Billie told me. "She's going to be big."

"Maybe we can get you to play something later," I told the young woman.

"I'd love that," Hazel replied.

We made more small talk before I moved on to greet other guests.

I spent more time than I liked to admit plotting out the day when I'd be able to host grand parties like this in my own place in the West Adams district. Though I had been known to throw a party or two, my current home was not fit for the type of entertainment I hoped to do, especially if I planned to invite notables like Billie and Count Basie, who was also here today. In fact, there were a number of Negro celebrities here.

I was sorry Carole wouldn't be here, but she was in New York promoting her new movie, *Vigil in the Night*. Clark's social secretary had laid out this gorgeous spread of deviled eggs, shrimp cocktail, scalloped potatoes, and lobster bites. But it was Clark's selfless generosity, inviting all these people into his home on my behalf, that was the real gift.

It was time to thank him, so I passed through the crowd in the living and dining rooms and headed into his den, where I knew he'd be sitting comfortably in one of his quilted wing chairs, surrounded by his closest friends. The sofas and chairs in the room were oversized, I guess to accommodate his large frame. There were about six people sitting around him, including Olivia de Havilland.

"Clark, I can't thank you enough for doing this for me." I flashed my signature cheeky grin, which he said always brought a smile to his face.

"Of course," Clark replied, putting his cigarette out in an ashtray in front of him. "It's my pleasure. It's not every day a woman gets recognized not just for her beauty, but her talent as well."

"Stop it," I said, heat filling my cheeks.

A journalist for the *Los Angeles Times*, Ellen Morgan, approached us. With her hard jawline and broad shoulders, she seemed like she would've been better served covering politics than entertainment.

"Clark, darling. I was wondering where the guest of honor and the host were." She waltzed over like she had received a personal invitation to join us. "This is a fabulous event." She turned to me. "Congratulations, Hattie. You are so deserving of that award."

"Why, thank you kindly," I told her, pausing to take a drink off the tray of a passing waiter. "I am most appreciative of Clark."

Ellen took it upon herself to sit down next to Clark, even though I was standing. "I love the friendship you two share." She looked at him as she spoke. "Is it true, Clark, that you fancy yourself a prankster?" she asked.

I was a tad irritated because this was supposed to be an informal affair and she was sitting down like she was about to conduct an exclusive interview.

"My dear, I have no idea what you're talking about," he replied with a sly grin, obviously not as bothered by her presence as I.

"Mm-hmm," Ellen said, pursing her lips.

"Oh, Clark is definitely a prankster," Olivia interjected. "Once, when we were filming, Clark replaced Hattie's iced tea with scotch."

The memory of that day caused Clark to break out into a fit of laughter.

"You should have seen the look on her face," he said, admitting his guilt. "But Hattie was the consummate actress. She swallowed that drink like it was sweet tea straight outta Georgia, made it through her scene, and then had a coughing fit afterward."

Just remembering that day caused me to swat his arm. He laughed as he ducked out of the way.

"Mr. Gable is more than a prankster. He is also a champion for Negro rights."

We all turned toward the voice that had just entered the conversation. It was Lennie Bluett, an eighteen-year-old actor who was one of hundreds of extras on set to film the burning of Atlanta scene in *Gone with the Wind*. He'd attended an arts school in Los Angeles and though he'd just been an extra, I could tell he had a promising career.

"A champion? Do tell," Ellen said, her nose twitching like a bloodhound's.

Lennie exchanged glances with me and I knew he was keeping his disdain for me at bay. He turned toward Ellen.

"Well, during the filming," he began, "I happened to notice that we had separate bathrooms for Negroes and whites, which is a shame given how hard we were all working." Lennie took a seat across from Olivia, his trousers rising to reveal his plaid socks. "We worked just as hard as the white actors. Plus, I knew Mr. Selznick had assured the NAACP that he would be sensitive to Negroes in the filming. There wasn't nothing sensitive about having the Negro actors traipse across half a mile to the very back of the lot to use the bathroom."

Lennie took a deep breath and brushed down his trousers and rushed his words out like he'd been wanting to tell this story since it happened. "I talked to"—he paused like he was fighting the urge to look my way—"some other actors about it, but they 'didn't want to cause any waves.'" He used his hands to emphasize his disgust.

I took the cheese tray from a passing waiter and set it on the table in the middle of everyone for a momentary distraction. Lennie was talking about me.

There were a lot of inequities on set. In addition to separate bathrooms, the studio sent cars for white actors yet the colored actors were forced to ride together in a single car that went around picking us up at our homes in the morning. I did get my own chair, but I didn't get any extra special treatment. I had seen the worst of this business between white actors treating colored extras as their own personal slaves to them making colored actors wait in the rain because a white actor didn't want to be confined in the same building as them. I think folks like Lennie just didn't know how good we had it, compared to the world outside our set. We weren't regulated to a colored section of the lot like at other production houses. This movie was the first time Negroes and whites had come together. We ate side by side. After a lifetime of mistreatments, I recognized the advancements we'd made. Yes, I would've liked to have made more but I understood that it was a slow process. Lennie wanted to complain about something the rest of the world was doing.

"So anyway," Lennie said, continuing his conversation, "it just wasn't right. There would be no *Gone with the Wind* without Negro actors. I couldn't get anywhere with anyone else. So I happened to tell Mr. Gable about it."

I half expected everyone to turn to me with accusatory expressions. But thankfully, Clark stepped in.

"He sure did. He burst up into my dressing room that day like his pants were on fire," Clark said.

"You weren't scared about approaching the star, the King of Hollywood?" Ellen asked, intrigued by this tale.

"Oh, of course," Lennie replied. "I knew we weren't supposed to bother the stars, but I didn't know what else to do. It just wasn't right."

"It sure wasn't," Clark said, his brow furrowing in anger at the memory.

"And do you know, Mr. Gable promptly exited his dressing room and went to the director and Mr. Selznick and demanded that they integrate the bathrooms?" Lennie continued, his voice laced with respect and admiration.

"Well, did they?" Ellen asked.

"They sure did." Lennie laughed. "I guess when the King of Hollywood demands something, he gets it."

"Wow," she said. "And that little nugget didn't get out to the public?"

"No, the focus was on the movie," Clark said. He had never been one to be showered with admiration outside of the limelight. "I just did what I thought was right."

"Let's not talk about the bad old days," I interjected. "This is supposed to be a celebration, not an interview." This conversation made me queasy. People always thought I had more power than I actually did. "We need to get in there and entertain our guests."

Clark knew how I wrestled with my station in Hollywood, and like the consummate friend he was, he stepped in to lighten the conversation. "You're so right." He slapped his thighs as he stood.

"Today is about you, my friend." He took my arm. He and I had talked about why I didn't feel comfortable pushing for the integration of the bathrooms on set, but what few people knew is that before Clark went to the director, he stopped by my dressing room to discuss the matter. And we'd both agreed it would be much more effective coming from him. But I was going to let Lennie think whatever he wanted.

"Thank you, my friend," I whispered as Clark led me back into the front room, where Ernest Whitman was entertaining the crowd with his impression of Paul Robeson singing "Ol' Man River."

"Come on, Hattie. Show 'em what you got," Ernest said, waving me up to the front of the room when he spotted me in the entrance with Clark. I was happy to shift thoughts from that incident on the set with Lennie. So I did what I do best, sashaying up next to Ernest and launching into impressions of the white comedian Fanny Bryce, and the crowd erupted in laughter.

Later, as I stood talking to Louise and Clark, Susan Myrick, who worked as our dialect coach on *Gone with the Wind* and just so happened to be a reporter and best friend of the author, Margaret Mitchell, approached me. "Hattie, why don't you show us that rendition of 'Swanee River' you did on set? You know the one where you do that hilarious tap dance and buck-eyed eye roll."

I just stared at her, unsure of how to respond. She'd written that in her column for the *Macon Telegraph*, but it was absurd because that never happened. I hadn't said anything about the lie because I knew that Susan took liberties with her articles in order to appeal to her white Southern readership, and a lot of the stuff she wrote arose from her racist presumptions.

When I didn't reply, Susan turned to a woman standing next to her. "Did you know that when I was on set covering the movie, I had the most terrible cold. Hattie whipped up a concoction of linseed oil, lemon juice, and bourbon. And almost instantly, my cold was gone. She took great care of me. I think that Hattie has played Mammy so long that she can't help but be a mammy in real life."

I had fixed her one of my mother's medicinal recipes on set. But had I known it would come back in this form, I might've laced it with turpentine.

"You really shouldn't call her that," Clark said. The right side of his mustache twitched, which often happened when he was getting agitated.

Susan had the nerve to look appalled. She used her hand to flick his words away. "That's ridiculous—everyone calls her Mammy."

Clark could never get used to the disrespect I experienced, but I'd had a lifetime of it, so I'd learned to let it roll off my back. Even the general public called me Mammy. But as long as it was clear that the reference was to my role in the movie, and not to any past or present condition of servility, it didn't bother me none. I'd come to see that my role often got more attention than those of some of the other players who were considered the stars, so I learned how to embrace it.

"No, everyone calls her Hattie, because that's her name. And as long as you're in my house, you'll show her some respect," Clark said. The harshness in his tone was startling and caused several people to stop mingling and gawk in our direction.

Susan stared at me, blinking as if I were the one who'd said something to offend her. Tension hung in the room like a dark cloud before a storm. Even the music had stopped playing. Susan's mouth opened, then closed, as if she couldn't find the words to reply.

This was not the atmosphere I wanted to celebrate in, so I smiled. "Turn the music back up. This is supposed to be a party!"

"Excuse me," Clark said, exiting the room, no doubt in an effort to calm himself.

As the big-band sounds filled the room, uncomfortable chatter slowly picked up. I turned to Susan and lowered my voice. "I tell you what." I pointed to the *Gone with the Wind* book that was peeking out of her large, monogrammed leather handbag. "How about I sign your book for you?"

She hesitated like she was still processing the humiliation. I wasn't sure how she would react to my offer since she was such a good friend of the author.

After a few unsure seconds, her shoulders relaxed, and she said, "Fine." She reached in her bag and pulled out the book and a pen. She handed both to me.

I scribbled, *Thanks for the support, Hattie McDaniel,* and then I paused . . . and added *Mammy.*

That seemed to settle Susan down and she moved on to talk to other guests.

I made my way back toward the den, where I assumed Clark had gone, but the room was empty. I noticed the doors closed to the first-floor bedroom that he'd transformed into a storage room to hold his growing collection of firearms, so I tapped on the door.

"Knock, knock," I said, easing the door open and peeking my head in. "Can I come in?"

Clark's back was to me and he was staring out the large bay window, taking in the moonlit garden.

"Sorry about that," he said, without turning around. "I know you hate me coming to your defense."

"I hate you doing anything that might taint your standing with your fans," I said, easing into the room and closing the door behind me.

Clark turned to face me, his eyes suddenly dark with sorrow.

"I hate that you have to endure stuff like that."

I shrugged. "I do too. But I've learned to deal with it. People are who they are."

"Do you get frustrated by all of this?" he asked.

"All the time," I said without hesitation. "My own people assail me because they think the roles I take are a choice. Though I guess I could choose to say no and go be someone's cook."

"Well, can I just say that I'm glad you're choosing acting because I would hate for your talent to be confined to the kitchen." He flashed a smile and I was grateful that the tension of the evening seemed to be lifting.

"I just needed a minute to cool down. Come on, let's get back to the party," he said, leading me out.

For the rest of the evening, I was able to enjoy mixing and mingling with my friends, catching up on who was starring in what movie and who had gotten entangled in what scandal. Word had spread about the tour Mr. Selznick was sending me on and everyone was extending their congratulations for that as well.

"Hattie, at a time when so many of us are feeling stifled in Hollywood, it's so refreshing to see someone breaking through the ceiling," said one of my friends, Nina Mae McKinney. She was standing next to two other actor friends of mine, Wonderful Smith and Bojangles Robinson. Nina had been one of the first Negro film stars in the country, but she'd moved to Europe in 1934 because she was fed up with the racism. She'd come back last year but hadn't been able to find work. "It's hard to stay positive when we're facing so many obstacles," she added.

"We've got to be optimistic," I said. "Mr. Selznick has assured me that my career is on the upswing. I believe that we all have a brighter future ahead in Hollywood. Mark my words, moviemakers are finally going to see the wisdom of creating a wider range of roles for colored performers."

"You have such a hopeful tenor," Nina said, her wide doe eyes flashing her respect. "I'm glad to see that the doldrums of Hollywood haven't tainted your attitude."

I knew that it was easy to get disheartened with our status in Hollywood. But I needed to convince my friends that my Oscar win was the beacon of hope so many of us needed.

"Let's toast," I said, motioning for the waiter who was distributing flutes of champagne. All of us took a glass.

"Yes," Wonderful said, lifting his glass in the air. "To Hattie McDaniel."

"No," I said as my friends all raised their glasses. "To all of us. The world may not be ready to give us our due. But here in Hollywood, let's all believe that we're on our way."

I was happy to see my friends toast to that. Now we just needed it to happen.

CHAPTER 7

July 1940

My light was still shining bright, and though my train was chugging along (as opposed to racing full speed like I wanted), the accolades continued pouring in. I had moved into my new house, just three miles from my old apartment. I'd bought new living room furniture, including an armoire to display my budding doll collection, honors, and awards. Everything was set up to my liking and the place felt like home.

The final touches were being put on my tour and the contract for my new radio show had been worked out. My post-Oscar employment might not have been instantaneous like that of Bette Davis and Luise Rainer, who were booked and busy within weeks of their wins. But I had to be optimistic that the expansion of roles for me would manifest soon.

I folded the last of my undergarments and slid them into the corner of my suitcase. It had taken me two days, but I was packed and ready to hit the road for my tour.

Ruby tapped on the door to my bedroom just as I closed my suitcase and set it on the floor. She entered looking like the consummate professional.

"Hey, Hattie, I have your itinerary written out for you, and per your request, I built in some time for you to catch up with friends when you get to New York," she said, handing me the folder she kept all my important travel papers in.

"Wonderful."

"And Mr. Meiklejohn is on the phone for you." Before I could point to my luggage, she added, "I'll have Bert bring the bags to the car," referring to my driver. I loved how Ruby was always one step ahead of me.

"Thank you so much." I dropped the folder in my purse and darted out of my room and downstairs to the living room to grab the telephone.

"Mr. Meiklejohn, how are you today?" I said, greeting him.

"Hello, Hattie," he replied. "I'm well. Are you all set for your tour?"

"I am. Being back out on the road will return me to my roots." Though I'd been reluctant about touring, I was actually excited now about getting on the road because it would give me a chance to drum up support for my radio show.

Mr. Meiklejohn hesitated, then said, "Well, I'm calling with some good news and some bad news."

I sighed, pulling out a chair next to the phone to sit and brace myself. "Give me the bad news first."

He didn't hesitate as he said, "They canceled your radio show."

I sat straight up in my seat. "What? Why?"

"Something about top brass not being able to gain more interest." He sighed. "Mr. Selznick had one of his people call me. They didn't have a lot of details. I'm waiting on a call back from Mr. Selznick now."

The radio show had been one of the only reasons I had agreed to do the tour. It was going to be promotion for the show. If it was canceled, I'd rather stick to doing movies.

"And the good news?" I finally said.

"Mr. Selznick is adding some more venues for the tour, so your run could actually go through the end of the year."

Puffs of exasperation filled my cheeks. So he was booking me in more theaters—probably colored venues. Had this been Mr. Selznick's plan all along?

"I know this is not what you wanted to hear," Mr. Meiklejohn said. "I am so sorry. But remember, many Negro actors would give their right arm to trade places with you."

I let the exasperated breaths escape. The "you don't know how lucky you are" diatribe was starting to feel like some kind of whip being used to keep me in my place.

"Fine, Mr. Meiklejohn," I said. "I must go, or else I'll miss my train."

"I'm sorry, Hattie. I'll let you know when I hear something more. Safe travels."

I hung up the phone and sat in disbelief, letting the silence mix with the ticking antique wall clock over my phone stand. Ruby found me just sitting there a few minutes later.

"Are you okay?" she asked.

I fell back into my seat, dejected. "No. My bubble has once again been burst."

I filled Ruby in on everything Mr. Meiklejohn had told me.

"It's so frustrating. I'm trying to prove I'm worthy and I'm hitting roadblocks at every turn," I groaned.

"You *are* worthy," Ruby said, moving to stand directly in front of me like she wanted to look me in the eyes.

"I know that. I just need the rest of the world to know it as well," I huffed. "Maybe I just need to tell them I'm not doing the tour."

"And they'll just get someone else who will," Ruby said matter-of-factly. "Hattie, I know this isn't what you wanted, but you need to keep your name out there while you can still ride the wave of your Oscar win."

I massaged my temples as she continued talking, reminding me of all the reasons I loved acting.

"It's your calling, and sometimes God doesn't take us on the path we think we should go."

I thought about all that I'd done up to this point in my life. From dropping out of high school to go on the road performing with my brother Otis, to being a blues singer on the radio, to a maid, to a nightclub singer, back to a maid, to a radio star—and now an Academy Award winner. My path had definitely been filled with twists and turns, mountains and valleys.

"You're right, Ruby," I finally said. "My radio show might have died before it even lived, but I can't let the same thing happen to this tour."

She smiled her pleasure. "Exactly. I know you weren't initially gung ho on touring, but now you have something to prove."

My friend was so right. I wanted everyone who didn't believe in me to regret their decision. "Tell Bert to bring the car around. I have a tour to sell out."

Ruby hugged me as I stood. "That's the Hattie McDaniel I know and love!"

• • •

Whoever said trouble don't last always needed to take a glimpse into my life. I'd been on tour for three weeks and though I'd gone in giving it my all, the interest just hadn't panned out. Mammy may have been a hit on the big screen, but I guess people weren't interested in seeing her on the stage. I had gotten notice that advance sales in Negro theaters were not going well, and I'd heard that Mr. Selznick was not pleased.

I was back in California for a show at the Roxy Theater, a venue in Glendale that could make or break a career. It gave me a chance to come home for a few days, but being here had done little to settle the nervousness that swept through my body.

"I doubt that colored people are used to buying seats in advance," Ruby had told me this morning over breakfast. She had been trying to soothe my angst about the declining ticket sales. "Couple that with the fact that most Negros have limited means and their cinemas are of poor nature, they'll see your personal appearance as special. I know they will."

After three weeks of playing to half-empty houses, I didn't know whether to actually believe that, so her optimism did little to soothe me. Still, I shook away any negative thoughts and tried to concentrate on tonight's show.

Tonight was the first time I was performing before a mixed venue. This was simply something I hadn't done before. At least not since grade school. As I stood backstage, I reminded myself to take slow, deep breaths to steady my nerves.

I peeked out from behind the heavy maroon curtains. The crowd was sparse and only one-fourth of the seats were filled. Nervous anticipation filled me at the scattered colored and white faces. Not only because of the crowd, but because Mr. Selznick had sent his production manager Ray Klune to watch the show.

I took another deep breath and turned to mentally prepare for my performance. I looked up to see Mr. Klune standing backstage.

"Break a leg, Hattie," he said with a grin. But just as quickly, the smile was gone. "I know I need not tell anybody with as fine a sense of showmanship as you, or anybody with the fine sense of taste that you have already demonstrated, that it is of the utmost importance to you and your race that your act be a dignified one, and on the highest possible plane."

I fought the urge to tell him what he could do with his ominous warning and instead gave a slight nod.

I knew his cause for concern. I was supposed to send Mr. Selznick a copy of the script I was doing weeks ago. I'd sent the first draft, which was why the studio was antsy. It made them nervous because I was more sassy than usual. And I'd thrown in a little sexiness. So they had suggested a number of changes. I had been avoiding sending the final draft because I didn't agree with their suggestions. I knew Mr. Selznick wouldn't be pleased but I didn't want him analyzing and trying to make more changes to my script. My plan was to ad-lib so Mr. Klune could only do a written report and not have a tangible script to make sure I was following.

"You 'bout ready, Miss Hattie?" the stage director asked as Mr. Klune returned to his seat.

I nodded and stepped into my dressing room. I always liked taking a couple of minutes to pray before each performance.

As soon as I finished my prayer, the stage director poked his head in the door.

"Okay, you're on in five," he said.

"Thank you. I'm ready," I replied.

This was my element. Always had been. As I prepared myself for my mental space to perform, I squeezed my eyes shut and for some reason I had a flash of a memory of my first real stage performance. My brother Otis had formed a traveling theatrical group and Mama wouldn't let me perform, so I snuck out and did it anyway. Mama had skinned my hide, but the way the audience had roared, whooped, and hollered their approval made every lash worth it.

I'd known I was talented all my life. Otis, who fancied himself a "producer" and "recognizer of talent" confirmed it. He was the one who convinced me—and Mama to allow me—to first step in front of a crowd in 1903, when he and I performed at a carnival trying to get money for food.

Every time I watched an adoring crowd, I knew more than anything, the stage was where I was destined to be.

My mama had never understood, but me, Otis, Sam, and Etta had gotten the entertainment bug from her. Mama was a good singer, probably better than us all, but she'd long ago traded her love of singing for domestic life. That wasn't going to be me.

My mother hated my constant performing. In fact, sometimes she would give me a nickel just to get me to stop singing and dancing.

She was religious and didn't believe in shows, but she'd raised me to be fiercely independent so it should've been no surprise that I was so driven to get what I wanted. And what I wanted was to perform.

I shook away the memory and took a quick glance in the mirror to make sure my head scarf was securely tied and my apron was free from wrinkles, then I headed toward the stage.

After a few minutes, the curtains parted, the house lights dimmed, and the slow sounds of Al Jolson's song "My Mammy" filled the room. Al was a white entertainer who first played Mammy—in blackface. As the piano keys clinked, I slowly lifted up my long dirndl skirt and eased to the edge of the stage.

"Oh, how do, folks?" I said in an exaggerated voice. "You know, I just about forgot I had a real honest-to-goodness audience, after lookin' at you all from the silver screen so long. It just does something to me in here when I see your smiling faces." I sashayed to the front of the stage, put one hand on my hip and the other to my forehead like a salute, and peered out into the crowd. "Yes, suh, there ain't nothin' like a real honest-to-goodness smile—that is, when you mean it." I widened my grin even more, exaggerating to convey my sincerity, and that was exactly what they were waiting for because the audience roared with laughter.

I then launched into a re-creation of Mammy's confrontation with Scarlett over Ashley Wilkes and the petticoat scene from *Gone with the Wind*, ending with my infamous scene with Clark where I said, "My goodness, Mr. Butler, you sho is bad."

Of course that line, which was word for word what I'd said in the film, elicited applause from the audience.

Performing the scene onstage gave me a chance to rework Mammy a little but also to parody the white characters now so firmly enshrined in white folks' imaginations. The funny part was that, the way the laughter filled the room, the white fans had no idea they were even being parodied. They were thoroughly entertained by the extra oomph I added to Mammy on the stage. I made Mammy a character and a characterization and the majority of the people in this room were none the wiser.

When I completed my act, I belted out two original songs.

"You can talk about your Mammy, dear ole Mammy, yes of yore, but things is changing nowadays, an' Mammy's getting bored. Mammy must have some rejuvenation, razzmatazz, and syncopation," I sang.

I loved this revision because I portrayed Mammy as casting off her household duties for some swingy music and a little fun. I got a chance to show white folks there's more to her life than serving them and raising their children. This Mammy was full of energy and sensuality.

But since I know what white folk want, I ended my act with, *"Oh, what's the use? I guess she'll always be, always of yore, people singin' songs about her around their cabin door."*

I took a seat on the lone chair positioned in the center of the stage, popping my corncob pipe into my mouth. *"I'se sorry for even contemplating rejecting my place. I want my chillen nestled to me breast, colored and white, with so much zest."*

I'd thought hard about performing the double entendre, but it was my way of making a mockery of the unjust system. The audience, ignorant of what I was really saying, gave me a boisterous round of applause at the end of each act.

Just when I had the audience thinking I'd always rather be a mammy than anything else, I took a deep bow and broke out in song. By the time I finished, the crowd was clapping and dancing. In their minds, I could dream of freedom, but true happiness really came from serving them. Nothing could be further from the truth, but I was giving folks the fantasy they desired.

At least some folks.

While my white fans were cackling and laughing, it wasn't until I saw a Negro couple in the back of the room get up and leave that I noticed the other Negro faces in the room. While a few smiled jovially, many sat stoically. While one white man in the front row doubled over with laughter, a Negro man sitting across the aisle from him glared at me with disgust, until he too got up and left.

I pushed aside the constricting feeling of hurt in my chest and delivered my closing line with a wide grin and expressive eyes—even though behind the smile, I wanted to cry.

By the time I changed out of my costume and headed out, I had pulled myself together. The theater was pretty much empty, but standing in the parking lot next to my car was Rawley Morris, a reporter with the *California Eagle*.

"Rawley, how are you?" I said, shaking his hand, grateful to see a familiar face, even one that had sometimes been critical of me. "Didn't know you were here."

"I'm well. I was in the back. Glad I was able to come," he continued, pausing for a moment. "Because, truthfully, I came expecting to pen a disparaging article of how you were once again kowtowing to white folks."

I inhaled sharply. "And now?"

The right side of his lip went up and his eyes lit with approval. "You're a wise woman, Hattie McDaniel."

"Whatsoever do you mean?" I asked, playfully batting my eyelashes, relief sweeping through me that he was not here to bash me.

"I watched that white audience in awe. They didn't even get it." He shook his head, impressed and disgusted at the same time.

"I know," I said, shrugging. "They usually never do."

"If they had really listened, they could tell that you found David Selznick's historical dramatization of slavery, the Civil War, and Reconstruction ridiculous. But it's like that just went over their heads," Rawley said.

I responded with only a knowing smile.

"Is that why you wanted to play to white audiences?" he asked, then continued before I could respond. "When I first heard that, I thought it was because you just wanted to entertain white folks." He wagged his finger and shook his head knowingly. "But this showed me there is more to you than people know. The more serious implications of your performance would escape most whites, but it's like being on that stage gives you the chance to look white people in the eye and undermine their racist fantasies with a confusing and unexpected alternative to the Mammy stereotype."

I wanted to breathe a sigh of relief that *finally* someone in the press understood me.

"And if they miss the point, it's all the more powerful, for the joke is really on them," I added, leaning in and lowering my voice. "They were laughing at an image that reflected back their own weaknesses and foibles, a mockery of themselves. But if you write that, I'm going to deny it to the very end," I quickly added.

He smiled again. "I can't believe I'm saying this, but your secret is safe with me. You're more than Mammy. I finally get it."

"Then I would say God led you here today." I chuckled as I headed to my car.

Yes, I was more than Mammy and I was so happy that Rawley could now see that. Now I just wished that the rest of the world could understand as well.

CHAPTER 8

August 1940

When I was just starting out as a performer, Otis would tell me the show must go on—no matter what. Otis could sing and dance and act. But most of all, he was the pushiest of directors, and he viewed me as his star talent. When I had a bad case of pneumonia at age seventeen, I learned then to power through my performances. When the Depression claimed our audience at the nightclub I headlined in Wisconsin, I persevered despite near-empty rooms. Otis was also my buddy, and I so wished he were with me tonight.

But even without him, I wasn't about to let the crowd standing outside the Lincoln Theatre here in DC stop me now. I'd been heart-broken when I saw the protestors picketing in front of the theater.

The signs read, "You'd be sweet too under a white man" and "*Gone with the Wind* hangs the free Negro." Out of all the tour dates, Mr. Selznick had picked this one to attend.

"There she is!" someone hollered.

I kept my head low and speed-walked toward the side door that I'd been trying to quietly sneak into since my driver pulled up to the theater.

Thankfully, they were on the other side of a long guardrail because I was sure the thirty or so protestors would've tackled me to the ground. They looked angry, as if I had personally wronged them.

"Hattie McDaniel, how could you be such a traitor to your people?" someone shouted.

"You make the whole race look bad," another person shouted.

"Hey, Uncle Thomasina, I hope your show flops!"

I tried to tune out the verbal brickbats, but each comment pierced my heart.

As they pummeled me with more disparaging remarks, I fought the urge to stop and try to make them understand my side. *No, that would do no good,* I quickly told myself.

Even if I wanted to engage with the protestors, my brother's voice rang in my head: *The show must go on.*

"Don't you care about the image you're setting for our young girls?" said a young woman wearing a Howard University School of Law sweatshirt over her dress.

It took everything inside me not to stop. *The image?* I wanted to shout. What image? The one of a working actress who made more money than most Negroes would see in their lifetime? More money than she and her protesting friends would make as lawyers. I fought back the urge to respond. Besides, I didn't have the energy. My last stop in Chicago had been spent battling a horrible summer cold. And though I wasn't feeling nearly as bad, I hadn't healed completely. The last thing I needed was a war of words with people who were intent on crucifying me.

My head was pounding and my chest was congested but when I stepped on the stage two hours later, it was like I was able to transform myself into a healthy individual.

Ray Klune might have been duped by my performance in Glendale, but Mr. Selznick wasn't buying it. Mr. Klune's only criticism of my show was that it was a little short, since it ran only ten minutes. But he had endorsed it to Mr. Selznick, even suggesting they add a full orchestra.

For some reason though, Mr. Selznick wanted to see for himself and had flown across the country to watch my performance here in DC. I could tell by the expression on his face as I took my final bow, he wasn't pleased. Throughout the show, when I sang, he frowned. When I sashayed, his brow furrowed. When I gave Mammy some sex appeal, by batting my eyes and shimmying my bosom, I thought he was going to fall out of his seat. So this displeasure on display as he stood outside my dressing room yelling at Mr. Klune was to be expected.

I was about to round the corner when I heard Mr. Selznick reading the riot act to Mr. Klune.

"Is that what you call a good show?" he bellowed. I stopped so I could hear. "That sloppy and sentimental mess? And then did you see how the material veered into inappropriately sexy territory? While I can accept the former, the latter has to go. A sexy Mammy? My God in Heaven." He threw up his hands in utter exasperation.

Mr. Klune was usually a yes-man, so I was surprised when he said, "Could you be overreacting? It wasn't that bad."

"Nothing is going to jeopardize my investment." Mr. Selznick jabbed a finger in Mr. Klune's direction. "If we don't watch out, she will rob herself of stature as a performer by stooping to cheap things."

I inhaled some courage and stepped around the corner.

"Mr. Selznick, Mr. Klune. So glad the two of you could make it to DC," I said, my wide grin belying my queasiness.

Mr. Selznick wasted no time with formalities. "Hattie, you're going to have to delete some of your act. And you need to stick to the script. All of this ad-libbing is unacceptable," he said. Though he had reeled some of his anger in, I could still tell by the way his brows met at the top of his nose, he was not pleased with me.

I swallowed the words screaming to get out. Ad-libbing allowed me to fit my mood and the audience and I'd be damned if he would take that from me.

"The fans don't seem to mind my saucy side," I told him.

"The ticket sales say otherwise," he countered matter-of-factly.

"Then you got all these folks out here protesting you and *Gone with the Wind*."

I wanted to explain to him that most colored folks had seen me only in white films and didn't know about my time in troupes traveling to colored theaters and my early days as the satirical Hattie. The only barometer they had of my talents was as Mammy, so that's where some of the disdain came from. But since that would do little to excuse the fact that his precious movie was being publicly disparaged, I didn't bother saying anything.

I decided to try and shift the focus. "Well, I have the play with Langston Hughes coming up," I said. I was participating in Chicago's American Negro Exposition, a celebration of the seventy-fifth anniversary of Emancipation Day. I was performing in the *Cavalcade of the Negro Theatre*, written by Langston Hughes and Arna Bontemps. Mr. Selznick hadn't wanted me to do it because he only wanted me participating in events his team had arranged so as not to sully Mammy. But he'd finally acquiesced when I reminded him of the colored audiences that performance would put me in front of, and I agreed that the event would be at my own expense.

"My understanding is that the organizers are anticipating a strong turnout," I continued, hoping that the specter of positive exposure would satiate him.

It didn't. "That show is none of my concern," Mr. Selznick snapped.

Before I could respond, the manager of the Lincoln Theatre walked up. His dark face was grim with distress. "Mr. Selznick, I was told I could find you back here," he said.

Mr. Klune stepped up. "Hello, Mr. Lawson, isn't it?"

"Yes. I manage this here establishment for A. E. Lichtman," he said, clasping the lapel of his too-big tweed suit.

"What can we do for you?" Mr. Klune said.

He looked at me, and the enthusiasm he'd had when he hosted a reception for me just this morning had been replaced with concern. "We've finished tallying the box office and, sir, we lost quite a bit of money," said Mr. Lawson. "We need for the studio to reimburse us."

Mr. Selznick looked at him like he'd lost his mind. He took a step toward the theater manager. I didn't know if he was trying to intimidate the man or get his point across, which was crazy since Mr. Selznick's six-foot-one frame still had to be a good three inches shorter than Mr. Lawson's.

"Mr. Lawson, I'm not sure how long you've been in business, but it doesn't work like that," Mr. Selznick said.

Mr. Lawson gritted his teeth. "We're a small theater, and your people told me that Hattie McDaniel is a star. You all assured me that her presence is a guarantee of full houses and enthusiastic audiences."

"She is a star." This time it was Mr. Klune who spoke.

Mr. Lawson looked at me again, then back to the white men standing before him. "I tried to give her a chance, but perhaps it may be that Miss McDaniel, despite her color, is better suited to the white theaters. Between the protestors and poor local ticket sales, colored folks don't seem to want any of Hattie McDaniel."

Mr. Klune and Mr. Selznick exchanged glances as I struggled to keep my head held high.

"I'm sorry, Miss Hattie," he said. Then to Mr. Klune he added, "If you hope to bring any future acts here, I sincerely hope we can talk proper compensation for our loss."

With that, he turned and left.

Mr. Selznick rubbed his temples, exasperation filling his face. He released a heavy sigh.

"I'm going back to my hotel. I have an early flight. Ray, handle this." To me, he said, "Hattie, I expect to see the revised script that you *will* stick to on my desk before you take the stage at your next stop in New York."

Mr. Selznick stomped off without saying good-bye.

"You okay, Miss Hattie?" the stage director asked once both men were gone. I'd seen him pretending to busy himself with boxes, but I knew he had listened to the whole conversation.

"I'm fine, thank you," I said, even though I wasn't. I hastily made my exit to my dressing room.

I sighed and sat down to begin removing my makeup. That's when I noticed that someone had set the NAACP's magazine, *The Crisis,* on a table in my dressing room. I picked it up and examined the photo that covered the entire front page. I'd been so happy when they'd come to take that photograph a week after the Oscar win. I naively believed it was the start of the next phase of my life. I recalled the words I'd given the reporter that day. "I know that in my business, popularity is here today, gone tomorrow. I've learned by living and watching that there are only 18 inches between a pat on the back and a kick in the seat of the pants."

I'd had no idea how prophetic those words were because right about now, I was at inch nineteen. I tossed the magazine in the trash can and began reworking my script.

CHAPTER 9

October 1940

I arrived in Manhattan with a watered-down script. The fire had been extinguished from Mammy. Mr. Selznick had poured a gallon of water on her by threatening to cancel the tour if I continued to ad-lib. I had no acting gigs on the horizon—though I called Mr. Meiklejohn weekly for updates. I'd lost the radio show; I couldn't afford to lose the tour. Right now it was all I had.

I needed to shake off the melancholy cloud that had hung over me since I left DC and focus on the flowers that were before me—literally. It wasn't every day that one received an honor from the First Lady of the United States, but here I was, in Queens, New York, at the World's Fair, receiving a bouquet of roses and an esteemed award from Eleanor Roosevelt.

The excitement in the air was palpable. This was Negro Week at the fair, so they had opened the doors to allow colored and white to mix. The crowd was buzzing with anticipation as they waited for the First Lady to take the stage. I stood off to the side of the stage, peeking out at the audience of more than two thousand people.

The band began playing "The Star Spangled Banner" and the crowd sang along. As the song concluded, the First Lady emerged from the other side of the stage to thunderous applause.

"It's a beautiful day," she said as the crowd roared their approval.

She welcomed the guests, then praised the fair's theme of "The American Common," which was patterned after the custom of New England towns where commons were established to provide an arena for townspeople to meet, discuss, and decide questions of local government.

"The American Common program for the World's Fair is allowing us to present the contributions to American culture of racial and ethnic groups in the United States," she said. "And during Negro Week, I am honored to assist in creating a living picture of the American Negro and their contribution to the cultural development of the United States. And I am especially honored that one of those women is here with us today."

She motioned for me to approach the stage. "Ladies and gentlemen, Hattie McDaniel, the first colored woman to win an Oscar for her role as Mammy in *Gone with the Wind*."

The crowd erupted into applause as I emerged from backstage. The First Lady squeezed my hands, then lifted them to the crowd like I was a heavyweight fighter. The applause grew louder.

As the noise settled, she handed me a beautiful plaque. "This is in honor of your groundbreaking role in cinema and your contributions to Negro culture. Thank you for being an outstanding member of the colored race in the field of theatrical entertainment."

Watching the admiration from the crowd and the First Lady of the United States, I was overcome with emotion. I had always admired and respected Mrs. Roosevelt because from the moment her husband took office, she was clear that America should not expect its new First Lady to be a symbol of elegance, but rather "plain, ordinary Mrs. Roosevelt." Despite this disclaimer, she showed herself to be an extraordinary First Lady.

Her smile softened her strong features as she read the award. "'For your esteemed contribution to the arts, we salute you,'" she said. I knew that she had pushed for her personal maid to play the role of Mammy, but judging from the admiration in her eyes, she bore no ill will.

Then, much to my surprise, she hugged me, a moment of unity and recognition that I was sure would go down in history.

The multiracial crowd erupted in applause again.

"I'd also like to present this special block of stamps commemorating the seventy-fifth anniversary of Emancipation," Mrs. Roosevelt continued.

More applause as I waved to the crowd to express my gratitude.

This honor was the only reason New York was added to my tour schedule at the last minute. Mr. Selznick didn't believe in wasting an opportunity. He figured that since I was going to be in New York, I needed to do a show at the Loews Theater, along with some other personal appearances.

My show was in three days, but I had plenty to keep me busy, including an interview with a New York newspaper. That's where I was racing to now and made it to the penthouse dining room of the Hotel Theresa with ten minutes to spare.

However, there was no time to rest as the reporter was already seated and waiting. We exchanged greetings and he waited patiently while I ordered a cup of coffee to rejuvenate my weary spirit.

"So, Hattie, what are your keys to success?" the reporter asked after the waitress had brought my coffee and I'd gotten it to my liking. I found myself distracted by his flaming-red hair, which was a sharp contrast to his pale peach skin. But the enthusiasm in his eyes told me he was a true fan, so I tried to redirect my attention.

"If you keep trying, something is bound to happen," I said, mustering the energy to remain cordial. "Whether or not it is in your favor is a matter only you can decide. I am optimistic about the future of Negroes in Hollywood cinema. It is just a matter of time." That had become my standard spiel, but as each day passed, I was wondering more and more if those were just empty words.

"The first time I ever saw you was in Sam Pick's," the reporter continued, referring to the nightclub I was working in in Milwaukee before I moved to Los Angeles.

I'd started there as a bathroom attendant in 1930. I hated that job, for seven dollars a week waiting on white women using the toilet. Then one night a group of rowdy anchor clankers came in near closing. They'd demanded entertainment but our nightly singer had already left. Sam, the owner, had reluctantly allowed me onstage and I brought the house down. From that one night, I became a regular performer until Sam had to close the club because of money woes and I piled into a car with some of the performers and headed to LA.

"I enjoyed my time performing there. Too bad the place never quite recovered from the Depression," I said.

He asked more questions and took extensive notes. "Just a few more things," he finally said. "What are your thoughts about the Loews declining to book you?" the reporter asked.

"What do you mean? I'm scheduled to be there at the end of the week," I said.

He frowned. "That's not what I was told."

I'd come straight to my hotel dining room after returning from the Fair. Had Mr. Meiklejohn tried to call me with this news?

The reporter looked at his notes. "The studio's official response is that Loews couldn't accommodate the last-minute request, but our sources tell us that their response derived from something deeper than an inconvenience. The Loews management has become leery of Negro acts prior to the election."

I knew that the pending presidential race with incumbent Democrat Franklin Delano Roosevelt against Republican Wendell Willkie had increased racial tensions in the city. But I didn't understand what that had to do with me.

The reporter must've recognized the confusion on my face because he said, "My sources tell me that the Loews's real fears are that you would draw integrated audiences to their theater and that violent clashes would ensue."

I was so sick of the racist tenor of this era. There had been no fights at the World's Fair. Negroes had never risen up en masse at any of my appearances so this whole diatribe was tiring.

"The idea that our mere gathering would incite violence is not only false; it's exhausting," I said.

The reporter scribbled furiously, then looked up at me and added, "Just a few more questions, then I'll be on my way. What do you say to those who criticize you?"

I released an exasperated sigh. Oh, how I wanted to simply end this interview, but Mr. Selznick would be upset, so I answered. "When I hear the claims that I am selfish in pursuing my dream of acting, it pains my heart. My true goal is to give my own interpretation to the role, to make Mammy a living, breathing character. The way she appeared to me in the book. I can't say this enough. It's a tribute to those women who had struggled in and against slavery," I said.

As I watched this red-haired, freckled-faced man, I wondered if he truly realized the two different worlds we lived in.

"What are your words of advice to those who want to follow in your path?" he asked.

I motioned for the waitress to come refill my coffee, as I thought about the perfect response. "I always offer words of encouragement to the younger generation based on my personal philosophy, a blend of Booker T. Washingtonian principles of hard work, self-help, and the power of positive thinking. I tell them, do not become discouraged. If the world does not accept your offering at first," I said, thinking of my own struggles, "remember 'success' is a word and thought put into action."

The response must have been fitting for him because he smiled, then waited patiently as the waitress refilled my coffee. I dropped two sugar cubes into the cup, as he said, "You are a very wise woman with a determined attitude, Miss McDaniel. Is this something that was instilled in you from your youth?"

I nodded as a nostalgic smile spread across my face. I paused for a moment to reflect on my family, especially my parents. "Yes, my parents worked very hard. My father was disabled from fighting in the Civil War and unable to work, so my mother worked from sunup to sundown to pick up the slack. We were not rich, but we had an abundance of determination."

"Your parents were born into slavery, correct?"

"They were." Images of my father sitting in his rocker, his unlit pipe dangling from his lips like a security blanket, brought a smile to my face. Memories of how he would calmly dispense life lessons made my heart swell. He could barely walk, was going blind, and had gotten his jawbone blown out in the war, so it was hard for him to work. Mama had given birth to thirteen kids, but only seven of us survived. She had a lifetime of heartache and our extreme poverty only made things worse.

"Our readers would love to hear more."

That made me relax. Talking about my family was something I'd never tire of. I told the reporter a little of my background. How my father, Henry, had been born a slave in Spotsylvania County, Virginia, where he plowed the fields until he was sold away from his family. How in 1863, when the Emancipation Proclamation was delivered, he'd joined a contraband camp—made up of runaway slaves—to fight in the war. He met my mother, a newly released slave, there. Both of them were smart and ambitious and dreamed of a better life for their children. I talked about his years fighting the government for his military pension, which he never received because the government kept asking for his birth certificate to prove his identity. But since he was a slave he couldn't prove where he was born, let alone when he was born.

"I always believed it was this final battle that killed him," I told the reporter. My heart ached as I thought of my father's feeble posture, long list of ailments, and deteriorating disabilities, which were a constant reminder of his service to a country that just five decades earlier had enslaved him.

"My mother did her best to hold our family together but her options were few," I continued. By the time I was finished, I noticed that the reporter had stopped writing and was listening intently as if I were a griot relaying a story.

Finally I said, "Well, I'm sure I've given you more than enough."

"Yes, yes," he said with a wide grin as he closed his notepad. "I'm sure I have enough for an interesting and thorough piece. It's been such a pleasure talking with you."

He stood and bid me good-bye. I sat for a moment thinking of my parents. My mother had come to terms with my love of the stage, but she never got to see the fruits of my labor before she died in 1920, two years before my father. I didn't realize I was crying until I felt a wet tear fall down my cheek.

I wiped my face and gathered my things. I needed to get to a telephone and call Mr. Selznick to find out whether or not it was true about the Loews canceling my show.

"Well, if it isn't the incomparable Hattie McDaniel."

I looked up from my table when I heard my name. My mouth was agape in shock at the figure before me, the wiry man I hadn't seen in fifteen years.

"Nym?" I struggled to contain my emotions at the sight of my second husband, Nym Lankford. "Nym? Wh-what are you doing here?"

He shrugged and didn't make eye contact as his eyes darted around the dining room. "Heard you were in town. Figured you'd be at the only fancy hotel that allowed colored people. Asked around and someone said you were up here. I just . . . I don't know . . . just wanted to come see you in person and say I'm sorry." He couldn't even look me in the eyes.

"You should be." He still had those enchanting hazel eyes that made my insides dance and a thin, devilish smile. He wore a dingy gray suit that swallowed his scrawny frame, but he was still as handsome as the day we'd met. But no matter how he looked, inside I felt nothing but shock and disdain. I hadn't seen this man since he walked out of my life with no explanation whatsoever. I couldn't believe he had the audacity to show his face to me ever again.

CHAPTER 10

October 1940

I stared at the man before me like he was a ghost. Well, he was a ghost—of my past.

"What are you doing here?" I repeated, sitting erect as I willed away the rush that had made my heart speed up.

"Like I said, heard you were in town, and I don't know . . ." Nym shifted his weight from one foot to the other, his tattered and stained tan loafers doing a slow tap dance. "Just felt like I needed to give you an explanation."

My chest slowly rose, then fell. "Fifteen years later? You finally decided you owe me an explanation?" I was incredulous.

"I-I don't know what to say, Hattie," he stammered, running his hand up and down the back of his neck. I guess he still had that nervous habit.

The emotions I'd felt about my parents moments ago had been completely obliterated—replaced by full-on fury. I'd loved Nym hard. After the death of my first husband, Howard, in 1915, I hadn't thought loving another man was possible. And then my daddy died after years of illness, and Nym, who worked in show business with me as a laborer on set, was there saying words like, "Hattie, we're going to do this, we're going to do that." Howard had been focused on providing a life for us, but Nym had been solely focused on making me happy. He pulled laughter from my crying. While Howard had been stodgy, Nym was alluring and full of life. Even sex with Howard had been trite and mechanical. Nym encouraged me to embrace my sexuality and be proud of every inch of my body. I had opened myself up to him in a way I never thought possible.

I shouldn't have married Nym amid my vulnerability over my father's death. But that's the thing about grief. It envelops you in darkness and makes you susceptible to the first ray of light. Nym was my sunshine.

We'd run off and gotten married, and for two years, we enjoyed a glorious life. Nym was a man who knew how to make me feel like a woman. He encouraged my career and was by my side as I recorded my first blues song. He toured with me as I performed across the country, and we lived it up on the road. He was my personal cheerleader at my various minstrel shows, where I was showered with love from attendees. (That's why it was so darned confusing that my people thought I was a sellout.) And then we returned to Denver, where I continued to play local theaters. Life was good. Or so I thought.

One day Nym left to get cigarettes and never returned. Just like that, I became a cliché.

I had heard of things like that happening, but I never dreamed it would happen to me. I was bedridden with depression for days. Initially I thought maybe something nefarious had happened to Nym. Perhaps he was gunned down by gangsters since he did like to play the numbers. Or maybe he had amnesia, anything that would explain how and why my husband would be gone.

But then one of his relatives told me that he was not dead but alive and well in New York City. I was heartbroken and tried to find him, to no avail.

I struggled to go on with my life, working, dating, never telling anyone I was married, because, was I really? And then, finally, when I could take it no more, I slid one of his cousins ten dollars and got his address in New York.

I showed up on his doorstep, ready to confront him. What I wasn't ready for was the bright-eyed, bushy-haired woman who answered the door with a curly-haired baby boy on her hip—a baby boy who was the spitting image of my husband. It wasn't just the baby's appearance that ripped my insides to shreds—it was her words. "You looking for Nym? He's not here. I'm his wife, Irene."

I was momentarily frozen, so she said, "Is there something I can help you with? You from the census?"

I couldn't find my words so I made up some excuse I didn't even remember all these years later. I couldn't get back to Penn Station and out of New York fast enough.

I cried all the way back to Colorado. And then the next day, I finally filed for divorce. I guess I hadn't done it in the three years that Nym had been gone because, deep down, I'd always hoped that he would come back. I never heard from Nym again. That's why I was dumbfounded to see him standing in front of me now.

"Did you hear me?" Nym asked.

I shook away my thoughts, wondering how long he'd been talking to me. "Huh?"

"I said, you're doing good for yourself," he said, sliding into the chair across from me as if I'd extended an invitation. Finally he made eye contact. "Congrats on the Academy Award win. I always knew you'd make it."

"What do you want, Nym?" I said. I was tempted to look around the hotel dining area for a security guard. Or a butcher knife.

"I told you I wanted to . . . I wanted to . . ."

"Apologize for breaking my heart? For being a bigamist?" I answered for him.

He looked down at his hands as he drummed his fingers on the table.

"All of that, I guess."

"Does your wife know that your marriage is invalid?" I asked, suddenly wishing I had said something to her all those years ago. Why had I left him to live happily ever after? I should've blown up his world the way he'd shattered mine.

Nym looked at me and bit his bottom lip. "It's not my marriage to her that's no good."

I stared at him, trying to process what he was saying to me. "Pardon me?"

"I've been married to Irene since we were kids," he confessed. His fingers drummed faster, matching the pace of my heartbeat.

"Oh my God," I said. "So *I* married a bigamist?"

He stopped drumming and lowered his head in shame. "You make it sound so ugly."

"Is there another way that it could sound?" When he didn't reply, I leaned back and sat erect in my seat. I needed to compose myself. I was not going to give this man the satisfaction of letting him know how utterly crushed I'd been. "I don't know if you came in here hoping to be absolved of your infidelity. I don't know if you came here looking for money. But whatever your reason, you wasted your time."

He held his head high as if I'd insulted him.

"No, I don't need your money," he said with conviction. But just as easily as the words left his mouth, he added, "But I . . . I was kind of hoping you'd help me maybe get back into show business. Work has been kinda dry, and when I saw you'd be here, I figured a good word from you would help one of these theaters bring me on board."

His audacity made me burst out laughing. One of those loud laughs that came out of nowhere, from deep down in my soul. Perhaps that was why the people at the tables next to me had turned to look at us.

Nym kept his gaze locked on me. "I know we had our issues, but you know I'm a good, hardworking employee."

"You have lost your mind," I finally told him, my laughter morphing into indignation. "It will be a cold day in hell before I help you do anything, Nym Lankford. Now get out of my face before I have you arrested and then call your wife and let her know you're a two-timing sap."

"Now, Hattie—"

"Get out!" I screamed, slamming my palms on the table, causing him to jump and more people around us to turn and stare.

He glared at me, I guess assessing if he should push me, then decided it would be in his best interest to leave.

"I really am sorry about everything, Hattie," he said, slowly standing. "It was fun being with you—our life and all."

It wasn't lost on me that he hadn't said a thing about love. So I'd just been something "fun" to do? That thought made me ill.

He continued, "I just didn't know how to tell you I was already married and Irene was demanding that I come home. So I just left. I don't expect you to understand."

"Good, because I don't. Good-bye." I pushed the chair back from the table, stood, tucked my purse under my arm, and strutted out the dining room.

It had taken me the longest to get over Nym. The last thing I needed was a trip down that memory lane. I didn't look back. I just wanted to get back to my room and try to erase the memory of this day altogether.

CHAPTER 11

November 1940

I had never set foot on the campus of Howard University in Washington, DC, but it was everything I'd ever imagined it to be. Flanked by beautiful redbrick buildings, lush landscaping, towering trees that hung over serene walkways, and lawns that were immaculate enough to be on the cover of *Architectural Digest*, the campus looked a colored paradise.

As one of the leading Negro colleges in the country, Howard was home to a diverse community of students and faculty from all over the country who were passionate about education and social justice. It was a vibrant center of cultural and intellectual activity. The school was celebrating its seventy-third year and one of their events was a Salute to Excellence luncheon for Negro women in the arts. I was honored that I'd been selected and invited to the campus.

There had to be 150 students in the medical auditorium, where today's ceremony was being held. The professor who organized the event had told me to expect about sixty students, mostly members of the Howard Players, a club for students hoping to work in film and TV. I don't know when I started allowing the negative voices criticizing my roles to override the positive ones, but it was refreshing to be reminded that for many colored people, the things I had done in my career were groundbreaking. It also wasn't lost on me that the last time I saw Howard University students, they had been protesting my presence at the Lincoln Theatre.

I'd just finished my twenty-minute speech about my career, where I talked about my commitment to acting and paving the way for future actors, closing with a promise to be there for all in need. Now I was standing at the podium at the front of the room, fielding questions, which, judging from the fact that half the room had their hands raised, were plentiful.

"Yes, we'll start with you," I said, pointing to a young lady in an indigo blue jacket in the front row.

The young lady stood and in a shaky voice said, "I understand you've been acting since you were little. But when did you get serious about it?"

"I was always serious," I responded. "I won a medal in dramatic arts when I was fifteen. One year later, my oldest brother, Otis, who wrote his own show and songs, persuaded my mother to let me go on the road with his troupe. I loved every minute of it, the tent shows, the kerosene lights, the contagious enthusiasm of the small-town crowds."

I loved that these young people looked at me as if they were sponges, ready to soak up every piece of the knowledge I could impart. Another student raised his hand and blurted out a question before I could even call on him. "With so many people who want to get into the business, can you tell us about your lucky break?" the young man asked.

That made me chuckle. I leaned against the podium. "Isn't it funny how people see your final destination but not your journey? I moved to Los Angeles with a shiny new pocketbook but very little cash in it. For years I sang in choruses, worked in mob scenes, thankful for the smallest thing. I was an extra in hundreds of films. Many extras complain about getting tired of sitting around on the sets. I never tired. For me, a soundstage was as exciting as an Agatha Christie mystery. I learned so much, just sitting and watching. But this wasn't an overnight journey."

Several more hands went up and I pointed to a girl at the back of the room.

"Do you feel like you have made an impact? And what do you

say to all of your critics?" I was impressed with the confidence in her voice. These students were truly exceptional.

"I know I have made an impact. In addition to the Academy Awards, I'm the first Negro woman in the Screen Actors Guild, a union for actors. That opened the doors for others," I said. "And many of those loudest in their condemnation of me are newcomers who do not remember the days when no Negro player was given a dressing room, when there were no hairdressers on the sets for Negro actresses, when no studio hired a Negro wardrobe girl. I have seen many changes in the film city and the trend has been one of increasing gain.

"I have never apologized for the roles I play," I continued to the captive crowd. "Several times I have persuaded the directors to omit dialect from modern pictures. Sometimes in our impatience, we want change immediately. But change often comes incrementally, a little here, a little there."

That garnered another round of applause. I answered some more questions before Lorraine, the young lady who had introduced me, stepped up next to me.

"We promised Miss McDaniel we would be respectful of her time, so that's it for the questions," Lorraine said.

"One more question," a young boy from the back of the room said, jumping up. And without waiting to be acknowledged, he said, "Is it true that Clark Gable is colored?"

Several students gasped, some snickered, and thankfully, the professor stepped in. I'd heard that rumor in Hollywood, but I wasn't about to get caught up in any gossip, especially about my friend.

"Mr. Robbins," the stern professor said, her displeasure evident, "I am highly disappointed in you. You know we do not traffic in gossip." The young man shrank back into his seat and she turned to me. "My apologies."

I nodded to let her know it was okay, but I was grateful I didn't have to address that rumor.

"Miss McDaniel is going to close us out with a special treat," the professor said to the crowd before taking her seat.

I moved back to the podium as a hush fell over the room. I cupped the mic in my hand and began to wiggle my shoulders as the music played for my 1929 song "I Thought I'd Do It."

I sang the first verse, invigorated by their anxious eyes.

"You never miss sweet cakes till your sugar's all gone."

The young audience started clapping along. Many of them had never heard my blues songs, but the way they were clapping and dancing as I paraded up and down the aisles let me know they were enjoying it.

"Ain't no use of sniffle, whimpering, and whine. I took you back for your last, last time," I sang.

All my blues songs were about men doing me wrong—probably not the most appropriate songs for this group of Howard University students, but the professor had asked me to sing some of my most popular songs, so I did.

It had been years since I'd sung some of the blues hits that had made me radio famous. Few people knew I was one of the first Negro women to sing on the radio in this country, but that was back in the 1920s, when blues dominated the music world. In all, I'd made sixteen slides between 1926 and 1929.

And now today, I was ecstatic about the chance to revisit some of my old music for this new young audience. I'd been thrilled when the administrators from Howard's drama department sent a telegram telling me they were giving me an award and honoring me for my work in *Gone with the Wind*. That in and of itself had been enough. But when one of the professors said she was a big fan of my music, naming every song I'd ever done, I was doubly thrilled. She'd asked if I would do the honor of singing a few songs at the ceremony. She just didn't know, it was my honor.

I finished the last song to a standing ovation, before taking my seat as Lorraine returned to the podium.

"Now, you knew she could act and dance, but who knew she had a voice like that?" Lorraine said to more applause.

"Miss McDaniel," Lorraine continued, "on behalf of the drama department at Howard University and the Howard Players, we want to say that you and your work are an inspiration to us all."

This was why I did what I did. For this sea of young faces, in all hues, and their futures. It felt good to be among my people without criticism. Young people who might one day walk through doors that I'd opened.

"We know that gardenias are your favorite," Lorraine continued. "So we'd like to present you with this bouquet." She handed me an amazing three-foot-tall bouquet of white flowers. I was going to have a bear of a time getting that back to Los Angeles on the train, but I was proudly going to do it.

"Thank you so much," I said, standing and taking the flowers. "May I quickly say something?"

She motioned to the microphone. I stepped up, feeling just as grateful as I had the day I won the Academy Award.

"To each and every one of you," I said. "I mean this. Please don't hesitate to let me know if I can be of service when you're ready to make your transition to Hollywood. I don't know what exactly I'll be able to do, but I am ready, willing, and committed to helping you."

Excited chatter filled the room and joy filled my heart as I returned to my seat.

"This concludes our program," Lorraine said. "Please stay and enjoy our reception, hosted by the members of Sigma Gamma Rho Sorority. For those of you who don't know, Miss McDaniel is a charter member from the Sigma Sigma Chapter in Los Angeles"—she grinned widely—"and my sorority sister, so you know that we made the reception extra nice. Enjoy!"

I didn't immediately make it into the reception area as I fielded more questions from eager young students. I was thrilled to see some aspiring writers and producers in the group. One of the students told me that the Howard Players were interested in not just acting and writing but technical work, makeup, stage direction, and scene painting. Hopefully, all of those doors would be opened to these talented young people.

The crowd had pretty much cleared out when I noticed a young girl hanging back. She had big doe eyes and a stained white dress. Her long black hair hung in two plaits. She looked as if she was scared to speak.

"Hello there," I said. "Did you enjoy the program?"

"You have no idea," she said. "I, um, I was h-hoping I could have your autograph."

That's something I would never tire of. When I was a little girl practicing dances we believed would make us famous, Sam, Etta, Otis, and I would also practice signing our names because we knew this day would come.

"I'd be honored," I said. I took her notebook and scribbled: *Wishing you bountiful blessings. Love, Hattie McDaniel.*

Her hands trembled as she took the paper. "Thank you so much. This is for my mother. She . . . we are huge fans. You're her favorite person in the whole wide world."

"Awww, isn't that sweet," I said. "What's your name?"

"Addie."

"Oh, that's my sister's name."

"I . . . I know. I know everything about you." She was so nervous, I just wanted to reach out and take her into a big bear hug.

"This is just, this is just so amazing. Today is my mama's birthday and I'm gonna give her this," she said, holding up the paper I'd signed. "We don't have much and I can't get her nothing else, but she's gonna appreciate this more than anything I can buy anyway."

I was moved by the pure joy in her voice. "Your family lives here in DC?"

She nodded. "Yes, ma'am."

"Well, I'm glad you'll get to spend the day with her."

"My mother . . ." She paused, then her enthusiasm tempered as she lowered her head. "My mama is a maid, but she says you're her inspiration. We watch all your movies together, even the ones where you didn't say anything."

The shame that filled her face saddened me. "First of all, thank you to you and your mother. Secondly"—I took her chin and lifted it—"don't you ever be ashamed of what your mother has done, or is doing. There is no shame in domestic work. She is putting food on the table."

"Yes, ma'am."

"My mother was a domestic too. Always remember that our mothers do the best with what they have," I told her.

She nodded. "I know, but when I graduate, I wanna be successful like you," she said.

"Don't be like me. Be better than me. But," I said, waving a finger, "if you know all about me, you know that I worked as a maid as well. You do what you have to do. But for some reason, I believe you're destined for greater things."

That made a smile spread across her face. "Oh, yes, ma'am. I'm gonna be a history teacher. Or a writer. I just . . . well, it's sorta hard because I feel like I need to help my mama and my brothers out."

"That's noble of you, but I'm sure your mother wants you to stay in school." I reached over to the chair I'd been sitting in and grabbed my mink stole and handbag, then pulled out a piece of paper and wrote my number down. "Here, take my number. And if you are ever in Los Angeles and need anything, give me a call."

Her eyes lit up and she watched in awe as I draped my stole over one shoulder. I was moved by this eager young girl and prayed that life would bring her all the blessings she could handle. Suddenly, I paused, then slid my stole off. "You know what would go well with that autograph for your mama's birthday gift?" I handed her the stole. "This."

Her mouth formed a perfect O as her eyes grew even wider. "Nooooo."

"Yesssss," I said, smiling. "The Lord has blessed me, so I can be a blessing to others. Tell your mother happy birthday."

Addie didn't reply. Instead, she threw her arms around my neck and cried.

CHAPTER 12

January 1941

If we weren't sitting in the middle of the Brown Derby restaurant, I would've let out a piercing scream. But this was the go-to spot for wheeling-and-dealing lunches. In fact, Greta Garbo was sitting two tables over and I'd heard she was up for a part in a new movie, *Two-Faced Woman*, so I knew those were movie execs with her. The last thing I needed was word spreading that Hattie McDaniel was making a fool out of herself in public.

But with the news my agent had just delivered, suppressing my elation wasn't easy.

"This is just what the doctor ordered," I said to Mr. Meiklejohn, who was sitting across from me, his eyes wide with excitement, as I read the script he'd given me twenty minutes ago.

Since returning from New York and that disastrous encounter with my ex-husband three months ago, I'd been in a funk more than ever. I'd come down with a horrible case of bronchitis that I couldn't shake for months. I spent most of my days in bed trying to heal and hadn't even been able to spend the holidays with my family like I'd hoped. Not being able to work gave me a lot of time to think. And I realized that I had little control over my own career. I'd decided to change that and had been pushing Mr. Meiklejohn to find me more work.

"I'm glad you like it," Mr. Meiklejohn said.

Mr. Selznick had loaned me out to 20th Century Fox to film a movie called *Maryland*, of course playing a servant, but I couldn't do anything that I really wanted to do. Mr. Selznick had rejected me for a number of roles and I was getting beyond frustrated because his possessiveness was stifling my career. Little by little, my enthusiasm and optimism were dying as I was relegated to simpleminded character after simpleminded character. I felt like he was in complete control of my life.

But this—this script in front of me—was an answered prayer. It was called *In This Our Life*. It was the perfect thing for me to break out of the box I was in. It was the story of a hardworking housekeeper whose ambitious son is accused of killing a little girl in a hit-and-run. It was a serious drama and I knew that I'd get some pushback because of my comedic background, but I wanted this role bad.

"I don't just like it. I love it. This role was written for me," I said, my eyes dancing in anticipation.

Mr. Meiklejohn smiled. "I knew it as soon as I read it," he said. "As a matter of fact, it's written by an up-and-coming screenwriter. And he said he had you in mind as he wrote the story."

"Oh, this is just magnificent," I said, tapping the paper. "Plus, this would definitely assuage any negativity that the NAACP has been throwing my way. This is the type of role they've been hoping for for Negro actors."

As I fingered the script, my mind raced back to Mr. Selznick and his constant limitations. "Do you think the studio will let me take it?" I asked.

In *Maryland*, I played a cook named Carrie, who amused audiences by scrapping with her no-account on-screen husband, Shadrach, played by the actor Ben Carter. I knew people felt the part was beneath me. Shoot, my friend Ethel Waters had even turned the role down because she felt it too demeaning. But Ethel had a husband and was starring on Broadway, so she could afford to be selective. I hadn't done a movie since *Gone with the Wind*, and since returning from tour,

I had made only eleven dollars so I'd needed to take whatever work I could get.

My underemployment stemmed from being caught between offers of conventional Negro roles and Mr. Selznick fretting that the part would be too close to Mammy. He didn't want any other movie projecting the Mammy image and that left me dangling since the reality was that those were the only roles really available to me. I truly was experiencing an Oscar curse, a term Luise Rainer had coined after winning two Oscars for best actress in the 1930s and being unable to find work after.

"Getting the studio on board is going to prove a challenge," Mr. Meiklejohn admitted, stroking his chin. "But I know how important this is to you, so I'll be working diligently."

I needed Mr. Meiklejohn to make this happen. I clasped my hands and leaned in so he could understand the magnitude of my request. "This is my chance, Mr. Meiklejohn. This is something that no one can complain about. This"—I tapped the script again—"will bridge the divide I have with both coloreds and whites. This is what I want," I said, nervous anticipation filling me. This role would definitely put me in the running for another Oscar. The writing was some of the most powerful that I'd ever seen for a Negro actor.

"I'm on it," Mr. Meiklejohn said. "One other thing: Did you give any thoughts to the request for recipes from the studio?"

"That's just ridiculous," I mumbled, my enthusiasm tempered. Mr. Selznick wanted me to get coverage in fan magazines, which movie consumers loved. But unlike white actresses, who were in the magazine offering fashion, beauty, and love advice, they wanted me to provide cooking tips.

"I don't use recipes to cook," I said dismissively. "So I'm unable to provide them. I do everything by instinct and care nothing for precise measurement. When Will Rogers asked for recipes for his party, it took me a whole day in the kitchen to re-create the recipes for cornbread, greens, and icebox cake in order to give him exact measurements."

"They also want fried chicken," he added.

I rolled my eyes. "Of course they do."

"They're going to call it Mammy's Fried Chicken à la Maryland."

"To plug the new film," I said with disgust.

Mr. Meiklejohn shrugged. "You know what? I'll send over the cornbread, greens, and icebox cake recipes and tell them that's all I have."

Before I could thank him, my eyes swept over his shoulder at the man who had just appeared at our table.

"Hattie McDaniel! What a pleasure to see you."

Unlike a few months ago when it had been Nym surprising me, I was grateful to see this friendly face.

"Well, I'll be," I said, standing to greet him. "It has been far too long."

After we hugged, I turned to my agent. "Mr. Meiklejohn, this is James Lloyd Crawford, an old friend."

"What? We're still friends? I haven't spoken to you in more than a decade," James joked, his gentle smile filling the room.

I chuckled as I draped my arm through James's. "I met James when I was performing in Wyoming with the Theater Owners Booking Association," I said.

"But we became dear friends when you were performing at Sam Pick's in Milwaukee," James said. He leaned closer to Mr. Meiklejohn like he was letting him in on a secret. "I'm the one who convinced her to get out of that bathroom tending to customers and get up onstage."

"That is not how that went." I laughed as I sat back down. James was a regular in Sam Pick's, one of the few nonperforming coloreds that was allowed in the popular nightclub.

"Well, whomever was responsible has my eternal gratitude," Mr.

Meiklejohn said, standing. "Now, if you will excuse me, I must get going. I have to go convince Mr. Selznick of your new destiny." He shook the script in his hand. "Claiming good outcomes."

"As am I," I said.

"I'm sorry. I didn't mean to interrupt your lunch," James said.

"No, we have concluded our business and I must get going to another appointment," Mr. Meiklejohn said as he held up the check in my direction. "I'll take care of this on the way out, Hattie." To James, he added, "It was a pleasure to meet you, Mr. Crawford."

After we both bid Mr. Meiklejohn good-bye, I motioned for James to take a seat. "Please tell me you can stay for coffee so we can catch up."

"I'd be honored," James said, taking the seat Mr. Meiklejohn had just vacated. "I'd just come through to grab a cup of java so this is perfect."

The waitress came and cleared our plates and utensils.

"Is there anything I can get for you, sir?" she asked James.

"I'll have a cup of coffee. Hattie?"

"I'll have the same," I told her. She smiled and scurried away and I reached out and took James's hands in mine.

"So what are you doing in Los Angeles?" James had been a dear friend, but I'd met him when I was dating a man named Roscoe Conkling Simmons. Plus, even though James had a stocky build and the prettiest white teeth I'd ever seen, I'd never really been physically attracted to him.

"I moved here a few months ago," he replied. "I kept saying I was going to look you up, but you're an Academy Award winner now, so I was sure your plate runneth over with potential suitors."

If only he knew.

"I'm never too busy for a friend," I said, squeezing his hands before releasing them.

Waiting for our coffee, we started talking about ten years' worth of stuff—his real estate ventures, the race riots in Chicago, Harlem, Detroit, and LA, my film work, the Academy Award, and more. I was reminded how astute he was regarding world events as he talked about President Roosevelt's "Four Freedoms" recent message to Congress and this new sculpture they were building called Mount Rushmore.

"So, who are you dating these days?" James asked.

I smirked, ignoring his question. "What happened to your wife, the one you used to always have on your arm at the club, who let everyone know she used to dance at the Cotton Club in Harlem? What was her name?"

"Pearl. And she wasn't my wife."

"Umm-hmmm, so you say." I chuckled.

He leaned in, placing his arms on the table. "I don't have a wife. I'm waiting to marry you."

"If you don't hush with that," I said, a wave of heat filling my cheeks. I'd known James was sweet on me, but I'd never taken it as anything serious.

His tongue wet his lips as his eyes ran up and down my body.

"I'm sorry. I don't mean to be rude," he said, catching himself. "You're just looking real nice, Hattie. Hollywood has been good to you." He leaned back in his chair as the waitress returned with our coffees. "Are you seeing anyone?" he asked after she set our drinks down and walked away. "Or are you still married to the stage?"

I flashed back over the loves of my life. My first husband, Howard Hickman, had said the same thing. We'd married when I was seventeen. He wanted a wife and I wanted lights. I used to think that was why Nym left (now I knew it was just because he was a toad).

"You really shouldn't concern yourself with who I'm seeing," I said, trying to feign indignation. But in reality, I was flattered. "But if you must know, no one at the moment." I let the latter question hang in the air. No man was ever ready for my answer about my love of the stage.

James spoke. "Well then, if there's no one around that I should be concerned with, and there's no one around that you should be concerned with, we should concern ourselves with each other."

I giggled, because the expression on his face was serious.

"Let me take you out to eat."

I motioned around the restaurant. "Uh, I just finished eating."

"That was lunch. Let me take you to dinner," he said matter-of-factly.

"Let's just finish our coffee and see." I pointed to our cups.

James acquiesced and we made more small talk for the next hour. Finally, I said, "Well, I must really be going as well. It was so good to see you and catch up."

"So, what about dinner?" he hurriedly asked as I pushed my chair back.

Hesitation swept through me. I had no interest in dating right now, but I really had enjoyed my conversation with James. I found his intelligence refreshing, his wittiness delightful, and his friendship enjoyable. Plus, I recognized that the best relationships always grew out of friendship.

"How is tomorrow?" I finally said.

"If I can't take today, I'll take tomorrow. Marian Anderson and Dorothy Maynor are having a concert and I'd love it if you'd accompany me," James said.

"Then it's a date." I smiled as I stood and retrieved my straw handbag. I pulled a piece of paper out, wrote my information down, and slid the paper to him. "Looking forward to it."

The next evening, James Lloyd Crawford picked me up and took me to dinner, then the concert. That was followed by lunch the next day, and dinner again the day after that. For three weeks straight, we spent every day together. It had been years since I had felt so alive, so desired. Over the years, I hadn't given much time to dating seriously, instead opting to, as James said, focus on my true loves of acting and singing. But before I knew it, I found myself in love again, and this time, I wanted nothing more than to build a future with James Lloyd Crawford.

CHAPTER 13

March 1941

In my forty-seven years on this earth, I'd only truly loved one man. As I sat in the small room of the Union Baptist Church waiting to marry James, thoughts of Howard Hickman filled my head.

We'd originally met in 1910, and the first thing I'd noticed was that he appeared to be on some sort of starvation strike. Though he had the smoothest umber-colored skin I'd ever seen, I just wanted to cook him a decent meal because it was obvious he hadn't had one.

My sisters were already married off by the time they were seventeen, and I had been determined that wouldn't be my story. So taking up dalliances with a man was not on my list of things to do, but there was something about Howard, with his crooked smile and hair that looked like it was freshly pressed.

I had married Howard exactly 121 days after meeting him. And I'd been heartbroken when precisely four years later, he'd died of the flu. Then there had been Nym, who at the time I thought I'd loved. He'd soured me on marriage altogether and made me vow to be single forever.

That's why I couldn't believe I was in this tiny Tucson, Arizona, church about to say "I do" again. After only two months of dating, James had taken me to dinner at Ivie's Chicken Shack. Though the place was small, it was one of my favorite restaurants because it was so tastefully decorated and you were liable to see any number of jazz greats taking a go on the spirit piano. I'd told James how much I liked

Ivie's on our first date and he'd remembered. After dessert, he shocked me even further when he got down on one knee and presented me with an impressive diamond ring while asking for my hand in marriage.

That was three weeks ago. James and I had planned a quick civil ceremony at the courthouse in Tucson, since you could immediately marry in Arizona. But while we were waiting on my bouquet, Ruby had talked us into moving the wedding to Union Baptist Church here in Tucson because she knew the pastor, Rev. Percy B. Cornelius, and she felt our union needed to be ordained in a church.

"Are we ready now?" Reverend Cornelius asked, his brow creasing with exasperation.

I knew he was aggravated with me as I'd delayed the service for four hours while awaiting the delivery of my bridal bouquet from LA. When we'd arrived in Tucson I'd discovered I'd left my bouquet cooling in the refrigerator. I'd spent two weeks having the most exquisite gardenias and orchids picked for the wedding. I wasn't about to walk down the aisle without them.

Now my bouquet was in hand, so I smiled, brushed down my dress, and said, "Yes, Reverend Cornelius. We're ready."

He nodded his approval and headed inside the sanctuary.

I glanced at myself in the floor-length mirror in the vestibule. I'd carefully picked out this white crepe gown with gold bead trim. I'd topped it off with a Juliet cap with gold sequins and gold slippers.

I had forgone a wedding party and told my friends I would celebrate with them upon my return to LA. So when Bobby Brooks, the twelve-year-old tenor I'd hired, began singing "Because," I slowly made my way inside alone.

My heart smiled at the sight of James in his black dovetail jacket, oversized tie, gray pants, and black oxfords. Though I'd known James for years, it was hard to believe that it was just a few months ago that I began to look at him in a different light.

"We are gathered here today . . ." Reverend Cornelius began his standard speech and I stood next to James smiling both inside and out. I clutched my bouquet as I promised to love, honor, and cherish—I'd been adamant that there was to be no "obeying" in any of my vows. I didn't want to start off my marriage lying to the Lord.

". . . And so, by the power vested in me by the state of Arizona, I now pronounce you, Hattie McDaniel, and you, James Lloyd Crawford, husband and wife."

Little Bobby and the five other people in the room (friends of Reverend Cornelius) erupted in applause as James leaned in and kissed me. There were no sparks like I felt when I was marrying Howard, no awakening of my soul. But that's because I was older and wiser. I loved James, but I'd been on this trek long enough to know that a good marriage needed more than love. It needed two people looking outward in the same direction. James and I had that.

As we exited, a reporter outside the church approached us. I didn't even know the press had gotten word that I was here.

"Congratulations, Hattie," the reporter said. "How do you feel about marriage number two?" In that moment I was glad I'd kept my marriage to Nym quiet. Few people knew about it. I guess that was how he was able to successfully be a bigamist.

My arm was draped through James's, so I pulled him closer. "I personally intend to stay married forever this time," I said.

I kept walking as the reporter blasted a slew of other questions. Normally, I welcomed press, but today was about me and my husband. And Act 2 of my new life.

• • •

I was in matrimonial bliss. In our short time together, I felt like James and I had created a harmonious partnership. He had shocked me by gifting me 160 acres of Montana farmland as a honeymoon gift. I didn't know what I was supposed to do with it since I never had any intention of moving to Montana, but I was touched by the gesture.

I still had to work, so instead of heading back to Los Angeles, the day after the ceremony, James and I went east on a train to New York City.

We made stops in Kansas City and Chicago, where I had an interview with the *Chicago Defender* after a fundraiser for war-torn Britain.

"Tell the truth, Hattie," the reporter, who had identified himself as Bob Lewis, had asked when James excused himself to go to the bathroom, "are you happy?"

I was a little insulted by the question, but Bob had made a name for himself prying into the personal lives of Negro celebrities, so I supposed the question was to be expected.

Bob, with his slicked-back hair and eyes that danced in constant search of a story, stood before me in his charcoal-gray suit that looked like it took his entire week's salary.

"I don't mean to be disrespectful," he said when I didn't immediately reply, "but this union seems more of, ah . . ." He paused as if he really was trying to find respectful words. "A partnership as opposed to love."

While I felt like James and I were partners, love indeed lived at the center of our marriage. My voice was firm as I replied, "Mr. Lewis, you have sat with me for all of thirty minutes. I'm not sure how you feel qualified to even make such an assumption, but I assure you, I have never been happier," I said, punctuating my declaration with a smile.

That seemed to have settled Mr. Lewis as he returned to the gossip of Hollywood, trying to get me to weigh in on the Bette Davis and Joan Crawford feud. Of course, I didn't engage. I didn't want people giving unsolicited insight on my personal affairs, so I made it a practice to avoid flapping my lips on matters that didn't concern me.

That interview had made me skeptical of others. I wasn't sure what it was they thought they saw, or if it was just reporters digging for a story, but I didn't want their negativity usurping my marriage.

However, immediately upon our arrival in Manhattan, Mr. Selznick delivered a telegram insisting that I capitalize on the news of my nuptials and do more press. So by the time we checked into the Hotel Theresa in Harlem, not only were we engulfed by a crowd of admirers but I had a list of press interviews. From the *New York Amsterdam News* photographer taking photos of James and me eating breakfast in our suite to a guest appearance on the *Eddie Cantor Show*, it was one event after another. I thought that James would tire of the fanfare since this was not a proper honeymoon, but he seemed to bask in all the attention.

When I went to visit the Riverdale Colored Orphan Asylum, where I spoke before two hundred children, delivering inspirational words, it was James who took to the podium and told reporters, "We are so moved by this visit that Hattie and I are considering adopting one of these young children."

My mouth fell open in shock. We had never spoken of adopting, or children in general, let alone one of these orphan children.

"Adoption," a reporter exclaimed as the room erupted in applause. "Wouldn't that be wonderful?"

All eyes were on me as I feigned a smile. I shifted uncomfortably as James squeezed my hand like we were a united front. "Nothing would bring me greater joy than motherhood," I finally said to the flashing cameras and reporters scribbling on their notepads. "My husband and I will surely consider that in the near future."

When we left the orphanage, James and I never spoke of adopting children again. He might have just been grandstanding, but he had no idea that his words had lit the fire of desire for motherhood inside me.

• • •

I'd spent a week in the Big Apple, and my goodness, was I ready to return home. But we had one more stop to make—my real home, Denver, Colorado.

It had been almost ten years since I'd been in Denver, the place my family had moved to when I was seven years old. My father had plans.

Practical plans that worked for a long while. He was a laborer and was going to take advantage of the city's booming construction market. Only the steady work he had hoped for never quite materialized and my father was only able to get odd jobs here and there.

Still, the city molded my love of the stage. It was the place where I'd come to know God. To understand that in spite of our meager circumstances, He took care of His children. And that's why I was excited to be back in my church, Shorter AME. It was Easter Sunday, so of course there was a large crowd. I was overwhelmed with showers of praise and blessings from my former friends and schoolboys and schoolgirls. I was even presented with a hat from a young hatmaker, Leon Bennett, who had made the specially designed hat for me when he heard I was coming to town.

"I am so happy to be among family and friends," I said from the podium. "I'm so happy to be home."

I had to pause for the applause that filled the room. I then shared with the crowd stories of my parents and the foundation they had laid for my siblings and me right here in Denver.

By the time I finished my speech, I was in tears. The crowd was too.

After the service, the nostalgic sadness was replaced by joy as I walked through the living room of my nephew, who was hosting a reception for me. It seemed like the entire church was here. Old friends, local Negro leaders, white lawmakers, even the Colorado governor, Ralph Carr, was here and he gifted me with an autographed picture of himself. The mayor presented me with the keys to the city.

"This is a return fit for a queen," James whispered as we were whisked off to an upscale tearoom at the Blue Parrot Inn, where a group of colored women, all state government employees, honored me. I wrapped up the day with another press conference with local journalists in the same tearoom. As I waited for the reporters to file in, my eyes connected with the lone Negro journalist in the room.

I stepped down from the podium and made my way over to introduce myself.

"Thank you for coming," I told the young woman, who couldn't be more than twenty-five. Yet, she was poised and professional in a tailored navy suit, her hair pulled back in a bun.

"No, thank you," she said. "I'm Justina with the *Denver Star.*"

"Well, Justina with the *Denver Star*"—I leaned in and lowered my voice—"stick around after the press conference and I'll give you a one-on-one interview."

The way her eyes lit up brought joy to my soul. "Yes, ma'am," she said as I winked and moved back to the podium. Minutes later, after the host had started the press conference, I wished that I could just take young Justina to dinner and escape the immediate barrage of Mammy questions.

"Did you draw on your own experiences to play Mammy?"

"Do you think you mastered that role because domestic service is in your blood?"

"Was your mother called Mammy?"

The questions were hurled at me. I remained gracious and cordial, but I was truly tired of them linking everything I said or did to Mammy.

"It just amazes me how similar you are to your fictional persona. You have that drawl of the old Deep South and a laugh as elemental as the sunrise or thunderstorm," said a *Denver Post* reporter who identified herself by the name of Frances Wayne. "It's like since you were a housekeeper in real life, you're able to eloquently bring that to the stage."

I locked eyes with James, who was sitting in the front row. He knew I was tiring of comments like that which were aimed at diminishing my light. I decided I'd had enough and wanted to let these people know I was Hattie McDaniel, not Mammy.

I smiled, though my eyes were meant to express there was nothing amusing about what I was about to say. "Let me be very clear so that your readers are aware. I play a maid. I am *not* a maid. In fact," I said, adjusting my mink wrap in dramatic form, "I am financially quite comfortable—hardly anyone's housekeeper."

My response was obviously unexpected and a heavy veil of silence hung in the room until Justina raised her hand.

"Miss McDaniel, what would be your dream role?" she asked.

The tension lifted just a bit. I grinned widely and said, "What a wonderful question. My dream role would be one where the viewer saw no color. Where I was simply a mother, a sister, a friend, dealing with issues that are universal to coloreds and whites. A role that allowed viewers to see the range and complexity of my acting abilities."

I wanted to say a role like *In This Our Life*, but since we'd still had no movement on that project, I left it at that.

By the time the press conference wrapped, I noticed Frances Wayne was still rattled. So I did something I'd never publicly done before. I walked over to Frances and with a wide grin, this one void of any exasperation, extended my hand toward her.

"Miss Wayne, it was a genuine pleasure to meet you," I said.

Frances's eyes slowly went down to my hand as it hung in the air, then her gaze returned to meet mine. She looked like she didn't know what to do. I'd bet my extended arm that she had never before intimately touched a colored person. Finally, she reluctantly shook my hand. Several individuals, including my own husband, looked on in shock that I would dare be so bold.

In that moment, I didn't care. I released her hand, flashed another smile, then turned and headed toward the exit. I'd returned to Denver a star and everyone in this room was going to recognize that.

CHAPTER 14

May 1941

I was returning to Los Angeles a married woman. And though we had spent four weeks on the road, I hadn't tired of James one bit.

It was a working honeymoon, yet James and I really did have a magnificent experience. We had busy days with me doing personal appearances and interviews. But at night, before we retired, we shared our dreams of building a life that would allow us to help others. At sunrise, he serenaded me with love ballads—even though he couldn't sing a lick. At sunset, he ignored his two left feet and lack of rhythm and we danced under the moonlight. And well into every night, he fed my sexual appetite. It really was everything I had hoped for in a marriage.

Now we were back home. James had moved most of his belongings into my place. And not only had Ruby ensured that everything was put away but she'd done an amazing job of pulling together a reception to celebrate our wedding. She'd transformed our home into a magical paradise, with cascading floral arrangements in hues of soft pink, cream, and lavender adorning every corner of my living and dining room. The fragrant scent of fresh flowers mixed with the smell of eucalyptus from soft glowing candles. A violinist was perched on a stool in the corner, filling the room with beautiful sonatas.

Clark and Carole were among the first to arrive. I'm sure it wasn't intentional, but they'd color-coordinated—she wore a sapphire blue dress, he a gray suit with a shimmering sapphire tie. They looked like two halves of a harmonious whole. It was no surprise that they would be in sync with their attire; they were in sync with all that they did.

"I'm so lucky to have Hollywood royalty at my lil ol' wedding reception," I joked, greeting them as they walked up the steps toward my front door.

Both of them hugged me, then Clark turned to James, who was standing next to me in the front entryway greeting guests.

"Well, let me get a gander at the man who swept in and stole my Hattie's heart," Clark said, extending his hand toward James.

"Hello, Mr. Gable," James said, not bothering to hide his excitement. "I've been waiting to meet you since Hattie speaks of you often."

"Yes, we could never get those schedules aligned, but I wouldn't miss this reception for anything." He motioned to Carole. "This is my wife, Carole."

James shook her hand as well. "Mrs. Gable, it's a pleasure. You look simply stunning."

Carole released her signature giggle and said, "Hattie, I like him already."

"Come on in and make yourselves at home," I said, motioning for them to enter.

We greeted more guests before moving inside. James gently kissed me before going over to mingle with some friends in the living room as I headed over to speak with the caterer.

I'd just finished marveling at the spread of hors d'oeuvres when the maid Ruby had hired for the evening approached me. "Miss Hattie, there's a man here to see you. He said his name is Roscoe Conkling Simmons." She looked over her shoulder toward my front door, then back at me, before lowering her voice. "He has somewhat of a small entourage with him."

This was just like my ex to arrive with people in tow, to my wedding reception. I expected to see a smiling Roscoe standing at my front door, no guilt or shame about crashing my party. Roscoe was the nephew of Booker T. Washington through Washington's third wife, Margaret Murray Washington. Between that and his own political endeavors, he had a sort of arrogance that was both annoying and attractive.

"Well, I'll be. If it isn't the debonair Roscoe Conkling Simmons." I hugged him, and his Old Spice cologne filled my nostrils. Of course he looked dapper in a tailored three-piece suit, the vest beneath emphasizing his polished look.

Normally, I would have been greeted with Roscoe's hearty smile. Instead, his expression was serious when he released me from his grip. His eyes went to the large wedding photo on an easel by the front door. He took in my white wedding gown, which I'd also donned for this event. His eyebrows raised just a bit. I'm sure that was because most people didn't choose white for their third marriage, and Roscoe was one of the few who knew about Nym, so he was aware that this was my third trip down the aisle. But I wasn't most people so it shouldn't have surprised him.

"Umm, well, I'm glad you dropped by," I said, his silent gaze making me uncomfortable. "How did you find . . ."

"It's the talk of the town," Roscoe said, interrupting me. "And one of my friends just happened to be invited to the reception." He motioned behind him, without bothering to introduce any of the six friends that were with him. There were over four hundred people squeezed into my home and backyard, six more wouldn't hurt.

"Well, you and your friends should come on in," I said, stepping aside. "There's plenty of food and libation."

I reached for Roscoe's hand to pull him back as they walked in. "What's going on?" I whispered. If there was one thing Roscoe was not, it was a man of few words. "I know you've always been bold but do you really think this to be appropri—"

He shook his head before I could finish my sentence. He glanced over my shoulder, into the living room, where James was standing on my white lambskin rug, engaged in some conversation that appeared to be thoroughly entertaining Count Basie based on the way he was doubled over in laughter.

"I just cannot believe you got married, Hattie," Roscoe whispered. "I love you and this is heartbreaking."

I pulled my hand from him. At one time, many years ago, after I finally accepted Nym wasn't returning, I fancied Roscoe and had dreams of a future with him. But just as I loved the stage, Roscoe loved the Republican Party. An accomplished orator, he spent every waking hour chasing political dreams. And since our dreams didn't align, a future wasn't possible.

"Roscoe, we haven't spoken in years. You don't think this is strange to show up at my wedding reception proclaiming your love for me?" My tone was just as hushed. I was attracted to Roscoe's ambition, but there was no part of me that ever thought we could truly work. Besides, it was moot now.

"Maybe. But I've been simply distraught over your marriage." He inhaled, his voice turning husky. "You don't remember the great times we had in Chicago? The way we made each other feel in those intimate moments? I love you, Hattie, and I have love for your husband for having sense enough to fall in love with you."

His words made me uneasy. "I must return to my guests. You and your friends are more than welcome to stay and enjoy the festivities," I told him, then excused myself to join James.

I'd never had a problem getting a man. (It was keeping them that seemed to be my issue.) When I closed a chapter on a relationship, I didn't go back and reread it, so I wasn't quite sure why Roscoe's declaration unnerved me.

I shook off thoughts of my past and focused on my future, as I spotted my husband and approached him.

"There you are, my love," James said when I rejoined him in the dining room, next to our three-tiered wedding cake. "Madame Sul-Te-Wan here was just marveling at the foliage." He motioned toward the living room, which was overflowing with white flowers and lush green plants.

"These gardenias are magnificent," Madame Sul-Te-Wan said, pointing to all the white flowers lining the dining room wall. I was a little surprised to see her here. We hadn't spoken since she lost the role of Mammy to me. She was the first Negro actress to sign a film contract and be a featured performer, so she felt she deserved the role. She'd had a small role in *Maryland* with me but hadn't uttered so much as a "hello."

"Thank you so much," I replied. "And I'm honored that you joined us to share in the festivities."

"Of course."

Her plastered grin let me know that she was here more to be nosy than in genuine support.

"Are you two ready to be presented?" Ruby asked, approaching us and giving me a welcome reprieve.

I nodded, excused myself, then took my husband's hand and followed Ruby to the foyer. She rang a handbell. "May I have your attention, please?" She waited a few minutes for the chatter to subside. "It is my honor to formally present Mr. and Mrs. James Lloyd Crawford." She stepped aside for us to enter.

James and I walked hand in hand into the living room to resounding applause from what I hoped were people genuine in their happiness.

I scanned the mixture of guests squeezed into my home. We'd set up tents outdoors, and thankfully, the weather had cooperated so everyone didn't have to stay stuffed inside. It was an interracial mix of famous Hollywood figures. Of course, Clark was here, but so were Vivian, Bette, Lillian, and Louise and a host of other actors, as well as friends, family, neighbors, and a few fans. Women from my sorority, Sigma Gamma Rho Sorority, Incorporated, which was an organization that uplifted the community through sisterhood, leadership, and service, were here, adorned in blue and gold and passing out cake to the guests. I was honored they had offered to assist in my special day.

"May I also have your attention, please?"

My mouth fell open in shock when I saw Roscoe at the front of the room, clinking a fork against a glass of champagne.

"Hello all," he said as the guests turned their attention to him.

James looked at me, his eyes questioning. I shrugged, hoping that my husband didn't notice the way my hands were nervously shaking. What in the world was Roscoe doing?

"Some of you may know me as the politician Roscoe Conkling Simmons," he began as an uncomfortable muttering passed through the room. Roscoe, an editor for the *Chicago Defender*, was vocal in getting colored folks to remain loyal to the Republican Party but anyone who wasn't politically astute most likely didn't know him. "Today, however, I stand before you as not a leader in the Republican Party but as a dear friend to Hattie McDaniel," he continued.

A tight grin spread on my face. I wanted nothing more for him to hurry along, particularly because I had no idea what he was about to say.

"I would like to take a moment to toast my dear friend, congratulate her lucky husband, and wish her all the happiness she deserves," Roscoe continued.

I don't know if James sensed something or if he was being genuinely affectionate, but he stepped closer to me and intermingled his fingers with mine.

"To Hattie and her husband," Roscoe said, raising his glass in salute.

The guests toasted us as well then the chatter resumed. Roscoe made his way over to us and James's grip tightened on my hand.

"Hattie, I am sorry I must be going but I wanted to personally wish you well. And your husband too," he added without taking his eyes off me.

"James. The name is James," my husband said.

Ever the politician, Roscoe smiled and extended a hand to James. "James, pleasure to meet you. Take good care of my girl."

"Since she's *my* girl now, you can be assured that I will," James replied.

I stepped in before they got into a top dog contest. "Thank you very much for dropping by, Roscoe." Roscoe knew me well enough to know that was his cue to leave.

"I'll be on my way. But might I have a hug for an old friend?" When I didn't move he looked at James. "That is, if it's okay with you, James."

I could see the slow rise of James's chest, but he nodded without comment.

Roscoe leaned in and hugged me and whispered, "Call me when this doesn't work out."

I struggled not to react, instead keeping my smile plastered as I pulled back and said, "Safe travels," before wrapping my arm through my husband's.

Roscoe returned his hat to his head, tipped it, then exited with his entourage in tow.

Thankfully, Count Basie returned to continue his conversation with James, so any tension James was feeling dissipated.

I was happy when eight o'clock arrived and Ruby began ushering most of the guests out as the caterer began dinner for a hundred of my closest friends.

"Hmph, Hattie, you got you a good-looking one there," Ethel said as we sat around one of the many rectangular tables that had been set up throughout my house. "Can he handle you, though?"

I took a sip of my sidecar and grimaced as the cognac slid down my throat. I set my glass down. "I'm the one in charge and intend to mold my husband to my liking." I wasn't trying to be domineering, but this was my third marriage and James's first. I knew what to expect.

"The inner man doesn't come out until you've got him," I continued. "It's my business, like in the Bible, to bend the twig to incline the branch."

My friends chuckled and said, "Amen" and "Good luck with that."

"This is all just a shock to me," Ethel said. "Because I seem to remember you vowing never to marry again."

"It won't be long before he'll be just like one of the family," I said, laughing as my friends raised their glasses in a toast.

"What are you ladies talking about?" James asked, approaching us.

As my friends smiled, I extended my hand toward my husband. "Just how happy I am to be your wife."

After the party came to a close, James and I assisted the maid as she started cleaning up.

"So what did you think?" I asked my husband after we'd put away most of the food.

"It was nice. Well, except for your boyfriend crashing the party," he replied.

"He's not my boyfriend. I haven't spoken with Roscoe in years and"—I kissed him on the lips—"you're the only man I have eyes for."

That brought a smile to my husband's face. "Well, I really did enjoy myself. Can't say that I've ever hosted a party of such magnitude."

"I do enjoy entertaining." I looked around the small house, surprised that we had fit so many people in here. "But I can't wait to move into the new house, then I'll throw the grandest parties."

James, who was picking up a discarded napkin on the floor, stood erect. "New house? I didn't know you were thinking of moving."

Excitement filled his face. "I was just talking with Paul Revere Williams—that's the architect who designed Frank Sinatra's house."

I knew who Paul was. What I didn't know was why my husband would be talking with one of the most sought-after Negro architects in all of Los Angeles.

James answered my question as he continued, "Paul says there's a beautiful plot of land opening up around the corner from the Dunbar. We could have him design us a place."

"Oh, I'm not staying in this area," I said, snapping a lid on the leftover potato salad and placing it in the fridge. "As much as I love it here, I bought a house in the West Adams district."

Confusion spread across my husband's face. "Ummm, Negroes aren't allowed there."

"Ben Carter and Norman Houston from the Golden State insurance company just bought houses there. And so did I," I announced.

James blinked, frowned, then blinked again. Finally, he said, "What do you mean you bought a house there?"

"I began the process a few weeks before we got married."

His head cocked, disbelief mixed with anger covered his face. "And you didn't think this was something that I needed to know?"

I paused, not quite understanding what the big deal was. "Well, can you buy a house?"

James was "in between" jobs right now, having left his real estate business when he moved here to LA, so we both knew the answer to that question.

"That's not the point, Hattie. I'm your husband," he huffed.

"I understand that and I was purchasing the house prior to us getting married." I chose my words carefully and spoke calmly. I don't know why I hadn't discussed this with James before today. Maybe I'd been so caught up in our honeymoon. Or maybe I didn't think his opinion on this really mattered because this had been a dream of mine since I first arrived in LA.

"I still feel like I should have a say. I know you're used to wearing the pants, but I'm the man of the house."

I didn't want to denigrate my husband but the way he was snarling at me, decked out in a suit my money bought, irritated me. "When's the last time you contributed anything to show you're capable of buying a house, let alone maintaining one?" The moment the words left my mouth, I wished that I could swallow them back. I inhaled. "James, I'm sorry, but . . ."

He threw his hands up. "You know what, enjoy your house."

"Okay, please don't be angry." I stepped closer to him. "I am sorry, you're right. I should've talked to you about the house."

I hugged him, trying to get him to smile. He wouldn't. "You're going to love it."

Curiosity overrode his anger because he sighed and said, "So is it really in the West Adams district?"

"Yes. That was one of the first neighborhoods I saw when I got to LA, and I promised myself one day I'd live there." I wrapped my arms tighter around his waist, recalling when my siblings Sam and Etta took me on a tour of the area my first day in town. They'd called my dreams of living there lofty. But I'd known it was just a matter of time.

"I thought white folks weren't supposed to sell to colored people in Los Angeles," James said, referring to the fact that homeowners in most of Los Angeles were required to sign racially restrictive covenants promising to never sell to Negroes as part of the deed to their properties.

"The Depression changed that. Many of those white homeowners just wanted to get rid of their homes and they sold to anyone with green money," I replied.

"Hmph," he said, his lips extending in a pout.

"We're still celebrating our wedding, sweetheart," I continued. "Don't be mad at me. I promise when you see it, if you don't just absolutely love it . . ."

The corner of his top lip crept up in skepticism. "Oh, so now you're a huckster? Because whether I love it or not, you're staying."

I couldn't help the smirk that popped up. "Okay, so you know me well. But you are gonna love it. I just know you will."

"I hope so," he said, finally hugging me back. "Come on, let's clear the rest of the stuff."

CHAPTER 15

June 1941

I'd won an Oscar. First colored woman in the history of this country. So why in the hell couldn't I find work? Where were the producers who should have been beating down my door to work with me? When Claudette Colbert won in 1935 she was booked with a full schedule in two more movies the next month. The same thing with Bette Davis and Katharine Hepburn. Hell, even Olivia, who lost to me, was filming a movie. The film I'd been so excited about, *In This Our Life*, was stuck in the perpetual land of preproduction, so I had no clue if or when that script would even see the light of day.

"You know why, Hattie," James had said to me this morning over breakfast after I lamented my lack of job offers. "You're still a colored woman in America. The rules are different."

I'd been so aggravated with his lack of understanding of my frustration that I'd retreated to our bedroom, where I'd been standing and staring outside into the backyard for the past thirty minutes.

I didn't want to admit that my husband was right. I truly believed this award would open so many doors. But as each day without work passed, it was getting harder to stay optimistic.

"Hey," James said, finally coming upstairs to check on me. He stood in the doorway, holding a cup of coffee, looking unsure whether he should approach me. "I brought you coffee."

I didn't reply but took the cup as he walked over to me.

"You okay?"

I didn't answer his question and instead took a sip of my coffee then said, "The *California Eagle* was spot-on in that article I read yesterday. They said that the problem for colored performers reached much deeper because filmmakers remain dependent on typecasting. They refuse to acknowledge the complexity of the Negro experience."

James sighed like he was tired of hearing this. "Honey, you live good for a colored woman in America," he said. "Rest on your laurels."

"I am fully capable of abandoning typecasting and taking on more complicated roles," I said, ignoring his comment. "I won the Academy Award on talent and trained ability, not because I'm a type. You read the article. They said if I only weighed a hundred pounds and had been four shades lighter in complexion, I would've earned the Oscar just the same."

"But you would've never even gotten the role if you didn't fit the type."

"You don't know that."

James bit down on his lip like he wanted to dispute that, but then decided against it.

"Well," James said slowly, like he was choosing his words carefully, "you are talented but the reality is, your roles are limited."

I flicked him off with the wave of a hand. He was making me feel even worse.

"Sweetheart, I know you're frustrated, but everything's going to be okay," he said.

"It's just disheartening. My money is running thin."

"I wish I could help more but my real estate ventures are drying up for now. The licensing requirements here are so stringent."

I released an exasperated sigh. I didn't have the wherewithal to address his lack of employment. I handed him the cup of coffee. "I've got to work. We need the money. We're about to get this house.

I promised my goddaughters I would help with their schooling. It's just a whole list of expenses that require more income, not less."

He set the cup down, then eased up to me and wrapped his arms around my waist. "I understand, sweetheart." He paused. "There's no shame if you have to go back to being—"

"Don't even say it," I snapped, cutting him off. "I'm not going back to domestic work."

The fact that my husband would dare suggest that irked me something terribly.

"I'm just saying, as a last resort. You worked as a maid when you filmed—"

"Not even as a last resort." I wiggled from his grasp. "I did that when I was just starting out. I'm not going to be someone's Academy Award–winning maid. Something will come along. I know it will. Now, if you'll excuse me, I'm going to go visit Sam."

James sighed as I walked around him, but he didn't try to stop me.

• • •

The sight of my brother's small white wooden house brought a smile to my face. I marveled at the brick-colored stucco roof and arched entry on the front porch. The entire neighborhood looked like some sort of colored utopia. Many of the houses on the street were similar to my brother's place. A group of boys were playing box ball while some girls jumped on the sidewalk in a game of hopscotch. Several people were sitting out in the front yards and waved to me as I pulled into the driveway. Sam and his wife, Lulu, didn't have any children, but they'd moved into a neighborhood that looked like the perfect place to raise them.

"Hey, Sister," Sam said, opening the door and welcoming me in.

I kissed his cheek as I made my way inside. I didn't make it over here often, but I loved my brother's place. I was impressed by the striking color combinations of gold and green. There was a sitting room to the right with velvet gold drapes framing the large windows, and a footstool appropriate for the corresponding chair. The parquet flooring and oversized Turkish rug were a long way from the shack that we'd grown up in.

"I'll make us some tea, then you can tell me why you're really here." He winked at me as he headed into the kitchen.

I eased over to the fireplace, hoping to get my mind off my dilemma, and a small smile crossed my face when I noticed the photo of Sam sitting behind a microphone.

It was a picture of Sam recording his radio show. He played a preacher named Deacon McDaniel on *The Optimistic Do-Nuts*. The variety radio show had become so popular it once aired up against *Amos 'n' Andy*.

Next to that photo was a picture of me in the radio studio in what had become my signature hat. I remembered that thing was twenty-eight inches high with a wide brim that folded up around the front. Tan netting wrapped around the front of the brim.

Sam had bought me the hat to surprise me with the role as Hi-Hat Hattie on his show.

My smile faded as I thought about the conversation that had transpired after my siblings had given me the great news about the radio show. Etta had turned around and given me a maid's uniform. She worked as a cook for a West Adams couple and had gotten them to hire me on as a maid.

"For most of us colored entertainers, acting is something we do on the side. It's a supplement. It doesn't put food on the table," Etta had said.

Etta and I had fought about my refusal to take that job. I'd been making as much as seventy dollars a week with tips at Sam Pick's in Milwaukee. I wasn't about to go be somebody's maid for seven dollars a week and I had told her as much.

I'd eaten my words just three months later, after I moved into my own place and had been forced to take a domestic job to pay my bills.

But that was before the Oscar. Now I should have offers waiting on my doorstep.

The problem was, I didn't. And I didn't know what I was going to do about that.

Sam returned and handed me a cup of tea. We talked for a while, and before I knew it, my brother had brightened my spirits with his proverbial humor and incessant joke-telling.

"What do you call a will?" he asked as he took a seat across from me.

"What, Sam?"

"A dead giveaway."

I couldn't help it, I burst out laughing. "You don't have a lick of sense," I told my brother as his telephone rang.

"Did you hear the one about the play that had a happy ending?" he asked as he stood and headed toward the phone.

"No," I said.

"Everybody was glad it was over."

"Go, go answer that," I said, trying to catch my breath as I shooed him away. "I'm supposed to be crying tears of sadness and you got me over here splitting my sides."

"No worries, you got plenty of side left." He chuckled as he picked up the phone.

"Hello . . . this is he . . ." My brother made faces at me like we were back in our childhood days, then his expression turned serious. "Why yes, she's here . . . of course." Sam paused, then extended the phone toward me. "Hattie, your agent is on the phone."

"What in the world?" I said, standing and walking over to take the receiver. "Mr. Meiklejohn?"

My agent's voice filled the phone. "Sorry to ring you over here but James said I could find you here."

"Yes, it's fine. What's going on? I hope it's some good news since you're tracking me down," I said.

"I hope you'll think so. Jack and Harry Warner from Warner Brothers are interested in you. They want to bring you over to make movies."

My brow furrowed in confusion. "But I'm under contract with Mr. Selznick."

"That's just it." Mr. Meiklejohn rushed his words out. "The Warners want you. MGM demanded twelve thousand dollars to loan you out."

"What?" No way would someone pay that.

"Oh, the Warners want you bad," Mr. Meiklejohn replied. "Jack Warner personally called Mr. Selznick to bargain for a lower fee. It was tense for a minute, but the Warners agreed to pay $9,640. And they'll take over your contract."

A myriad of emotions raced through me. My future was being navigated and I felt like I had no say. But at the same time, if the Warners were willing to buy out my contract, they must have work for me.

"So, I'm out at MGM?"

"No. Warners is just borrowing you for a year. And they want you to start immediately. They have a film for you called *The Great Lie*, with Bette Davis, Mary Astor, and George Brent. I just heard they also offered a role to your brother." I looked at Sam, who was standing staring at me like he too wanted to know what was so urgent that my agent would track me down.

"What's my role?" I finally said.

The silence that filled the phone answered before he did, so I said, "A maid." It wasn't a question.

Finally, Mr. Meiklejohn said, "Yes, but . . ."

I tuned his explanation out. Everyone raved that *Gone with the Wind* was going to be a celebrated classic. But for me, it was just a springboard to more maid roles.

As much as I wanted to complain, I really had only two options: either go play a maid, or go be one.

"Fine. When do I start?" was all that was left to say.

CHAPTER 16

August 1941

I asked for work, and I got it. Maybe I should've been more specific in my prayers because the role of Violet in *The Great Lie* was worse than I could've ever imagined.

Not only was I forced into filming with little to no preparation, but the film had been besieged with problems from day one. Besides technical issues, it was swathed in negative publicity. The star—Bette Davis—hated working on the film so much that she had taken to bad-mouthing the production. Bette was a perfectionist and had stormed off the set, calling her role "inferior." A lot of people thought she was rude, but Bette didn't believe in sugarcoating things and therefore didn't bother with pleasantries. The Warners had banned journalists from the set and made efforts to block Bette from doing any more interviews because she would tell anyone and everyone how unhappy she was.

"What are you over there thinking about?" James's voice pulled me from my thoughts. I was behind the wheel of my Packard sedan, following the movers to our new home.

"This film," I replied as I turned off Figueroa toward Crenshaw Boulevard.

James reached over and squeezed my hand. "Not today, honey. You're off and today you're supposed to be completely focused on moving into your dream home—that you bought without your husband's input."

That made me smile, but only because in the last few days, James had gotten excited about the move.

As we turned onto South Harvard, all thoughts of the Warners evaporated. James was right. Today was about the celebration of another dream come true.

"These are some nice houses," James said, peering out the window at the Craftsman and Victorian-designed mansions. I'd convinced him to wait and be surprised since it wasn't going to change anything. Now, watching the expression on his face, I was glad he'd obliged.

The white-and-green Mediterranean two-story mansion perched on the hill at the corner of South Harvard and West Twenty-Second Street stood as a beacon of hope, welcoming me into the West Adams district, Los Angeles's first suburb dating back to the 1880s. A suburb that until a few years ago didn't allow any colored folks to live here.

"I can't believe the white people are leaving here," James said, his eyes wide as he took in the manicured lawns and massive houses.

"There was an exodus westward to new neighborhoods like Beverly Hills," I said.

When I'd first toured the seventeen-room mansion, I knew that this home had been made for me. It had everything I wanted, including a safe in the basement where the previous owners had secreted their money. I planned to use it for storing canned goods and as an air raid shelter.

Norman Houston had been the first colored person to settle in West Adams in 1938 when he bought a mansion a couple of doors down. Norman had cofounded the influential Golden State Mutual Life Insurance Company in 1925, which had been formed to provide colored Californians, who were often denied policies or charged outrageous premiums, with quality life insurance. My friend Ben Carter had moved in shortly after that. And now me. Ben had told me, colored folks had already started calling the neighborhood Sugar Hill in homage to the affluent colored New York neighborhood of the same name.

Louise and Ethel were also looking at houses in the area, along with a host of other Negro celebs with money. Lillian and her fiancé, Jack, had tried to move in and had even bought a house. But their white neighbors had successfully kept them out with restrictive covenants.

Thankfully, I hadn't had any issues in purchasing my home because I paid ten thousand dollars above the asking price and the previous owner was all too anxious to sell.

The minute we pulled up to the home, James's eyes lit up in awe—just as I expected.

"Wow," he said. "This is it? This is our home?"

I couldn't help but chuckle at how just moments ago, it was my home. Now it was ours. This place would be more than just a house. It was a symbol of how far I'd come. And the fact that once again, I had come full circle. My sister Etta had worked two houses down as the Kelsey family's housekeeper. The same family she'd tried to get me to go work for when I first arrived in LA.

I exited the car and slowly walked into the front yard, my gaze glued on James to gauge his reaction. I'd already taken in the beauty of the estate.

"Okay, you were right, honey. This is magnificent." He pointed to the gardenias that lined the pathway. "Did the house come with your favorite flowers?"

I laughed. "It's perfect, but that would've been a bit much. I had the landscapers fill the ground with gardenias."

He leaned down and sniffed the white flowers. "Yes, you love some gardenias." He pointed to the shade trees and neatly sculpted shrubs I'd had installed as well. "This really is beautiful, darling," James said, fingering the American flag that hung on the front porch. "So you've been knowing about this place for a while?"

"The area anyway." I nodded. "Since my first day in LA."

I noticed an elderly white couple in front of their home across the street, talking to a younger white man and woman. They were staring at us.

"Hello there!" I called out, enthusiastically waving from my yard.

"We're your new neighbors." James stood and put his hand in the small of my back as he followed me to the front of our lawn.

A hearty smile filled my face as we walked across the street. "I'm Hattie McDaniel and this is my husband, James Crawford." But my greeting was not returned. The elderly woman pursed her thin lips as her nostrils flared. The man with her bore a scowl that looked like he had just bitten into something sour. Both of them turned and scurried up the walkway and into the house.

The younger couple didn't make a quick exit, but they didn't greet us either.

"You might know my wife," James said, stepping up. "She's the Hattie McDaniel from *Gone with the Wind*, who won an Academy Award." I guessed he thought if we let the neighbors know my credentials, they wouldn't have such disdain.

He thought wrong, as neither of the two responded.

An uncomfortable silence filled the space between us. Finally, James said, "Well, we just wanted to say hello. We need to get back to getting everything inside."

"Why did you move here?" the younger man asked just as we turned to walk away.

"Excuse me?" I said, taking a step toward him.

"There are plenty of places you could move here in California, Watts, Compton. Why here?" His tone was filled with disgust.

The audacity! I held my head high as I said, "Because I wanted to. Because I can afford to."

"So Mr. Murphy really sold to you?" The woman spat out her words as if they tasted repugnant. The undertones of her olive skin said she most likely had some ancestors come over on a boat herself, so I was trying to understand how she dared stand in judgment of me.

"He did. And at ten thousand dollars above the asking cost," I replied.

She had the nerve to huff, then take the man's hand. "Come on,

Albert." She looked at me in vile condemnation, then they both made their way into the house next to the elderly couple's.

I was used to racism, but I didn't understand this. I could afford to live here just like each of these homeowners, yet that didn't matter. My money was green but my skin wasn't white and that's all that mattered to these people.

James shook his head in disgust. "Welcome to Sugar Hill," he said, before turning and walking back across the street.

CHAPTER 17

September 1941

I'd created a utopia inside my Sugar Hill home. I spent my days just wandering through the large dining room, butler's pantry, and oversized kitchen. I would spend hours sitting on the service porch that backed up to the kitchen or reading in my library. Over the month we'd been here, I'd redecorated the drawing room, den, and all four bedrooms in light colors with beige carpets and French Provincial ivory furniture.

Ruby's husband, Lee, had repainted the house's interior using a variety of uniquely contrasting colors. Even James had gotten on board, crafting the lounge into his own personal area. I had meticulously made this place a home.

My career may have been in tatters, but I found comfort in my home. I'd already had multiple parties, but the one going on right now was by far the biggest since I'd moved in. Nearly seventy-five people were mingling about, packing the wide hallway.

Hosting my parties was my way to celebrate my continual survival. I couldn't put into words how it felt to be surrounded by good food, friends enjoying Pall Malls and overflowing wine goblets. These parties truly soothed my soul. I also loved the fact that they broke the color lines in segregated Hollywood. There was no white domination of talents. Inside the walls of 2203 South Harvard, we were all equal.

Right now Billie Holiday was playing on the Victrola. My maid was pouring and passing around after-dinner brandy.

I loved drifting through my sitting room, mingling with entertainers like Thelonious Monk, who gave impromptu performances. Oh, how I wished my mother could be with me now. She would have loved this scene. Sometimes, in one of my spiritual moments, I imagined she knew what her daughter had accomplished, that she and my father were sitting with ease, with no pain, comfy in their rocking chairs, looking down at me.

This was more than a home; this was a sign of success. This was what my father had left Tennessee in search of over sixty years before.

I went out back and talked with guests who were sitting on my oversized porch, smoking. After about fifteen minutes of jovial conversation, the sound of my white Wurlitzer spinet grand piano lured me back into the living room, where Duke Ellington was tickling the ivory. Judy Garland was marveling at my growing collection of figurines, and Bing Crosby was studying my Oscar plaque, situated on the fireplace mantel. My eclectic passions and achievements were on full display—from my variety of books on Negro art and history to my doll collection.

I had no problems getting colored stars out, but it wasn't until word spread that Clark never missed one of my parties that I started seeing white actors, directors, and Hollywood movers and shakers coming out as well. Clark was an irresistible drawing card. He'd gotten folks out when my parties were at my previous place, so it was no surprise they came out even more here.

"I'm just trying to figure out where my picture is," my dear friend and fellow actor Wonderful Smith said as he pointed to the numerous autographed photographs of Hollywood colleagues and other dignitaries that lined my living room wall.

"Well, as soon as you give me an autographed photo, I'll put it up." I winked as I headed to the door to greet more guests. I'd bought two dogs last month, a Dalmatian I'd named Danny and a Spaniel named Frisky. They too had made this their home. In fact, they stood next to me as I greeted guests like they were my personal butlers.

Even when they weren't partying, those artists had been coming to my home to relax, practice their craft, and exchange information on their progress in their careers.

Just last week, Cab Calloway and Ethel Waters, who had recently moved in across the street, spent over an hour at the piano in the corner working on a song. It was private and intimate, but it was also free of white interference. It reminded me of the original and independent productions staged by my siblings for colored audiences back home in Denver.

A reporter from the *Los Angeles Times* was here tonight. Martha Davis was having the time of her life, it appeared, the way she was hanging all over Clark and Laurence Olivier.

"Wonderful party, Hattie." I stood next to her as her gaze scanned the backyard. "Lots of people here too," she said, dragging out her words for emphasis. I eyed the brandy in her cup and wondered how much she'd had to drink already.

"Well, you know I like to entertain," I said.

She let out a loud hiccup then a small giggle before leaning in toward me like she was letting me in on a secret. "Hattie, you're getting too prominent to continue mingling with so many common people. You'd better begin eliminating them."

I was instantly reminded of my father's words, *"The truest feelings flow with alcohol."*

I stared at her for a minute, before replying, "You're right. That's a good idea. I'll start by eliminating you."

I motioned for the security guard I'd hired because an unruly guest had gotten out of hand after too much hooch at my last party. "Miss Davis will be leaving now," I said once he walked over.

Martha looked on in shock as my security guard pointed toward the door.

As she was being escorted out, my friend Ruby Dandridge, whom everyone just called Ru, was coming in. I'd been knowing Ru since I first moved to Los Angeles. She had moved here with her two young daughters, Vivian and Dorothy, and her special friend Geneva Williams, a few years before I did. Ru was one of the few people in Hollywood who was open about being in a relationship with a woman. Well, she wasn't really open. She didn't really talk about it. She and Geneva just *were*. They went places together, did things, lived together, raised children, all like it was perfectly normal. I knew both of them had been in unhappy marriages, Geneva to some man she never talked about and Ru to a draftsman named Cyril Dandridge in Cleveland. But Cyril was quiet and unassuming. Ru was all energy and chatter and ready to talk to anyone, especially if she thought they could help her.

"You already throwing people out?" Ru said, watching as the security guard ushered a grumbling Martha out.

"Ru," I exclaimed, ignoring her question. "I didn't think you would make it."

She hugged me, then handed her straw bag and lightweight jacket to the maid. Ru wore a blue-and-white polka-dot shirtwaist dress and white gloves, looking like she was ready to be cast in a movie on a moment's notice. "Oooh, we've been on set all day. I almost didn't make it, but I told myself, 'Self, you know everybody who's anybody is gonna be at Hattie's party so take your tired behind on over there,'" she said with her signature sass.

I laughed, even though I knew Ru wasn't kidding. If ever there was someone determined to make it, it was Ruby Dandridge. And if she wasn't going to make it, she was going to make sure her girls did. She and Geneva had taught those girls to sing, dance, perform acrobatics, and recite poetry. Dottie and Vivy (as we called them) were pros, performing at colored churches, schools, and organizations. At one point, they even had a group with a young singer named Etta Jones called the Dandridge Sisters, though they'd disbanded the previous year.

"How are the girls?" I asked as she walked over to the dessert table and grabbed a slice of high lemon pie that had been set out on saucers.

"Oh, they're doing well." She slid a piece of pie in her mouth, closed her eyes as she savored the taste, then opened her eyes and said, "Dorothy has a few small roles she did this year, and she's making a mark with soundies," she added, referring to the film clips that were displayed on jukeboxes. "Right now, she's doing *Sun Valley Serenade* with the Nicholas Brothers, so hopefully something will take off. Geneva will make sure of that."

A pain shot through my heart. Both Dottie and Vivy had confided in me that they hated Geneva. She was a strict taskmaster and often punished the girls for the slightest infraction. They were terrified of her so I could only imagine what they were enduring. I had tried to talk to Ru about it, but she didn't want to hear it and all but told me to mind my business.

"Is she still pining after that Nicholas boy?" I asked.

Ru shook her head like the mere thought of her daughter dating exasperated her. "She is. I told her Harold Nicholas can't do anything for her but get her a gig. But you know these kids. She doesn't want to listen. But thankfully, she'll be gone on tour soon so that will no longer be an issue." She looked over at James, who was now laughing with Judy Garland. "How's married life?" Ru asked.

"The best," I said, to which she groaned like I'd said the impossible.

"Well, as long as you're happy," she said.

"I am," I replied.

"Are you going to the *Gone with the Wind* celebration?" Ru asked, then returned to her pie.

Her question made me groan. I'd received an invitation from the city of Atlanta to appear onstage for the one-year-anniversary celebration of the premiere (the same one I wasn't originally invited to). The city had made an exception for the anniversary, I guessed since I'd won an Oscar. Nearly a million people had shown up for the original premiere. I could only imagine what this year would be like. And I couldn't attend. The director of *The Great Lie* tried to blame me, saying I'd delayed production by flubbing my lines. While there were whispers that I was doing it on purpose, that wasn't the case. I had been handed two new pages of dialogue cold, but rather than rapidly learning the part as I normally did, I simply could not remember the lines. James said I was unconsciously resisting the role, because Violet was another servant who cared only about making sure her mistress was happy. But now I was set to reshoot my scenes whenever we resumed filming.

"Well, I thought I was, but we're still working on *The Great Lie*," I told my friend.

"Still?" she asked.

"It seems like it's one problem after another. The baby hired to play Peter was sick during much of the filming. That caused delays. Then a nurse dropped the poor infant, injuring him so badly he had to be replaced."

"Oh, that's a serious lawsuit," Ru said with her mouth full.

"Of course. And then it seems like everybody caught the flu," I continued. "Mary Astor is having marital problems and it's just one big disaster. Luckily, Bette is getting married on New Year's so she's demanded that we be through filming by Christmas. But for now, I have to decline the anniversary celebration because we'll still be filming."

"Well, at least you're working," Ru said.

"Barely . . . I don't have anything lined up after this."

A look of surprise swept across her face. "I would've thought they'd be banging down your door."

"That's exactly what I thought. But nothing could be further from the truth."

"Well, let's hope that's only temporary, because if Hattie McDaniel can't find work after winning an Oscar, there's very little hope for the rest of us," Ru said, setting the saucer and the half-eaten pie down as if she'd suddenly lost her appetite.

CHAPTER 18

November 1941

For Clark, hot tea was the answer to everything. In his world, maybe. But in mine, all it did was burn my tongue.

Usually, from the moment I passed through the white iron electronically controlled fence on the perimeter of Clark's home, the acres of citrus groves would transport me to a place of peace. I could look out across his front yard at the fields of oats and alfalfa, the stables and barns, the pigsty, which had no pigs, and I would instantly feel comforted.

Not today, though.

"Drink up," Clark said, motioning toward the cup of hot mint tea in front of me. I did manage a small smile at the tea rose he'd plucked from the bush that adorned the brick steps to his front door when he welcomed me in. He'd laid it on the saucer as an ornament. I knew he was trying to lighten the angst that had been on display since my arrival.

I'd come to Clark's ranch distraught over the news my agent had delivered to me today.

I'd called Mr. Warner to voice my concerns with the film, and my efforts had backfired. I'd always said colored actors shouldn't complain. If only I had listened to my smart advice. Instead I'd moaned about how Hollywood was always plugging white stars while completely neglecting colored ones. I'd also listed all the needless delays with *The Great Lie*. Mr. Warner had listened intently, then the very next day called my agent to say that he was terminating my contract after I finished reshooting my scenes. I'd cried all night long. Mr. Meiklejohn had said he'd all but begged the Warners to reconsider—to no avail.

James only made things worse, talking about how maybe this was a sign it was time for us to leave Los Angeles. He wanted us to move to Chicago. Leave? I'd just bought my dream house; I wasn't going anywhere.

But what if I couldn't get any more work? How would I pay for this dream house?

I'd rushed over here to talk to Clark since he had a knack for cheering me up.

"So what did they say was the reason?" Clark said, taking a seat across from me in a green quilted wing chair.

"That I just didn't fit their needs. And it's not like I can go back to Selznick International either. They basically sold me off because they also don't want me," I scoffed as I sipped my tea. It had been years since I'd been out of work and the thought of returning to extended unemployment made me physically ill.

"That's a bunch of gobbledygook," he said. "What other roles do they have a need for since they've limited what they'll allow you to do?"

He was visibly perturbed as he paced. "You know Warner has been trying to steal me from MGM," he said. "I'm gonna tell them they can forget about me doing anything with them unless they renew your contract."

"You'll do no such thing." Clark had one film slated to come out next year, *Somewhere I'll Find You*. I knew that he didn't have anything else lined up, so I was not about to let him make waves because of me.

"What good is it to have all of this so-called power in Hollywood if I can't utilize it?" he protested.

My hand went to his arm to calm his rising voice. "Clark, I so appreciate your unwavering friendship, but there are some battles you have to let me fight alone, okay?"

Clark puffed but let the matter drop. I wished there was something he could do. But the reality was that the Warners had made even fewer attempts than Mr. Selznick at securing assignments for me. And now they were letting me go.

I didn't have anything to worry about immediately. But with money going out and very little coming in, if I didn't get work in the next six months, the life I'd fought so hard to achieve was going to come tumbling down.

• • •

The sunlight bounced off the beams in the vaulted ceiling and shined their rays directly on the petite frame of Mrs. Katherine Mayweather. The way her delicate eyebrows dipped, forming a V as she pursed her lips, revealed her displeasure.

She lifted her damask hemline, stepped into the kitchen of her six-bedroom colonial house, sauntered over to the white refrigerator in the corner, then ran her index finger along the side, before holding it up toward me.

"This is highly unacceptable," she said, shaking her head in disgust.

I peered at her finger. Granted, I was a few feet away, at the oven making tea for her friends, but her white-gloved finger looked clean to me.

Mrs. Katherine wagged her finger in my direction. "Mr. Mayweather was not pleased with the lack of proper cleaning last week."

The sound of Mrs. Katherine's high-pitched Southern voice annoyed my soul.

"The milkman will be here this evening and I don't want him thinking we keep a dirty refrigerator," Mrs. Katherine ranted as she leaned in and ran her fingers across the top of the freezer.

Satisfied, she stood and commenced removing her gloves. "I do declare, I do not know what's gotten into you. You used to be such a reliable Negra." She tsked as she ran her finger along the counter. "I swear, ever since that Booker T. Washington was allowed in the White House to dine, the Negroes have been losing their minds. Take the tea out to my friends and get back in here and clean this up!"

"Yes'm," I said, scurrying into the parlor, where four women sat watching

television. I set the tea on the table in front of them. Not one of them looked my way, as I was invisible to them.

"Here it comes! This is my favorite part," one of the women squealed.

"Frankly, my dear, I don't give a damn," the women said in unison, along with Rhett on the TV. Then they all burst out into a fit of giggles.

When I noticed them watching Gone with the Wind, *my hand trembled and some of the tea spilled onto the table.*

"Goodness' sakes, you clumsy thing," one of the women said.

"I'm sorry, ma'am," I said, rushing to clean it up.

Another one of the women leaned in and peered at me. "Has anyone ever told you that you look like Mammy?"

Mrs. Katherine appeared in the doorway, releasing an evil laugh. "That is Mammy. She's my maid."

I bolted upright in my bed. That dream—no, that nightmare—had given me heart palpitations.

"There are just some things a colored girl ain't never gonna be able to do. Society will compel you to follow me into domestic service. It's imperative that you have the proper skills," my mother would always tell me.

I threw back the covers and made my way into my office and started going through my list of contacts. I could try to find out where the producers were with *In This Our Life*. Or I could call everyone I knew in this business until someone gave me a job. I would start back at the beginning. Call the agent Charles Butler. See if he had anything.

"No, I'm just going to have to appeal to Mr. Warner directly," I mumbled. I'd tried to be professional and leave my career in the hands of my agent, but it had been three months since I'd had a job.

I punched in the number to Warner studios.

"Hello," I said, when the chirpy receptionist answered. "This is Hattie McDaniel. I need to speak to Jack Warner."

"Umm, Mr. Warner is unavailable. Can I take a message?"

"He is available because I know for a fact that he eats breakfast in his office from seven thirty to eight thirty." I glanced at the clock on my wall. "It is eight fifteen. I also know that he is not opposed to conducting business during that time, so it is imperative that I speak with him."

I guess I caught her off guard because she hesitated, then said, "Please hold, Miss McDaniel."

Just when I thought the receptionist was about to come back to the phone with an excuse, I heard a click on the line, then, "Hattie McDaniel! Just the woman I wanted to talk to."

Now I was the one caught off guard. "Excuse me, Mr. Warner?" My angst tapered as I had not expected to be greeted so enthusiastically.

"I had you on my to-do list today. I planned to call your agent."

"For what?"

"Well, after some reevaluating and assessing, we've decided that we would indeed like to renew your contract after all." His tone was filled with cheer like I was the luckiest woman on earth.

Out of all the things I expected him to say, this wasn't one of them.

"Unfortunately," he continued, "we're going to have to do it at a lower salary. But I'm sure with the shortage of work out there for colored comedic actresses, you'll appreciate the opportunity to get back in the fray with a new role we found for you."

I inhaled. Exhaled. I should've seen this coming. This fire-and-rehire thing was becoming a common practice in Hollywood. Actors were supposed to be so grateful that they'd been rehired, they would work for less money. But he was right, what choice did I have? Louise hadn't been in a role in four months. Neither had Lillian or Ethel.

Still, I wanted to have some dignity and not just agree without question.

"What's the role?" I asked.

"It's a feature by Raoul Walsh called *They Died with Their Boots On*. It's a bit part, but you'll play a superstitious servant."

Of course, I wanted to say. A laughable female servant. The same thing I'd played in my last seventy-plus films.

Mr. Warner must've sensed my apprehension, because he quickly added, "But, Hattie, that's just the first one. We'd like to sign you on for another role I hear you've been dying to play."

I could feel his smile through the phone. "The movie is called *In This Our Life*. And I already have Bette Davis and Oliva de Havilland on board."

The script I'd been dying to play in? Was he really offering that role to me?

"We want you to play Minerva Clay, their housekeeper." The script I'd wanted. The role I'd wanted. "But you'll be more than just a housekeeper. This role is more about being a mother. Your son, Parry, is arrested for a hit-and-run that Stanley—that's Bette's character—actually did." I wondered if he knew just how bad I'd wanted this role. "And Hattie," he continued, "I know you don't have any kids, but I believe you can bring the compassion that's necessary to this role."

I felt my eyes welling with tears. Yes, I was still a housekeeper, but finally, I got to focus on something else, motherhood.

• • •

My role in *In This Our Life* had only three scenes, but it was the most meaningful work I'd done in my entire career. I was able to put some of my old sass into the first two scenes and even snuck in a couple of disapproving glances. But it was the third scene that had everyone on set predicting another Oscar win.

In the scene, I was able to deliver to Roy Timberlake, Olivia's character, a soliloquy about the fate of Negroes in the justice system. I had never before had the opportunity to be on screen with such quiet dignity. Hell, with any dignity at all. I'd poured all of my emotion into that scene and I couldn't wait for the world to see it.

"You all packed, sweetheart?"

I turned and smiled at James, who was standing in the doorway of our bedroom.

I motioned toward my bags on the floor. "I am."

"Wow, you really did get two weeks' worth of clothes in those suitcases," he said.

I nodded, proud of myself. The Warners had been so excited about my performance in *In This Our Life* that they had arranged for me to immediately go on tour with the Count Basie Orchestra, starting at Manhattan's Strand Theatre. They figured touring would be good promotion.

"Time will fly, don't you worry," I said, kissing him on the cheek.

"Well, I'll miss you while you're gone."

I gave a faint smile at our cordial formalities. The reality was both of us would be just fine with our time apart. Over the past few months, we'd been spending more and more time away from each other. I busied myself with church, community engagements, and work. And he busied himself with everything but work. I guess the newlywed phase had worn off.

"Well, I'll take your bags down," he said. "I'm listening to the game. The Brooklyn Dodgers are giving the New York Giants a run for their money."

"The baseball team or the football team?" I asked.

"It's winter, obviously football."

"It's silly that two teams would have the same name anyway," I said.

I couldn't care less about sports, but these days it was as if we struggled for things to talk about.

I grabbed my purse as he took my bag downstairs. As we made our way across the living room, a loud, piercing noise filled the air.

"We interrupt this broadcast to bring you this important bulletin from the United Press. Flash. Washington. The White House announces

Japanese attack on Pearl Harbor," the announcer's voice boomed throughout the room.

Both James and I froze and stared at the radio like it was some sort of foreign object. The phone shrilled, startling me.

"Hello," I said, after racing to answer it. James had moved closer to the radio to hear better.

"Oh, thank goodness I caught you before you left for your train." It was Evelyn, Mr. Warner's assistant. Her voice sounded panicked. "Are you listening to the news?"

"I am," I replied.

"It's just tragic. Just unbelievably tragic," she said. Her voice sounded like it was about to crack.

It was, but I was sure that wasn't why she had called me. "I will have to finish listening later. I must get to my train."

"Well, that's why I'm calling," she said. "Mr. Warner wanted me to stop you. He said his sources are telling him this is not good."

"I'm sure it's not. The Japanese attacking America, it's just heartbreaking. But what does that have to do with my tour?" I asked.

Her sigh filled the phone. "Miss McDaniel, I'm afraid there won't be a tour. Mr. Warner has canceled not only the tour but the release of *In This Our Life* as well."

CHAPTER 19

January 1942

Our country was in turmoil. More than twenty-four hundred Americans had died the day the Japanese attacked Pearl Harbor and nearly a thousand more had died in the month since. With the loss of so many lives in this unspeakable tragedy, guilt had kept so many of us confined to our homes.

Despite how much I loved my house, I was going stir-crazy inside and announced to James that I was going out to Club Alabam. Though he'd refused to go, up until the moment I walked downstairs, dressed and ready to leave, I'd hoped that he would change his mind.

"So, you're really not going?" I said, when I saw him in the sitting room listening to a special war report on the radio. That's all he did these days, consume hours and hours of war reports. We seldom talked now, and when we did, it was to argue about something. "Billie Holiday is performing tonight."

"Americans are dying like crazy, we don't know what the future holds, but yes, let's go drink and be merry at the club as we bop to Billie Holiday," James deadpanned.

It was crazy how any topic—tonight it was going out to a club, two days ago it was the amount of groceries I was buying—would become a battleground for our conflicting desires. But lately, it felt like if I said, "Let's go right," James was going to be adamant about going left.

"You're being ridiculous," I said. "We've been cooped up in the house for more than six weeks. There is nothing wrong with trying to resume our lives."

A disconnect had settled between us, so it was no surprise that he didn't reply.

"I was thinking we could go together, have some fun." I hoped for a glimmer of enthusiasm from him. I desired socializing and he longed for solitude.

I continued, "Everything feels so strained between us, it would be good to get out."

"Going to a party won't magically fix things," he responded.

"It's not about fixing everything in one night, but at least making an effort to be together, to be a team again," I said softly, hoping to convey my need for connection.

Talking to James these days often left me emotionally drained. Even my moments of vulnerability didn't seem to reach him.

He leaned over and turned up the volume on the radio, using the news announcer's voice to dismiss me. "Enjoy your partying."

Although fewer people were at Club Alabam than usual, there was still a crowd of thirty or forty. I guess some were still like James, hesitant about being out partying when the world was in chaos, but I had to do something lest I stay in my bed and cry about my tour and movie being canceled, the state of the world, and my failing marriage.

That's why when I heard Billie Holiday was performing tonight, I wanted to attend, especially to support a colored entertainer. All of us had basically been sidelined by the war.

After James made it clear he wasn't coming, I'd called and asked Ru Dandridge to join me. As expected, she was grateful for an escape from the confines of her home as well. We'd been sitting for the past hour talking about Dorothy, who had shocked everyone when she announced she and Harold were getting married.

"I just can't believe it," Ru said, tapping the pack of Pall Malls until a lone cigarette popped out. "I think she just wants to get away from me and Geneva. She's just too young." She retrieved the cigarette.

I was glad Ru kept talking because I didn't want to tell her that was exactly why Dorothy was marrying Harold.

One of the regular waitresses approached our table. "Another round for you ladies?" she asked. I nodded. "Coming right up," she said before turning to me. "By the way, Miss Hattie, I'm sorry to hear about your friend?"

"What friend?" I asked.

"Carole," the waitress replied. "She died last night." She said that like she was giving me the dinner special.

"Carole who?" I asked.

"Lombard. Clark Gable's wife. It's in today's paper. I knew you all were friends."

"What?" I exclaimed, jumping from my seat so fast I almost knocked my chair over. I'd been in bed all day and hadn't read the paper or listened to the news. I couldn't believe James hadn't heard the news either, or at least he hadn't said anything to me if he had. Ru didn't bother with daily news unless it was in a trade magazine, so I wasn't surprised that she didn't know either. I glanced around the room and spotted a newspaper sitting on the end of the bar. I raced over and snatched it up.

"'Carole Lombard, fun-loving wife of Clark Gable, and 21 other passengers, including 15 army fliers, were presumed killed last night in the crash of a Transcontinental & Western Air transport near Las Vegas, Nevada,'" I read.

My hand instantly went to my chest. Carole dead? That meant a part of Clark was dead too. Images of him succumbing to the grips of grief flashed through my head.

"Oh my God. I need to get to Clark." I tossed the newspaper back on the bar and raced over to my table, grabbing my purse and coat.

"Where are you going?" Ru asked as I slid my arms into my wool coat. "What happened to Carole?"

"She was killed in a plane crash. I've got to get to Clark." My hands were shaking and I could barely get my coat on.

"Go, go," Ru said, shooing me toward the club's exit. "I got the tab."

I thanked my friend, then raced out, jumped into my car, set the choke, turned the ignition, hit the starter button, and sped toward Encino. My pounding heart filled the silence of what I normally enjoyed as a smooth ride.

Thoughts of a smiling Clark and Carole danced in my head. Tears filled my eyes as I thought of how they bonded over unpretentious things. She learned how to hunt and fish because that's what Clark liked. She also learned how to handle a shotgun. He gave her the ranch life she craved.

I turned on the radio and within five minutes, the story was running again.

". . . Lombard had raised two million dollars for war bonds," the radio newsman said. "As you may recall, war bonds were created by the US Treasury Department and allow everyday Americans to invest in the war effort as well as their own futures. The bonds support the war in the short-term but can be cashed in for their full value a decade later. Lombard had traveled to her home state of Indiana with her mother, Elizabeth Peters, and the press agent Otto Winkler—who worked with her husband, Clark Gable—for a three-day event to encourage citizens to buy those bonds."

I gasped. I didn't realize Mrs. Peters was with her. Clark was close to her as well.

• • •

I arrived at Clark's place in half the time that it normally took for me to get to his ranch. To my surprise, his gate was open, so I pulled in, then jumped out and used the manual switch to close it so the press wouldn't take it as an open invitation to enter.

I maneuvered up his winding driveway, expecting to see a number of cars parked in front of his house. But the driveway was empty except for Clark's treasured 1935 Duesenberg Model JN.

Maybe Clark wasn't home, after all, I thought as I jumped out and made my way up the pebbled walkway to the porch.

"Clark!" I yelled, banging on the door. I leaned in, peering into the small window, trying to see inside. "Clark!" I pounded for a few minutes until I heard a groan.

"Go away," he moaned.

I banged again. "Clark, it's Hattie. You know I'm not about to do that. Open the door."

The man who tended to his horses walked up to the edge of the porch. "He's not gonna answer. Been holed up in there alone since he got the news yesterday," the man said. "He won't answer for nobody. You're the third person that has been over here."

"Oh, he's going to open this door," I said, banging harder. "Clark, open the door and let me in! You know I'm not gonna leave! I'm gonna stand on this porch and sing Negro spirituals at the top of my lungs if you don't open this door, and you know I'll do it!"

I stood for a few minutes until I finally heard the lock click. Clark slowly opened the door and my breath caught in my chest. His eyes were bloodshot, his face ashen, his hair disheveled. His normally erect posture had been replaced by slumping shoulders and flailing arms. He had a bottle of whiskey in his hand and his whole body reeked of anguish. This was the Clark no one saw. He was maniacal about his image, which had been carefully constructed—by his ex-wives, himself, and the studios. But in this moment, I wasn't talking to Clark, the King of Hollywood. I was talking to a heartbroken husband.

"Oh, Clark, I'm so sorry," I said, taking his hands in mine. He grasped my hands, pulled me to him, hugged me, and sobbed. I held my breath. Anguish wasn't the only thing he reeked of. The smell of hooch assaulted my nostrils.

I shook off the stench burning my nose and guided him back inside. I had just sat him down on the sofa when I noticed a life-sized mannequin sitting at the end of the couch. She was dressed in a flouncy nightie and had an uncanny resemblance to the actress Lana Turner. The sight was a strange one to behold, but before I could ask him about it, Clark spoke up.

"It's my fault," he cried. "It's my fault that she's dead."

"Come on, now. You can't blame yourself for that. You had nothing to do with this."

"But I did though," he cried. "Carole had been advised by the pilot to take a train home, but she insisted on flying instead."

"That doesn't even sound like Carole," I said. "It's been in the news that air travel was expressly forbidden because of the fear of accidents in wintry weather or sabotage by Hitler's spies. Why would she not follow the pilot's advice?"

He looked like giving me the answer to that question pained him. Finally he said, "I . . . I . . . I had an affair."

That was heartbreaking news. Everyone knew Clark was a ladies' man, but with Carole, I thought he'd changed his philandering ways. "But wasn't she in—"

"Yes," he snapped, before falling back on the sofa, "but you're not listening to me! She was in Indianapolis when she found out I had an affair with Lana Turner when we were filming *Honky Tonk*, and that's why she got on the plane and came home," he cried.

Before I could ask more questions, Clark said, "I'm leaving, Hattie. I can't do this. I'm burying my wife, then I'm leaving."

"Leaving to go where?" I asked.

"Ma wanted me to go fight," he said, using his pet name for Carole. "I'm going to be an army tail gunner," he said.

I frowned, thinking it had to be the whiskey talking. "Are you serious? Isn't that an extremely dangerous position?"

Clark nodded, using the back of his hand to wipe the tears trickling down his cheeks. "I'm going in and I'm not expecting to come back." He reached for the glass I was still holding and when I moved it away, he leaned over, grabbed the bottle of whiskey off the coffee table, lifted it to his mouth, and took a long swig.

"Clark! I know you're grieving, but you're an actor. And you're well past draft age."

"Making movies seems so frivolous when you've lost the love of your life," he bemoaned.

Watching my friend was heartbreaking. Gone was the tenacity that had made him a star in Hollywood. Grief had swallowed his confidence whole.

Before I could say anything else, Clark's back door opened and his friend David Niven entered.

"Hey, Hattie," he said. "I was wondering whose car that was."

"Hi, David." I glanced over at Clark, who was laid out on the sofa. "I just got the news and rushed right over to check on him."

"Yeah, I was with him as the list of names ticked out of the teletype," David said. He lowered his voice and leaned in. "It was awful."

"It's simply heartbreaking." I just knew Carole through Clark, but with the pain I felt right now, I could only imagine what he was going through. "Is he gonna be okay?" I asked.

"I can hear you, you know," Clark moaned. "I'll be fine if everyone just goes away."

"President Roosevelt sent a wire with his condolences," David said, ignoring his request.

"Did you get rid of the car?" Clark slurred his words.

"No, Clark, we're not going to worry about that right now," David replied.

"What is he talking about?" I whispered.

"You know how he and Carole loved that Duesenberg. He wants me to sell it outside of California so he never has to see it on the road again," David said.

I shook my head. "You're right. That's something to deal with later."

Suddenly, Clark cried out, "We were supposed to be married for life!"

I walked over and eased the bottle of whiskey from his hand. I expected him to protest, but he just let his arm drop, moaned, and closed his eyes.

I motioned for David to follow me into the kitchen. He looked at Clark, who seemed to have passed out into an alcohol-induced slumber, then he released a heavy sigh as we exited.

"He said he had an affair," I whispered once we were out of earshot.

David nodded. "With Lana. But Carole found out about that right when she left for Indianapolis and they've been wiring one another since she's been gone. They had made up and Carole just wanted to get home as fast as possible." He pointed to the mannequin in the other room. "That was a joke he was going to play on her. He'd dressed the thing up and was going to get Carole riled up for nothing."

I knew they'd loved playing practical jokes on each other. However, this one didn't seem funny to me. But I'd have given anything to have her walk through the door right then, look at that mannequin, and start fussing. Or laughing. Or crying. Or anything.

But that wasn't happening. It would never happen again and I didn't know how my friend would ever survive that.

CHAPTER 20

May 1942

The casualties from World War II now topped two hundred thousand. Hollywood had all but shut down as the fictional world of movies took a back seat to the real world. I worried each day about Clark, who had not only gone into war but had taken one of the most dangerous jobs in the military. But I'd be lying if I said I wasn't devastated over having the most important work of my career shelved. The last time I talked to Mr. Warner, he told me *In This Our Life* was on hold indefinitely as Hollywood now had to try and navigate how, and if, to entertain Americans in the midst of a war.

I tried not to focus on my personal loss and instead turned my attention to the thousands of Americans who had been killed when Japan had bombed Pearl Harbor. Ruby and I had been talking about this regularly.

"Here you go, Miss McDaniel," said Amisha, the Turkish immigrant whose skilled needlework rivaled my mother's.

Her thick accent boomed throughout the tiny seamstress shop. "I made the dress perfect for you," she said, handing me the long damask gown I'd brought in several weeks ago to be tailored.

I don't know why I was bothering to take my clothes to the tailor anyway. The war had stopped all personal appearances, and I hadn't left my home in Sugar Hill in the past three months.

"Thank you, Amisha."

"If you have more work, I'd be happy to do it." There was an air of desperation in her voice. I imagined she hadn't been getting much employment in the past few months.

"I'll keep that in mind," I told her before bidding her farewell and walking back outside.

"Good day, madam."

I smiled at the young colored man standing outside the seamstress's shop smoking a cigarette. Though his threadbare garments swallowed his thin frame, his smile was warm and welcoming.

"Hello, how are you?" I replied.

"As good as a colored man can be," he said, tipping his worn-out fedora. "Know anyone looking for a good jack-of-all-trades? I'm real good at fixing things," he said.

In the past, I might've searched for some work around my house that could help this young man out, but I needed to conserve every penny.

"I'm so sorry. I wish I did," I replied.

"No worries. Thanks, anyway. You have a good day."

I nodded and took a few more steps on the sidewalk when I heard someone running up behind me.

"Excuse me." I turned toward the voice calling out after me. "Aren't you Hattie McDaniel?"

The lanky white man in a tweed jacket and pageboy hat stood giddy with delight.

"I am," I said, expecting him to ask for an autograph for his wife or something of the like.

Instead, he said, "I am Frank Milligan with the Office of War Information. We actually had a telegram sent to you."

"I haven't received anything."

"It just went out today. So I do believe this is divine intervention that I would bump into you today." He was bouncing with excitement and could barely keep still.

"And why, pray tell, would you be trying to get in contact with me?"

The Negro man smoking the cigarette looked on as if he wanted to know the answer to that question as well.

"Well, as you know, President Roosevelt is trying to mobilize Negroes and ensure their involvement in various aspects of the war," Mr. Milligan said.

"I'm aware of that, but what does that have to do with me?"

"My office wanted to see if you'd be interested in starting or doing something with the Negro troops. The troops could really use some brightening up. We also need your help in promoting American racial harmony."

I had just been talking with Ruby this morning about how I felt the need to do something to help those serving in the war. Maybe Mr. Milligan was right. Maybe this was divine intervention. I knew that more than two million colored men had registered for the draft and a new group of Negro fighter pilots called the Tuskegee Airmen was hard at work in the war.

"I do think that's a splendid idea. My father was a veteran so I'd love to help," I said. "I do have a telephone. Please take my number and have someone call me with the details." I opened my purse and removed a fountain pen and paper and scribbled my number.

"Just spectacular!" he exclaimed. "My superiors are going to be so ecstatic to hear this." He tucked the paper in his jacket pocket. "I'll have them call you expeditiously."

He had just scurried off when I noticed the man smoking the cigarette staring at me. Only now the warm smile was gone from his face.

"What?" I asked, wondering why he was staring at me like a disappointed parent.

"So you really 'bout to support that white man's war?"

"I'm not supporting a war. I'm supporting the colored troops fighting in the war."

"This here war ain't got nothing to do with us." He flicked his cigarette to the ground, smashed it with the heel of his tattered loafer, then took a step toward me. "The majority of colored folks round here living in segregation and poverty. We can't get a decent education or employment."

I took a step back. His proximity made me nervous. "M-maybe the war will bring us together, foster an environment favorable to the colored cause," I managed to say.

"If you believe that, you'll believe a colored man gon' be president one day," he quipped. "That whole mess that man was talking about FDR trying to ease division is just superficial. He wants us fighting his war so we don't pay attention to the war going on here at home."

I don't know why I felt compelled to defend a president I had never met—to a man I'd never met—but I did. "Even before the US entered a war, the president signed an executive order ending discrimination in defense hiring," I said.

"Yeah, under immense pressure. It's propaganda," he snapped. "Mark my word, they're just using you. They want you to show us good colored folks that this war is worth us putting our lives on the line. They want you to convince us that we're supposed to sacrifice our lives to live as half an American." He jabbed a finger in my face. "Is this America even worth defending? Will colored Americans suffer the indignities that we've been enduring forever?"

His negative outburst had taken me aback. All I wanted was to continue on my way. "Good day, sir," I said, walking away as he shouted more ominous warnings after me.

At home, I pushed aside that man's words and immediately went to work. I called the Office of War Information and was patched right through. By the time I hung up with the director, I was excited.

I decided to start by forming the Hollywood Victory Committee. I brought on Lillian, Louise, and some of my actor friends—Eddie Anderson, Leigh Whipper, Ben Carter, Fayard Nicholas, Nicodemus Stewart, Wonderful Smith, and Mantan Moreland—and they all agreed to serve on my steering committee. Our goal was to keep morale up among our colored military. Thankfully, all of us were in alignment with that mission and none of us were like the man outside the seamstress's shop with his "this ain't our war" negativity. We began planning tours of military bases as well as activities directed at assuring that colored citizens backed the war.

But still, the cigarette man's words haunted me throughout my planning. He was right about one thing—I strongly believed that victory abroad would be meaningful only with a victory at home in the long, ongoing domestic struggle for civil rights. No way could the United States continue to brag about its superior democratic institutions while sustaining widespread Jim Crow laws and disenfranchisement of Negro citizens.

My committee stayed busy over the next few months entertaining the troops, traveling to military camps across the country, raising funds, and disseminating war news to Negroes to rally them behind the long, hard fight through the war.

I also won an appointment as a captain in the American Women's Voluntary Services organization and often posed proudly in my smartly tailored uniform for publicity photos for colored newspapers. I played hostess to a group of colored soldiers touring the Warner Brothers lot in a different set of press materials geared toward white audiences. I dressed as Mammy and served meals to white GIs. The 28th Infantry made me an honorary first lieutenant. I received citations from the Red Cross. Several Negro servicemen on layovers in Los Angeles stayed in my home since the city still had very few hotels that welcomed colored patronage.

My actor friends and I welcomed the distraction. Work for colored actors remained slim. The war in Europe had cut off crucial international markets and forced American studios to downsize their output, so work was even more scarce than before.

I enjoyed being appreciated by my people for a change. Not since the cigarette man had I been peppered with criticism. It was as if the war had given my people a reason to unite.

I hated what brought our country to this point, but it wasn't lost on me that with my war efforts, I'd finally found an area where I was appreciated.

CHAPTER 21

July 1942

Hollywood was adjusting to the war. After several bleak months, I was back at work, playing in a movie called *The Male Animal*. It was a bit part, and of course, it was for a maid. Since the role was modern, I had been able to convince the producer to dispense with the traditional demeaning Negro dialect. I even tried to put more back talk in.

I dragged myself out of bed and downstairs. I had a few hours before I needed to get to the set. Maybe I should see if my husband wanted to eat breakfast together since that was yet another thing that we'd stopped doing.

James was already eating at the breakfast table. The place setting for one indicated he had no intention of waiting for me to join him. In the past two months, silence had widened the gap between us. It was as if we simply had nothing left to say to one another. Even still, I decided to force a conversation.

"We wrap on *The Male Animal* today," I said, pulling a plate out of the cabinet.

"Is that right?" James said, his voice monotone as he took a crumpet from the center of the table and slathered apricot jam all over it.

"I'm so ready for it to be over, though I have no idea what's next."

"Find another movie production house," he said nonchalantly.

"I'm under contract with the Warners," I said, exasperated. Since he hadn't bothered to look at me since I sat down, I felt compelled to add, "I either have to play the parts the studio gives me or leave the industry altogether. And if I did that, who would keep you in your fine suits?"

He glared at me as he bit into his crumpet, though he didn't respond. I didn't mean to be snippy with him, but these days I couldn't seem to help it.

I continued, "I still believe the industry will improve for colored folks, but . . ." I couldn't believe that I was letting a "but" enter my thoughts. I hated to admit it: my optimism was officially fading.

James set his fork down and picked up the folded *California Eagle* sitting next to his plate. He opened the paper up and began reading the inside. And while he did that, I couldn't help but stare at the photo on the front page. Walter White glared at me across the table. His smug face made my insides fume. It was bad enough that all these producers were relying on formulaic stereotypes to hold me back. But this face. The pale face staring across my breakfast table was the real reason I'd been unable to get any decent roles.

Walter White had been a persistent irritant. He'd tried to get *Gone with the Wind* shut down before we even started filming because of its "negative portrayal of Negroes." Then he wanted Mr. Selznick to hire a colored adviser to be present on the set during filming to give advice. As the executive secretary of the NAACP, he leveraged that position to get Mr. Selznick to take him seriously. Mr. White did get a Ku Klux Klan scene that was in the book dropped from the movie, but I think that was more so because of a scathing column Earl Morris at the *Pittsburgh Courier* wrote.

"Are you reading that NAACP article?" I asked.

James set the paper down, exhaling an exasperated breath. "Yes. It's just about how Walter White is trying to get studio heads to include Negro military contributions in newsreels."

"Hmph."

"He apparently has the support of the First Lady."

"Why would Eleanor Roosevelt want to have anything to do with him?" I balked.

James shrugged. "Not sure. The article said she is sincerely interested in this problem of colored stereotyping and hopes that Mr. White will meet with success."

I rolled my eyes. I didn't know how Walter White had been able to fool all these people into thinking he spoke for our entire race, but he did not have sincere intentions when it came to colored film vets.

"Seems to me you guys should be appreciative of the fact that he's out there fighting for you all," James said, taking another crumpet. "Don't you want better roles?"

"Of course, but I'm offended by Walter's refusal to consult with me and other Negro actors. He only wants to deal with studio power brokers. Do you know he had the audacity to tell Louise that our willingness to play maid roles makes us suspect? That's why he won't include us. He said we had little pull and would hardly be useful allies in the struggle."

Just talking about Walter White got me steamed.

"But he's really been working to get the industry to stop portraying Negroes as buffoons or humble servants," James said.

I slammed my palms on the table. "I don't want to hear that. It's a criticism of my artistic skills and a statement of his intention to exile me from Hollywood." I huffed. "He had a luncheon last week and seventy people were there. Not one member of the Negro film community was invited."

"I read somewhere that he passed for white and infiltrated white supremacist groups to gather info for the NAACP," James said. "So while you might not agree with all his methods, he really is working for colored folks. That's why I think you should go to the NAACP meeting tonight." James looked at me like he'd been trying all morning to figure out a way to convince me to attend the closing meeting of the NAACP's national convention. I'd received a personal invitation via telegram and promptly discarded it. James had retrieved the invite from the trash and now he slid it across the table toward me.

"No. Walter White has been the bane of my existence." I huffed. "I refuse to even breathe the same air as him."

"Okay, don't go for Walter White. Go for your fans. Go for all the young actors who are looking at you like a guiding light. Show that you rise in spite of hate."

James knew how to get to me. I would never acquiesce to Walter White, but for the fans and the young actors, maybe he was right.

It was that line of thought that led me five hours later to the Shrine Auditorium for the NAACP National Convention keynote address.

The Who's Who of colored Hollywood was at this event. I didn't usually feel intimidated when I walked into a room, but standing there in the foyer of the Shrine, between the intricate columns and red velvet curtains lining the wall, looking at what amounted to Negro royalty, gave me an apprehension I seldom had. There were at least three hundred people at this private reception. I spotted Mary McLeod Bethune deep in conversation with John H. Johnson, the publisher of the *Negro Digest*. Los Angeles mayor Fletcher Bowron was standing with the guest speaker, Wendell Willkie, and A. Philip Randolph, who was receiving the Spingarn Medal for his accomplishments in the field of labor with the Brotherhood of Sleeping Car Porters.

"Hello, Miss McDaniel."

I smiled at the towering man with the thin mustache and houndstooth suit who had walked over to greet me.

"Reverend C. L. Franklin," I said, greeting the young pastor from Memphis, who was making a name for himself as a great orator. His wife, Barbara, was a gospel singer who I'd met back in my singing days. "How are you?"

"Just splendid. Happy to be here. I just began working with the NAACP, so I'm serving as a delegate." He tapped his name tag.

"Is your wife here?" I asked.

"No, Barbara couldn't make it. She just gave birth in March. Another girl. We named her Aretha."

"Well, congratulations. Give her my love," I said, squeezing his hand and making a mental note to send a congratulatory token to the Franklin family.

James cleared his throat as if he was waiting to be introduced, but Reverend Franklin had moved on before I could do the honors.

"It would be nice if you would acknowledge me," James said, a scowl across his face.

Believing it would be easier if I just agreed, I simply said, "Sorry."

That pacified him and he continued scanning the room. "Everybody who's anybody is here," he said in awe.

I took in the sea of people who had begun filing inside the auditorium. "It's the last day of their national convention, and outside of Walter White, you were right about the impact the NAACP has on our community. So I guess it's a good thing we came."

James seemed to appreciate my acknowledgment of him and kissed me on the cheek before excusing himself to go talk to someone he'd spotted.

I was surprised that even Lincoln Perry, or rather Stepin Fetchit, was here. And with his head held high. If there was anyone on earth who caught it worse than me, it was him. He'd billed himself "The Laziest Man in the World" and had parlayed that into a successful film career. He was the first Negro actor to earn a million dollars, but the cost he paid for it was high as he was crucified for being "embarrassing and harmful." But from the way he laughed and moved among the crowd, you'd never know that it bothered him.

I moved about the room, talking with more people, including my friend Clarence Muse, an actor who also worked as a reporter for the *California Eagle*.

"Clarence, don't you look dapper."

"Thank you. I do clean up well, don't I?" He laughed, striking a pose as he stroked the collar of his navy suit. "You look lovely yourself." He motioned toward my fitted charcoal-gray silk jacket and calf-length skirt.

I used my gloved hand to pat the feathers on my pillbox hat. "Thank you, darling."

We shared a chuckle before I added, "You here working for the *Eagle* or on behalf of the NAACP?" since he was active in the local branch.

"A little bit of both," he replied, his eyes darting over to Mr. Bowron, who had just wrapped his conversation. "Matter of fact, let me see if I can get an interview with the mayor."

He excused himself just as I noticed my sorority's national president, Bertha Black Rhoda. She waved me over to the table where she sat with a group of distinguished women.

"Sister McDaniel, what a pleasure," she said, standing to hug me as I approached them. Each of the women looked dignified and esteemed in their sorority colors.

"Hello, Madam President," I said, admiring her blue-and-gold bell-sleeved dress. "I didn't know you'd be here."

"Yes," she replied, motioning toward the table of women. "All the national sorority presidents are members of the NAACP. We are slated to talk about the programs each of us are doing for women in wartime. This is Beulah Tyrrell Whitby with Alpha Kappa Alpha Sorority, Incorporated."

The petite woman in a salmon-pink, rhinestone-lined hat and two-piece light green suit stood and extended her hand.

"Might I say that we are super proud of your wartime efforts—of course, that's in addition to your screen work," Beulah said before motioning to a poised and distinguished woman sitting behind her, draped in strands of pearls and a cream wedge silhouette dress, a pink-and-green rose on her lapel. "If I may, I'd love to introduce you to another fan. This is Ethel Hedgemon Lyle."

The regal woman stood and used both of her hands to cover mine. Her smile illuminated the entire room. "Miss McDaniel, it is an extreme pleasure to see you. We met briefly when you were in Mississippi a few years ago speaking at our Mississippi Health Project program."

"Ah, yes," I replied. I had a rare personal appearance in Mississippi when I'd heard about the AKA's public health initiative to provide proper health care for Negroes. I had made it a point to volunteer and ended up speaking at a reception. "You all were so welcoming and I was honored to be part of such a worthy cause."

"Yes, that was one of our most successful programs," Ethel replied. "I think I speak for all of us when I say your perseverance in spite of adversity is admirable and we will be here to support you in all your endeavors."

Her words meant a lot, especially because she was in a different organization. But in this moment, not only did I feel seen; I felt embraced by fellow Negro women.

"Thank you very much," I said.

As Ethel returned to her seat, Bertha held her hands out to introduce the other women. "And this is Blanche Thompson with Zeta Phi Beta Sorority, Incorporated, and Helen Elsie Austin with Delta Sigma Theta Sorority, Incorporated."

I greeted each woman, thanking them for their work and outreach efforts during the war and beyond.

"We'll have to get you out to speak at our new program where we focus on employment counseling and career development for Negro women," Helen said.

"It would be my pleasure," I replied.

We talked for a few minutes about some of their sororities' programs. I gave each of them my information and told them not to hesitate to call me if I could ever be of service.

I had just made my way back to James, who was deep in conversation with another man, when a fair-skinned woman, who looked like she couldn't be more than twenty years old, approached us.

"Hello, Miss McDaniel." The woman was simply angelic with creamy, smooth butterscotch-colored skin and a svelte figure that looked like it was made for dancing onstage. "I just wanted to tell you that I am such a huge fan. I admire your work tremendously."

"Why, thank you," I said, returning her smile, which originated from her eyes.

"I'm an actress myself," she said, her hands trembling nervously. "Well, I haven't really done anything yet. But I just moved to Los Angeles in hopes that I can one day follow in a fraction of your footsteps."

I took out a card and handed it to her. "Well, I am always about helping the next generation and would love to stay in touch. What's your name?"

She was giddy as she took the card. "It's Lena. Lena Horne."

I squeezed her hand. Her infectious personality had instantly brightened my mood. "Miss Horne, it was a pleasure to meet you. I look forward to speaking with you soon."

She smiled. "Thank you so much."

"They're telling us to take our seats," James said, nodding toward the usher who was ringing a bell to summon everyone inside.

"I'll expect your call," I said.

"Most definitely," she excitedly replied as James took my hand and led me away.

I felt good with all the interactions I'd had in the past thirty minutes, so I was on a bit of a euphoric high when I followed my husband into the auditorium.

"Oh my," I said, looking around. The auditorium seated nearly seven thousand people and it looked like every seat was taken.

"I had no idea this many people would be here," I said.

"Yes, an impressive turnout. I understand there are NAACP delegates from all over the country, as well as guests. Now, aren't you glad we came? When I checked us in, they said we have reserved seating in the front row," James said, brushing the collar of his suit as if he wanted to make sure we were seen as we maneuvered the narrow aisle toward the front.

The program began with a hearty song by the Second Baptist church choir. After a few acknowledgments and introductions, Wendell Willkie, the 1940 Republican presidential nominee who lost to Franklin Roosevelt, took the stage and delivered a riveting speech about how the war was breaking down color barriers. After he finished, Walter White took the podium.

"Thank you to everyone gathered here today," he began. "I am happy to wrap up our conference and hope you go back to your respective cities fully energized and charged to do the work of our esteemed organization. I also want to take a moment to urge us to remember the mission of the NAACP, and that is to champion equal rights, eliminate racial prejudice, and to advance the interests of colored citizens. One of the things we're fighting is the deplorable state of race relations worldwide. And no greater area is that being manifested than in Hollywood," Mr. White said to rambunctious applause. "I have worked tirelessly to urge filmmakers to make a complete break with the tradition of showing Negroes as menial characters, who were nothing more than cretinous, grinning Uncle Toms. We are sending a direct message to colored Hollywood veterans regarding their responsibilities in the struggle."

I began shifting in my seat as all feelings of euphoria dissipated.

Mr. White continued, "We are asking Negro actors to play their roles with sincerity and dignity instead of mugging and playing the clown before the camera."

I could feel the heat of people's stares while he spoke. I kept my gaze on the stage.

"Many of you may have been reading the news about my discussions with the studio heads about our portrayal in cinema," he continued. "I have been negotiating directly with the studios to change the roles available to colored actors in Hollywood. I am happy to report that my nearly three years of meetings have been successful and I anticipate that in the near future, colored cinematic characters will receive significantly more respectful and realistic treatment."

He paused as more applause filled the room. I didn't clap until James bumped me with his elbow to let me know people were watching. I inhaled and turned my attention back to Walter White as I did a slow clap.

"And to show you that these producers are listening to our concerns, I have some wonderful news to share with you," he continued.

"I would like to invite an amazing actress to the stage." Mr. White paused and motioned toward where I was sitting in the front row. Oh, my! I definitely hadn't expected him to acknowledge me. I guess that was why I'd been extended a personal invitation. I moved my pearl bag to the side, preparing to stand, though I was thoroughly confused. But before I got out of my seat, the young actress I'd met earlier, who was seated three seats down from me, stood.

"Please help me welcome Hollywood newcomer Lena Horne," Mr. White said, leading the audience in applause.

My face was flushed with embarrassment as I sank back in my seat. Thankfully, no one noticed. They were too busy loudly applauding Lena as she ascended the stairs, her yellow satin dress framing her body like she was a goddess.

Lena hugged Mr. White. He stepped from behind the podium, took her hand, lifted it, and twirled her around like they were in the middle of a ballroom dance. "Ladies and gentlemen, may I present to you the perfect image of the New Cinematic Negro." His voice boomed, the acoustics in the room seeming to amplify every syllable. "She's articulate, sophisticated, thin, fair-skinned, and extraordinarily beautiful." The room erupted in applause again and I felt physically ill.

Lena smiled as she waved to the audience. "Miss Horne got her start at Harlem's Cotton Club, and she is well known among the Negro leadership elite in Manhattan."

I couldn't believe the way he was prancing her around, or the way the crowd seemed to be lapping it all up.

He wrapped his arm around her waist as he pulled her to him. "Now, I'm a close friend of her family, and yes, I urged her to try Hollywood. She has no history in the movies and therefore has not been typecast as anything so far," Mr. White continued. "That makes her the perfect person to establish a different kind of image for Negro women." He released his hand from Lena's waist and leaned in closer to the microphone. "It is time that we get rid of the grinning-darky stereotype, the swivel-eyed cretins, who shuffle, jig, and drop consonants throughout the films that reach not only America but the whole world, white and colored. America . . ." He paused and glared down at me where I sat in the front row. "Hattie McDaniel's Mammy is no more." He turned back to Lena and used both hands to motion up and down her body like she was a contestant in some kind of competition. "This is who we want representing us in colored Hollywood," he said with a grin as wide as a Cheshire cat's.

I kept my gaze on the stage, refusing to turn to look at the legions of people I was sure were staring at me, aghast at my humiliation or feeling sorry for me—neither of which I would ever be okay with. James had squeezed my hand as if it was his way of calming me. There was no calming the fury that railed inside me. Not only was Walter White demeaning my profession, but I was the only actor he explicitly called out. My dignity broke the haze of rage and I kept my head held high as Lena exited the stage. I felt her apologetic eyes upon me, but my gaze remained steadfastly forward.

The rest of the ceremony was a blur and I wanted to scream with joy once the program wrapped. My hope was to escape the NAACP convention unseen, so when everyone stood to applaud the planning committee, I made a hasty exit out the side door. But Clarence stopped me just as I reached the hallway leading out of the venue.

"Hattie," he called out.

I paused, debating whether I should just keep going. I didn't want to stop, talk to him, and have others pause and look at me with pity and embarrassment. But since I knew Clarence walked a similar path as me—his work as a forceful activist was often overshadowed because he was typecast as a bowing and devoted servant—I stopped.

"I'm sure you're not happy about what just transpired in there," he said.

That was an understatement. He looked just as aggravated as I did. Clarence often wrote in his column that Negroes seldom praised us for our good performances, but invariably accused 90 percent of us as being "Uncle Toms." He was a fierce fighter to get the Negro community to rally behind Negro film stars. If anyone would understand my plight, he would.

"Is this Clarence my friend talking or Clarence the reporter?" I asked.

He closed his notepad and dropped it in his jacket pocket.

"If I had disdain for Walter White before, it just quadrupled," I whispered.

James, who had followed me out, shifted uneasily, like he wanted to escape before someone he knew came over to us.

"Can we talk about this outside?" James said, eyeing the scores of people who had started filing out.

As I noticed the sorority presidents exiting the building, genuine concern on their faces, I suddenly didn't want to simply run away.

"Now, if I can have Clarence the reporter back, please?" I said, standing erect and ignoring James's fidgeting.

Clarence didn't hesitate as he pulled his notepad back out and flipped it open.

"Clarence, I have no quarrel with the NAACP or colored fans who object to the roles some of us play," I said, speaking loud enough that those passing by could hear. "I naturally resent being completely ignored after I have struggled for eleven years to open up opportunities for our group in the industry. I have tried to be a credit to my race. I've had exemplary conduct both on- and off-screen. You can imagine my chagrin when the only person called to the platform was a young woman from New York who had just arrived in Hollywood and had not yet made her first picture. I take nothing away from her, but I wonder why something must always be taken from me."

Another reporter I didn't recognize appeared at the side of Clarence. "Walter White says he's fighting to change things. Do you believe that there have been advances in the industry?" the reporter asked.

"Of course. And there is much room for improvement," I replied.

"What types of improvement?" he asked, scribbling on his notepad.

I debated answering, but this bag was opened, so I might as well empty it. "There has been an evolution of some colored roles from incidental to central characters, as well as the better treatment of colored players on the studio lots," I continued. "The battle must be fought outright here by the actors and it cannot be won if outside pressure from individuals and groups hurts the doors of opportunity for us. It takes time to change things and I don't believe that will be gained by rushing or attempting to force studios to do anything they are not readily inclined to do. That's all I have to say. Excuse me." I let James take my hand and lead me away.

Thankfully, no one else tried to stop me, though Clarence did catch up with us. His notebook was closed again.

"Between me and you," he said once we were outside the building, "Walter White is an audience of one. Negro film stars have always been more conscious than he that Negroes should have better roles. His lone-wolf approach is going to do nothing more than throw the studios into a panic that will, in turn, compel them to delete darker-skinned, working-class, and comic characters from the screen."

"I couldn't agree more," I replied, not slowing my pace.

"I just don't understand why Mr. White thinks he's the best person suited to wage the struggle to improve our representation," Clarence said.

"Exactly. We are the ones best suited for that," I replied, pausing as an idea swept into my head. "Matter of fact, I think it's time we did something about it."

"Something like what?" Clarence said as we approached my car.

"I don't know. Mr. White has the NAACP. We should form our own committee. Just for Hollywood," I said. I'd had such success with the Hollywood Victory Committee. Maybe I should duplicate that to help our cause.

Clarence's eyes lit up. "Yes. An organization to hold the studios accountable."

"Mr. White's interests are self-serving and not in our best interest," I said. "We could call our group the Hollywood Fair Play Committee. We will not only force Walter White out of the film debate but preserve our own livelihoods."

A wide smile spread across his face. "I like that. Count me in."

"I'll do that. Look to hear from me soon." I tucked my purse under my arm and eased into the passenger seat with a renewed sense of determination.

"Are you sure you want to make waves?" James asked once we pulled out of the parking lot.

I leaned my head back against the seat. "The safe approach isn't working," I said. "It's time I stop sitting back and waiting on Hollywood to make room for me. I'm going to effect change on my own."

My husband didn't ask any more questions as we navigated our way home.

CHAPTER 22

August 1942

When I was growing up, my mother used to always say that delayed is not denied, and now today, as I celebrated the release of *In This Our Life*, I finally knew what she meant.

I was overjoyed that the role I had longed to do would now be seen by the masses. Maybe this would silence Walter White. Maybe it would help the Hollywood Fair Play Committee I'd formed last month. Maybe it would get Negroes to see that I was capable of more than Mammy—if only given the opportunity. A myriad of maybes swirled through my head.

The theater was packed for the premiere, even though they'd announced the release only three weeks ago. I hated that Clark couldn't be here. He had been promoted to officer in the army, so I didn't foresee him getting out anytime soon. But Louise, Ru, and Lillian were here at the Hollywood Theater in Los Angeles.

We'd just finished watching the premiere and had now gathered in the large foyer of the theater for a reception.

As proud as I was of the role of Minerva, I was a tad perturbed because a lot of my lines had been cut from the three scenes I had filmed.

"Your performance was simply exceptional," Mr. Meiklejohn said, approaching me as I stood in a corner greeting fans.

"Thank you so much." I wanted to talk to him about the cuts, but I didn't want to do it in front of people and there were about a hundred folks in the room, including most of the cast.

Bette approached as well, taking my hands and giving them a gentle squeeze. "I'm so proud of you and I have to agree that it's your best performance ever. No way can Walter White complain about this role." She pointed toward Olivia, who had just walked up with the director. "It's obvious he already likes the movie since he sent Olivia a letter thanking her for her performance."

"Excuse me?" I said.

Olivia exchanged glances with the director. The blank expression on her face said that she would rather not have shared that information, but since Bette had divulged it, she slowly nodded.

"Yes, Mr. White sent me a letter last week. He called my performance a high watermark on the treatment of the Negro," Olivia said.

The audacity of that man. Walter White had never even acknowledged that I was in the path-breaking project and he's out here sending Olivia accolades. This felt like just another mark in a long line of disrespect. Not to mention that the studio had shown him the final copy before I'd even seen it.

Olivia must've been able to discern the look on my face because she quickly added, "I think he just decided to send me the letter because I had been telling a mutual contact that I had hoped *In This Our Life* would be a less conventional story of romance in trouble and that it would have dealt more deeply and extensively with the story of Parry and Minerva and their relationship with the principal characters."

"Well, all I know is this is a movie that we all should be proud of," Lillian said, lifting her glass to try and break the growing tension.

The guests near us lifted their glasses in a toast, and the mixing and mingling resumed. I relaxed. Lillian was right. This was a project to be proud of. I wasn't going to let Walter White dampen such a joyous occasion.

The sight of Jack Warner approaching brought a genuine smile to my face. A stout man with wispy blond hair and a woman who looked like a Catholic school matron stood beside him.

“Hello, Hattie, I’d like you to meet Alonzo Richardson and his wife, Zelle,” Mr. Warner said.

The way the couple’s lips were pursed wiped the emerging smile from my face.

“Hello, Mr. and Mrs. Richardson, it’s so nice to meet you,” I said, nodding my head in greeting.

Mr. Richardson didn’t bother with formalities as he crossed his arms over his protruding belly and looked at his wife.

Her tone was just as stiff as her appearance. “Miss McDaniel, as head of Atlanta’s film censorship board, I must tell you that I deplore this movie.”

I was at a loss as to what I was meant to do with that information. “I’m sorry to hear that,” I managed to say. “I actually think it is one of my best performances to date.”

Mrs. Richardson bristled as if it was taking everything inside her to contain her disdain. She brushed a string of bright blond hair out of her face, as if it would dare get out of order. Finally, she said, “This movie is an insult to Southern whites everywhere.”

“I’m afraid I must agree,” Mr. Richardson added.

To Mr. Warner, Mrs. Richardson said, “I’m shocked that Warner Brothers would even film scenes where Negroes objected to the racial status quo.”

Mr. Warner’s eyes widened. Did he not have a conversation with this couple before he brought them over to me? Could he not see the disdain that was almost oozing from their pores?

Mrs. Richardson’s lips were in a thin tight line before she said, “This is just the film industry’s continued unwarranted sympathy for Negroes, who complain in spite of the things that we have done for their own good.” She balked. Her indignation was palpable. “We know how to handle our coloreds. White Southerners love the Negro. We appreciate his ability as none other can and we put up with his frailties as none others do.”

I was speechless. This woman had the audacity to be insulted because my character wanted a better life.

"This must never be shown in the South," Mr. Richardson continued. It felt as if he and his wife were tag-teaming me.

Added Mrs. Richardson, "I am going to have to delete all mentions of racism from the movie before it can be shown anywhere in the Southern box office. Though if I had my druthers, I would toss the entire film in the trash." She didn't give me time to reply as he added, "Good day," then hobbled away with her husband scurrying behind her.

I stood dumbfounded as they walked out of the theater. When I looked at Mr. Warner, he too appeared frazzled before he excused himself without offering any words of comfort.

Bette, Olivia, Louise, Lillian, and the others who had just moments ago been celebrating stood, stunned silent just like me.

• • •

Mrs. Richardson's words had haunted me for the past week, James was out of town, and I'd been stressed for days at the thought that Southerners would see an altered film. I was relieved when Ruby walked in through the back door since she was so good at calming my frazzled nerves.

"Hi, Hattie," she said. Her luggage was by her side, indicating she'd come straight here from the train station.

"Hello, Ruby. How was your trip to Harlem?" I asked.

"It was fine. It was great to spend time with my cousin and her new baby." She poured herself a cup of coffee. "I went with some friends to see the movie," she said. From the blank expression on her face, I couldn't instantly tell if she'd liked it or not.

I slid into a chair at the kitchen table and began adding sugar cubes to my coffee. "What did you think? I'll have to tell you about what happened at the premiere last week."

Ruby looked uneasy as she took a seat across from me. She slow-sipped her beverage. Finally, she said, "It . . . wasn't what I expected.

I know you said you had a scene where you talked about racism, but I didn't see that and I'd had really been looking forward to it."

I blinked. "What do you mean, you didn't see the scene? It was the last one that I was in."

Confusion crossed her face. "You were only on-screen twice, so—"

"No, I have three scenes."

She frowned. "Not in the movie I saw."

"What do you mean?" I had figured we'd get blowback in the South, but New York was censoring the movie too?

"I guess the movie was cut. It's like your character was there, then just wasn't seen again," Ruby said, shrugging.

"This is insane," I muttered as I stood and scurried over to the telephone and picked it up to call my agent. "William Meiklejohn, please," I said as soon as his secretary answered. "It's Hattie McDaniel."

When he picked up, I immediately began talking. "Mr. Meiklejohn, do you know anything about them deleting scenes in *In This Our Life*?"

Through the sigh in his voice, I could tell that he did.

"I just heard," he said. "I was in the process of trying to verify what happened before I brought it to you. I was actually on the phone with them when you called. The studio says cutting those scenes is the only way they could get the film shown in the South."

"New York isn't the South!" I exclaimed.

"Well, the Warners say they don't know who ordered the cuts for the theaters outside the South. So they're looking into it."

I sighed. If I believed that, I should believe I would play Cary Grant's love interest in my next movie.

"Trust me, I'm trying to get to the bottom of it," he said.

"Please keep me updated."

"I will. But I also think this is something that deserves an in-person meeting. Can you be in Mr. Warner's office tomorrow at eleven A.M.?"

"I most definitely can," I said. We made arrangements for the meeting tomorrow and I could only pray that it would make a difference.

I fell back in my seat after hanging up the phone. Once again, Negro moviegoers would see me only in a comical way. The cut scene, as well as my deleted lines, was a step forward in securing equality and it was being withheld from my community.

"Don't worry," Ruby said, sensing my dejection. "Once word gets out about the cuts, people will file complaints with the NAACP."

As if Walter White would ever let those complaints go anywhere.

• • •

At promptly eleven A.M. the following morning, I found myself sitting in Jack Warner's office, questioning why things in my life could never go smoothly. Neither he nor Mr. Meiklejohn had arrived yet, but Mr. Warner's secretary had suggested I come on in so I could meet with the publicity team before he arrived.

I had no desire to do any promotions on a movie that had butchered the best scenes of my career. But since I didn't want to end up without a contract—again—I agreed.

"Hello, Truman," I said when the man who headed public relations walked in along with two other men, who I assumed were part of the marketing team.

"Hi, Miss McDaniel. I'm so glad we were able to meet up with you. We'd like to get your sign-off on these press releases before they go out. We got good traction on the movie announcement. Now we want to do another wave of publicity highlighting our talent."

I blew a disgruntled breath, but took the paper he'd handed me. The first release was about Ernest Anderson, who played my son in the movie. My eyes stopped the slow scan of the release. I looked up at Truman in disbelief, and then went back to reading, only this time out loud.

"'Ernest Anderson was working as a service attendant on the Warner Brothers lot when he was discovered. He was a favorite of Bette Davis, who loved his dedication to serving and got him the part in *In This Our Life*.'" I stopped reading again and looked back up at Truman.

"Ernest is a graduate of Northwestern University's theater department. Why are you making it seem like he was some servant on the lot?"

Truman's eyes darted around the room, as if he expected one of his colleagues to step in and support him. When no one said anything, he replied, "Ummm, my job is to sell a movie. And what I wrote sells better."

"What you wrote is a lie." I continued reading. "'During the scene where Hattie McDaniel cleans and frets over Roy, impeccably played by Olivia de Havilland, Hattie said after filming wrapped one day, "Land sakes, I sho like showin' the world that colored folks can be happy as servants."'"

My mouth fell open as shock filled my throat. "What in the world? I never talk like that off camera. And I for sure wouldn't say anything like that! Why are you putting words in my mouth?" I waved the paper at him. He stood with a smug expression as if he knew he would emerge victorious in this debate.

"It's all a show," he said, his cockiness on full display.

I didn't know what was worse, this rewriting of history, the blatant lies that further perpetuated stereotypes, the cutting of my lines, the fact that I couldn't get decent roles, or the fact that Mr. Warner couldn't even bother to show up for this meeting when Mr. Meiklejohn had stressed its importance. This was the last straw.

CHAPTER 23

September 1942

I was playing a waiting game. Mr. Warner had verbally agreed to let me out of my contract. Yet I continued to wait for the official release. It had been six weeks. I'd been sitting at home, fretting my future, wondering what in the world I would do if I couldn't act. I'd probably still be sitting there immersed in my downtrodden circumstances if today hadn't been such a special day. Dorothy had tied the knot. She was now Mrs. Harold Nicholas. And so everything needed to be pushed aside so that I could celebrate with my friend.

Ru had done a 180 when it came to this marriage. She said Geneva had reminded her of all the doors that would be opened if Dorothy became the wife of the famous Harold Nicholas. Ru had even started talking about Dottie becoming a dancer with them and doing films, since Harold and his brother Fayard were among the most sought-after Negro dancers in Hollywood.

The wedding was an intimate affair—only about forty guests. Dorothy looked like she should be on the cover of *Brides* magazine. Her white wedding gown with its fitted bodice and cascading train looked so classic as she stood under the arch at the front of the Hollywood Gardens. The colorful blooms of roses, lilies, and peonies provided the perfect backdrop as she and Harold exchanged vows.

After the wedding and reception, we moved the celebration to Brothers, a popular after-hours joint.

We pulled up to the white house tucked in a corner a few blocks off Central Avenue. During the day, "Brother" (I don't think anyone even knew his real name) worked as a bartender at the Dunbar Hotel. But he ran a speakeasy after hours that had become the highlight of a night out. Probably because of its exclusivity and the fact that the Dunbar closed at midnight. Brother knew people wanted to keep partying, so while he was bartending, he would glide over to different people and whisper "See you later." That was your personal invitation to his place.

Brother would head from the Dunbar to his house on Adams Boulevard, where the fun continued until the sun put a period on it.

Me, Ru, Louise, and Lillian were still floating from the nuptials when we knocked on Brother's front door about twelve thirty A.M. Brother swung the door open in his usual dramatic fashion, wearing his signature red, black, and white Chinese tunic, a long cigarette resting between his fingers. At the Dunbar, he was always immaculately dressed in a white vest, jacket, black tie, and black trousers. But here, in the comfort of his home, Brother greeted patrons every night in some kind of exotic look, complete with mascara, rouge, and shimmering lips.

Brother eyed the four of us standing on his doorstep. It was common knowledge that not everyone was allowed entry into his exclusive "nightclub." It didn't matter how famous or infamous you were, if he didn't want you in, you didn't get in.

But luckily, all four of us were regulars so Brother grinned widely as he extended his signature greeting: "Hello, darlings, how are you? Come in."

We all gave him air kisses as we entered the dimly lit sitting room. Actually, every room here was a sitting room since people took a seat wherever they could find one. A haze of swirling cigarette smoke drifted through the air, mixing along with soft piano music and quiet chatter. The windows were draped in luxurious velvets, their deep hues of crimson and emerald reflecting the flickering glow of the vintage chandelier suspended from the ceiling. It was lit just enough to see and be seen.

Another thing Brother didn't play about was attire. He wanted his mixed crowd of patrons to don their best outfits, so there were men in tailored suits, donning fedoras, women sitting around with fur stoles and dresses and jewels, flanked with heavy Jasmine-laced perfume that danced in the air, dying to be noticed. We were all still in our wedding attire: I wore a cream floor-length gown and black satin jacket and my friends were all in semiformal attire as well, so we fit right in with the folks dressed to the nines, smoking, drinking, and nibbling on light bites. Laughter mingled with the sound of ice clinking in glasses as we headed to an empty table in the corner.

I spotted Dorothy in a corner talking to Orson Welles and Rita Hayworth, who he was dating. I waved and Dorothy blew me a kiss. I could still see the glow in her eyes. I glanced around and Harold was nowhere to be seen.

"Is that Lena?" Louise said, tugging on my arm and pointing across the room.

I hadn't expected to see Lena Horne here. We hadn't been in the same room since that disaster at the NAACP convention. My friends were looking at me as if I'd turn around and leave.

"Looks like her," I replied blankly. When I noticed the expressions on their faces, I added, "She had nothing to do with Walter White's shenanigans, so I bear no ill will toward her."

That seemed to settle them. Still, it felt good to know that my friends were in my corner, ready to dismiss Lena should I instruct them to do so.

"Let me go check on my daughter," Ru said as we watched Lena make her way over to talk to Dorothy.

It was unusual to see both Lena and Dorothy in attendance in the same place, almost as if Hollywood couldn't handle two beautiful fair-skinned women in the same room.

We took a seat at an empty table in the corner and had barely settled in before Brother had drinks sent over to us. I took a sip of my Cognac and leaned back, closing my eyes as the melodic sounds of the piano wafted through the room. A relaxed sigh escaped my lips.

"Hey, I've been meaning to ask, is it true that Adolf Hitler is a fan of yours?" Lillian asked after we'd been sitting for a few minutes.

I shook my head. "Not mine, personally," I replied. "He's a fan of *Gone with the Wind*, and from what I hear, he's obsessed with Clark."

Apparently, Hitler had a bootleg theater copy of the movie and he loved it. And once he'd learned that Clark was in the war, he'd offered a generous incentive for his capture.

I'd written Clark weeks ago when I first heard the story and had been surprised to get a quick response. He'd confirmed the Hitler story and wrote, *If Hitler catches me, the son of a bitch will put me in a cage and send me on a tour like a gorilla. If a plane I'm in ever gets hit, I'm not bailing out*. His words had haunted me for days and were just a reminder that I couldn't wait for this war to end.

"That's one fan I think I'm okay with never having," Louise said. A heavy silence passed over us as we thought about all the horrible things we'd heard the German dictator was doing. It was hard to fathom some of the rumors, but Clark had said most of them were true.

"Hello, ladies." The high-pitched voice of Fredi Washington broke the silence. None of us had even seen her approach our table. Fredi had starred in *Imitation of Life* with Louise. She'd played her daughter, Peola, so I knew Louise would be cordial. But the rest of us just side-eyed Fredi. We didn't want to speak because she'd aligned herself with Walter White and she'd been bashing us in her brother-in-law's Harlem newspaper. Up until that point, we'd considered Fredi one of us. But she was just a female Walter White with no power.

"Fredi," I said, deciding to respond. "Saw your article in Adam

Clayton Powell's paper." I looked at Lillian, who'd lit a cigarette and had it resting between two fingers. "What was it she said?"

Lillian inhaled the cigarette, then blew a puff of smoke in Fredi's direction. "That she was weary of Hollywood racism and our accommodationism," Lillian replied, never taking her eyes off Fredi.

"Accommodationism," I repeated, looking at my friends. "Is that even a word?"

Fredi moved a strand of her naturally curly hair behind her ear. "I just call it like I see it," she said, folding her arms across her chest. "Your little Fair Play Committee is nothing more than obstructionism."

"Ooooh, there she goes with another big ism word," Lillian said.

For a moment, we all just glared at one another. Fredi'd left Hollywood in 1937 to work in theater and civil rights activism in New York. Now she fought alongside Walter White for better roles for Negroes, most of the time at our expense. But she could do that. Like Mr. White, she was fair, with blue-gray eyes, a pale complexion, and light brown hair. She could easily pass.

"The fair-skinned section is over there," Lillian said, pointing across the room to where Dorothy and Lena were engaged in conversation.

"Really? That's the best you have?" Fredi said, unfazed by the attack. It really wasn't fair. Fredi wore her race like a badge of honor, never hesitating to remind people that it didn't matter what she was mixed with, she considered herself 100 percent Negro.

But again, she had the luxury of being loudly colored. She could be vocal about her mistreatment because she could assimilate into their world if she so chose. The rest of us had to do so in nooks and through back doors, lest we never work in the industry we loved.

"Your half-white comments don't bother me," Fredi said, her hands resting defiantly on her hips. "Been dealing with that my whole life."

Lillian shrugged. "Everyone thought you were white anyway from *Imitation of Life*."

"If I made Peola seem real enough to merit such statements, I consider that a compliment and it makes me feel I've done my job fairly well," Fredi replied.

"Look," I said, "we don't have a problem with you embracing your race with everything inside of you. But you don't have to hate us in order to love yourself."

"I've spent most of my life trying to prove to those who think otherwise . . . I am a Negro and I am proud of it," Fredi said.

"Yeah, well, you can take your Negro behind and go jump off a bridge," Lillian interjected, as she resumed smoking her cigarette. "You were one of us and you aligned yourself with a man who said we believe if people are too hard on the producers, they won't let us play our Uncle Tom roles anymore. That's a direct quote."

I turned back to Fredi. "Fredi, we're not interested in your personal attacks or your alliance with a man who spends a considerable amount of energy cozying up to, and even defending, Hollywood notables, all while trying to tear us down."

Fredi was unfazed as she said, "I heard you were trying to meet with the Screen Actors Guild?"

I knew that she had cofounded the Negro Actors Guild of America in New York with Noble Sissle, Paul Robeson, and Ethel Waters to financially assist colored actors in the industry, but we were trying to get in with SAG, which was crucial to helping actors navigate their contracts and deal with labor issues.

I had requested a formal meeting with the union representatives from SAG regarding the issue with Walter White. They refused to meet because they contended that their involvement would undermine their standing in Hollywood and that the clash was not a labor issue. They refused to take sides in what they called "a political fireball" within both Hollywood and the colored community.

"Thank you for your pseudo-concern, Fredi, but we'll handle this on our own," I said.

Fredi shrugged. "Don't say I didn't try to help," she said, before walking off.

Once she was gone, Louise said, "I can't stand her now, but she's right, leadership is the problem at SAG. They barely let us in. I don't know if we'll ever be able to get them to help us."

"That just means it's time to change the leadership," I said. "We need to get more Negroes in upper leadership positions." I glanced back over at Lena, who was still talking to Dorothy. But this time, at least Harold had appeared. I watched them for a moment, then an idea hit me. "Lena is perfect for that position."

"Lena? Are you kidding me?" Lillian said, her mouth agape. "You know folks don't care for her."

Since she'd arrived, and perhaps because of how she'd arrived, Negro actors regarded Lena as an interloper and always shut her out.

"That's because of how she was brought into the fray," I said.

"Hmph," Lillian said.

"We have to be welcoming of the next generation of colored actors," I told them. I didn't blame Lena for how Walter White was using her. And I thought she was the perfect choice to lead the Screen Actors Guild. She had youth and Hollywood's standard of beauty on her side. So I guess, in essence, we were using her too.

Much to the chagrin of my friends, when I was able to get her attention, I waved for Lena to come over. Within minutes, an apprehensive Lena stood over our table. The expression on her face said she had no idea what to expect.

"Hello, Lena," I said. "You know Lillian Randolph and Louise Beavers?"

Thankfully, both women smiled like they weren't just sitting here talking about her.

In that moment, Ru reappeared. "And Ruby Dandridge," I added.

"Hello, ladies," Lena said.

We exchanged small talk, then Lillian said, "I'm going to tell

Brother to put on some Cab Calloway or something. All this soft piano music is making me sleepy."

I took her exit as an opportunity to pull Lena aside to a corner so that we could speak in private.

"Thank you for agreeing to step aside and talk with me," I said once we were alone at a side table. I had to admit, she looked stunning in a pale pink blouse and matching skirt. Soft curls framed her face. I would take nothing away from her beauty. I just would never understand why hers had to be the only standard of beauty for Negroes.

"Would you like something to drink?" I asked. The way she quickly shook her head told me she was just anxious to get to the point of why she'd been summoned to the dark recesses of Brothers.

"First, I know this really isn't the venue for this, but I must make clear that I bear no ill will whatsoever over what happened at the NAACP conference."

Her shoulders sank in relief. "Thank you. I had no idea . . . I mean, I've just been hearing so much," she said.

I leaned in and lowered my voice, though no one could hear me anyway. "Let me let you in on a little secret. Hollywood is fueled by rumors. Trust me, I have no issues with you." I patted her hands. "We are here to look forward, not backward."

I'd done my due diligence on Lena. She belonged to the well-educated upper stratum of colored New Yorkers. Her father owned a hotel in New York and her mother was an actress, but she seemed like the type who was determined to make it on her own.

"Thank you for that. I am extremely realistic and have no misconceptions of the roles I am allowed to play in the white movie world," Lena said. "But I would never want it to be at someone else's expense. Especially someone of your stature who has paved the way for aspiring actors like myself."

"I appreciate that," I replied. "And I encourage you to push ahead in spite of any obstacle you may face, and you will face many obstacles. It is my understanding that you have two children?"

"Yes, ma'am."

"Remember to always put your family's welfare first. I know some people question my roles. Though I don't have children of my own, I do have people who depend on me. So you have to remember that you must earn a living. You've got to work, so just do what you must do," I told her.

My words seemed to blanket her with comfort. "Thank you so much for this," Lena said. "I'm having an awkward and difficult time adjusting so this means a lot."

I took that moment as the perfect time to interject the reason for my private conversation. "The ladies and I were talking and as you may know we're all members of the Screen Actors Guild."

"Yes, I was told that I needed to be a part of that in order to advance in Hollywood," she said.

"Well, we want you to not only be a part of it but to be in leadership."

Lena's eyes widened like that was the last thing she expected. I explained to her all the ways it could benefit her, why we felt she was suited to lead, and what she needed to do.

By the end of our conversation, not only was Lena on board, but I felt like a fire had been lit under her, and I had a strong feeling she would be a viable force in Hollywood—and not just in front of the camera.

CHAPTER 24

June 1943

Today was one of those days that felt like it stretched out from Los Angeles to Louisiana. As my hands gripped my steering wheel, I struggled to keep exhaustion from catapulting me off the Arroyo Seco Parkway.

I was on my way back from Pasadena, where I'd filmed a scene for my latest movie, *Johnny Come Lately*. I had stopped for groceries and was now headed to Clark's ranch. He'd returned last week from the war and I was worried about how he would do returning to his empty home.

Clark met me at the door with a huge smile. Someone who didn't really know him would have thought he was fine. He seemed to be in good spirits, his grin wide as he greeted me in his usual jovial manner.

"If it isn't my dearest friend in the whole wide world," he sang, his voice booming like a circus announcer's. But I knew it was an act; his smile and pleasantries a mask that he wore like a necessary piece of clothing.

Even still, I plastered on a smile. "Hello, old friend!"

He hugged me, a long hug that felt like it was designed to suffocate the grief that raged inside.

"Come on in," he said, releasing me and motioning for me to enter.

I entered and took a seat on his living room sofa. "What is this?" I asked, picking up a brown aviator boot with a missing heel that sat on his round pine coffee table. I flipped the boot over and immediately noticed a big hole in the bottom.

He took the boot out of my hand, stroking it like it was a newborn baby. "At one point during the war, there was a raid," he said, plopping in his quilted chair across from me. "Our aircraft came under attack and was hit fifteen times. A shell penetrated the plane, deflecting off the floor and missing my head by inches." I gasped as he held the boot up. "But it did knock off the heel of my shoe."

"Oh my God," I said, horrified. "You came within inches of dying?"

He shrugged, like it was no big deal. "Never thought I'd be returning."

In his letters, Clark had seemed to come to terms with the possibility of impending death. But the callousness with which he spoke made it seem as if he was disappointed that he'd survived the war.

My mind struggled to wrap around the magnitude of his war experience. "So you were really over there fighting and not just, you know, a figurehead?" I asked.

Clark laughed as he set the boot back down, took a seat, grabbed the bottle of scotch, and refilled his glass. "You sound like my fellow airmen. My presence instantly aroused suspicion and doubt. They felt like they had been risking their lives daily over enemy Europe, and here I come, older and a major movie star. They thought it was a publicity stunt."

While I didn't think that, I also didn't think he'd be put into actual combat. "How did you convince them that it wasn't?"

Clark ignored the way my eyes lingered on his glass. "I was just myself. I refused special living quarters, and opted to share with the men. I joined them in action. Before long, most of them warmed to me." He smiled as he took a long swig of his drink.

Clark was a modest man, slightly bewildered by his own fame, so it was no surprise to me that he would be easily accepted by his fellow servicemen.

"And you're a captain now?" I motioned to a photo that sat on his mantel of him in a captain's uniform getting out of a plane.

Pride filled his face as he nodded. "Actually I've since been promoted to the rank of major. But I'm super excited about the fifty thousand feet of color footage I got for this documentary I'm working on called *Combat America*."

"So you were fighting and filming?" I asked.

"Yep, apparently my enrollment was a boost to the air force recruitment campaign so they gave me a team of film industry men who joined me on combat missions and simulated attacks. Got it all on film. Can't wait for folks to see it." He took another swig as I sat in the silent power of his words.

After a few minutes, I asked, "So how are you, you know, being back here?"

He sat in his thoughts for a moment. Finally, he admitted, "I miss Ma." He didn't sound as heartbroken as the last time we'd talked about her. But I could tell by the expression on his face, he would never truly be over her. "When I was at war, I gave up my leave days to write letters of consolation to wives of aircrew who never returned from missions. I saw so much death and destruction." His voice was solemn as a mist covered his eyes. After a pause he said, "I realized I hadn't been singled out for grief—that others were suffering and losing their loved ones just as I lost Ma." He shook away his melancholy thoughts.

Officially, Clark was still in the Army Air Corps and he'd even shared that he was still receiving seventy-five hundred dollars a week from MGM, although he was adamant that he would film nothing until the war ended. I knew that wouldn't dissuade the movie producers. They would milk Clark's patriotism for everything they could. But I was concerned that not working meant Clark had nothing but time to date and drink. Word around town was that Clark had been spotted multiple times in the few days he'd been here, drunk. Even today, I couldn't help but notice his glass of scotch had been refilled twice and I hadn't been here an hour.

"Enough about me. What's going on with you?" Clark said, the smile returning to his face.

"Sadly, nothing has changed. Walter White is still after me. And this rationing is driving me crazy," I said.

The country was in the midst of gasoline rationing. Since last December, the government had banned pleasure driving. Drivers with A stickers, which I had, who were caught going anywhere for "pleasure" were penalized by losing their gas rations. The A coupons entitled the bearer to purchase three to five gallons per week. B tickets were reserved for commuters, who were allowed the most purchases per week. I hated using up my gasoline, but my trips to Pasadena and to see Clark had both been necessary. I knew the country was trying to deal with the shortage of necessities, but this rationing system was a huge inconvenience.

"I need a new washing machine but not only can we not buy new appliances, clothing, and scores of other items, but now they want to dictate when and how far we can travel. It is all just so exhausting," I said.

"I'm glad that you broke the gas sanction to come see me, Hattie, but really, I'm going to be fine. I'm going to work on this documentary and do my part for war efforts."

I didn't know what Clark's definition of "fine" was, but as I watched him swallow the rest of the liquor in his glass like it was iced tea, I was determined to be there to help my friend through this most difficult time.

• • •

I was thankful to make it home with no issues from law enforcement.

I had just removed the last of the groceries from the trunk of my car when I spotted my neighbor Hazel Lee racing out her front door.

Hazel was one of the first Negro physicians in Los Angeles, though she was retired now. She and her husband had moved in a year ago.

He'd died of cancer three months later. So we'd grown close as I'd taken to checking on her almost daily.

"Evening, Hazel," I called out as I waved to her.

She ignored me and swung the front door of her car open and jumped inside. I couldn't make out the expression on her face, but she had on slippers and looked extremely disheveled. Before I could move closer, Hazel had revved her car engine and backed out of her driveway so fast, she ran over her mailbox and into the ditch in front of her house. But instead of stopping, she put the car in drive and tried to speed out. The tires in the front spun aimlessly, trying to gather traction as she continued flooring the ignition. The roar of her Oldsmobile sedan filled our street.

"Hazel!" I called out, dropping the bags of groceries back in my trunk and rushing over to her. "Are you all right?"

Again she ignored me and just kept gunning the car. I made it to her vehicle and quickly tapped the hood. "Hazel! What are you doing?"

She opened the car door and jumped out. Fresh tears fell from her eyes as she raced to the front to examine her tires. "Oh no, oh no, oh no," she cried when she saw the car. "I don't need this right now." Her hands were shaking as she rested both palms on her temples.

I took her by the arms to get her to calm down. "Talk to me. What's going on?"

She opened her mouth, but instead of words, sobs escaped. She struggled to speak, and then finally managed to say, "It-it's . . . oh my Lord. It's LJ."

"Your grandson?" I asked.

She nodded as she used her sleeve to wipe her tears.

"Is he okay?"

Hazel's grandson Leonard Junior, or LJ as everyone called him, was one of her most cherished relationships. The twenty-three-year-old with bright eyes and deep dimples was one of the kindest young men I'd ever had the pleasure of meeting. After his grandfather's death, he practically lived there, helping Hazel out.

"No," she cried. "He's in the hospital. On life support."

"Oh no."

"I need to get to the hospital." She took a look at her car again and started crying even harder.

I rubbed her arms. "Okay, breathe. Come on, I'll take you to the hospital."

I had barely finished my sentence before Hazel said, "Thank you so much," and headed next door to my car.

On the way to the hospital, Hazel told me how her grandson had been attacked by white servicemen stationed in Los Angeles because of his zoot suit. The flashy outfits with tapered, high-waisted pants, fingertip coats, fedora or porkpie hats, and a long watch chain had been made popular by Cab Calloway and Duke Ellington. They were all the rage among young Angelenos of color. I'd read about some violence behind the suit because of war rationing, but the media had made it seem like the young men were in the wrong.

"I thought they were just targeting Mexicans," I said as I navigated out of our neighborhood.

"It started out as attacks on Mexican Americans," Hazel said, wringing the tissue she'd retrieved from my glove compartment. "But you know they put all us minorities together." She shook her head in disbelief. "These servicemen say the suits are unpatriotic and wasteful. It doesn't make any sense that they're targeting those boys over some clothes. And do you know there's an article in the *Times* this morning putting the blame for this violence on the victims? Lord, when I read that, I had no idea then it would be happening to my own grandson."

Hazel dabbed her eyes as she glanced at my speed gauge, no doubt willing me to speed up. But I was already going ten miles over the speed limit.

"So what exactly happened?" I asked, hoping conversation would keep her mind from imagining the worst.

"LJ was at a movie theater in Long Beach today when a crowd of sailors had the movie crew turn on the lights and they hunted anyone wearing a zoot suit. Do you know they chased my baby onto the stage and tried to strip his clothes right off of him, then commenced to beating the hell out of him. And folks in the audience just sat and watched. Didn't nobody try to help!" Hazel cried.

My hand went to my heart. "My Lord."

"Hattie, if they kill my boy . . ." Her words trailed off as her sobs returned.

"Shush," I said, patting her arm. "You know LJ is a fighter; he's going to pull through this." I didn't know that, but if felt like the appropriate thing to say.

We arrived at the hospital and I dropped Hazel off and went to park. By the time I made it to the emergency area, Hazel was with her family, LJ's mother, Patricia, and father, Hazel's son, Leonard, who was pacing the waiting room.

"He's gonna be okay," Hazel said as I entered. "Doctors said he just got out of surgery, so the worst is behind us. He's banged up pretty bad, but they said he'll make it." She raised both hands to the ceiling. "Thank you, Jesus."

I noticed a young man sitting in the corner, holding a portable radio in one hand, the other arm rested in a sling. He had scratches on his face and his left eye was swollen.

"This is my nephew, Otis," LJ's mother, Patricia, said, gently squeezing the young man's shoulder. "He was with LJ. They stripped him of his clothes, beat him right in the street, and stole his money."

"It had to be about forty of them just stomping and beating me," Otis said, fear still filling his wide eyes.

"When Otis asked a white police officer for help, the man refused," Patricia said, her voice cracking. "It's a wonder they didn't do more damage. Radio stations were broadcasting the locations of where the next round of violence was expected and taxi drivers are giving free rides to any white person that wanted to go."

Before I could respond, Otis sat erect. "Hey, they're talking about it on the news." He held the radio up so we could all get a better listen.

"The Theatre Defense Bureau called an emergency meeting and it appears the riots have subsided," the news announcer said. "The navy and Marine Corps have declared Los Angeles off-limits to all soldiers, though their official position is that their men acted in self-defense. We'll continue to follow this story."

Leonard Sr. knocked the radio onto the floor. "Turn that mess off. I don't want to hear their lies. Neither one of those boys bothered anybody." He loosened the collar on his porter's uniform as he paced back and forth across the room.

"Honey . . ." Patricia said, trying to calm her husband by rubbing his arm. He snatched his arm away and, in that moment, our eyes locked.

"Hattie McDaniel?" he said, stopping just feet from me and staring as if he was just realizing who I was. "What you doing here?"

"She drove me here," Hazel said before I could reply.

I was standing about fifteen feet away from him, but the slow, calculated steps he took toward me seemed to take an eternity.

"Hattie McDaniel, the war's favorite spokesperson," he spat.

I struggled to contain the fear his words sent shooting through me. Was this man really about to verbally attack me when I was here supporting his son?

There was rage in his eyes as he stood nose to nose with me. "This the country you always speaking out for? These the servicemen you want us colored folks to get behind?"

The venom in his tone frightened me and I took a step back. Thankfully, Hazel stepped up beside me.

"Now, Leonard. All Hattie was trying to do was help me get here.

I understand you're upset, but you're not right to attack her," Hazel warned her son.

He glared at me, unmoved by his mother's words. "Thank you for bringing my ma. But you can go now. You can take your white-lovin', shuckin' and jivin' self on outta here."

"Leonard!" Hazel and Patricia said in unison.

"It's okay," I said, holding up my quivering hand. "Tensions are high. I understand. I'll pray for LJ," I told them, before turning to Hazel. "Let me know if you need anything."

Her eyes were full of apology, but I couldn't provide any more comfort.

CHAPTER 25

July 1943

The words wouldn't stick. I'd been sitting at my dining room table, studying this script for three hours. My mind was scattered, drifting from thoughts of whether Hazel's son was right in his assessment of my war efforts to whether I should move my china collection from the right corner to the left corner. I was thinking about everything except the words in front of me.

"Good afternoon."

James was standing in the entryway to the dining room. He was dressed as if he'd just come from a polo match, wearing plaid pants and a cream shawl-collared cardigan that he had to be burning up in. He had reappeared yesterday, in a cheerful mood, like he hadn't been MIA for three weeks. James had left the day after I'd returned from the hospital with Hazel and LJ, claiming he was going to handle some real estate business. And I hadn't heard from him since until he walked in the front door yesterday.

He didn't wait for me to respond. "Let's go see that new exhibit at the Los Angeles County Museum of History, Science, and Arts building at Exposition Park," he said.

Before I could reply, a cough filled my throat and I released it for a full two minutes before I was able to answer him.

"I don't . . ." The cough returned and I doubled over trying to clear my throat. My Dalmatian, Danny, jumped into my lap. I patted his head to assure him that I was okay just as my Spaniel, Frisky, came and nuzzled on the other side of me.

"Are you okay? Do you need some water?" James asked, shooing both dogs away. Neither of them moved. I guess they had no respect for my husband either.

I'd been dealing with this cough for three weeks now. The doctor said I'd gotten a respiratory infection from the dry ice that was used on the set of *Johnny Come Lately*. They'd used tons of the stuff to make fake clouds, and I felt it had permanently set up residence in my throat.

"I'm fine," I said, stifling the cough this time. "I'm trying to learn these lines for this film. We start shooting this scene next week. So, I'm sorry, but I can't go off gallivanting across Los Angeles with you."

He frowned, his annoyance on full display. "So now spending time with your husband is considered gallivanting?"

I set the script down and released a long sigh. I knew that bitterness was boiling over with me and, try as I might, I couldn't keep my feelings suppressed. I was not only frustrated with his frequent absences, but I truly felt like my husband had sold me a bill of goods. He was a cattle rancher with no cattle or ranch. A real estate mogul with no real estate. I'd yet to see the fruits of all his so-called wealth and success. When he was home, he dressed daily like he was among Hollywood's elite, lunching with executives and hobnobbing with movers and shakers. But he had no real job. I'd even paid for him to attend real estate school. He sold one house, lost all interest, and was on to the next thing.

I massaged my temples. "James, I really can't do this. Perhaps your time would be better served looking for a job."

James had held a government job in San Francisco prior to meeting me and even worked for the studios at one point as a movie consultant. But he did not stick with anything for long. He said he wanted to "explore everything," and because of that, he succeeded at nothing.

"Please don't start with me about a job," he said peevishly. "I do well for myself. And it's not like I ask you for one silver nickel."

He was right about that. Since the day we said "I do," James hadn't asked me for any money. He just used the money we had in our joint bank account and let me pay for everything.

"You're right." I paused and released a cough. I didn't even have the energy to debate. "You'll have to pardon my snippiness. I'm just tired and not feeling well."

He sat down at the table across from me and took my hand. "That's because you work too hard. You don't enjoy life. *We* don't enjoy life."

I wanted to tell him that someone had to work hard to pay for this life, but that would only prolong the conversation and I just wanted him to go do whatever it was he did during the day.

I pulled my hand away and went back to my script.

"James, this is all I know. I've been performing since I was eight years old."

"Exactly. And after forty-plus years, it's okay to retire. You even talked about it when we first got married."

"That was frustration talking then. You've seen the difference I was able to make during the war. I can't walk away." James knew how much this meant to me. How much it had always meant. He knew what type of impact I had on the soldiers. So this was more than just wanting to be in the limelight. Acting was my calling.

"This is a hard business and you've given it your all, and had success. I think you should just let it go," James said.

I flung a page of my script to the side to display my exasperation. I wanted to scream and ask who was going to pay the damn bills around here if I retired.

"Sweetheart," he said calmly. "You've had a good run. You have more than enough money in the bank. I think you should retire from the screen and move with me to Chicago."

"Chicago?" I balked, incredulous. "I know you're always there but since when are you thinking about moving to Chicago?"

"I told you I wanted something different. Chicago is wide open for new real estate. My sister has some connections that could really benefit me."

I dismissed his comment with a wave of the hand. No way was I about to sacrifice what I had fought so hard to create, especially to follow a man.

Anger filled his face at my nonverbal reaction. "You know what, Hattie? I don't even know why you have a husband. You're married to the screen and you'll sacrifice everything and everybody for a career that doesn't love you back."

He stood, pushing back so hard the chair toppled over.

His words pierced my heart. The last time a man had uttered those words to me was when Howard had complained about the very thing that James was lamenting. Howard had died feeling neglected and it had torn my soul. Even still, I couldn't give James what he wanted.

"I'm going back to work," I said, not wanting to continue arguing.

I expected him to protest, but he simply turned and stormed out of the room.

The sound of a suitcase dragging across the floor pulled me from my script about thirty minutes later. I stared at the brown leather suitcase, then back at my husband.

"You leaving again?" I asked.

He stopped and glared at me. "Yeah. I need some time away."

"When are you coming back?"

"I don't know." He shrugged.

"I have that National Council of Negro Women event next week. Everyone is bringing their spouses," I told him, a sliver of panic setting in. Had I pushed my husband away?

"And I'm sure you'll do well," James replied. "Like you said on many occasions, you don't need me."

"Howa . . ."

James frowned in confusion. "What did you just say?"

I stared at him with a blank expression. I couldn't believe I was about to call him by my dead husband's name.

"Who did you call me?" he repeated.

"I-I . . . I was about to say, how are you just going to up and leave?" I fumbled my words together.

That explanation must have satisfied him because he released an exasperated sigh, then said, "I'll be back, Hattie." His expression was serious as he added, "I love you. But I just need to clear my head."

Danny came and snuggled at my feet and James looked at him with disdain. "You have your dogs and your script, so you'll be fine."

With that, he carried his suitcase out the door.

CHAPTER 26

February 1944

The harmonious blend of the Nash Singers humming beautiful a cappella melodies in the lobby of the Second Baptist Church couldn't quiet the conflict raging inside me. I couldn't help but question if all of this—the constant appearances, the never-ending interviews, the love-hate relationship America had with me—was worth it. My marriage was in shambles. When James had left for Chicago last July, he'd stayed gone for six months. Though he did write that he'd found work and would be home soon, he hadn't returned for the rest of the year. I'd spent Christmas and New Year's alone. I wondered if James had another woman. Had the man I'd treated like trash become someone else's treasure? *Stop it,* I told myself. I would run myself wild with what-ifs.

If James and I were meant to be, we would be. I needed to focus on the things that really mattered. Dorothy had given birth to a beautiful baby girl and the two of them were home resting. I'd had a chance to spend some time with them this morning and was now here at the Second Baptist Church doing what I loved best next to acting, celebrating our youth.

The NAACP's Youth Council was holding its first annual Motion Picture Unity Award Assembly. Several people were on the program to be honored for their contributions to interracial unity during 1943, including Lena Horne, Rex Ingram, Dooley Wilson, Carlton Moss, Ben Carter, and others. I was happy to be the keynote speaker, but I was even happier to see Bette Davis getting her due from the organization with an award for her efforts to harmonize and create goodwill between the races.

During the war, Bette had joined me in performing for colored troops, the only white participant in a troupe that I had formed. Bette had been one of the most ardent supporters of colored causes, even going so far as to demand that the Hollywood Canteen, a club for active servicemen where they could dance with starlets and get served food by their favorite Hollywood actors, be integrated. When I heard that, I was floored. Open interracial mingling was something that was just *not* done. Not even in the USO, which was strictly white-only and colored-only. But Bette told them either they integrate or she'd quit. And without stars, there wasn't a canteen, so they acquiesced.

Bette was a fierce, five-foot-three New England dynamo who proved that with hard work, guts, and determination, a woman could conquer the world.

"Hello, gorgeous," Bette said as I entered the holding room where the guests were gathered.

"Hello, beautiful," I said, returning our standard greeting to each other.

"Are you ready for your keynote speech?" she asked as she took a match and lit her cigarette.

"I am." I walked over to the wall mirror and adjusted the gold ribbon on my royal blue Stetson felt hat.

Bette took a puff of her Lucky Strike cigarette. I eyed her in the mirror as she tapped her foot in excitement and stared at me like she had a secret she was dying to share.

"What's got you in such a jovial mood?" I asked.

She glanced around the room to make sure no one was watching then whispered, "It was supposed to be a surprise, but I get to introduce you."

Well, wasn't that a pleasant revelation? Bette was a two-time Academy Award winner and the highest-paid actor in Hollywood and she was introducing me?

Bette squeezed my arm. "It's always an honor to uplift you, Hattie. I'm just so proud of you and the work that you do."

Our moment was interrupted by the organizer, who escorted us into the auditorium. The crowd was integrated and large. I didn't realize just how many people were here until I took my seat at the front of the room. There had to be over three thousand people in the auditorium. The Master of Ceremonies, Dr. Harold Kingsley, opened the program, quickly guiding us through until it was time for Bette to introduce me.

My heart swelled with pride as Bette spoke with such admiration as she rattled off my extensive body of work.

"And now, ladies and gentlemen, may I bring to the stage, my friend, the talented Hattie McDaniel."

The applause was instant and in that moment, all the criticism that I had received over the years didn't seem to matter. As I took my place at the podium, I felt loved.

I unfolded my speech and looked out into the sea of finely dressed Hollywood notables and then spent the next thirty minutes giving the speech that Ruby had helped me write on the history of Negroes in Hollywood. I noted some of the colored film pioneers and outlined the progress that Negroes had seen in the industry. And since I had a captive audience, I took the opportunity to defend my fellow actors.

". . . So I come to you today on behalf of my colleagues who have had a war waged against them for simply trying to work and provide for their families," I said. "As artists, we reserve the right to accept the parts that we can portray with sincere artistry, objecting to the push to delete menial roles. Roles that are not demeaning. Roles we attribute to our foreparents, who had to start from somewhere." I inhaled and glanced out, unsuccessfully gauging reactions. I continued, "I don't doubt that running through some of your minds is: the reason that Hattie McDaniel is speaking on the subject of cooking, washing, and ironing is that she has done so much of it herself. I'm not ashamed to admit that I have. Entertainment has always been my primary profession, but I have never shied from relying on domestic work to get by."

I was grateful to hear resounding applause. I paused, allowing the applause to die down, and then concluded with a tribute to those young colored GIs fighting abroad by reciting Paul Laurence Dunbar's "The Colored Soldiers," an homage to those of an earlier generation who had, like my father, taken up arms to protect the country.

Before I sat down, though, I took a moment and went off script. "I'm proud of my work, and at the same time, I'd like to acknowledge the next generation of Negro actors, like Lena Horne." I gave a warm smile to Lena, who sat about three rows back. I returned my attention to the audience. "Lena is a newcomer to Hollywood and she represents a new type of nigger womanhood."

As soon as the words left my mouth, I caught myself. "I mean, she represents a new type of Negro womanhood."

I'd be kidding myself if I didn't silently acknowledge the audible gasps that filled the room. Shame blanketed Negro faces. Horror filled white faces, including Bette, who had literally clutched the strand of pearls around her neck. I was mortified that I would make such a mistake. I didn't even use the word in my daily conversations, so why in the world would it slip out? My heart raced and I had to steady my hands. Whatever the reason, I knew stopping would only draw attention to the faux pas, so I forged ahead. I finished my speech, then returned to my seat with my head held high, though beads of sweat peppered my forehead.

After the program, I couldn't get out of the auditorium fast enough. Unlike when I sought an escape from the Shrine for the humiliating

Walter White experience, this was a deeper embarrassment. I was heading out of the theater when Robert Smith, an editor with the *Los Angeles Sentinel*, approached me.

"Miss McDaniel, care to comment on why you called Lena Horne such a derogatory name?" he asked, his tone dripping with disdain. He was one of those Walter White supporters who thought I'd be better off shining shoes than playing servants.

"I have no idea what you're talking about." I quickened my steps toward the door.

He raised his voice. "You called Miss Horne a nigger."

I stopped, took a deep breath, then forced a smile as I turned around to face him. "No, you're mistaken. I said 'Negro.' I have no other statement to make."

I darted away, leaving the reporter confused, maybe even questioning whether he'd misheard. I don't know what made me deny it. I think I was just focused on getting out of there before anyone else could stop me—especially Lena Horne.

• • •

The morning sun tickled me out of my restless sleep. James had returned late last night and crawled into bed. Even though I was awake, I didn't bother turning to him and he didn't bother saying anything to me. But I had only dozed off and on all night as my awful mistake haunted my dreams.

I rolled over and saw that James was already out of bed. I released a heavy sigh, then forced myself up to begin my morning routine of showering and grooming.

All morning, the weight of yesterday threatened to suffocate me. I knew what I had to do.

After I was dressed, I searched for the Whitman notebook where I had written Lena's number. When I found it, I carried the notebook downstairs to the telephone, lifted the receiver, exhaled my fear, inhaled courage, and dialed the two-letter exchange and five-digit number.

"Hello," Lena said, her soft voice filling the phone.

"Good morning, Lena. This is Hattie McDaniel," I said before I lost my courage.

"Good morning, Miss Hattie."

I didn't want to dawdle so I quickly said, "I wanted to extend the most heartfelt apology to you for yesterday. As I have expressed to you, I have the utmost respect for you. I would never intentionally embarrass you or myself with such an egregious slur."

I was grateful to hear sincerity in her tone. "Apology accepted, Miss Hattie. I do believe that it was not intentional."

I closed my eyes in relief. I had wrestled with this all night and was grateful that she had accepted my apology. Thankfully, she didn't belabor the issue and the call was brief. I bid her good-bye and returned the receiver to the base.

I blew a sigh of relief, then stood and made my way into the kitchen. James was at the table having coffee and reading the newspaper.

"Good morning," he said.

"Good morning," I replied, walking over to the kettle and pouring myself a cup of coffee.

He eyed me over the paper. "I see the event yesterday didn't go too well."

"Why do you say that?" I slid into the seat across from him as he folded the newspaper and gently pushed it across the table.

I picked up the paper and the headline screamed "A Slip of the Lip May Sink a Ship." I immediately started reading. "'As Hattie McDaniel delivered her speech, Lena Horne reacted with embarrassment and shock. She dripped with great beads of sweat and wrung her hands at the offensive epithet.'"

I had to hold my breath to suppress the cry forming in my throat. I'd been battling the charges of Uncle Tom and racial self-hatred on a daily basis. This would only serve to ignite the fire even more.

I kept reading. "'Miss Horne continues to be the epitome of grace.

When asked to comment, she expressed admiration for McDaniel, whom she regarded as one of her few friends among Negro film players.

'The audience contained a number of white representatives from the studios. Many of whom had actually done very little to promote a new image of Negro womanhood, or did this indicate the depth to which racism has warped Hattie McDaniel's own sense of self and pride?'" the article concluded.

Lord knows, while I disliked Walter White's tactics when he introduced Lena, this wasn't purposeful or even subconscious. I respected Lena. I liked Lena. For this reporter to write this was absolutely horrid!

"I can't believe the *Sentinel* published this," I yelled. "You'd think the colored press would be more understanding of a simple mistake!" I angrily pushed back my chair, stood, stomped over to the counter, and snatched open a drawer. "I'm going to write a letter and have the *California Eagle* publish it."

"Do you think that's wise?" James asked.

"I cannot continue to have my name sullied. You know what? I'm going to write the *Sentinel*, too." I sat back down and began pounding words onto the notepad.

In my letter, I wrote that I had already apologized to those who were worthy of such consideration. *It was a regrettable error,* I wrote, *much like those countless typographical errors which the columns of your paper constantly and continually contain.*

I knew I probably shouldn't have stooped so low to degrade the Negro newspaper, but fury was guiding my hand.

> Mr. Smith, your article is unauthentic and falsely exaggerated, and you have threatened wartime unity by sowing seeds of discord and malicious antagonism. I had barely uttered the offensive term before correcting myself, followed by a sincere apology. My dear friend Lena Horne quickly forgave me and hardly broke

out in a sweat, per your fictitious story. In truth, Mr. Smith, Miss Horne confidentially told me, she just does not sweat.

You, Mr. Smith, are a Judas and an unscrupulous Pharisee. If account for my error, I could, it would be only to truthfully state that the radiotronic mental reflections of minds such as yours . . . like ether waves of mental telepathy, electrically lodged in my subconscious the instance you released them.

And in answer to the telepathic atmosphere of your unholy and prejudiced mind, my friend Miss Horne became the victim of my subconscious mind. And she, in turn, most unjustly received what I undoubtedly and unquestionably must have meant for you. And I am now quite sure and fully convinced—I did!!!

I didn't bother seeking input from anyone and expeditiously mailed my letter. I was tired of being assailed and it felt good to fight back for once.

Five days later, I was back at my kitchen table with both James and Ruby waving the *California Eagle*, like I was the one who had committed some egregious atrocity.

"Hattie, you covered a half page of the *Eagle*," Ruby said. "I'm afraid your tirade did nothing to help your cause. It makes it appear that you refuse to take responsibility for the appalling comment, and then you turn around and used the horrendous term against the editor." Her voice was filled with frustration. Ruby often saved me from myself and I knew she was aggravated that not only had she not been able to stop me from sending the letter but now she'd have to clean up my mess.

"Welp, anyone who originally may have been willing to give you the benefit of the doubt is now walking away even more offended," James added, shaking his head like I'd embarrassed him. "This rant is just over-the-top and makes it appear as if you've lost your marbles."

I usually gave no merit to the things he said regarding my career, but the expression on Ruby's face echoed his.

She nodded as her brow creased with worry. "I'm sorry, Hattie. This is bad. I wish you had let me read it before you sent it off. It certainly sounds spiteful and indeed troubling."

"It makes you seem angry, bitter, and insecure," James said.

I fell back in my chair, torn. If I stayed silent, it was a problem. If I spoke out, it backfired. I couldn't help but wonder if my constant losses were preventing wins. I was just trying to speak up for myself. And now I was a helpless bystander, watching both my career and reputation within the colored community slip away.

This was not the Hollywood dream I thought I'd have after winning an Academy Award. This was not a dream at all. It was a full-blown nightmare.

CHAPTER 27

May 1944

For three months, I'd been paying for my response in the *California Eagle*. I'd heard everything from I "was becoming unhinged" to I "was jealous of Lena's beauty" to I "was trying to grandstand for white folks." Some of my friends had distanced themselves, with the exception of Lillian, Louise, Ruby, and Ru, who all admitted it was bad but assured me that it would die down. James acted like I had shamed him and even went so far as to say the article was why he'd lost out on an advising job he was up for. I refused to let him place that blame on me. There probably wasn't even any job.

But the stress was taking its toll. I'd been hopping mad on set today of the movie I'd been filming, *Three Is a Family*, when one of the wardrobe girls had the nerve to balk at carrying away my clothes after I'd changed out of them. She'd said "touching colored clothes" wasn't part of her contract, then she'd quit, simply walked out. I was hurt and livid. And found myself screaming and tossing things in my dressing room. It wasn't until I caught a glimpse of myself in the mirror—and saw that I indeed looked unhinged—that I pulled myself together.

Then on top of that, my monthly visitor hadn't come and I was fatigued and on edge all the time. I'd been working overtime on the film, a comedy that centered on the mishaps surrounding a set of infants who were the result of a careless stork. I had gotten to the point where I could barely make it through the day. I'd thrown up this morning and when I'd arrived home early, disheveled and exhausted, Ruby was concerned and called and set up an appointment with the doctor.

Dr. Wyatt examined me, checking my temperature, my heart, and asking me several questions. After I told him how I'd been unable to keep any food down, he pointed to my chest.

"May I?"

I nodded as he slid on a rubber glove, gently unbuttoned my blouse, and began lightly pressing my breasts.

"Ow," I said, jumping at the pain from his touch.

"How long have your breasts been tender?" he asked.

I shrugged. "A week or so. Does that have something to do with my fatigue? And don't bother telling me it's the weight," I said, trying to muster a smile.

A light flashed in his eyes. "Well, I think you're about to put on a little more weight."

"What?" I asked, confused.

He clasped his hands. "Hattie McDaniel, you're about to be a mother."

"Wh-what are you saying?" I don't even know how I managed to get the words out of my mouth. My hand covered my stomach. James and I were obviously troubled in our marriage, but what hadn't changed was our lovemaking. We both had healthy sexual appetites and had many sessions where we'd started out mad at each other. We still made love regularly—when he was in town.

"I do believe your fatigue is not the result of your hectic work schedule, but rather because you are with child," the doctor continued. I guess he was trying to gauge my reaction to the news because his grin had tapered a bit.

A child? I was about to be a mother?

"I-I'm pregnant?"

The doctor nodded. "That's my diagnosis. You are a little older than our usual first-time mothers, but as long as you take it easy, you'll be fine. I hope that news makes you happy."

I had never believed that I would be blessed with children, but I had silently coveted motherhood since James and my visit to the orphanage. I buried my face in my hands and wept tears of joy, giving Dr. Wyatt his answer that I was indeed happy about this news.

• • •

I dove into pending motherhood with a fury. My fatigue had been replaced with a burst of adrenaline that kept me fueled. We'd wrapped filming the day after I got the news, and for the past four weeks, I'd spent every day shopping to decorate my baby's rooms. Yes, plural. My child would have two rooms. James, who was ecstatic about the news, thought two rooms was too much, but I didn't care. One room was going to be the nursery and the other a playroom, though right now it was holding the avalanche of gifts that had begun to arrive, since I'd shared the news with my closest friends.

I decorated the nursery in a combination of blue and pink colors because I wanted to be prepared either way. There were drawers full of baby clothes, rows of baby books, stuffed animals, and a bassinet and rocking chair. I'd had an artist paint baby ducks at a pond on the wall. This would be a utopia for my baby. It would engulf her with a daily reminder of how much she was loved. Or he. It truly didn't matter.

I'd been godmother to so many of my friends' children. I loved spoiling and cuddling them. I had so many plans for this child. She (or he) would have a strong Christian upbringing like I did. This baby would know that no matter what obstacles were placed in their path, they could achieve their dreams. Maybe by the time my child grew up, things would be different in terms of race relations. The thought of all that was in store for my child made me sporadically weep tears of joy.

Word of my impending arrival spread quickly, probably because I told everyone that I knew. James felt I should wait until I was further along, but I could hardly contain myself. Besides, Dr. Wyatt had said based on his measurements, I was ten weeks pregnant. That was more than enough time. Plus, anyone who knew me could tell something was up anyway because, as Clark said, I "glowed."

Louise and Lillian had shown up at my house today with even more gifts. None of us had children, so even if I didn't spoil my baby, these two surely would. Louise brought seven different layette sets and Lillian had found a bassinet-shaped flower vase to match the bassinet I'd ordered from New York.

"Ooooh, Hattie, this is beautiful," Louise said, handing me two more boxes. She fingered the handcrafted rocking chair I'd had commissioned from a local woodworker.

"I know, isn't it gorgeous?"

Louise sat down in the rocking chair. "Have you thought about names?" she asked as Lillian rearranged the stuffed animal selection and made room for her gift.

"Yes," I said. "If it's a boy, I'm going to name him Otis. After my brother. If it's a girl, I will call her Hattie McDaniel Jr."

Louise laughed, then suddenly stopped rocking as she studied me. "Wait, you're serious?"

"I am." I nodded.

Lillian, who had stopped her rearranging to stare at me, said, "What does James have to say?"

"About what? My being pregnant?" I shrugged. James had been shocked at first like me. But then he had quickly embraced the idea of fatherhood and often talked about all his plans for our child. "He's thrilled. He wants children. In fact, it's already helping our marriage. We haven't had an argument since I found out I was pregnant."

"No, what does he say about the names?" Lillian asked.

"Oh, he's leaving that up to me."

My friends chuckled.

"Only you would make your daughter a junior," Louise said, resuming her rocking.

"Do you know your due date?" Lillian asked. Now she was unfolding and refolding clothes, I'm sure so they met her standards of perfection.

"Not exactly. Just that I'm due in the fall," I said.

The two of them exchanged glances before Lillian said, "Are you a little worried? You know, you are forty-nine . . ."

I winced. I'd been shaving years off my age and even my friends didn't know my true age. "Well, I believe in the ninety-second Psalm: bring forth fruit in one's old age," I said with a wink as all three of us laughed.

We were interrupted by the shrill of my ringing phone. Ruby was gone and I'd given the maid the day off so I raced to answer.

"Hattie, hello, it's William Meiklejohn," my agent said.

I hadn't spoken to Mr. Meiklejohn in weeks.

"Hi, Mr. Meiklejohn, how are you?" I said, cheer filling my voice.

"Great! I'm calling with good news. I got a call from Jack Warner. They have a role they wrote with you in mind. Not only that, they want to send you on a grand tour of South America, where you have thousands of fans, especially in Brazil. It should be a remarkable experience for you."

Without hesitation I said, "I do apologize, Mr. Meiklejohn, but I must decline." My hand went to my stomach. It didn't matter how much money I would lose out on. "I am expecting and the stork is near. Bringing a healthy baby into this world is my sole focus."

I was surprised he hadn't heard the rumors by now. But judging by the silence that filled the receiver, he most definitely had not. To say Mr. Meiklejohn was shocked would be an understatement. But then he wished me well and reminded me of a meeting we had next week with the Warner team regarding marketing for the movie we'd just completed.

"Can I tell the folks at Warner?" he asked, just before he bid me farewell.

"Of course."

I was thrilled to share the news with the publicity department. The studio had begun sending a limo to shuttle me back and forth. I was often tired in the last few weeks of filming, but I'm sure they simply thought I was coming down with some ailment.

"So, Hattie, how many months along are you?" Hal, the publicist, asked once we were in the studio offices for our meeting.

I lovingly touched my midsection. "I'm about three months."

His eyes danced like a variety of marketing ideas were running through his head. "I've been doing some thinking, and I believe we should play up the baby theme. You know Arthur's wife is pregnant?" Hal said.

I nodded. My costar Arthur Lake had been ecstatic about his firstborn.

"It's all he talks about," I said. "And I understand because it is a joyous experience."

"And the married couple that authored the play on which the film was based just had their first child," the marketing assistant Rose added. "And don't forget Cindy."

I let out a hearty laugh. Our studio cat gave birth to three kittens last week, so something was definitely in the air.

"Let's also say Arthur's goldfish is having twins in the press release," Hal said, and chuckled.

Under any other circumstances, I might have felt some kind of way about the studio using me to such measures. But I was so happy, it didn't even matter. Not just because of the baby, but because any publicity that could make the world forget about that awful slip at the NAACP Youth Conference was welcomed.

We handled some more promotional business until Hal said, "I hope you don't mind, but I took the liberty of summoning Louella Parsons here." He looked up to the receptionist, who had appeared in the doorway. "Is she ready?"

The receptionist nodded. "Yes, sir."

"Perfect," Hal said.

Louella Parsons was a gossip columnist. She and Hedda Hopper had a huge rivalry, but they both were extremely popular. The studios tried to balance coverage between the two. Personally, I would've preferred to break the news with the Negro gossip columnist Harry Levette, but it was too late now.

As soon as I entered the room they'd set up for the interview, Louella stood with her arms outstretched. I placed my hands in hers and she squeezed them in a hearty greeting.

"Hattie McDaniel, what a pleasure."

"How are you, Louella?"

"Antsy. I came here expecting an interview about your new film, but I understand you have some exclusive news for me."

"Yes, darling," I said, my smile spreading as I took a seat. No sense in making small talk. "Betty Grable, Lana Turner, Maureen O'Hara, Gene Tierney, and the rest of those glamour girls have nothing on me. I, too, am taking time out to welcome the stork."

Louella released an audible gasp. "Will wonders never cease? I made every guess imaginable regarding your news. But I must confess that motherhood escaped my list. Really, dear, I am too happy for words, learning about your coming event," she said.

"Yes, my dear, it really is a gift from God." I caressed my stomach, hoping my child could feel my love in my womb.

I'd been happy to share my news with the studio. And now, through Louella, with the world. And it wasn't lost on me that I was more excited to be talking about my baby than acting.

CHAPTER 28

October 1944

Yesterday, my neighbor Hazel had told me that I was "holding my baby well" to be eight months along.

I'd patted my midsection and joked that I was so fluffy it was hard to tell what was baby and what was collard greens and cornbread.

But today, as I stared at my naked reflection in my bathroom full-length mirror, I really was starting to get concerned. There had been no change in my body.

Shouldn't I see some kind of bulge by now? Shouldn't I feel the baby moving?

I dressed and headed into the kitchen, where our cook (who James had insisted we hire so I no longer had to stand on my feet for long) had a big spread of bacon, eggs, ham, salmon croquettes, and grits prepared. James was already eating and reading the newspaper. The joy of us being parents had worn off and we'd settled into that stagnant place that had become our norm. But at least we weren't fighting and arguing at every turn.

I skipped the greeting. "Don't you think I should be showing more?" I pressed down on my dress to reveal my stomach.

His eyes rose slightly up over the paper. "Good morning to you too."

"Sorry. Morning. I was just examining my stomach. Don't you think I should be showing by now?" I did the profile pose again.

He shrugged nonchalantly, his attention back on his newspaper and his breakfast. "I don't know. When do pregnant women show?"

"Definitely by eight months." I glanced down at my stomach, which was no different from when I first received the news. "What if something is wrong?" I said.

"Oh, stop worrying yourself. You've had monthly doctor visits and the doctor has never given you cause for alarm."

"But he just checks my blood pressure and asks questions. What if something is wrong?"

He must've seen the distressed look on my face, because he set his fork down. "Look, why don't you call Dr. Wyatt and see if he can get you in today? We can go in to his office rather than have him make a house call and he can check and ensure everything is okay to put you at ease."

"Yes, let's do that." My insides were a bucket of nerves as worst-case scenarios danced in my head. What if something was wrong?

Forty-five minutes later, I sat in the waiting room of Dr. Wyatt's office.

"Mrs. McDaniel Crawford," the receptionist said. "Dr. Wyatt will see you now."

I rose and entered the doctor's office where he poked and prodded and listened to my heartbeat, then my baby's. After sending me to the bathroom, he sent my urine sample to the lab, where he said he would inject it into a frog.

"I don't understand why that's necessary. Isn't that just to find out whether I'm pregnant?"

"It is. But the intensity of the results can sometimes give us insight into other issues," Dr. Wyatt said. I didn't want to take a chance on any other issues, so I did as he requested. Since it took twelve to twenty-four hours to get results, I tried not to think the worst as James led me back to the car.

"I hope once he assures you that everything is fine, you'll get somewhere and sit down," James said once we were in the car. "You can't be doing all that working and running around like crazy carrying my baby."

"*Our* baby," I corrected him.

"Our baby," he replied.

For once I was listening to my husband. Nothing else mattered but a safe delivery. My hand went to my stomach, gently rubbing it as I made promises to my child that I would take a hiatus, do whatever was necessary to safely bring her into the world.

I never thought anything could make me give up on acting, but I would do it with a quickness for my baby. But in my heart, I knew that this child was a sign of great things to come. I'd be able to have my child and my career. I'd have it all— the life I finally deserved.

• • •

Twenty-four hours had become thirty-six and I was about to go out of my mind. That's why I'd insisted James and I go wait in Dr. Wyatt's lobby until he could tell me what, if anything, was going on with my child.

After a torturous hour of waiting, the receptionist summoned us back to an examination room. When Dr. Wyatt entered, the distressed expression on his face set off a dry churning in my gut.

"Dr. Wyatt? What's wrong?" Now I was really nervous.

"Hattie, um, I-I . . . I don't know how to tell you this." He eased down into the chair next to the examining table.

My heart quickened with each syllable.

"Just tell me. Is my baby okay?"

His shoulders slumped, then he said words that would haunt me forever. "There is no baby."

I sat up, my face contorted with confusion. "What?"

"Yeah, Doc," James said, stepping beside me, his hand resting on my shoulder. "What are you talking about?"

"There . . . is . . . no . . . baby," he repeated. He was slowly blinking his eyes like he'd seen something traumatic.

Those four words were like a spear through my heart. "What happened to my baby?" I screamed.

"There . . . I don't know quite how to say this . . ." He shook his head like he was in a trance. "There appears to never have been a baby."

"What? You—you must be mistaken," I cried. James took my hand to calm me, though he looked just as perplexed as me.

"We ran the test multiple times. That's what has taken me so long." Finally, his eyes met mine. "I'm so sorry."

"No!" I yelled. "Test again. I am pregnant."

"I'm sorry, Hattie," he said once more, as if those two words would rectify this situation.

"No." My voice was lower now, quivering as I struggled to make sense of what this man was saying. I grabbed his white jacket, startling him and James. "You told me there was a baby. I know there is a baby."

He flinched but didn't pull away. "I'm sorry."

I wanted to scream at him to stop saying that but when I opened my mouth this time, nothing but guttural moans came out.

He continued, "You . . . well, you're a large woman and I guess that's why your condition was misread for so long. I don't know what to tell you. I don't know what happened, but based on my exam, not only were you never pregnant, you're likely unable to ever have children. I believe you have what we call psychogenic infertility."

My world was spinning. He might as well have just taken his scalpel and dug out my heart.

"What happened? How is this possible?" James stammered. "What is psychogenic infertility?"

Dr. Wyatt looked at me with pity. "It's when a woman is too anxious, ambitious, or not in tune with their own stress to get pregnant.

It happens to career-driven women who often harbor antimaternal unconscious thoughts that hijack hormones from their brains and ovaries."

James dropped my hand. "So she will never be able to get pregnant because she's too career-driven?"

Dr. Wyatt's silence reeked of judgment, but I could not get my mind to formulate this idea that I would never get pregnant. I needed to understand what happened to the fact that I was already pregnant.

My voice quivered as I said, "Dr. Wyatt, I need you to explain to me how I lost my baby?"

His voice was firm now as if he'd had an injection of professionalism. "You didn't lose the baby, Hattie. You were never pregnant. We've seen cases like this before. You had a false pregnancy."

"What the hell is a false pregnancy?" I screamed.

"It's where the mind convinces the body that you're pregnant. I've consulted with my colleagues and it's a rare disorder called pseudocyesis."

Pseudocyesis? Psychogenic? None of this was making sense. "I'm not crazy. I was pregnant. You said it. I felt it. Who put you up to this? Did Walter White do this? Did some reporter? One of the producers?" I hurled accusations at him.

"Hattie . . . ," James said, finally reaching for my arm.

"No!" I screamed, jerking away from him. "This man is the one who's crazy."

"I can give you something to calm your nerves," the doctor said, standing and walking toward his medicine cabinet.

"You can give me my baby!" I cried, grabbing him again and spinning him toward me. This time James was able to grip both my hands and unclench them from Dr. Wyatt's coat as I cried, "Give me my baby! That's what you can do!"

Those were the last words I remember before the weight of this devastating news pushed me to the floor and the sounds of my baby's lost soul mixed with the wail of my disappearing hopes and dreams sent me spiraling into an abyss from which I didn't think I'd ever return.

PART 2

HEDDA HOPPER'S HOLLYWOOD

October 1944

"Hello, everybody, Hedda Hopper reporting to you from Hollywood, that fabulous place where everyone wants to live but seldom does. This reporter may have been scooped on the story about Negro actress Hattie McDaniel's bun baking in the oven. But I have an exclusive juicy tidbit. It appears the stork won't be making a stop at the home of the Academy Award winner after all. Apparently, Miss McDaniel's pregnancy was in her head and not in her body. Such a tragedy, especially since everyone in Tinseltown knew how happy Miss McDaniel was about motherhood.

"As your in-the-know reporter, I've heard the rumors that this was all a publicity stunt to promote her new movie, Three Is a Family, *but I saw the light in Miss McDaniel's eyes. She truly thought she was about to be a mother.*

"Now, I'm no psychotherapist, but I can only imagine the mental toll a phantom pregnancy will take on someone. Let's pray Miss McDaniel doesn't spiral downhill from this.

"You're listening to Hedda Hopper's Hollywood. *Good day, America!"*

CHAPTER 29

November 1944

I had mourned for thirty days and thirty nights. My body had betrayed me, tricked me, played a cruel joke on me, and in return, I had cursed it, damned it, and finally, come to terms with it.

The loss—or whatever you called it—had widened the canyon between James and me. He never mentioned that claim from the doctor that my career was to blame for my inability to ever have children, but it lingered in the air like a cloak of death. Yet I had no energy to give the claim any life.

After weeks of trying to reach me to no avail, James had shouted something about me not being the only one in pain, then he'd announced he was going back to Chicago for a while. I hadn't even said good-bye. I didn't have the stamina to concern myself with his pain. I was fine with our solo grieving.

A heavy fog was my constant companion. Even now as I made my way down the stairs and into the kitchen. I stopped just outside the door when I heard voices. It sounded like Ruby and my neighbor Hazel.

"So, Ruby, be honest. Do you think she was really pregnant?" Hazel whispered.

"What? Why would you ask something like that?" Ruby replied.

"Well, I heard Hedda Hopper's show. Plus, I know her health is declining," Hazel said. "Maybe her mental state is too. Though I was talking to my doctor friends about it and we are all in agreement that sometimes women mistake menopause symptoms for pregnancy symptoms. Maybe she is in menopause. It's just so sad. But I believe God carried the matter off for the best."

Not only did I have to deal with my loss, but now I was fodder for professional banter?

Silence momentarily filled the room, then Ruby said, "I appreciate you dropping by to bring this casserole, but I really need to be getting back to work."

I debated making my presence known, but honestly, I didn't have the energy.

I turned around, with every intention of heading back into my bedroom and slipping under my covers. Instead, I headed to the nursery. I eased open the door that I hadn't touched since the day I discovered I would forever be childless. I stood in the doorway, taking in all that I'd done in preparation of my beloved infant.

My eyes went to the small cross that hung over the baby's crib. The sight of the white metal ignited a rage in my heart.

What kind of God would plant a fertility seed in my brain but not my body? What kind of God would give me the joy of motherhood only to snatch it away?

Was Hazel right? Was it my health that had caused my body to morph into delusion? Was it the cessation of my menstruation? Maybe it was the weight gain that the studios had pushed on me all these years? Or maybe it was the fact that as much as I lied to the press about my age, my body knew the truth: I was fifty-one, and past child-bearing years.

But the thought that scared me the most raced to the forefront: Had my desire for children caused my mind to have delusions?

I walked into the nursery, picked up the white elephant lamp I'd bought after seeing it in the Sears catalog, lifted it in the air, and slammed it onto the floor. The minutia of relief was instant, so with my arm I swept all the books off the shelf, then knocked the crib over, then the matching rocking chair, then the bassinet. With every item I destroyed, the river of tears cascaded harder. I didn't stop until I heard Ruby's voice.

"My God, Hattie. What are you doing?" she said.

I was sure I looked like I needed to be in a sanatorium.

I opened my mouth to answer her, but all that came out was another gut-wrenching sob, and I fell back against the wall, my entire body sliding to the floor.

Ruby took me in her arms and rocked me as I bawled. Nothing she said could ease my pain. And I cried until I had nothing left.

I'm not sure how Ruby got me to bed, but she did, and I remained there for three weeks. Though for me, time didn't exist.

"Hey, Hattie."

My eyes fluttered open toward the voice coming from my bedroom door. But even the sight of Clark Gable with his golden-watt smile and brow furrowed with concern couldn't reach me. I continued lying in the bed, staring out the window.

"Ruby said it was okay for me to come in." He fidgeted with his collar and tiptoed like he was fearful of being discovered in such an intimate space. Although we were close, he was still a consummate gentleman and wouldn't find it proper to be in a lady's bedroom, unless of course, it was one of his many conquests.

"I would ask how you're doing, but I know the answer to that." He sat on the edge of my bed when I didn't move. "I know you're pretty faithful. God will help you through this trying time."

I wondered if my friends all had a script they read before coming to visit me because they all gave me the same spiel about God making no mistakes. Well, I'm sorry but I would never understand God's rationale on false pregnancies and barren wombs.

After weeks of silence, I found my voice and simply told Clark, "The Old Man upstairs has deserted me. It's damn hard for me to believe in God or anything."

My words shocked him, but I meant them. God had forsaken me, so I wasn't going to sugarcoat my feelings.

"You know I had a hard time with Ma's death," Clark said after a few minutes. "The army chaplain gave me this." He reached in his pocket and pulled out a purple ribbon. He gently fingered the raised yellow cross on it. "It has a quote from Psalm 147, verse three—'He heals the brokenhearted and binds up their wounds.'" Clark gently laid the ribbon next to me. "I wanted you to have it in hopes that it could bring you comfort like it brought me."

Clark was more spiritual than religious. He was baptized at a Roman Catholic church in Ohio, but when his mother died, his father refused to raise him in the Catholic faith. So he didn't have a strong faith foundation. But I appreciated him trying to reach me through my language. Or at least what used to be my language.

I reached for the ribbon and pulled it to my chest. In this moment, I didn't know how my broken heart would ever heal, but I held the ribbon close to me anyway.

"Maybe you need to get away," Clark said after a few minutes. "Just some time to clear your head."

Ruby had suggested that same thing. She'd tried to get me out of the house to attend a Women's League gala. Then she suggested I retreat to the quiet solitude of her family's ranch in Fullerton, which was about forty minutes outside of LA.

After a few more minutes of silence, Clark said, "I just wanted to check on you. I'm gonna go." He stood and took my hand. "I know you're hurting, my friend. Trust me, I know pain. I know the stronghold of grief." His voice shook. "But like you told me, you have to fight your way out of this darkness. I'm here if you need me." Then he leaned down, kissed my forehead, and walked away.

I'd dealt with death, from my parents to my brother Otis. While that had hurt, this pain felt different. My baby had lived only in my mind. How was I supposed to grieve that?

The memory of Otis reminded me of his words the last time I had been suffocated by grief. It was after Howard died and I had taken to bed much like I was doing now.

"You don't get over it. You get through it, Hattie. And you do that by fighting. You're the strongest person I know. Get up and fight," he'd told me.

Otis had died of pneumonia shortly after telling me that, and I had wanted to sink deeper into my pit of despair, but his words became my constant companion and catapulted me forward. If he hadn't given me the will to fight through my depression, who knows where I would be today.

"Get up and fight, Hattie."

My brother's voice filled my head. I wanted to plead with him and tell him losing a child you never had was different. That was an unimaginable pain. But I knew if Otis were here, he wouldn't want to hear it. And it was that knowledge that made me read the scripture on the purple ribbon again, then finally throw back my covers and get out of bed.

CHAPTER 30

December 1944

The month at Ruby's family ranch had done me good. I'd spent days meditating, reflecting, and resting on the wrap-around porch that overlooked sprawling trees and mature vegetation on the two-acre ranch where Ruby lived with her husband and five children. I thought being around so many people wouldn't be good for me, but it was exactly what I needed. They'd provided me with light and laughter and just the right amount of space.

Most of all, I'd had a few powwows with God and, in the end, I'd come to terms with something my mama used to always say: "We may not understand the why, but God does everything for a reason."

When I returned to South Harvard I dove into my work in true Hattie McDaniel fashion. Louise and I appeared in two floor shows for a fundraiser for the American Women's Voluntary Services organization. I tried to do personal appearances and speaking engagements at least four times a week.

As long as I stayed busy, I felt no pain. That's why I decided to celebrate my return with a New Year's Day party. Today was the big day. As the caterer bustled about, I felt something I hadn't felt in months: happiness.

James, who had returned right before Thanksgiving, didn't bother to attend, because he didn't think I needed to be throwing a party. But that was fine. I was on my road to recovery and his absence wasn't going to change that.

Ethel Waters was finishing her rendition of "Stormy Weather" when I noticed a colored man in an army uniform talking to my neighbor and fellow actor Ben Carter, and decided to introduce myself.

"Hi, I'm Hattie McDaniel. Thank you for coming to my party and thank you for your service," I said, extending my hand.

He shook my hand, but his expression was tense. "Hello, Miss McDaniel. I am a guest of your neighbor Hazel Lee."

"Well, I'll have to thank her for bringing you. I'm always happy to meet our beloved servicemen."

Someone else might have been bothered by Hazel inviting strangers into their home, but I had a revolving door here at Sugar Hill. Everyone was welcome and my friends knew that.

He shifted uncomfortably as his eyes darted from me to Ben. "Well, you may not feel that same way once you hear what I have to say."

My smile faded. "Pardon me?"

Ben wrung his hands, then said, "I'll let you two talk," before excusing himself.

"Miss McDaniel, I agreed to come here with Hazel so that I could personally deliver you these." He lifted a bag onto the table.

"These are letters from GIs stationed in Panama," he said.

I guess my expression was one of bewilderment because he patted the bag.

"Miss McDaniel, when my fellow servicemen found out I would be coming here, they asked that I not only deliver these to you but also deliver a message."

"What kind of message?"

"It's about your role in *Three Is a Family*, where you played a laughing lunatic who forgot her name in the movie." His voice was rife with disgust.

A laughing lunatic?

Before I could respond, he said, "I mean no disrespect, but I think it's important that you know the feelings of the colored soldiers who are putting their lives on the line for this beloved country."

"I'm sorry. What's your name again?" I asked.

"Lieutenant John Emerson. And please, just hear me out. In the movie, you were referred to by your white employers as 'Colored Mammy' or 'Whatchamacallit,'" he continued, sounding as if he'd rehearsed the speech all the way from Panama. "As we watched the movie, the white fellers laughed their heads off, while every man of the Negro race burrowed his head in shame. Most of the colored soldiers watching the movie got up and left, feeling just as low as a group could after a shameful performance by one of his own race. I never hope to have to undergo such an ordeal again."

"I was acting, playing a character," I protested.

"Many Australians saw the movie," Lt. Emerson continued. "Unfortunately, motion pictures are their only conception of life in the United States. And then a soldier pulls occupational duty, drills the fields all day, does guard duty, and that night, he sees a plantation picture with a Negro in it playing the part of a servant or maid and acting crazy. You and people like you who play the comical, illiterate roles lower the colored soldiers' morale and make them wish they were never even born. I am proud that I am a Negro, but I don't like to see my people act as though they were just in America to take up space."

"Lieutenant Emerson, do you know that seven percent of American Negroes belong to the artistic and professional groups, while the other ninety-three percent are cooks, butlers, street sweepers, sharecroppers, porters, maids, and washerwomen? Thus, I could argue that my roles are more lifelike than not."

He was not to be dissuaded. "It's everything, from the roles you take on to your expressions. You grin inanely in all your movies."

This was ridiculous. Now I was being belittled for my facial expressions? "Does the mere fact that a Negro is called upon to smile during the filming of a picture come under your definition of 'grinning inanely'? I don't know of a single Negro comedian with a deadpan expression, and I am certain that my broad smile could never be termed an inane grin. Are we to forgo all comedy parts because we are Negroes?"

He raised both hands in defense. "I'm really not trying to upset you."

It's too late for that. I took a step toward him so we were face-to-face. "You come into my home on what's supposed to be a festive occasion and belittle how I earn my living," I snapped. "Why are you singling out us, anyway? Our images are flitting across the screen for just a few moments—and that's if we're fortunate. Why not ask yourself or your fellow soldiers whether you've been doing anything constructive?"

I didn't deserve this kind of treatment. My wartime efforts were many. I'd worked with the American Women's Voluntary Services, had constant USO tours, and made numerous trips to bond rallies. But all that should be discredited because I played a maid in a movie?

"I'm doing my best at the few roles that are offered to me." I didn't care that a small crowd was staring at us. "I don't understand this double standard. No one has ever accused Gracie Allen, Joan Davis, Lucille Ball, or Martha Raye of being ignorant because they play silly parts."

"I can see I've upset you, and that was never my intention. I will see myself out. But please, take time to read the letters."

He walked over to Hazel and whispered something. Hazel shot me an apologetic look and followed him toward the door.

I don't know how, but I made it through my party. The guests were all gone and I was now seated at the kitchen table, the letters stacked in front of me. Slowly, I took a letter opener and slid it underneath the first envelope, carefully opening it, then removing the letter. I read it and forced myself not to ball it up. I opened each envelope, my stomach sinking further as I read each one. Some of the letters were signed individually. Others carried names of up to fifteen men. They all came from Panama.

Your characterizations are a demoralizing embarrassment to the Negro race.

How can you sleep at night?

You should be ashamed of yourself.

You're a discredit to our race.

One after another, the letters blasted me.

I threw the stack onto the dining room table and summoned Ruby into the room.

"You called," she said, appearing in the doorway. She had hired a cleanup crew and was working with them.

"I need to hire some secretaries to help me respond to these letters," I said, pointing to the stack.

"Respond?"

"Yes. To each one. They are criticizing me for my portrayals and I want to assure them that I would never disgrace them but, at the same time, remind them that I can't afford to forsake my life's profession, which is the means of my livelihood."

"Umm, okay," Ruby said, her eyes going from me to the mounds of letters. "How about we go to bed and talk about this in the morning."

"I need at least three ladies here tomorrow," I barked. "I'm going to start responding to these letters tonight."

I could tell she wanted to advise me against that, but she simply said, "I'll get right on it." She paused. "Then I'm going to bed, and when I wake up, we can tackle these with a fresh mind."

But the next morning, when Ruby returned to the kitchen, I was still at the table, furiously writing.

"Oh my God, Hattie. Have you been to sleep?" she asked.

"I've responded to over forty." I'd dozed off and on here at the table, but I was determined to get through these letters. "But we still have about three times that."

She sighed. "Okay, I have two ladies coming later this morning."

"That's fine."

"Why don't you go get some rest and let's let them handle it?" Ruby said.

"No." I kept furiously scribbling. "I'm going to write until I can no longer keep my eyes open."

"I think you've made your point." Ruby gently patted my back.

I stopped and looked up at her. Not because I agreed with her, but because with each letter, my rage grew. This whole letter-writing campaign had one person written all over it and it was infuriating. Every single letter sounded the same, and all the phrases were ones that had been thrown at me before.

"I know Walter White is behind this," I said.

"How do you figure that?" Ruby slid into the seat across from me.

"He's touring military outposts near Panama. I know he's responsible for this hailstorm of negative mail." I pushed the piece of paper I'd been writing on when she walked in across the table.

"That's why I wrote this letter to the War Department and other branches of the United States government. I'm telling them about Walter White," I said.

"And why are you doing that?" Ruby asked, her eyes scanning the letter that I'd handed to her.

"They need to intercede on my behalf. I know that I'm a public target and criticism is all around me, but Mr. White is going beyond what is normal or fair," I said. "He's consistently singling me out. And I'm the only one he refers to by name. I plan to do whatever I can, regardless of how malicious or desperate, when it comes to stopping or seeking revenge against Walter White."

"Whoa, Hattie. I need you to breathe." Ruby eased over to me and gently stroked my arm.

While I'm sure I looked mad, I was completely in my right mind. "No, this is long overdue." I snatched the paper back. "You know what, maybe I should tell them how he covets white women."

"And what good will playing to racist fears do, especially when it's not true?" Ruby asked.

I started feverishly writing. "We don't know that it's not true. Or better yet, maybe I'll just tell them that he's firing up our troops. Let the government know so when the colored GIs return home, they'll be angry and threaten our domestic tranquility. I think I'll even say one of the letters I got from a serviceman says that Walter has a grudge against the world. I'm gonna tell the government that thirteen colored GIs signed that."

"Hattie, do you think that's wise? The specter of colored violence will trigger the worst kind of white repression." Her voice was calming, and managed to soothe my wrath, but not my anger.

We faced off for a minute until the tears I'd been fighting since I started reading the letters burst through.

"Remember what happened the last time you let your rage guide your response," Ruby said, reminding me how I'd only made the situation worse the time I responded to the slur against Lena Horne. "You're striving for a better life for colored people. Don't sabotage all your efforts."

"What am I supposed to do? Just sit here and take this? You don't understand, Ruby. I've known the worst of poverty and Walter White's campaigns are threatening not only my stature in Hollywood but my ability to support myself and my family."

She patted my hands and I pulled my arm back.

"No! I have to do this! I have to do something," I exclaimed.

Ruby grasped my hands to keep me from writing.

"Hattie, stop," she said firmly.

I gave her a look to remind her that she worked for me. She gave me one right back that said being my friend was more important than that.

Finally, in a low, trembling voice I said, "Do you know that when I was three, I remember feeding locusts to a kitten."

"Okaaaaaaay," she said, dragging her words out. "It just shows that you've always been nurturing."

"No," I said, pounding the table with my palms. "We fed locusts to the kitten because we didn't have anything else to feed him. I refuse to have a life of hunger."

Ruby would never know how the terror of hard times haunted me. It was the fuel for my success, and yes, it may have even been what drove me to my extremes, but I would not go back to starvation. I would fight with all that I had against any threat—real or perceived. And that included the powerful and respected Walter White.

CHAPTER 31

April 1945

It had been three months and still, no one from the government would help me.

I had been looking forward to the veterans' luncheon in the Dunbar's elegant ballroom. I was hoping that a sea of servicemen dressed proudly in their military uniforms, with their medals and ribbons displaying their achievements and sacrifices, would rid my mind of the havoc Walter White was causing in my life.

Since the luncheon hadn't started, I took a moment to run to the ladies' room. I had just rounded the corner when my eyes locked with Mr. White's. My immediate instinct was to turn and go the other way, lest I take off my slingback heels and bludgeon him to death. It was obvious that I had seen him, but I didn't care as I spun around and headed in the direction from which I had just come.

However, I may not have wanted to speak to Walter White, but he wanted to speak to me.

"Miss McDaniel!" We were in a long hallway that was flanked with tall ornamental plants that I had hoped would shield me from his view.

"Miss McDaniel!"

At first I debated whether I should just keep walking toward the front and out the heavy double doors. But I stopped and spun to face him.

I didn't bother to hide my displeasure. "Yes, Mr. White? Is there a reason you're screaming my name like an old coyote?" He was wearing his usual patterned wool-rayon suit and tiny spectacles, which did little to mask the deep blue tint of his eyes. Had I not known his heart, I would have thought he was a sweet old man.

Mr. White composed himself as he stood erect. "Miss McDaniel, might I say that I am extremely disappointed in the news that I've been given," he said.

I folded my arms across my chest. "And what news would that be, Mr. White?"

"That you have waged a campaign to discredit me, even attempting to get the government involved." His tone was so haughty it made me want to laugh.

"Let me be very clear with you," he continued without allowing me to reply. "Yes, I told the GIs to write. But to the *studios*, not to *you*. Perhaps your erratic behavior is to blame for any backlash you might be receiving." His air of superiority wiped away any desire to laugh.

"You have had it in for me since the day I stepped foot in Los Angeles," I said.

"I for you?" he asked, incredulous. "You actually wrote a letter purporting that I don't work for my people?" His blond mustache twitched with aggravation. "I've been fighting for my people since I was twenty-five years old. And I worked tirelessly fighting lynching and other causes since I joined the NAACP in 1918. So don't tell me I don't work for the betterment of the Negro race."

Two ladies passed us, scurrying toward the restroom. Once they'd rounded the corner, I replied, "Mr. *White*, I find it mighty ironic that you championed anti-lynching, considering you—Mr. White, and I mean that literally—are on a crusade to lynch me."

He blew an exasperated breath. "First and foremost, I am a Negro. My skin is white, my eyes are blue, my hair is blond. The traits of my race are nowhere visible upon me, but do not be mistaken. I am a Negro. Secondly, I am not the only one who thinks your role in *Gone with the Wind* was a setback for our race."

"You act as if I did something wrong by winning an Academy Award," I snapped. "Roles have declined as you—my most vocal critic for some reason—and the NAACP campaigned for Hollywood to stop including so many servile colored characters in films. These were and are trailblazing roles."

"Trailblazing?" he scoffed and folded his arms across his chest. "Hmph. More like traitorous."

I glared at him, not responding. Finally, I said, "You have some kind of nerve, Mr. White. Discredit? You want to talk about discrediting someone?

"Do you understand that the NAACP, and organizations of the like, were started and kept alive by dollars dropped from the gnarled hands of the common laborer, the washerwoman, and the cook?" I continued. "I took the role of Mammy with pride because she represented the type of womanhood that has built our race, paid for our elaborate houses of worship, and sustained our business, charitable, and improvement organizations."

I held up my hand to stop him as he tried to speak. "Let me finish," I snapped. "I am proud that I am a Negro woman who earned her living with her swollen chapped hands. Members of that class have given so much. Bending their backs over washtubs, they have smiled encouragement to daughters who wanted an artistic career. Hobbling about kitchens, they have inspired their children to become doctors of philosophy and law. Enduring the unwanted advances of their masters."

I knew all about Mr. Walter White. He was the descendant of an enslaved woman concubine and her owner, so that quip was meant to sting. "It is because of women like me that you are able to sit perched in your powerful position, raining down judgment."

He folded his arms, his expression trying to remain indifferent. But I could tell that my words had pierced. "I take nothing away from where we've been. I am trying to motivate and propel Hollywood to see us as more than the stereotypical servants and slaves. It has nothing to do with discrediting you."

"It appears as if that is what motivates you each waking day, discrediting me. Tell me, do you criticize colored males or only women? How about you advocate for colored actors to have more diverse roles instead of shaming me? I'm making the best choice for me out of the dismal options I've been given. What types of roles am I expected to play? Do you think I like being a servant or slave? Do you think that given the choice, I'd rather play a maid, or the president? Or a business owner or, hell, a superhero. I would love to be a colored Wonder Woman. Tell me, Mr. White, where I can go sign up for those roles, and I will gladly leave this event and go."

I didn't give him a chance to respond.

"Unlike you, Mr. White," I continued, ignoring his pursed lips, "I don't dare to dream. My dark skin, ample girth, and coarse hair dictate that no matter how talented I am, my options are few. I wish I could change that. I pray that one day it will change. But in the meantime, much like my ancestors who toiled in the fields, I take the scraps I'm given and make the most marvelous supper I can. I give a dignified performance that opens doors so that the Negro actors of tomorrow can be all of those things that you think they should be, but America has not yet given us. So I make no apologies that I don't fit your standard of beauty. But this"—I motioned up and down my body—"is beautiful to me. It's the body, the face, the skin color God gave me. So you try to discredit me all you want. I will continue to stand strong, continue to persevere no matter what you throw my way to stop me."

He looked taken aback. I guess he had expected to get the high-road Hattie. Not today.

I continued, desiring to add one more thing before I finished. "You're well-heeled, Mr. White. You don't have to worry about earning a living. Maybe wealthy Negroes should invest in the film industry, or better yet, the NAACP could drop some coin into film production; then they can make pictures suitable to the organization. I'd be only too happy to play in them. Until then, Mr. White, how about you refrain from uttering my name at all. Good day."

I left without giving him an opportunity to reply.

CHAPTER 32

May 1945

My film career had come to a complete halt. No one would give me a role. I was watching the careers of Mary Astor, Ginger Rogers, and Joan Fontaine flourish. Despite what Mr. White said, I knew he was to blame, but his words got me to thinking. How much of this was on me?

The sound of pounding on my front door snapped me from my thoughts. I looked down at the sudsy water. I'd been engrossed in my thoughts so much that I had only washed one bowl in the thirty minutes I'd been standing at the kitchen sink.

The banging on the door grew louder. People dropped by all the time but usually they were cordial. So the pounding startled me.

I wiped my hands on my apron, then removed it because I made it a point to never greet guests in my apron.

"I'm coming. Hold your horses," I called out as I walked into the living room. I looked out the window and saw Dorothy on my porch. Her eyes were wide and she was wringing a handkerchief in one hand and grasping her daughter Lynn's hand with the other one. I swung the door open. "Dottie?"

She looked like she had been crying. "Oh my goodness, what's wrong?"

"I-I . . ."

I stepped aside and ushered her in. "Come inside."

Dorothy picked Lynn up, then shuffled past me. The toddler was dressed in a pink ruffled dress with a white petticoat, bobby socks, and patent leather shoes. White ribbons wrapped around four pigtails. With Dorothy's pink pastel dress, the two of them looked like they were on their way to a mother-daughter tea.

"Is everything okay? Is it Harold? Where is he?" I asked.

"Gone. As usual," Dorothy cried. "Performing in Paris."

I helped her remove her light sweater. "Okay, sit down and catch your breath so you can tell me what's going on," I said.

She sat Lynn on the sofa, kissed her on the forehead, then walked back over to me.

"Is that what you're upset about, Harold?" I knew Dorothy had regrets. She'd basically given up her career to be a housewife and take care of Harold and Lynn. And Harold hadn't missed a beat in pursuit of his career.

"Of course I'm upset about Harold," she sniffed. "But I had to see you because . . . it's Lynn." She looked over at her daughter.

I glanced at the doe-eyed little girl, who wasn't even two years old yet. She sat stoically, like her body was here, but her mind wasn't.

"What's wrong with Lynn?" I asked.

"That's just it," Dorothy said. "I don't know what's wrong. I've been to a bunch of different doctors because she won't talk, she won't move, she won't do anything but sit here and moan." She buried her face in her hands. "I just want my baby to say 'mama.'"

Lynn sat on the sofa, staring blankly. Her eyes were open but they didn't seem to have any life in them. It was like she was just staring into the abyss.

"She's been like this for months now. I keep telling everybody something is wrong and nobody will listen," Dorothy cried. "We just left the doctor, who said she'll grow out of it. But, Hattie, I know my daughter. Something is wrong with her. Yes, she learned to walk early, but that's it. She doesn't talk, she doesn't play. She doesn't even cry. She just does that," she said, pointing to Lynn on the sofa swinging her legs but exhibiting no other movement.

"Maybe she's just a late bloomer," I said. Even as the words left my mouth, I knew it was wishful thinking. Something was definitely wrong.

"But she should be talking, showing some emotion," Dorothy said.

I walked over and lifted Lynn's chin to study her face. Her legs continued swinging. Her eyes remained expressionless. "Have you talked to Ru?"

"Mama, the doctors, everybody keeps dismissing me, telling me that I'm panicking for nothing, but I know." She paced my living room.

"Okay, calm down. What exactly is your doctor saying again?"

"The same thing, that I'm overreacting, but a mother knows." She threw her hands up in exasperation.

"Okay, I'm going to call my doctor. She is one of the best in Los Angeles." After the fiasco with Dr. Wyatt, I'd found another doctor and was hopeful she could help Lynn.

"Thank you so much." Dorothy hugged me, and I could feel relief seep from her pores.

I went into the kitchen and, just out of earshot, dialed my doctor's office. "Hello, this is Hattie McDaniel," I said once the receptionist answered. "May I speak with Dr. Elliot?"

"She's just wrapping up with a patient," the receptionist said.

"I'll hold. It is of an urgent nature," I said.

"Okay," she replied before placing me on hold. Ten minutes later, Dr. Elliot's voice filled the phone.

"Hattie, how are you? What's going on? My nurse said it was urgent."

"I have Dorothy Dandridge here with her daughter and we are almost sure something is wrong. Not in an immediate, dangerous way, but the child seems lethargic and out of it. Dorothy is extremely concerned and unable to get assistance anywhere else. I am hoping that you can help."

"I was just about to head out for the day. How soon could you get to my office?"

"Right away."

"Then I'll wait on you."

• • •

It seemed like we'd been in this waiting room for hours, but judging from the clock on Dr. Elliot's wall, it had been less than two hours.

Dorothy hadn't stopped weeping. "What child do you know can sit still for this long, Hattie?" Dorothy said, pointing at Lynn, who was just staring out Dr. Elliot's fourth-story window.

"Let's just wait on the doctor," I told her, patting her leg.

When we first arrived, Dr. Elliot had immediately examined Lynn, then asked us a bunch of questions. Luckily, she had been able to get access to Dorothy's and Lynn's medical records, so she was already abreast of her case.

When the door opened and Dr. Elliot reentered, both Dorothy and I sat up.

"Were you able to find out anything? Is there some medicine I can give her? It's something wrong, right? I knew it was." Dorothy pummeled her with questions.

Dr. Elliot held up a hand to silence her, and surprisingly it worked. The doctor slid into her seat behind her desk.

"So I was able to review Lynn's medical records." The calm yet resigned tone in Dr. Elliot's voice made my stomach knot up. She was usually a straight shooter and had mastered blending compassion with professionalism. "I am so sorry to tell you this, Miss Dandridge, but it appears that Harolyn has brain damage."

Dorothy fell back against her seat as my breath caught in my throat. "B-brain damage?" Dorothy said.

Dr. Elliot continued, "That is the reason she is not fully developing. After consulting with my colleagues, we believe that her brain was damaged during birth." She looked down at her notes. "Were forceps used to get her out?"

Dorothy's chest started heaving. The day she'd gone into labor, she endured horrible pain but refused to go to the hospital until Harold returned from the golf course. The only problem was, when we called to tell Harold that Dorothy was going into labor, he'd said Dottie was "just being dramatic." By the time we finally made it to the hospital (without Harold), mother and daughter were in serious danger.

"Y-yes. I . . . was late getting her to the hospital. I mean, I was trying to wait on Harold. And by the time I arrived, she had turned and they had to use forceps to get her out." Dottie buried her face in her hands. "Oh God, what have I done?"

My heart ached for Dorothy. She wanted to be a good mother and wife so bad. She even had blamed herself for the fact that her husband couldn't keep that one-eyed rattlesnake in his pants. Harold's cheating was well known in Hollywood, and instead of calling him to the carpet for it, Dorothy blamed her lack of sexual experience for his wandering eye. Because of some childhood trauma involving Geneva (where Geneva abused her), Dorothy hated sex. She'd confided in me how hard it had been to even get to a point where she could let Harold make love to her. She felt his philandering was because she was so inexperienced in the bedroom, so she always excused the reports of his infidelity.

"This is not a blame you should place upon yourself," Dr. Elliot said. "Plenty of families raise disabled children. Don't look backward. Look forward and at what you will now have to do for Lynn's quality of life."

"Dr. Elliot, what does this mean?" I asked. "Lynn will never have a normal life?"

The doctor's expression was forlorn. "It means that Harolyn will forever be two years old. She will never be able to speak or function and will require a lifetime of twenty-four-hour care."

Dorothy's sobs grew louder, and as I watched Lynn sit there, expressionless, unaffected by the devastating news that would shape her life, I wept along with my young friend.

• • •

It had been a long day. Now, as the moon illuminated the night, I made my way up the steps to my house. I'd sat with Dorothy most of the evening and was now utterly exhausted. Ru and Vivy had finally arrived about midnight.

"You're going out of town again?" I said when I walked inside and saw the two suitcases by the front door.

James was sitting in a chair, as if he was watching the door and waiting on me to come home. He'd been home only a few days and now he was leaving again? He slowly rose from his seat. "No, Hattie. I'm leaving."

"That's what I asked. You're leaving again?"

"I'm leaving for good." He released a heavy sigh. "Let's not kid ourselves. Neither of us is happy. You don't care about anything but your career, your dogs, and that ridiculous vendetta against Walter White and the NAACP. Your disdain for everyone who dares question why you take the roles you take is exhausting. You live in a perpetual state of 'woe is me.'

"Oh, and above all else," James continued, "I'm not enough for you."

"So, because I won't be some little woman—"

He cut me off. "Because you won't be a *wife*," he snapped forcefully before catching himself and lowering his voice. "We're emotionally disconnected."

I balked. He was talking like this was solely my fault. "You're never here. And even when you are, you aren't. That's why there's a disconnect!" I said.

"I can't keep sacrificing my happiness for your success," he replied. "I need a partner who's present and invested in our marriage."

I stood staring at him, his words not completely registering. No, I wasn't happy. No, I wasn't the best wife. But he wasn't the best husband. Yet he was leaving me, even though neither of us had really tried to make it work?

I opened my mouth, but no words would come out.

James just shook his head, grabbed his bags, and headed out the back door. As the door slammed behind him, I stood in the middle of my foyer in disbelief. Had I lost another husband?

CHAPTER 33

June 1945

This had been the longest month of my life. Over the past year, James had stayed gone more than he was home, but something about knowing he was gone for good was devastating.

I pulled onto South Harvard, my mind on happier times with James. When I turned onto the street, I spotted a fire truck and my neighbors filling the street.

I eased into my back driveway, then walked around to the front, where my neighbors Bessie, Francis, and Earlie Richards stood on the sidewalk watching the commotion.

"What's going on?" I asked no one in particular.

"They done burned a cross on Norman's front yard," Bessie said, shaking her head and pointing to Norman Houston's place two houses down.

I knew many of the white residents had moved out when we moved in because they didn't want to live near us—it was crazy that they would give up their nice home rather than be neighbors with Negroes. But who would go to cross-burning lengths?

"I bet this has something to do with that lawsuit," Bessie said.

"What lawsuit?" I asked, peering at the smoldering four-foot white cross.

Bessie spun to face me. "You haven't heard?"

"Heard what?" I asked.

Bessie, Earlie, and Francis exchanged glances, and I felt like I had been left out of some schoolyard secret. Finally, Bessie said, "Several of the white residents in the neighborhood have gotten together and they're filing a lawsuit against us."

"Who is us?" I asked. I really was confused. I usually stayed abreast on the happenings of the neighborhood, but I had missed the last two neighborhood parties while dealing with all my personal drama.

"The Negro homeowners. All fifty-seven families, including you, Louise, Ethel, and Dr. Somerville and his wife. I mean, how are you gonna tell all these movie stars and prominent business folks they can't live in the mansions they bought several years ago?" Francis replied. "What's crazy is Norman isn't even in the lawsuit. He and Ben Carter are two of the few who live in covenant-free lots."

"Sue for what?" I knew the white homeowners in the area didn't care for me—or anyone who looked like me—that was evident from the first day I moved in. But I didn't think it was to the extent that they would sue to try and push us out of the neighborhood. They'd been successful at keeping Lillian and Jack out, but that had been one case, and Lillian and Jack had given up without a fight.

"Basically, they're saying the restrictive covenants barred us from even moving into the neighborhood in the first place. They said only people whose blood is entirely of the white race can live in this area," Francis said.

"And just how, pray tell, are they determining whether someone's blood is pure?" I asked.

Francis shrugged as she long-heaved. "Exactly. I've been fighting these restrictive covenants and I've organized some Saturday workshops to talk over strategy and make plans for court appearances. Everybody has their own attorney and nobody is having any success. Sixty of the hundred and two lots in this area are owned by Negroes. It's more of us than it is of them. But we're all operating in silos. I had been hoping that everyone would pool their efforts and fight this case, one street at a time, but I'm not having much traction."

"Why is this my first time hearing about this?" I asked. I knew all about restrictive covenants. They were established during a time when a lot of colored Angelinos owned their own homes as a way to keep them confined to certain areas.

"Well, to be honest," Francis said, again exchanging glances with Bessie, "I knew you were going through a lot, with the baby and your husband moving out."

Francis continued, "We were waiting to see how this all unfolded, but they just filed the lawsuit a couple of weeks ago."

The firefighters removed the last of the charred cross, and a frazzled Norman talked with a white-haired man in a wrinkled suit who I assumed was an investigator.

"So, you've been holding meetings about this?" I asked Francis.

She nodded. "Trying anyway. I'm having trouble because the lawyers want to handle the matter on a case-by-case basis. They think it's just a better financial deal for them than if they collectively fought the battle."

"Oh no," I said. I couldn't believe I'd been so preoccupied with my life drama that I hadn't seen this boulder steamrolling toward me.

"This is just atrocious," Earlie added, finally speaking up.

"I know," Francis said, her hands going to her plump hips. "They are trying to nullify our contracts. They've even had the audacity to complain about property values."

"Just ridiculous," I snapped. "My lawn looks better than any white folks' on this street." All of us had generously enhanced the value of their properties since we each took pride in our homes.

Louise had just bought a house here that belonged to a previous mayor. Pearl Bailey and Juan Tizon, a member of Duke Ellington's band, both lived around the corner. Some of the most respected elite had settled in Sugar Hill.

"I don't know, guys," Earlie said, nervously rubbing the back of his neck. Fear filled his eyes. "They had some racial clashes over on the south side. It might be time for me to go. I don't want to stay anywhere I'm not wanted."

"Then you must not gonna stay in America," Francis said.

"And you have just as much right to be here as anyone else," I said. "We all do."

"Well, it's crosses today, lynching tomorrow," Earlie said. I knew that Earlie had lost his father and two brothers to lynching, so no amount of money would ever make him feel secure.

"So what you gonna do, Earlie? Just give up? Give 'em your place?" I asked. Earlie owned a string of barber shops and other businesses in Los Angeles so I couldn't believe he was ready to give up on his home.

"I'm just saying," Earlie replied. "My cousin was telling me about one case where this judge said that even though Negroes couldn't be prevented from buying real estate in the area, they could be forbidden to live in their homes on the property."

"Nobody's going to put me out of my house," I said defiantly.

"If these white folks around here have their way, that's exactly what they plan to do," Bessie said.

I thought for a minute. "Let me make a call. Sugar Hill is my home. I'll be damned if I let them take what I've worked so hard to build." I looked at Francis. "You're right. We need to do this together."

We squeezed hands in solidarity.

• • •

I ended up calling Loren Miller, a Negro civil rights attorney who had done some work with Sam when he moved into a white neighborhood on Van Ness Avenue. Sam had been fighting an attempt to take his home under a restrictive covenant—that's how I'd first heard about it. The ACLU and the NAACP, which were pushing such cases as a step toward ending residential segregation in the United States, were providing him with representation.

Loren had worked with the USSR and Langston Hughes publishing articles in the *California Eagle* in support of the Soviet Union and attacking racism in the NAACP's *Crisis* magazine. He was already deep in the fight against housing discrimination in Los Angeles.

Loren was a critic of the film industry and colored cinematic images, but he had developed tremendous respect for me when he ran for a congressional seat on the Democratic ticket. I had openly supported him, and he said he would be there for me if I ever needed anything. Well, I needed this.

He'd suggested I meet him at the courthouse as he was closely watching another case on restrictive covenants.

I agreed, but I hadn't been ready for the scene that was unfolding in this Los Angeles district courtroom.

A white, skeletal-looking man, his lanky arms locked behind his back as if he was deep in thought, paced in front of the judge.

"Your Honor, my client, Alex Burnell, was in pursuit of the American Dream," the attorney said. "A native of Corona, California, Alex worked hard all his life, got married, and started a family. Within a few years, he had saved enough money to buy a moderately priced house in the area of Fullerton, which is where he was raised. It was a dream come true, but that dream quickly turned into a nightmare when, within days of moving his young family into the house, he was told he couldn't live there because he was Mexican."

The attorney continued, detailing how track 448, as it's called, was first developed in 1923 with an express restriction that Mexicans and other non-whites couldn't live there.

"White residents were outraged that the Burnells moved into the neighborhood," the attorney continued. "The young couple even had someone break into their house and move the family's furniture onto the street. Other residents filed a lawsuit seeking to have the court enforce the racial covenant by removing them from the residence and permanently adjoining them from living there. My client did not report the burglary, but he refused to give up without defending his rights. It's bad enough that Alex paid $4,250 for his house when everybody else in the area paid about $3,000."

I looked over on the other side of the room. There were six stern-faced white people behind the attorneys. They appeared to have no shame at the things Alex's attorney was saying, as if they had been given some birthright to keep out anyone who didn't look like them.

As Alex's attorney took his seat next to the meek-looking Hispanic man, the attorney on the plaintiff's side stood and cleared his throat.

"That's Gus Hagenstein," Loren whispered, leaning in. "He's a piece of work."

Gus began talking with a Southern drawl. ". . . Is it so wrong for my clients to want a homogenous white community? My clients believe Mexicans living in their neighborhood will cause them irreparable injury because it would require that they come in contact with lower-class Mexicans."

I gasped and Loren shot me an admonishing look.

Gus continued, "Their presence in the neighborhood will devalue my clients' properties by twenty-five to fifty percent. I will bring forth expert witnesses who will testify that Mexicans are dirty, noisy, and lawless."

For the next hour, I listened as Alex's attorney presented his side. He put on a good case, even using America's Good Neighbor Policy with Latin America that President Roosevelt had established. I sat captivated in that courtroom for over five hours.

After they wrapped for the day, Loren walked me outside to my car.

"Now I see why you suggested I come here," I said.

"After you told me about your case, I wanted you to see what you would be up against," he said.

"But didn't you just win a case with a colored family in Pasadena?"

Loren nodded. "*Fairchild v. Raines*. Yeah, I won that when the judge reversed the covenant, but he did so because of inadequate trial court findings, not on the grounds that the racial covenant violated either public policy or equal protection."

I immediately felt dejected. "Does that mean we didn't really have a chance with our case?" I asked.

"Whoa, I'm not saying that. This is a passion for me. These covenants are relentlessly crowding us out of all the desirable, new real estate developments, pushing us in blitzkrieg fashion into the city's most unattractive and unhealthy residential areas. We have every right to live wherever we want and I'm going to fight with every breath in me until I can get a court to agree. I'm just letting you know what lies ahead and that we're in for a fight."

"I never ran from a fight," I said. I might not have fought my battles the way some people thought I should have, but I knew how tenacious I could be.

"Well, you're in for one if you take on the white folks in West Adams. I firmly believe these covenants are illegal under the Fourteenth Amendment. However, a judge has never agreed to this in court," Loren said.

"Well, we can be the first," I said with confidence as I remembered Francis's words. Then I recalled what my mother used to always say to me and my siblings about being there for one another. "There is strength in numbers" was one of her favorite sayings.

I continued, "I was talking with some of my neighbors and we have all these individual suits. What if we consolidated our defense into a class suit? My mother used to always say a fist is mightier than a finger."

His eyebrows raised in interest. "How many do you think we could get in the class action suit?" he asked.

"At least fifty."

Loren nodded and I could see the wheels turning in his head.

"Okay, that's good. I'm heading to Chicago for an NAACP convention and meeting. This is a problem across the country. There are more cases in Los Angeles than in any other city, with twenty different suits in progress." He pulled out what looked like a pocket calendar and studied it for a moment. "We have a meeting with Thurgood Marshall because the organization is ready to tackle racial covenants, so this couldn't have come at a better time. We should meet next Thursday."

I breathed a sigh of relief.

"The whites are going after the colored homeowners, but it's the real estate investors they need to focus on as well," Loren said, closing his calendar.

"What do you mean?" I asked.

"There are investors who will purchase three or four houses in a white neighborhood. Their sole motive is to make money. They use straw parties to buy the property, then they'll get a Negro buyer and move him in there. Then the buyer sits back and waits to see what happens. If there is no objection, they buy up more property because they know it can be sold to Negroes at a profit. Sometimes the covenants are enforced; sometimes the brokers get into trouble with the Department of Real Estate and lose their licenses. This profiteering needs to be addressed. That's why I like the fact that this is a class action suit.

"At the NAACP, our belief is that we should not let one Negro be stuck out there all alone," Loren continued. "Negroes do not break covenants. They are broken by whites selling to Negroes when the property becomes less desirable for white occupancy."

His words had given me hope.

"So look, you get your people together and I'll begin laying the groundwork," Loren added.

"Thank you, Mr. Miller. Thank you so much," I exclaimed, excitedly shaking his hand. He covered my hands as if to temper my excitement.

"Hattie, I'm gonna be honest, having you on board will make this a high-profile case and your involvement gives us a major shot at striking a blow against housing discrimination. This is a tough and dangerous battle and I'm armed for the fight," Loren said.

He'd just spoken my language. If my racist neighbors wanted a fight, they were going to get it.

CHAPTER 34
December 1945

I didn't often get nervous, but today my nerves were on ten. When I looked around the courtroom, there was not an empty seat. Folks were even lined up against the wall in the back. I recognized some people from the local clubs, others from church. Of course, Louise, Lillian, Ethel, Dr. Somerville and his wife, and several of my neighbors sat in the first two rows since they were all defendants. We'd agreed that since I had the relationship with Loren and had spearheaded the suit that got us here today, I would sit at the defendants' table.

In all, there had to be over two hundred people here in the LA County courtroom. They were dressed like they were going to some fine affair. Colored and white. Some celebrities. Some spectators. Some spectators here to see celebrities. The stylish atmosphere in the court made one wonder if the judge would pour tea during the afternoon recess.

I didn't know how many people were here to see Loren at work, but that would be the real show. I'd seen him back in 1938 when he defended George Farley, a man who killed two officers evicting him from a home that had been auctioned out from under him over a street assessment bond. George was headed for the death penalty and Loren expertly got it reduced to manslaughter. I was praying we would see some of that legal magic here today.

"All rise," the bailiff said as the judge walked in.

I had briefly heard of this judge, Thurmond Clarke, back when he worked in the district attorney's office. But I didn't know anything about his views. Loren had told us he was fair, but he was still white. So the likelihood of him ruling for those who looked just like him was strong.

Loren had told us this trial could take over a month, but he'd reminded us just before court began today that he was using an argument that had never worked in any US court before—that restrictive covenants violated the California Constitution and the Fourteenth Amendment, which mandates equal protection under the law. It was a long shot and so he couldn't be confident that it would work. I knew we had to at least try.

We took our seats and Judge Clarke called the trial to order.

One of the attorneys representing my white neighbors, former Los Angeles mayor George E. Cryer, stood when it was his turn. He didn't even look our way, instead keeping his attention focused on the judge as he eased from behind the desk where the elderly man and his wife that I'd met when I first moved in sat. Several of the other white residents whom I'd seen around the neighborhood sat behind him. None of them would look in my direction.

"Your Honor," Mr. Cryer began, "my clients come before you today, extremely concerned about the place they call home. They have taken great care and pride to make it a place where they want to spend out their days. If restrictive covenants are not enforced, my clients in West Adams Heights are fearful that their property will lose value. One need look no further than the slums of Los Angeles to see what happens when Negroes overtake neighborhoods. Racial clashes will inevitably ensue."

He ran his hands up and down his navy suspenders as he spoke directly to the judge. His voice was calm, like he was talking to an old friend. Then it dawned on me: Mr. Cryer was a former mayor. The judge had worked in the district attorney's office. Of course they were friends. A sinking feeling filled me.

Mr. Cryer continued, "Negro West Adams residents were in violation of the law that restrictive covenants were protected under the Constitution, and therefore Negro property owners must be required to surrender their homes. Immediately." The way he said that—like it was a statement of fact—sent grumblings throughout the courtroom.

None of these people trying to force me out understood how I was ready to fight with every fiber of my being. This house was everything my childhood home was not. My parents had spent many nights pacing our creaky floorboards back in Denver, fretting over how to fix the gaping hole in the roof that turned our living room and my sleeping quarters into a pond every time it rained. My house on South Harvard was everything my parents could've never dreamed of. Police would have to drag my dead body out of Sugar Hill.

Loren brushed down his charcoal Shetland pin-striped suit and walked in front of the judge. His triangular mustache and naturally curly hair were impeccably groomed, he looked like a man on a mission.

"Your Honor, the Fourteenth Amendment rights mandate equal protection under the law for American citizens. My clients, who are American citizens, have not been afforded that right," Loren began. He launched into an opening statement that quieted the entire courtroom. His presentation was electrifying.

"We see it daily," Loren continued. "Some whites are using terrorism as they endeavor to preserve neighborhood segregation. The Ku Klux Klan burned crosses on the front lawns of colored Angelenos fighting restrictive covenants. Several Negro families have fled other white neighborhoods after enduring constant insults and threats. One family found themselves in jail. Another was bombed out of their home. It is this atmosphere of racial hostility that must be confronted."

The issue of race hung in the air like a pungent odor, yet Loren paced in front of the judge and the plaintiffs, unabated and unintimidated. He too was calm, authoritative, and without fear.

He continued, "It's time to end California's poisonous custom of ignoring the constitutional guarantees and validating restrictive property covenants. It is staggering to realize that ninety-five percent of this great, sprawling city is off-limits to Negroes," he said.

"Your Honor, these covenants are invalid on numerous technical grounds. But let's talk about the elephant in the room." He turned around and glared at the six sets of white eyes sitting across from me at the plaintiffs' table. "The plaintiffs are here today arguing that only persons whose blood is entirely of the white race may occupy a home in Sugar Hill."

One of the men, Wilbert Carey, who I'd heard was the lead plaintiff, turned red with rage. He glared right back at Loren, his nostrils flaring. But if he had hoped to intimidate Loren, he was sadly mistaken. Not only did Loren not flinch; he spoke directly to him. "Mr. Carey, your lovely wife has a hint of golden undertone," Loren said, motioning to his wife, who sat in the row behind the plaintiffs' table. "I imagine she gets that from the Cherokee side of her great-grandmother."

Mrs. Cryer gasped and Mr. Carey looked like he wanted to jump out of his seat and strangle Loren right in the middle of Superior courtroom 6.

Loren was unmoved as he spun toward another man, sitting next to Mrs. Carey. "And Mr. Winn. Census records show your grandfather is actually Li Nguyen . . . spelled N-G-U-Y-E-N. Is it possible that he was among the forty-six thousand immigrants from China in the 1800s?"

My heart dropped as more gasps filled the room. Of course I wanted to win, but Loren was treading in dangerous territory.

Loren turned back to the judge.

"Judge Clarke, the most populous state in the union became so because so many people from other states and other lands have moved here," he said. "Not only was Los Angeles founded by Mexican families, but twenty-six of the first forty-six settlers were of African and mixed-race ancestry. And then the city was further developed with Indian labor."

Mr. Cryer jumped up from his seat. "Objection, Your Honor. Mr. Miller's history lesson is completely unnecessary."

"Oh, but it is very necessary, Your Honor," Loren challenged.

Again, he turned to the plaintiffs. "Do tell, how are you gauging this pure blood that is a precursor to homeownership in your neighborhood? Do potential homeowners fill out a survey? Do you take their blood and test it in a lab?" He turned to the judge. "You don't gauge it because you can't. Most scientists agree that it is impossible to tell whether any given person's blood is pure and unmixed in this day and age."

"Somebody needs to hang that boy!" some man in the back of the courtroom shouted as he jumped up. Judge Clarke banged his gavel and demanded order as the deputies escorted the man out.

Loren continued, unfazed by the threat or the outburst.

"My clients were optimistic that the war's end would bring surcease. But that was not to be the case. The migrants kept on coming, the children kept on being born, and the population kept on growing. For most Negroes, the areas where they were allowed to live remained the same, causing overcrowding and lack of housing," Loren said.

For the next two hours, both sides presented their cases, calling people to support their side. There were so many instances when Mr. Cryer made me want to spring from my seat with the vitriol he was spewing. But I didn't want to give him any reason to say "See, I told you they were uncouth," so I restrained myself, especially in light of the three different outbursts the plaintiffs' side had displayed.

Finally, after both sides had presented their cases for the day, I expected the judge to ask for more testimony. Instead, he said, "I've heard enough. I would like to visit this neighborhood."

All of our eyes grew wide as an owl's. None of us had expected that.

"I shall do that this evening and we will reconvene at nine A.M. tomorrow. Court is adjourned." He pounded his gavel, stood, and headed out of the courtroom.

• • •

This had been a long and drawn-out night. I'd kept looking out my window all evening, hoping to catch a glimpse of Judge Clarke visiting the neighborhood. But I never saw him and assumed he never came.

Even still, I was optimistic this morning as I headed into court. As soon as Judge Clarke took the bench and called court to order, Loren stood.

"Your Honor, we call for the court to find in my clients' favor as restrictive covenants violate the Fourteenth Amendment, as well as the California state Constitution," Loren said. He hadn't told us he was planning to make such a bold request. Asking the judge to end the case with a ruling? Surely the judge would laugh at that or instantly admonish him.

Mr. Cryer stood in objection. "Your Honor, I understand some may feel the white owners slept on their rights," he said. "But these Negroes have just gotten beside themselves. The audacity of Mr. Miller to think that you would throw out this case."

Chatter filled the courtroom.

"Quiet in my courtroom!" Judge Clarke had to bang his gavel to restore order. He sat for a moment as he waited for the noise to settle down before saying, "Mr. Miller, your motion is granted. I will also follow up with a ruling."

My head whipped toward Loren, who took my hand under the table and squeezed it.

"Granted?" I mouthed.

"Rights of citizens shall not be abridged because of race, color, or previous condition of servitude," the judge said, speaking over the noise that had started trickling through the courtroom as people tried to determine whether they had heard correctly. "There is certainly no discrimination against the Negro race when it comes to calling upon its members to die on the battlefield in defense of this country. It is time that the members of the Negro race are accorded, without reservations and division, the full rights guaranteed under the Fourteenth Amendment of the federal constitution. It is so ruled."

He pounded the gavel again and the courtroom erupted. Residents yelped and cried and hugged everyone as the judge exited the bench. I could barely move.

"They're going to appeal," Loren said, touching my arm to pull me from my daze. He obviously hadn't expected such a quick response either, the way he was batting his eyes. "So this isn't over. But you'd better believe, I'm in the fight. We'll take this all the way to the Supreme Court if necessary."

Those were just the words I wanted to hear to snap me back to this victorious moment.

"We won?"

"We won. For now, celebrate," Loren said, as he gathered his things. He motioned with his head to my neighbors and friends who were gathered by the exit door.

I could not believe this. This was opening the door for the end of residential segregation throughout the United States. I threw my arms around Loren's neck and hugged him. "Thank you so much."

He hugged me back and then I raced over toward my neighbors. After more congratulatory hugs, we moved out into the foyer, where we were instantly surrounded by press.

"Miss McDaniel, care to make a statement on behalf of Sugar Hill?" a reporter said, thrusting a microphone into my face.

I looked over to Francis, who had taken a spot right next to me. She'd been the one to start this fight, but she smiled and motioned for me to go ahead and respond to the reporter.

I turned toward the extended microphone. "Words cannot express our appreciation. This victory is about more than simply winning the right to stay in Sugar Hill. It is about giving Negroes in Los Angeles access to a better life," I said.

They threw a few more questions out, which I answered with ease and determination.

"Why are you crying?" I asked Francis after the reporters left. She was standing with Louise and they both were puffy-eyed.

"Hattie, this is so wonderful," Louise said.

Added Francis, "This is bigger than just us in Sugar Hill. This opens those avenues for us to move beyond the one part of Los Angeles designated for Negroes. We can have our children in better schools. We can find jobs in the area. Housing opens the door and we owe that to you." She hugged me.

I relished her embrace. This was the feeling I wanted to have, making a difference in the lives of my people.

I released an elated sigh, then turned to leave, just as a man in a brown tweed jacket approached me.

"Hattie McDaniel?" he said.

He looked like a reporter, and I really didn't feel like doing any more interviews, but I knew this ruling was momentous. So I said, "Yes?"

He handed me an envelope. "This is for you. Have a nice day."

Then he scurried away before I could ask any questions.

"What's that?" Louise asked as I began opening the large manila envelope.

My eyes scanned the paper as any elation I had moments ago been feeling escaped me.

I looked up at Louise in shock. "Divorce papers. James is filing for divorce."

CHAPTER 35

January 1946

I thought losing a husband to death was bad. It held nothing on losing a husband to divorce. Death had a finality to it. There's nothing you could've done to stop it. With divorce, you wondered, analyzed, and scrutinized all the ways things could've been different.

I brushed down my plaid blazer and dark skirt and stood as Judge Goodwin Knight entered the courtroom. James had arrived at the Los Angeles County courthouse before I did. He was dressed impeccably in a gray double-breasted suit. His attorney looked just as clean in a darker gray pin-striped suit. My attorney, Reginald Murray, had assured me this should be an easy process.

Judge Knight motioned for us to be seated.

"In the matter of *Hattie McDaniel v. James Lloyd Crawford*, let the divorce proceedings begin." He called me to the stand, then swore me in before saying, "Miss McDaniel, I understand you'd like to make a statement."

I couldn't believe that we had come to this. I mourned the fact that not only was I losing a husband but I was losing a friend.

"Your Honor, I ask that you grant me a divorce on the grounds that our marriage is irretrievably broken," I began, dabbing my eyes with my handkerchief. I inhaled, then glanced at my attorney. He nodded encouragingly. "For the longest, I believed that my marriage was dying because of the loss of our anticipated child. But if I'm being honest, the reality is that we were on life support long before that."

I finally looked over at James, expecting to see an angry expression. Instead, he looked sad, as if this was the last place he wanted to be.

"Miss McDaniel," Judge Knight said after I stopped talking.

"I'm sorry," I said, turning back to face him. I swallowed the air that felt like it was suffocating me. "It pains me to say that my husband is jealous of my success. As a struggling and modest Realtor, he simply could not handle the enormity of my career," I added.

James loudly scoffed and the judge shot him an admonishing look.

I continued, "Mr. Crawford's speculations on the real estate market had fallen on hard times, despite the housing boom of the immediate postwar period. His vast holdings of property in the West were as imaginative as real." I looked at my husband, preparing to unveil the news that he didn't yet know I knew. "For our wedding, he gifted me 160 acres of Montana farmland. I have since discovered that was bogus. He does not own any farmland in Montana or anywhere else."

"Now, that's a lie," James barked. The anger I didn't see just moments ago was on full display now. I should have been angry too. My attorney had been thorough in his discovery, and when he'd brought that news to me, I'd felt like such a fool.

"Mr. Lewis, will you please advise your client of the protocol in my courtroom and explain to him that I do not tolerate outbursts," Judge Knight said.

James slunk back in his seat, muttering under his breath.

"Mr. Crawford wanted me to bankroll some new real estate ventures and then travel with him to their various locations. Our problem is he constantly lived in my shadow. Add to that our lack of common interests and it led to a drifting apart," I said.

"So, y'all just gonna let her sit up in here and lie?" James exclaimed. "I was her manager. She's acting like I never contributed nothing!"

"Mr. Crawford, this is my last time warning you," Judge Knight said.

I ignored his outburst. Nothing I said was untrue. I continued,

"He never showed he could do any kind of business. He thought because he married me, he shouldn't have to work," I told the judge. "My marriage has been filled with unhappiness. Mr. Crawford has contributed little to the household income and refuses to find steady work. When he did, he took a job purposefully embarrassing to me." Since the courtroom was open to spectators, and about fifty of them had filled the seats, I didn't go into detail. I had prevented the world from knowing that James had taken a job as a garbage man, which I 100 percent believed he did out of spite. "I'd had to agree to give him an allowance to get him to quit that job before he even started."

"Do you think he was jealous of your picture fame?" Judge Knight asked. He seemed genuine in his questioning, though I was sure he was just trying to do a thorough job.

"Yes." James had initiated the divorce, but now I thought I wanted it more than him. I just wanted this part of my life to be over.

"I guess fame doesn't bring happiness, does it?" the judge commented.

"No, sir. That's why I am pleading with you to grant my divorce so that I may resume my life and close this painful chapter," I softly said.

The judge scribbled on his notepad, then said, "You may return to your seat now."

I stood and returned to my seat, grateful that for the most part I had kept the tears at bay. I turned and looked at Ruby, who was sitting behind me in the courtroom. She nodded her head in support.

"Mr. Crawford, I take it you have a rebuttal to these allegations?" the judge asked.

James stood defiantly, as if he'd been waiting on this moment. "I sure do."

The judge motioned for him to take the stand. He was sworn in and began speaking before he even sat down.

"Your Honor, I too wish to obtain a divorce. In fact, Miss McDaniel only counter-filed for divorce so that the newspapers could report that she was the one who filed."

I scoffed from my seat (even though it was true).

James continued, "The world knows Hattie McDaniel, the actress. I know Hattie McDaniel, the woman who has no respect for the authority of marriage." He pulled a piece of paper out of his pocket and held it up. "You will see from this article from the Associated Negro Press of Chicago that my wife has taken up dalliances with a Lieutenant Booker of the armed forces. As well as rekindled her relationship with the politician Roscoe Conkling Simmons, whom she even had in our home at our wedding reception."

I was stunned. "That's a lie!" Lieutenant Booker was a friend and nothing more. And I hadn't even talked to Roscoe since the reception.

The judge banged his gavel. "Miss McDaniel, the 'no outburst' rule applies to you too."

"I'm sorry, Your Honor." To my attorney, I whispered, "I want you to sue that news agency and demand a retraction."

"One thing at a time," Mr. Murray said.

"Mr. Crawford and Miss McDaniel, I have reviewed both of your statements, and since there is no community property involved as Miss McDaniel purchased the South Harvard property in her name, I hereby grant your divorce without prejudice."

He banged his gavel again, and just like that, marriage number three was done.

Mr. Murray patted me on the back, grateful for another victory. I'd won, gotten what I wanted. So why in the world did I feel so bad?

Ruby came over and hugged me. "You okay?"

I nodded. "I suppose. It's done."

James didn't even look my way as he headed out of the courtroom. I tried desperately to fight back tears. When a reporter approached, the waterworks began drizzling out.

"Miss McDaniel, would you ever marry again?" the reporter asked.

I dabbed my eyes. "I'm loath to get married again. The only requirement is that next time, I want a man who amounts to something by hisself and won't just latch onto me."

Ruby draped her arm through mine and led me away as I wondered if that desire was even realistic. I was truly starting to believe I was destined to be alone forever.

CHAPTER 36

January 1946

The best way to get over one man was to get you another. At least that's what I thought as I watched the naked man traipse across my bedroom.

His firm body was a reflection of his youth—abs that were perfectly chiseled, calves that were solidly formed, and biceps that looked like they pumped iron daily. Yes, he was fourteen years my junior, but he was looking for a good time and so was I. So we were a perfect combination.

I hadn't taken Winston Richardson seriously when he'd first flirted with me at the Lighthouse nightclub. He was an aspiring actor who had just gotten out of the military. I was . . . old enough to be his aunt. So no matter how much he flirted, I wasn't interested. But he'd been persistent and hadn't stop chasing me until he ended up in my bed.

My doorbell rang as he exited the bathroom. "You better count yourself lucky. I was ready for round four. You stay here till I come back. Rest up so you'll be ready." I winked at him, grabbed my dress, and slipped it over my head. I checked myself in the large six-foot mirror leaning against my bedroom wall. My hair was a mess. The back was matted from sweating and I had not a curl left. I quickly grabbed the brush, ran it over my hair, and raced downstairs just as the doorbell rang again.

I opened my door to see Thomas Griffith, the president of the Los Angeles branch of the NAACP. Thomas was also a local attorney.

We'd met only in passing, so I couldn't for the life of me understand what he would be doing at my front door.

"Mr. Griffith, to what do I owe this pleasure?"

He tipped his hat. "Good evening, Miss Hattie. If you don't mind, I'd really like to have a word with you."

I looked over my shoulder upstairs toward the bedroom where my young guest was. He'd been over several times in the last few weeks and I felt confident that he knew not to come out.

"Of course," I said, motioning for Thomas to enter. "I was just about to prepare dinner. Perhaps we can talk as I commence cooking."

Thomas followed me inside as I made my way into the kitchen.

"Please, have a seat," I said, pointing to the kitchen table.

"I'm surprised a woman of your stature does not have her own personal chef," he said, removing his hat as he slid into a chair.

I began taking pots from the cabinet. "Oh, I use a chef for my parties and when I have an abundance of guests, but I love being in here cooking."

He removed his coat. "That's right. I did hear you were thinking of opening a fried chicken restaurant."

"Oh, that's some gossip Hedda Hopper started," I replied. "Though a restaurant may be in the cards for me in the distant future, I have no plans to do any cooking outside these walls.

"Now, what is it you'd like to talk to me about?" I asked as I sat down and began snapping the peas for the big dinner I was cooking for myself and Winston.

He inhaled like it gave him strength, then began, "I'm here on behalf of the NAACP . . ." He paused. "And more specifically, Walter White."

I stopped, a pea in my hand mid-snap. I cocked my head at him, then dropped the vegetable in my bowl and stood. "It's been a pleasure speaking with you, Mr. Griffith. I'll show you out." I took two steps toward the kitchen door.

He reached up and put his hand on my arm. "Miss Hattie, just hear me out. Please?"

My eyes slowly went to his hand and he removed it, holding his palms up in defense. "My apologies."

I had never had any issues with Mr. Griffith. For that reason, I reluctantly eased back down into my seat.

He reached into his jacket pocket and retrieved an ivory-colored envelope. "I wanted to personally deliver this to you."

I hesitated, then took the envelope from him, tore it open, and began reading. *You're invited to the Crystal Tea Room for a meeting with NAACP President Walter White on February 21, 1946. Enjoy food, the pleasure of drinks, and fellowship as we discuss the state of the Negro in Hollywood.*

I tossed the invitation back on the table. "I am not about to break bread with Walter White. That man has openly insulted my intelligence and disparaged my artistic accomplishments."

Mr. Griffith's shoulders sank in defeat as if he had convinced himself that this would be easy and had suddenly realized that it was not.

"I know you have your differences with Walter," Mr. Griffith continued. "But despite all the progress in Hollywood, nothing is changing. And the cinema bosses think they're off the hook. So they've reverted to prewar status quo. I think Walter is just trying to publicly unveil his plan and get back in their good graces."

"And he's using us to do it." I snapped a pea and tossed it into the bowl. "I thought that he said us Negro actors have nothing to add."

Mr. Griffith released a weary breath. "I'm trying to set up the meeting with the colored performers," he said. "I was thinking if we just scheduled it over a meal with a drink, we could work through our differences."

"Because whiskey can wash away all the pain that man has caused," I said, not bothering to hide my sarcasm. "No, thank you. You all have your jolly good time without me." I stood, grabbed my peas, and walked over to the sink to fill the bowl with water.

"Come on, Miss Hattie. Louise, Lillian, Clarence Muse, Carlton Moss, even your brother Sam will all be there. Almost everybody who is anybody in colored Hollywood will be there," Mr. Griffith said.

Sam was going? I hadn't talked to my brother in weeks, but he knew how I felt about Walter White so I couldn't believe he was giving that man the time of day. And Louise and Lillian too? After everything that man had done to derail our careers? Hmph!

"Well, *everybody* won't be there because Hattie McDaniel won't be there." I turned off the water and turned to face Mr. Griffith. "So you let Mr. White know what he can do with his invitation. That man is prejudiced against those with darker complexions."

Mr. Griffith opened his mouth to interject but I stepped toward him and kept talking. "There's none of us that wouldn't welcome better parts. Maybe when we move up the real world's occupational ladder, we can move up in film."

"But Miss Hattie, it's time for us to move forward. We must present a united front and your participation—"

I cut him off. "Mr. White has tried to imply that I would accept any role just to be working," I said. "You know, that's not true. I'm trying each day to lift the position of my people and to create a deeper respect from the other side for us. Mr. White's crusades only amount to declining employment for all Negro actors." I leaned in and wagged my finger in Mr. Griffith's face. "Did you hear that the role that MGM had for a Negro actor for their next film is going to a white man because of all this foolishness? And now Mr. White wants to come break bread with us? You're whistling Dixie, Mr. Griffith. All of this would've been prevented if your esteemed executive secretary had been working with us from the beginning. We could have effected change more quickly."

"Okay, I know you're hurt and bitter, but—"

"Mr. Griffith, if I never make another picture, I will be okay. God has endowed me with other talents that Mr. White and no other person knows about." I returned to the sink, finished with this conversation. My euphoria had been ruined with this foolishness. "So, if there's nothing further, you have a splendid day."

With no other protests, I heard his chair slowly scoot against the linoleum, then the slow drag of his footsteps as he headed out the front door.

I took a moment to compose myself before heading back upstairs.

"Where were we?" I said.

Winston was laid out across my bed. He had slipped some lounging pants on, but the way his chest glistened instantly wiped the past fifteen minutes from my memory.

He patted the bed. "We were taking a resting break and you were telling me about your new role."

I shook away the trance his body was luring me into and sat down on the edge of the bed. My attraction to Winston was beyond physical. He had a delightful blend of maturity and youthful enthusiasm that made me feel alive and cherished.

"Oh yeah. The movie is called *Family Honeymoon*. I play Phyllis, a grumpy, sourpuss cook."

He ran a gentle finger down my arm, caressing my skin until it tingled. "How do you feel about playing grumpy?"

"It's a mistake to portray persons as always cheerful, gay, and obsequious. Has it become a sin to laugh?" I said. "In real life, sometimes, the reverse is true. But who knows? I'm going to get criticized anyway, so what does it really matter?"

Winston was pensive for a moment, then said, "Can I ask you a question?"

I nodded as I removed my shoes and shifted my legs onto the bed.

"I heard a rumor that the studios are in turmoil not just over Negro images but because the House Un-American Activities Committee is saying a lot of high-profile Hollywood figures were communists."

I released an exasperated sigh. Just an allegation of leftist sympathies was enough to end a career. Movie producers were scared to death of communist claims. They had gotten rid of any cinematic content that might be interpreted by conservatives as left leaning. And it was nothing for people to link civil rights activism with communism.

Lena was among those high-profile celebrities Winston had heard about. She'd affiliated herself with Paul Robeson, who everybody knew had communist ties, and it was starting to affect her career as producers were shying away from casting her.

"I . . . I even heard your name mentioned." Winston's words were measured, as if he wasn't sure how I would react.

"Come on, now, Winston," I said, turning to face him. "You know I'm no communist. Those rumors are starting because I'm an active SAG member and such union involvement provides the anticommunist forces with supposed evidence that we're all communists."

His shoulders dropped in relief. "Whew. I mean, I knew, but . . ."

"No worries." I patted his cheek. "However, if that rumor is floating around, I need to handle it. I can't afford to be targeted in the anticommunist sweep of Tinseltown."

"I'm sure you'll figure it out," he said, his angst over the communist claims now gone. "But in the meantime, break time is over." He pulled me back on the bed while I giggled like a schoolgirl.

• • •

As soon as Winston left the next morning, I called Mr. Meiklejohn and shared my communism concerns and the rumors Winston had told me about. He suggested that I appear in a photo opportunity with the white politician Jack Tenney, a state senator who everyone called a communist hunter because he was on a one-man crusade to expose communists in Hollywood.

Mr. Meiklejohn thought if I could show people Jack Tenney liked me, it would end any speculation about me having communist ties. I also worked with Ginger Rogers's mother, Lela, to organize the

Motion Picture Alliance for the Preservation of American Ideals. Both Lela's organization and Mr. Tenney's Senate committee on Un-American Activities had come under fire because a simple accusation from them could ruin a career and blacklist someone from ever working again. Many people felt they were unjust and unfair in their attacks. I felt some kind of way about aligning with them simply because they were vicious in their attacks. But Mr. Meiklejohn convinced me that it was necessary to shut down all talks against me. Lela was so pleased with my work that she assured a newspaper reporter that I was "a good American."

But not everyone was pleased with my support. Charlotta Bass wrote a scathing editorial in the *California Eagle* demanding I repudiate my association with reactionary politicians like Jack Tenney. I didn't, and now it felt like I'd made an even bigger enemy of the colored press.

Now as I sat reading a critical article about how I was aligning with the very people who were ruining the lives of entertainers like Lena and Paul, all I could think was—if it wasn't one thing, it was another.

CHAPTER 37

February 1946

Death didn't wait for me to get my life in order. My sister was gone, and the hole inside my heart had widened.

Etta had been sick but I'd been wrapped up in my drama with James and that communist mess, and I hadn't made the time to go see her. We'd buried her three days ago and I'd been once again consumed with my grief.

I'd wanted to throw a party—a pity party—only my friends refused to attend.

Louise, Lillian, and Ruby had taken turns coming to comfort me, but no one would stick around long enough to feed into my wallowing.

"We're not letting depression engulf you," Ruby told me as she flung open the curtains in my bedroom, allowing the sun to tumble in like it had been waiting on an invitation. "Yes, mourn Etta. Mourn your divorce, but find whatever bright spot you need to in life that will give you strength."

When I flung the bedspread over my head, she said, "Call your little beau hunk over here."

My eyes widened as I poked my head out. I'd been discreet so I had no idea how she knew about Winston. She saw my expression and answered my question.

"It's my job to know everything," she said with a smile.

It took a few weeks but I slowly began breaking through the cloud of grief.

"Just keep moving." Ruby's words catapulted me out of bed most days.

Today, I decided that maybe cleaning would help rid my mind of the platter of negative thoughts my brain served me every day. I grabbed a rag and bottle of vinegar to begin wiping down my counters. I spotted Walter White's invitation to the dinner at the Crystal Tea Room. I had forgotten that was today. I tossed the invitation in the trash. I had a whole other set of problems and did not have the wherewithal to focus on the unfixable situation with Walter White.

There had been no shortage of people trying to get me to "open my mind" to dining with Mr. White. And I told everyone the same thing—you're wasting your time, especially since the man was back at it, boycotting my latest film, *Song of the South*.

Almost immediately after the film opened last week, critics said it was a "devastating animalization of Negro images that only perpetuated racism's most harmful and disparaging elements." That was a direct quote that I'd committed to memory from one of the Negro papers.

Pickets went up protesting the movie in Manhattan and other parts of the nation. Several colored theaters refused to screen the film, and some said my role was particularly objectionable. I received a barrage of letters protesting my appearance in the film. And that was just this week, all while I was trying to bury my sister.

I decided to take Ruby's advice and summon Winston, who, in his defense, had been trying to spend time with me for weeks.

• • •

My night with Winston had dulled the pain I'd been feeling and had been a welcome distraction. Now, as the morning sun made its appearance in my bedroom, I left him sleeping while I went downstairs to make a cup of coffee.

I'd only been downstairs about twenty minutes when he trudged down fully dressed in army fatigues and looking spry with energy.

"Good morning, beautiful."

"Good morning. You were sleeping soundly and I didn't want to wake you," I said, smiling as he came over and started massaging my neck.

"After that good loving, was there another alternative? I'm so glad you called me. I was missing you." He kissed my neck, then took a seat across from me. "But for real. What's wrong?"

I sighed, then said, "What's right?"

He picked up an apple that sat in a bowl in the center of my table and took a bite. "Talk to me. I know you're sad about your sister, but it seems like more than that."

"Naturally, I'm devastated by the loss of Etta, but you're right. There is so much weighing on me."

"Call me Dr. Winston." He crossed his arms and got serious like he was a bona fide therapist.

My shoulders drooped. It probably would be better for me to talk about it rather than holding it all in.

"You know that movie I did, the Walt Disney production *Song of the South*?"

A nostalgic smile spread across his face.

"Yeah, remember I told you my dad used to read those Uncle Remus folktales to me when I was little?" he said.

"At first I'd been excited about the role because these tales have been told for generations within the Negro community. But when Disney got ahold of the stories, they made them into another extension of racist ideology and I knew from the first day of filming it was going to be an issue."

"Did you say anything?" he asked.

"I wanted to, but it's one thing you'll learn in this business, Winston, if you rock the boat you will get tossed in the water." I exhaled heavily as guilt filled me. "I had hoped that I could bring change from the inside. An authenticity that would make people not hate the people we used to be. I am sorry to say I failed miserably."

My doorbell rang, interrupting our discussion.

"Dang, you're just a regular Grand Central Station here," Winston teased. "I'll go out the back."

I took in his appearance as he stood and placed his patrol hat on his head.

"You know what? It's been three months. We're grown, enough with the sneaking in and out," I said, standing and heading into the living room. "You can go out the front."

He followed me. "What! Does that mean we're official?" he joked.

I kissed him on the cheek without answering his question. The doorbell chimed again. Winston stopped my hand just before I opened the door, leaned in, and planted a wet kiss that made my knees weak. "Official or not, I think you're the greatest, Hattie McDaniel. See you later," he said. "Don't wait too long to call me next time."

I opened the door to reveal Louise and Lillian on the porch. Winston smiled and tipped his hat.

"Good day, ladies," he said as he stepped past them and bounced down the stairs.

Both Louise and Lillian, mouths agape, turned to watch him walk away.

"Y'all just gonna stand on my porch like some clucking ducks or are you coming inside?" I asked.

"Holy smokes . . . you wanna tell us what that's about?" Lillian asked, cocking her head in feigned shock.

"I don't," I said, grinning as I turned and walked back inside.

"You know you're not right?" Louise said as they followed me inside, closing the door behind them.

"Hush and mind your business." I laughed, then turned serious as I added, "How was the meeting?"

"You were right not to attend. It was awful," Lillian said, removing her jacket.

"Hmmph," I replied, taking a seat in my leather chair in the sitting room.

Lillian said, "I would ask how you're doing, but . . ."

"Ha . . . I'm okay. Winston does help dull the pain. . . ."

"The way your eyes just lit up, I'd say he sure does." Lillian chuckled before turning to Louise. "And to think when we left her, she was going into a decline."

"Well, that young whippersnapper looked like he could pull anyone out of a depression."

"I'm sure you all didn't come by to talk about my beau," I said. "What happened at the luncheon?"

Louise set her purse on the sofa, then sat down. "Do you know Walter White revealed plans to open a Hollywood office solely dedicated to improving colored cinematic representation. By the time he finished outlining his plan, the room erupted in protest."

Lillian made her way over to the bar and poured herself a glass of brandy.

"Clarence Muse was livid as a hornet, saying we didn't need another branch in the region since we had the NAACP Los Angeles office. You know how hard he works with that." She sipped the hooch, closing her eyes and savoring it like it was instant medication.

"Ummmph," I said, suppressing the "I told you sos" screaming to be released.

Louise continued, "I stood up and told Mr. White how we felt about his continued circumvention of Negro performers. And I brought up the letters he had those colored GIs in the Pacific send to you."

"Well, I'm glad you came to my defense," I said.

"It didn't matter," Lillian replied. "Walter denied all responsibility, but I tell you, Louise was on a roll. She got up under his skin. Even brought up what you said about him being prejudiced against darker-skinned Negroes."

"Good," I replied.

"Poor Lena, though," Lillian said. "They lit into her, called her an Eastern upstart and a tool of the NAACP."

"Shoot, forget that 'poor Lena' stuff. Lena got some Hattie in her." Louise chuckled. "She held her own and defended her career. She did refute the charges that Walter was prejudiced, but she said, however it was that she got on the Hollywood scene, it was her talent that was keeping her there. Still, her remarks did little to quell the crowds. Though it's all just a shame. We're battling each other when our real foe is the white studio system."

I tsked. "So nothing came of this meeting?" I asked, rolling my eyes. "Surprise, surprise."

"We were there for three hours and it was nothing but berating of Walter White and going back and forth. We left there more incensed than ever," Louise said, reaching for Lillian's glass.

"No, ma'am, get your own." Lillian moved the glass out of reach. "Louise called the NAACP a new type of streamlined gangsterism," Lillian continued. "Fortunately, I was in a non-belligerent mood and I laughed at their cracks."

"Walter had the audacity to call us selfish," Louise said, then released a defeated sigh. "But I think he's gonna go ahead and build the Hollywood bureau."

"Well, just like he continues to fight, we gotta continue to fight as well," I said.

Louise's tone turned serious. "Ain't you tired of fighting, Hattie?" she asked. "Everything and everybody? When all we want to do is make a living and live in peace." I could see the weariness in her face.

"I am, but I can't stop fighting till the day I die," I told her. "I know I have my days, but I didn't come this far to give up now."

"Well, I've had enough of this stressful talk," Lillian proclaimed as she leaned back in her seat. "I want to hear all about Mr. Stars and Stripes Forever."

"Lillian's right. Let me live vicariously through you. Do tell. It all."

All of us laughed as I decided to let my Winston secret out of the bag to my friends. We enjoyed the rest of the day talking about everything but Walter White and the NAACP.

• • •

Over the next couple of weeks, news of the meeting at the Crystal Tea Room was everywhere. The *Pittsburgh Courier* ran articles supporting Walter White and his plan to open a Hollywood bureau. They even ran a news story where they placed a significant amount of blame for lynching, disenfranchisement, unequal educational opportunities, and job discrimination on us. That was ludicrous. How Negro actors were responsible for the woes of the world was beyond me.

Mr. White had done an interview with the *Chicago Defender* where he continued his tirade against me. I'd just gotten my hands on a copy and was infuriated as I read. "'What is more important—jobs for a handful of Negroes playing so-called "Uncle Tom" roles or the welfare of Negroes as a whole? If a choice has to be made, the NAACP will fight for the welfare of all Negroes instead of a few colored stars, such as Hattie McDaniel.'"

Why this man insisted on badmouthing me was one of the world's greatest mysteries. I tossed the newspaper aside.

"How is he gonna blame us for racism?" I muttered to my dog Danny, who came and nuzzled up against my leg. "No matter what we do on the screen, he blames us for the racism in the world."

Danny just stared at me with his tongue hanging out. I reached over, rubbed him behind the ears, and stood.

I had to remember the words I told my friends, that the fight could never end until I took my last breath.

CHAPTER 38

October 1946

I was the first one on my feet applauding the magnificent performance I'd just witnessed here in the Biltmore Theatre in downtown Los Angeles. Winston, who was sitting next to me, seemed bored. I chalked it up to his youth. He didn't understand the magnitude of what we had just seen. *Anna Lucasta* was a Negro-cast drama in a different kind of theater. And the star, a young woman named Ruby Dee, was a different kind of actress.

The play told the story of a young prostitute in conflict with her family and herself. It took the colored experience from a segregated existence in Harlem, and it had come to the Biltmore. I'd heard that originally, playwright Philip Yordan had written the romantic story to be about Polish Americans but decided to make the cast colored. That was the type of progress I was ecstatic about seeing.

I knew the actors were from an ambitious young theater group called the American Negro Theatre and I couldn't wait to meet them. When the show wrapped and the cast had received a double standing ovation, I turned to Winston. "Do you see how the characters didn't have to be labeled?" I said, my enthusiasm brimming over.

"Ummm, I guess." He shrugged. He'd been disinterested from the first scene. As an aspiring actor, I thought for sure he would appreciate the brilliance of this performance.

I ignored his lack of excitement as I continued talking. "I mean, I know Anna was a prostitute, but she was also sort of a heroine. It was just magnificent."

Winston stared at me, blinking, before he said, "You think the concession stand is still open?"

I rolled my eyes and looked over to the other side of the theater where Louise had been sitting with her date. She'd share my excitement. She was already out of her seat and heading with others up to the stage.

The excitement of the all-Negro-cast drama was vivacious. When the curtains went down, actor Charlie Chaplin and some other local performers had already made their way up onstage. Everybody was embracing and raving about the play.

"Can we go?" Winston said as I tried to navigate the folks crowding the stage. "I just heard someone say the concession stand is closed and I'm hungry."

I took a deep breath and turned to him. "You can go on," I said. "I want to meet this young actress."

Winston seemed grateful for the reprieve and kissed me on the cheek and said, "I'll catch up with you later," before darting off. I didn't even bother asking how he was getting home since I'd driven to the theater. My attention was focused on Charlie, who was vigorously applauding Ruby Dee, as well as a man next to her that I remembered them calling Ossie at the curtain call.

I finally made my way onto the stage, taking a spot next to Louise.

"I'm not kidding," Charlie was saying just as I walked up. "This is something that Hollywood would want to do—we need to get this made into a picture!"

His enthusiasm lifted everybody. I'm sure that none of these actors had come to California looking to get into movies, but if Charlie Chaplin suggested it, the likelihood of it happening was strong.

"Thanks for the information," Charlie said, patting a card in his hand. "You will definitely be hearing from me!"

I smiled as I watched him dance away.

"Oh my God," Ruby Dee said when she spotted me. "Hattie McDaniel!" She squealed as she raced over and hugged me like we were old friends.

"So nice to make your acquaintance," I said.

She released her embrace and struggled to compose herself. "I'm sorry. It's just that you're one of my favorite actors," she said. This petite young woman, who couldn't have been any more than twenty-three years old, was even more beautiful up close. She wasn't light enough to pass, but she had the smoothest fair skin I'd ever seen. With big bright eyes and an innocent smile, she was going to have a long career in show business.

"Well, from that show you just put on, I can tell I'll be saying the same thing about you one day," I replied, my smile genuine.

She looked like she was going to pass out from excitement. I squeezed her hand. "You really did put on a spectacular performance." I looked around at the other cast members who had started to gather when she squealed my name. "You all did."

"Thank you so much," Ruby Dee said.

The young man stepped next to her and extended his hand. "Ossie Davis. And you have no idea how much it means to hear you say that." His grin was wide as he shook my hand like he was trying to put out a fire.

"Well, it's the truth," I said, pulling my hand back before he broke it. "I'm sure you all are exhausted. Where are you staying?"

Ossie gave a one-shoulder shrug. "You know how this goes. The theater didn't extend hotel accommodations to anyone but Ruby Dee," he said, and I saw guilt instantly fill Ruby Dee's face. "The rest of us are staying here and there. Some are staying with people in the community," Ossie continued.

That was no surprise. Several of us local actors served as a floating hotel for entertainers who came through town.

"I'm staying in San Pedro, down near the railroad station," Ossie said. "There's lodging there for railroad sleeping-car porters and a few of us are staying there."

"Well, as long as you're comfortable." I turned to Ruby Dee. "Are you enjoying our city? Are they giving you the star treatment?"

She leaned in and whispered, "I've never had a wardrobe person dress me or prepare me." The way her eyes danced warmed my heart. "And to see people like you and Humphrey Bogart and Ben Johnson, Anthony Quinn, Charlie Chaplin . . . Oh, it's just a dream come true," she exclaimed.

I greeted some other cast members before saying, "So, where are you all going to celebrate, because I know you can't be calling it a night?" I asked.

"Unfortunately, we have to turn in because we have another show tomorrow, but we'll be ready to hit the town after that," Ossie said.

Louise stepped up before I could extend an invitation. "Well, you all go get some rest, have an amazing show, and tomorrow, come to my place after the show and we'll throw you a private cast party."

The reaction from the cast members was instantly joyous.

I looked up to see Hedda Hopper heading over toward us. I hadn't even noticed that she was here.

"Why, Hattie McDaniel, I thought that was you over here," she said, adjusting her white gloves as she sashayed up to me.

"Hello, Hedda. I'm a little surprised to see you here." As usual, she wore her signature hat, this one with black feathers protruding from the right side.

"Why? I've heard great things about this play and wanted to check it out. Plus, I heard you were going to be here and wanted to see if we could get that exclusive about your divorce from James Lloyd Crawford." She batted her big doe eyes as she pulled out her notepad.

"This is their night," I said, pointing to the cast. "So that's all I'll be talking about."

"Well, I'm going to hold you to that promise of an exclusive interview." She paused and turned to the staff. "Pardon my manners. I'm Hedda Hopper, columnist to the stars."

"Gossip columnist," Louise murmured.

Hedda ignored her and said, "I must say I enjoyed the show."

"Thank you, ma'am," Ruby Dee said.

"It's my understanding that the show was originally written for Polish Americans?"

"Yes, ma'am. But we think the story is universal," said Ossie.

"It was interesting to see a colored woman playing such a powerful main role, but I guess it was okay since she was portraying a prostitute," she said.

"What is that supposed to mean, Miss Hopper?" I snapped.

"Don't get testy, Hattie," Hedda said. "I'm just saying, it's not far-fetched to imagine a colored actress as a prostitute."

Hedda was another one who would swear she didn't have a racist bone in her body—despite that disparaging comment.

"You people think the public is more naive than it actually is," I said. "Arthur Treacher is indelibly stamped as a Hollywood butler," I continued, referring to a popular white actor. "But I'm sure no one would go to his home and expect him to meet them at the door with a napkin across his arm." I tapped Hedda's pad. "Write this down. Theatergoers, film watchers, et cetera, need to comprehend the distinction between farce and factual comedy. It's supposed to be unreal. That's exactly its appeal. I have never apologized for the roles that I play and this young, talented actress should never do so either."

Louise stepped up beside me and touched my arm, no doubt trying to reel me in before I went down this path. Too late. I couldn't appreciate Hedda trying to taint Ruby Dee's moment and I was going to let her know.

"Well, I'm just repeating what the NAACP says." Hedda was defensive, which I knew never ended well.

Even still, I said, "The NAACP is not God. I haven't worked but two times this year and they want to give me a hard time, so you'll have to excuse me for not giving a fig what the NAACP says."

"It seems that it's not white moviemakers standing in your way, but rather Negro leaders and journalists," Hedda said indignantly.

"It's both," I replied. "They won't be happy until I really do have to open a fried chicken restaurant to survive. And others won't be happy unless I stay in subservient roles."

"Hattie," Louise whispered, using her eyes to motion to the audience that was glued to our exchange.

I took a deep breath and turned to the cast. "Apologies for my outburst. You all put on a magnificent performance and are destined for great things." I scowled at Hedda, whom I'm sure was shocked because I was usually so amenable. "However, I warn you that with success comes much scrutiny. Swath yourself in armor because you're going to need it. I hope to see you all tomorrow."

Then I turned and exited before I dug yet another hole I'd have trouble climbing out of.

• • •

The moon illuminated the twelve sets of bright eyes on Louise's front doorstep.

"So glad you could make it," Louise said, stepping aside so they could enter her palatial home.

Ruby Dee walked inside Louise's house, her eyes wide in wonderment at the majestic foyer and sweeping staircase heading up to the upper level. Other cast members had similar reactions as they marveled at the plush velvet sofas and ornate armchairs.

"This is what life is like to live in a fine house and drive a fine car," Ruby Dee said in awe as she peered at Louise's Jacob Lawrence art collection on the wall.

I smiled as I watched Ruby Dee slowly and gently touch Louise's drapes, furniture, and grand piano. It was as if she wanted to commit everything to memory. It was moments like this that gave me joy. Colored people were just as human as anybody else. We survived so long because we had a determination to accomplish the things that we wanted. So to see these young actors appreciate that meant a lot.

"What is this neighborhood called again?" Ossie asked, peering out Louise's floor-to-ceiling window. "The houses here are mighty fine."

"Sugar Hill," our neighbor Bessie said, walking up and introducing herself. She motioned toward me. "And you're looking at the Queen of Sugar Hill."

"Stop it," I said, laughing as I shooed her away.

"Why do they call you the queen?" Ruby Dee asked.

"People call me that because I am very proud of our neighborhood. I live around the corner," I replied.

"And she's being modest. She saved our homes from restrictive covenants," Bessie said.

"Oooh, I heard of those," Ossie said.

"This whole neighborhood is a point of pride for visiting Negroes," Louise said. "We had a bunch of ladies come through this morning from Zeta Phi Beta Sorority. They're having a convention in town. Each and every one of the visitors to their national conference, who remained over for a vacation, were just dying to see Sugar Hill."

Though Louise was a member of Sigma Gamma Rho Sorority like me, we'd happily hosted a reception for the members of Zeta Phi Beta as they filled the neighborhood with blue and white. We'd done the same thing when the members of Alpha Kappa Alpha and Delta Sigma Theta sororities were in town last year. We relished being a source of pride for such successful and inspirational Negro women.

"Did you know those sorority ladies, or you just let strangers in your house?" Ruby Dee asked.

"Hattie never met a stranger," Bessie joked.

"No, I didn't know them personally," I said. "But they knew this was where famous motion picture figures, and business and professional families lived in fine mansions and they just wanted to see it up close and personal," I said.

"If I lived in a place like this, I'd show it off too," Ruby Dee said.

An outsider might think we were showing off, but that wasn't the case. We were sharing in our good fortune. "We really just want to inspire people," I said.

"Well, I'm inspired," Ruby Dee said, twirling around the room. "One day, I'm gonna be famous just like you ladies and buy me a house just like this."

"I have no doubt you will," I said before joining the rest of the cast for the party.

CHAPTER 39

January 1947

I loved my friends, but sometimes I wondered if I had enough room in my life for my drama and theirs. Dorothy was on my phone. She was up for a lead role in a movie called *Pinky*, a drama about a light-skinned colored woman who passes for white. The studio had nixed her love scene because they couldn't risk provoking a backlash with an interracial romance, so Dorothy was livid and had called me to vent.

I listened, advised, and after forty-five minutes decided that I couldn't focus on anyone else's issues but my own. Ruby had boxed up everything from my nursery years ago and changed the room into a comfortable guest bedroom. But this morning I had come across one of the stuffed animals I'd purchased for my baby and it had sent me spiraling back down to that painful time. I'd busied myself trying to pack for my upcoming tour but my heart wasn't in this extended conversation with Dorothy.

Luckily, she had to go, as the nurse she'd hired to care for Lynn needed something. I was in my room trying on different hats I'd just purchased when I heard Winston come up the stairs.

"Hello, Winston. How'd your audition go today?" I knew Winston had been trying hard to break into the business ever since he moved here from New Orleans. He'd served four years in the army, even fighting in World War II, and after being honorably discharged, he'd come to Hollywood with high hopes.

"No luck." He sat down on the foot of the bed and buried his head in his hands. Then after a few minutes, he took a deep breath and looked up at me as I tried on another hat. "So, um, I have some bad news. I may have to move away, go back to New Orleans."

I spun around, my hat clutched in my hand. "What do you mean, move away?" I enjoyed Winston's company. He made me feel alive. He was fun. And after all that I'd been through, I looked forward to what he brought to my life.

"They went up on my rent and I just can't afford it anymore, especially since I'm having such a hard time finding work." He moaned, exasperation all over his face. I'd never been to his place but I knew he had a one-bedroom flat that he struggled to pay for each month.

"Well . . ." I paused, common sense trying to capture the words before they poured out of my mouth. But lust won out and I said, "Why don't you just stay here?" I motioned around. "This place is big enough."

My friends and I were always helping out young actors who needed a place to stay. Usually, I sent them to Bessie or Louise since they'd both taken in boarders. But with Winston, I didn't want him anyplace else. I wanted him here.

Winston looked shocked at my offer. "Oh, I wasn't suggesting that, Hattie. I would never disrespect you like that."

That actually made me feel better about my offer. "Nonsense. You're not disrespecting me. If I didn't think it was a good idea, I wouldn't have suggested it." I resumed trying on hats.

Winston stood and paced my bedroom like he was heavily weighing my offer. "Are you sure?" he finally asked.

"Yes. You, um, you could stay in the guest bedroom. It's a twin bed, but it's comfortable."

He smiled devilishly and eased toward me. "If I get lost in this big ol' house and end up in your bedroom from time to time, will that be okay?"

I giggled. "Why don't you just try it and see?"

"Okay, I'll start now." He pushed me down on the bed and pounced on top of me while I laughed and pretended I didn't enjoy every minute of what he was doing.

The next few weeks with Winston were euphoric. I didn't think about Walter White, or the NAACP, or the fact that, though I still did appearances, I hadn't had a film in two years. I just relished in his attention. We made love while Billie Holiday blared in the background, played pinochle in the basement, and ate dinner under the stars among my hydrangea bushes in the backyard. He'd even cooked me breakfast for the past five days. I was on cloud nine and hadn't felt this alive since my time with Roscoe Conkling Simmons.

Winston had to leave today for another audition and I longed for him while he was gone. When he returned, I'd hoped we could enjoy a romantic lunch before I had to head out of town for my ten-day tour.

The instant he walked through the door, I could tell the audition hadn't gone well. His head was bowed and the light that usually danced in his eyes was gone.

"No luck?" I asked.

He shook his head. Defeat blanketed his face.

He sat down on the chaise in the corner of the bedroom and, with his voice full of apprehension, said, "You think you can, um, call one of those producers for me and tell them to put me in a movie?"

I was taken aback. In all our time together, Winston hadn't asked me for anything.

"Winston, none of us out here are working. We are all struggling. That's why I'm even going to do this tour." I was scheduled to go on tour with several performances across the Midwest. I tucked some undergarments into my suitcase. I didn't even know if Winston could act. So how could I get a producer to give him a role if I couldn't vouch for him?

Winston stood, came up behind me, and wrapped his arms around my voluminous hips. "Please, baby?" he said, snuggling my neck, sending electricity shooting through my body.

I released a heavy sigh. "All right. I'll see what I can do," I said, wiggling out of his grasp. "Now, would you stop and get on outta here? You're gonna make me miss my train."

His infectious smile had returned. "I'm gonna miss you, Hattie McDaniel," he said, blowing me a kiss.

"It's just ten days," I said.

"I'll be thinking about you every day," he said.

"And me, you," I replied, planting another kiss on him before scurrying around him to continue packing.

Fifteen minutes later, Winston walked me to the car and we enjoyed a long kiss. Normally, I would've been concerned about what the neighbors would say, but with Winston, I threw caution to the wind.

"Bye, beautiful. I'll see you in ten days," he said as the driver opened the car and I got in. A warm feeling washed over me as I realized I was leaving him in my home alone for ten days and I wasn't worried in the least bit.

I waved to Winston, my heart aching as I pulled away. Marriage was out of the question, but I was looking forward to where this thing with Winston Richardson would go.

• • •

Sometimes, I felt that if I didn't have bad luck, I'd have had no luck. After only six days on tour, the producer in Memphis canceled the show because of low ticket sales and I found myself heading back to LA. I was sad because I really needed the money we were going to make on this tour. But I was excited to see Winston. We'd talked every other night. I wanted to call and tell him I was on the way home but I'd had to hurry to catch the last train out of Memphis.

By the time I arrived back to Sugar Hill, I was dog tired. I made my way inside the house, putting my purse on the counter when I entered. I was just about to call out for Winston when a sight on my kitchen table made me pause. It was a woman's clutch purse. I walked over, picked up the purse, examined it, and then opened it. I pulled out an identification card. Pamela Caruthers. Maybe Ruby had found the purse somewhere.

I was about to set it back down on the table when I heard it—a squeaking noise coming from upstairs. I set the purse down and eased to the edge of the stairs. The squeaking was going faster and faster. My brow furrowed as I followed the noise up the stairs and to my bedroom. It sounded like someone was jumping up and down on my bed.

I opened my door and almost passed out. Winston was in my bed on top of some white woman, both of them as naked as the day they entered this world. The sheets on my king-sized bed were hanging off as if they'd been in an intense lovemaking session for hours.

"What the hell are you doing?" I screamed.

Winston instantly stopped, his head whipping toward the door where I stood. He scrambled off her and to the side of the bed, pulling the bedspread to cover himself and leaving her exposed.

"Hattie . . . it . . . it's not wh-what it seems," he stammered.

"'What it seems'?" I yelled, rage filling my body like a volcano. "It seems like you brought some tramp into my home. It seems like you're having sex in my bed!" I lunged toward him. He dove out of my reach.

The woman scurried from the bed and grabbed her clothes off the floor, but then she paused after she slipped her dress over her head. "Oh my God. Mammy! My mother is a big fan."

I stood trembling with rage. "Get. Outta. My. House!"

Fear blanketed her face as she reached for her shoes. "Your mother is acting so weird," she muttered to Winston as she slipped her shoes on.

"Mother!" I screamed to Winston, who was cowering in the corner. "You told her I was your mother?" I picked up a lamp and threw it at him.

Winston ducked as the expensive ceramic smashed into the wall. Pamela took off running out of the room.

"Hattie, come on, now, calm down," Winston said, scrambling and slipping his pants on. "You're overreacting," he said, stepping toward me to try and pull me into a hug.

"Don't tell me to calm down!" I shouted, pushing him off me. "You sorry piece of . . ." I swung in his direction, my arm connecting with his bare chest.

Before I knew it, he slapped me across the face, and instinctively, I slapped him right back. We tussled in my bedroom, knocking over photos on my nightstand, sending the other lamp tumbling. I couldn't tell if he was trying to stop my blows or deliver his own.

"Get out, get out . . . GET OUT!" I shouted, falling back into a corner to catch my breath. My pillbox hat was cocked on the side of my head and the lace around my collared dress was ripped.

"I ain't going nowhere," he said, getting a burst of cockiness I'd never seen. "You said I can stay here, so I'm staying."

I glared at him. It was my turn to be shocked. I'd left a doting, loving young man in my home and returned to this . . . this monster. After a minute, I calmly said, "Okay, fine."

I pulled myself up off the wall, then with measured steps, walked down the hall to the guestroom where he kept his belongings. I grabbed armfuls of clothes, walked over, and tossed them over the railing. The clothes landed with a thud by the front door.

"What are you doing with my stuff?" he said, following behind me.

I ignored him as I made three more trips until all his stuff was in the middle of my foyer. I stomped down the stairs and into my basement, snatched open drawers until I found what I was looking for. I grabbed the matches, looked on a shelf, and pulled out some kerosene. I headed back upstairs and straight over to the pile of clothes. I squirted the liquid on the pile. By that point, he came running toward me. I spun around and squirted the kerosene on him. I struck the match and his eyes lit up at the sight of the flame.

"You crazy . . ."

"Get. Out." I jabbed the lit match in his direction. "Now!" I screamed as I chased him out the front door.

Bessie was in her front yard next door, pruning her rosebushes. She saw the commotion and called out, "Hattie, is everything okay?"

"She's crazy," Winston yelled as he raced out of my front yard.

"Hattie!" Bessie yelled.

I ignored her as I chased Winston out of my front yard and through the iron gate. Then I watched as he took off running down the street. I turned and my rage—now quiet—guided me back inside.

"Hattie, you all right?" Bessie said, following me in.

I didn't respond as I stood over his pile of clothes in the foyer. They were standing there taunting me. I struck another match.

I was tired of everything and ready to burn it all to the ground.

I was about to toss the match when I heard Bessie's voice. "Hattie, no! Put it down, Hattie, please. Put it down."

She was standing in the doorway, poised and ready to jump in to save me or take off running. I didn't know which one. I don't know when the tears started but I felt them dripping down my cheeks as Bessie eased over and gently took the match from my hand. And then she held me as I collapsed to the floor in tears.

CHAPTER 40

September 1947

The heaviness filled me, weighing down my eyelids and causing me to drag across my kitchen floor. Even the sunlight peering through the small window over my sink couldn't break through the cloud that hung over me.

It took everything inside me to fight off the depression demon that was sneaking up on me again, whispering in my ear that I'd fought a good fight on earth and now it was time to go to the other side. That was my thought as I stood in the kitchen, the phone pressed to my ear, listening to my agent. He'd called just minutes ago and I don't even know why I had answered.

"Hattie, are you listening?" Mr. Meiklejohn asked.

"Yeah, yeah," I said, forcing my attention back to the phone call. He had immediately started rambling as soon as I picked up and I had no idea what he was even talking about.

"I asked, do you listen to *Beulah*?" he repeated.

"The radio show?" Even though I was answering him, I felt as though I was just going through the motions. I pulled my housecoat closed, silently willing him to get to the point.

"Yes."

I took a seat in the chair next to my phone stand. "I do. Why?" *Beulah* was actually one of the only things I listened to these days. The radio show was a hit comedy series about a live-in maid who expended most of her energy trying to extract a marriage proposal from her boyfriend, Bill. Bob Corley, a white voice actor who mimicked a Negro woman, played Beulah.

Another actor named Marlin Hurt had first played Beulah until he died and Bob took his place. While Marlin was great, Bob was not. My friends and I often talked about how ludicrous it was that they'd rather have a white man play a colored woman than give the job to a colored woman. Still, I loved the show because Beulah reminded me of myself, feisty and funny. Well, me before life had started stripping me of my joy.

"What do you think?" Mr. Meiklejohn asked.

I shook off my wandering thoughts. "Sorry, what do I think about what?"

"Procter and Gamble replacing Bob and giving you the part!" he exclaimed.

That made me sit up and give my full attention to the conversation.

"Say it ain't so," I said, finally giving him my undivided attention. If this was true, this was huge. No Negro woman had ever headlined her own radio show.

"Were you not listening?" he said. "They're the sponsors, and what they want, goes. And they want you to play Beulah."

"Are you for real?" I asked.

"I wouldn't call you playing around about this. It's very real." I could feel Mr. Meiklejohn's enthusiasm through the phone.

I stood and began pacing. It was as if someone had injected me with a burst of energy, which I desperately needed.

"They want me to play Beulah?" I asked. I think I needed to hear it again.

"Yes. They've gotten so many complaints about Bob. Then someone had the bright idea to get a Negro woman to play a Negro woman." He chuckled.

"Oh, my. I've been saying that forever."

Giddiness filled me as I started thinking about all the ways I could make Beulah my own.

I stopped pacing and sat back down so I could focus. Something—I don't even know what—made me decide to do what my friends had been telling me to do for years, make some demands.

"Okay, if I take this part," I finally said, "then it must be without that contrived and humiliating colored dialect they like." I expected some pushback, but when Mr. Meiklejohn didn't interrupt, I continued, "I also want my friend and assistant, Ruby Berkley Goodwin, to write some episodes, and another friend, Ruby Dandridge, to play my side-kick in the show."

"I'm sure they'll be amenable to that." Mr. Meiklejohn sounded relieved that I was on board. If only he knew. He had quite literally just saved my life.

We discussed some other details like pay and time off for shooting movies. Then finally he said, "So, can I tell them it's a go?"

"It's definitely a go," I said, smiling as I felt the depression fog lifting. I guess a return to what I loved was exactly what I needed.

• • •

I had been playing Beulah for less than a month, and it was already more popular than anything else on the radio, with the exception of *Amos 'n' Andy*. Not only had Procter & Gamble agreed to all my demands, but they'd also given me final say over scripts and allowed me to hire my own staff.

For the first time in my career, I had flexed some star muscle and it worked. If only I'd had this kind of power in all my films, I'd have been able to do so much for Negro actors. I immediately set out to overhaul the show and successfully created a new interpretation of Beulah.

I'd brought to the role entirely new commercial possibilities. I was more than just a voice and the company used me visually in commercial endorsements. I was doing soap ads in my housekeeper's uniform, hawking personalized greeting cards and dishwashing detergent, and wearing clothes as part of paid sponsorships.

Within six months, Procter & Gamble had boosted the show from one to five days a week for fifteen minutes, every Monday through Friday at four o'clock. We broadcast live from Hollywood's Sunset Playhouse. I was making fifteen hundred dollars each week during the broadcast season, which ran fall through spring, and took the summer off to pursue movie roles. It hardly had the prestige of cinematic work, and the demands of radio made it hard for me to accept other engagements. But I was making the steadiest salary I had ever earned and finally felt like something in my life was going favorably.

I transformed Beulah from a man-hungry, lightweight giggler into an intelligent and mature woman who knew what she wanted and was going to get it one way or another. I still had moments where I would play Beulah a little dumb, but not because she was ignorant—rather as clever setups that she used in witty exchanges with her white employers.

The one thing I had not yet been able to do was move Beulah from a loyal Negro servant to a white family, always fussing over the Hendersons' needs, cooking and cleaning for them, to her own woman. But in time, that was my goal. This was what I meant by affecting change from the inside. This was my seat at the table.

Dorothy was in the studio with us today and I couldn't help but notice the exasperated expression on her face as she watched her mother in her role as Oriole. We had just wrapped a scene where Oriole was dancing with a broom to practice in hopes that a man would ask her out on a date.

"Dorothy, you don't seem to be enjoying the show," I said to her during our break. Her lips were pressed together as she sat rigidly in a chair in the corner. She opened her mouth to speak, but then closed it as Ru's boisterous laugh filled the studio.

"Speak your piece," I said.

She glanced over at her mother again, disappointment filling her face. "I don't mean any disrespect, Miss Hattie, but I don't like that my mother's character is so silly and dimwitted."

I'd been used to that criticism regarding the roles we played, but it landed different coming from Dorothy. Hers was peppered with concern and that concerned me.

"Oriole, like Beulah, is a comedic character," I said.

"But does it have to be so overdramatic?" She looked over my shoulder toward her mother. "Is it really necessary that she use such a high-pitched, squealing voice?" Dorothy asked.

Dorothy had decided not to take any stereotypical roles early on in her acting career. Though she'd really only done uncredited roles, she was adamant about the roles she would take. She said those roles were "Hollywood's way of keeping us in slavery."

But it wasn't like her stance had made her life that much better. Yes, her looks had her more highly regarded. But at the end of the day, she was still a Negro woman in Hollywood struggling to be seen for her talents and not her appearance.

I sat in the chair across from her. "Don't judge your mother, Dottie. I'm gonna tell you like I told Lena, Fredi, and every other fair-skinned woman working in Hollywood. You have the luxury of turning down roles. Folks like me and your mama, this is it. If we don't do this, we do nothing."

"I have troubles too," Dorothy said. "If I were white, I would capture the world. I'm an actress . . . I can do most anything. But they always want me to play a passionate woman of easy virtue because I'm Negro. I'm not going to do any more roles like that if I can help it."

I leaned back. "Well, again, you have that option. We don't." I loved Dottie with all my heart, but as similar as our paths were, they were on different ends of the spectrum. She hated the sexuality that Hollywood bestowed upon her, but she didn't even realize that Mammy's sexuality had been removed at birth.

"Your mother loves what she does. But the world doesn't see us as any more than what we are," I continued. I'd come to realize that fact a long time ago. "Let me show you something. Hang on." I stood quickly and headed down the hall to my office, where I flung open a desk drawer and retrieved a folder. A few minutes later, I was back, sitting in front of Dorothy. I took a newspaper article out of the folder and slid it toward Dorothy.

"This is a newspaper article from when your mother performed in *Hit the Deck* at the Philharmonic."

"I remember that. Mama was spectacular in that performance."

"Yes, but it got very little coverage. And when it did, guess who they attributed the wonderful performance to?"

Her eyes scanned the article. They widened, I assumed when they got to the part that said, "'Dorothy Dandridge was amazing in this role.'"

"Why am I listed here when it was Mama in this role?"

"Because people like your mother and I are invisible to so many. The reporter liked the role. It was memorable. But to him, Ru was forgettable."

I pulled out some more newspaper clippings and slid them in front of her. "When these newspaper writers—including my own people—describe me, they say she"—I paused and read one of the clippings—"'has a round beaming face, great size, expressive eyes, and versatile talent.'" I pulled another clipping and read. "Or 'she has wide, grinning teeth and brilliantined hair. Her walk is jaunty, with arms a-swinging.'"

I gave a faint smile. "And those are people giving me praise." I tapped another article and read. "'Dorothy Dandridge is talented, modest, beautiful, svelte. The dainty little Miss is a real trouper.'" I looked at her. "Now, don't get me wrong, I want you to receive your accolades because you are, indeed, all of those things. But your mother and I understand how people see us and we try our best to just live in the confines of that vision, else we won't work at all."

A mist covered her eyes. "I guess I never looked at it like that, but it's not as easy for me either," Dorothy said. "I'm not fully accepted in either world, colored or white. I'm too light to satisfy Negroes, not light enough to secure the screen work, the roles, available to a white woman."

I nodded in understanding. "But just like we understand your dilemma"—I looked over at Ru, who was replaying her broom-dancing scene as other cast members looked on—"you have to understand ours," I said, turning back to Dorothy.

I didn't know if it was because she was living it in her own way, or because she'd really heard me, but the heavy cloud of pain seemed to lift from my young friend's eyes. And when a small smile crept up on her face as she watched her mother, I knew that she understood.

CHAPTER 41

May 1948

The rigorous radio and film schedule was taking its toll. I'd gotten on the scale yesterday and was down another seven pounds. The stress of maintaining *The Beulah Show* and caring for my home in Sugar Hill had left me with no appetite and little energy.

My energy level was around a negative ten. That's why it hadn't surprised me that I'd slept a solid six hours. I really wasn't rested, but Francis had shown up at my place and all but demanded that I come to a party at her house tonight celebrating another court ruling on restrictive covenants. I didn't feel like getting out, but apparently, the whole neighborhood was in celebration mode. Though our Sugar Hill lawsuit was languishing in the higher courts on appeal, news had spread today about Mr. Miller's victory in a Missouri case over racial covenants. He'd taken that case all the way to the Supreme Court (even argued before Justice Thurgood Marshall), and today the court ruled restrictive covenants were unenforceable—a huge victory in the civil rights movement.

Mr. Miller had called me right after the ruling. "This wouldn't have been possible without you, Hattie," he'd declared.

The news was all over the radio and front pages of colored and mainstream papers.

Francis had shown up at my place in tears because this ruling meant that Negro families throughout the entire nation could now live in their own homes, buy homes wherever they chose, or rent homes in any section of the city. Overnight, race-restrictive covenants became no more than worthless sheets of paper, unenforceable in any court in the land.

I had wanted to rejoice but I could barely muster the strength, I was so exhausted. Francis had gone door to door in the neighborhood, demanding we all gather for a celebratory dinner at her place.

She'd brought me soup and some liquid mixture and ordered that I lie down, and then be up and at her place by seven P.M.

Though I agreed, it had just been to get her to leave me alone. I hadn't really expected her medicinal concoction to work, but it had. And I was feeling well enough to head to Francis's right at seven.

Now, as I entered her home and saw the more than thirty people mixing and mingling, I was glad I'd come. Within minutes, I found myself feeling much better.

"Thank you so much, Francis," I said, when I saw her shortly after my arrival. "I can't believe how much better I feel. What was that you brought over?"

She flashed an "I told you so" grin. "Just a little recipe my grandmother used to mix up. She always said that it could cure whatever ailed you," Francis replied.

"Well, she needs to bottle that up and sell it," I said.

We shared a laugh, then I told her, "I love what you've done with the place." I pointed to her large bay windows. The living room window was flanked with floor-to-ceiling champagne satin curtains and rose-colored tiebacks. "And those drapes look like something out of a magazine."

"Thank you. I had my entire living room redone last month. My interior decorator is to die for." She looked around the area as if searching for someone. "Matter of fact, he's here. Larry," she called out to a strikingly handsome man in the corner talking with some of our other neighbors.

Normally, I didn't find fair-skinned men that attractive, especially ones that were younger than me, which I could look at Larry and tell he was. But this man had piercing eyes and a thin mustache that sat atop full lips. His wavy hair was slicked back and held firmly in place by glistening pomade. He had to be the most handsome man in the room. Larry looked at Francis and waved as she summoned him over.

His smile arrived before he did and I swear my insides tingled.

"Larry Williams, meet Hattie McDaniel," Francis said when he stopped in front of us.

"It is a pleasure to meet you, Miss McDaniel," he said, taking my hand and kissing the back of it.

"Hello," I replied, immediately captivated by his presence and impeccable charm.

"Larry is considered one of the foremost interior decorators of the Negro race," Francis said. "He's from Michigan, but he's always doing things for the acting community. I can't believe you haven't heard of him."

"I can't believe I haven't either," I said, then caught myself. I didn't want to come off as some desperate broad. "I mean, your work is simply amazing," I said, motioning around the living room. "I was just telling Francis how I loved everything she'd done here. And those drapes. Are they Victorian?"

The right side of his lips went up in a smile. "I love a woman who can immediately spot luxury."

Francis grinned like a Cheshire cat, as if she was proud of herself for making a love connection.

"Well, let me get back to my other guests. You two continue to talk . . ." She looked back and forth between the two of us. "About drapes. And enjoy yourselves."

She all but danced away.

"How do you know Francis?" Larry asked when she was gone.

"She's my neighbor."

"Oh, you live here in Sugar Hill?"

"Yes, over on South Harvard."

"This neighborhood is simply spectacular," Larry said. "The architecture of the homes is impressive. I heard W.E.B. Du Bois himself had marveled at these homes."

"Yes, during a visit to LA for an NAACP conference, Du Bois said that nowhere in the United States is the Negro so well and beautifully housed than in Sugar Hill," I proudly proclaimed.

We moved into the sitting room, which overlooked Francis's large backyard. Larry told me a bit of history about the area that I didn't know. He also talked about his past and how as a child, he astonished everyone with his skill in blending colors in paint and designs in garments, which he made on his mother's sewing machine. He was a college graduate and though I discovered he was thirteen years my junior, I was intrigued with his career. And impressed when he told me he had decorated some of the most beautiful homes in Hollywood and Beverly Hills.

I was also impressed with his knowledge of the neighborhood. Unlike James, who just enjoyed the beauty of living in an exclusive area, Larry appreciated the beauty of the craftsmanship and all that went into making the neighborhood what it was.

After about two hours of talking, I noticed we were some of the last guests in attendance. I wanted to continue talking to him, simply because I enjoyed his conversation.

"You know, I'm serious about loving the work that you've done for Francis. Would it be possible to hire you to redo my drapes?" I asked.

"Of course," he answered without hesitation. "I'd be honored."

I pulled a piece of paper out of my straw purse and scribbled my number.

"Please call me tomorrow so that we may begin," I said, handing him the paper.

He took it without looking at it. "You say you live nearby. I could come over and take a look and give you a quote now."

I paused, every vein in my body screaming "Yes, come now!" But I simply smiled and said, "No, Mr. Williams. It's late. Tomorrow will suffice."

He returned my smile as he tapped the piece of paper. "Tomorrow it is."

"I look forward to seeing you then," I said, standing.

He stood along with me. "Not as much as I."

I walked away wishing I had indeed invited him back to my place. But my heart could take no more aches. So my admiration for Mr. Larry Williams would have to be at a distance.

CHAPTER 42

May 1949

From drapes to dates. That's what the first visit to my home by Mr. Larry Williams had led to—him designing some drapes for my living room, then taking me on a date. And another one, then another. That had been our story for the past twelve months. Larry had become a good friend, and I enjoyed his company. We could talk for hours about everything, from politics to movies. He was open about his dreams and I lost myself in stories of his childhood.

I also liked that I had become the envy of the town. Larry had accompanied me to a number of events since we'd been dating. From red carpet premieres to concerts at the Hollywood Bowl to the Doll League gala, Larry had been on my arm, his infectious charm wooing everyone he encountered. His doting made women side-eye their own dates. And he was usually the best dressed man in the room, not to mention the most charming.

Today, he was joining me for Clark's wedding to the British model and actress Sylvia, Lady Ashley, who Clark had been dating for only three months.

This was Clark's fourth marriage and he swore it would be his last. I wasn't so sure because although I could tell that he cared for Sylvia deeply, it didn't appear to be on the same level as his love for Carole. Carole would forever hold his heart. I didn't expect Clark to be alone forever, but I did want him to find someone who could bring him as much joy as he'd experienced in his marriage to Carole.

Prior to Sylvia, he was dating an actress named Nancy Davis, who had turned down his marriage proposal. Nancy knew Clark would never change his philandering ways, no matter how many promises he made. She'd told him if he wouldn't stop being a ladies' man for Carole Lombard, he wouldn't stop for anyone. Personally, I thought Clark was rebounding with Sylvia because Hedda Hopper had announced in her column that Nancy had started dating Ronald Reagan, whom Clark considered his competition.

Just three months after proposing to Nancy, Clark was asking Sylvia to marry him.

Sylvia was an oil baron heiress and I think my friend just wanted to marry someone like her to dull his pain over losing Carole. But I was worried because Clark had little tolerance for superficial women and Sylvia was the most shallow woman he'd ever dated. Plus, she loved to spend and party, which I knew would be a recipe for disaster for Clark, who despite his image, was a penny-pinching homebody.

But I was 0–3 in the marriage department, so who was I to judge?

I turned my attention back to the wedding, which was at the Alisal Ranch. The Alisals were longtime friends of Clark's and their picturesque western deluxe ranch was the perfect backdrop for nuptials—no matter how contrived.

The ceremony had been beautiful, taking place on a gentle slope, overlooking rolling hills and verdant meadows. We'd watched the two of them exchange vows while we were seated on handcrafted wooden benches adorned with delicate floral arrangements.

Now, we'd moved inside for the reception, which was taking place in a living room that was twice the size of mine. The room was decorated with palms, white chrysanthemums, and evergreen boughs. Clark and Sylvia stood in front of the huge fireplace taking pictures.

"Hattie, I must say, that man of yours is looking mighty fine."

I turned to see Hedda Hopper, who had walked up behind me as I stood talking to my friends Tallulah Bankhead and Gene Tierney.

Larry was a few feet over talking with a man I'd never seen, which was strange because the way he was laughing, they definitely seemed familiar, which meant Larry should've introduced us. I hadn't met many of his friends and was always asking when I would get the opportunity.

Hedda's eyes did a slow scan up and down Larry's body, taking in his suit and his two-tone brogues. His hair was slicked back and he looked like he was ready to be in a movie—if only they allowed good-looking Negro men in movies.

"Do tell, where did you find him?" Hedda smacked her lips like she wanted to slap some syrup on Larry and sop him up.

"Maybe he found me," I said with a wink.

"Is it serious?" Hedda leaned in like she was ready for some exclusive gossip.

"If it becomes serious, I'll make sure and let you know," I said.

She stood erect as if those were just the words that she wanted to hear.

"First?"

I thought about our last exchange, at the *Anna Lucasta* play. In this business you didn't hold grudges with people that could make or break you with a stroke of the pen. That's why I said, "As always."

She wagged a finger at me. "You didn't give me an exclusive, even though you promised me one when your last marriage failed."

"That was a little too painful." My hand went to her arm reassuringly. "But I promise, when I'm ready to share the details, I'll call you first."

She nodded, satisfied. "Evening, ladies," she said, speaking to Tallulah and Gene. Both of them gave her cold "hellos." Hedda didn't seem to care as she smiled, then waltzed away.

"Hello, *mi amore*," Larry said, easing up behind me just as Tallulah was about to say something about Hedda. The smiles on my friends' faces were instant. "Do you ladies mind if I steal this beauty away?

She's been out of my sight for almost thirty minutes and I'm beside myself."

Tallulah and Gene smiled their approval.

"Well, aren't you the charmer," said Tallulah.

"I want a man who misses me even when I'm in the same room," Gene added.

I smiled as Larry took my hand. "Good-bye, ladies," I said as he led me away. I felt like a giddy schoolgirl whose crush had just chosen her.

Larry nuzzled my neck as we stood at the bar. "Ummm, you smell divine."

"Would you stop?" I said, not really wanting him to.

"Can't help myself. I just wanted to do this," he said, planting a kiss on my lips. "And"—he stepped back—"I was hoping you could introduce me to Fred Astaire." His eyes darted across the room to where Fred was dancing with Ginger Rogers. Since they'd broken up their dance duo and hadn't been seen together in almost ten years, they had a little audience.

"I heard Fred was tapped to host the Academy Awards next year and I'm trying to get the stage design contract," Larry continued. "Can you help make that happen?"

I instantly felt a cautionary rumbling inside my stomach. Was another man trying to use me? Was Larry like James and Winston, only interested in what he could get out of a relationship with me?

I shook away that thought and simply said, "I'll see what I can do."

As the night wore on, I could tell that Sylvia was in her element. She danced, sang, and greeted her guests. Clark, on the other hand, seemed mechanical, as if he was just going through some motions. Even when I'd introduced him to Larry, he'd been dry.

I made a mental note to have a conversation with Clark at another time. He and Sylvia were heading to Hawaii on a honeymoon tomorrow. But I wanted to find a way to help him focus on making this marriage work.

As Larry and I were heading to the car, a man and a woman wearing waitstaff uniforms approached me.

"Miss McDaniel, I don't mean to be outta line," the man began. Anytime that comment came, a person was about to get outta line.

Even still, I stopped and said, "Yes?"

He looked to the woman and she huffed her disgust at his hesitation. She took a step in front of him. "Do you not have any shame in the roles that you play?" she asked.

I stared at this duo standing in front of the Alisal Ranch, clad in white waitstaff uniforms, dirty from an evening of serving. I was exasperated that I once again had to explain my desire to work for a living, especially at such a grand event. But before I could respond, Larry stepped up.

"The audacity," he said. "You're at this function *working* as the help and you want to belittle Miss McDaniel for *playing* the help?"

The woman looked taken aback. The man finally spoke. "She . . . we . . . we didn't."

"She, we nothing," Larry continued, his disdain on full display. "You're disrespectful and out of line. I should have Mr. Gable fire you on the spot and make sure you never work in this town again." The worker looked horrified as Larry took a step toward him. "Please don't ever approach my lady again."

With that, Larry took my hand and led me away. It felt good to have someone else come to my defense for a change. I was getting tired of fighting and it warmed my heart that I finally had someone fight for me.

I pushed aside my apprehension from earlier when Larry had asked about Fred Astaire. That was just nerves talking. Hedda was right. I'd lucked up with Larry Williams, and as he led me to the car, I decided I would stop fighting what felt so natural with the man I had grown to love.

CHAPTER 43

June 1949

I was twenty-two hours away from turning fifty-six and Larry had planned an exquisite evening. We dined at the Dunbar. We danced at Club Alabam. And finally, under the sunset, we sipped champagne and toasted my fifty-six years of life.

We had been sitting on a blanket on the ground, taking in the silence of the cool night air, when Larry said, "I read somewhere that you told a reporter that you were reluctant to get married again." He paused, then reached into his jacket pocket and pulled out a small, champagne-colored box. "I hope that this will change your mind."

He handed the box to me. I opened it to reveal a beautiful princess-cut diamond ring. The white-gold band was inset with flecks of glistening diamonds.

"What is this?" I asked, stunned at the sight of the ring.

"I want to marry you, Hattie McDaniel," Larry said. "I told Francis that the night we met, I wanted you to be my wife."

I was shocked. Neither of us had ever talked about getting married. I'd failed at it three times. I had no desire to do it again. I'd just assumed that he had no desire, though he'd never been married.

"Larry, I can't do another wedding," I told him, closing the box.

He gently opened it back up. "Let's not do a wedding. Let's just go tomorrow to Arizona and get married in front of the justice of the peace."

"Tomorrow?" I asked, incredulous. "Arizona?" A flash of my wedding to James filled my head.

"Yes. There's no waiting period. We can get the marriage license, then marry immediately."

The expression on his face told me he was serious and had given this a lot of thought. I sighed as I recalled my intentions to remain single forever. I guess that's why you never tell God what you're not going to do. Because looking at Larry, I knew that despite what I'd said, in this moment, all I wanted was to be Mrs. Hattie McDaniel Williams for the rest of my life. This time, maybe it would all work out for me. After all, I had a hit show, loads of money coming in, and a new man who wanted to spend his life making me happy. It had taken me years to get to this point. My time was now and I was ready to seize it.

"Yes," I said, throwing my arms around his neck. "Yes, Larry Williams, I will be your wife!"

• • •

Twenty-four hours after my proposal, I was married again.

Larry and I had driven to Yuma this morning, where we had a quick ceremony at the home of some friends I had in the area. When I'd called Mason Huston and his wife, Valarie, they'd enthusiastically offered their place for the ceremony. They'd even adorned their large patio with an array of flowers, which Larry had fawned and fussed over for an hour until they were positioned just right.

Mason and Valarie served as best man and matron of honor for the double ring ceremony. I wore a navy dress and a hat that had been personally designed for me for one of my personal appearances. Larry looked dapper in a double-breasted navy suit. There were a few photographers there and they'd already begun snapping photos.

Our ceremony was quick and painless and as the sun was sinking into the west, I said "I do" for what I hoped was the last time. We had an amazing dinner buffet on the patio afterward. And I walked out of the Hustons' house as happy as could be.

That happiness lasted about two hours.

Larry was a little perturbed that I had to return to work immediately, but I had to be back on the radio on Monday. He'd wanted to take some grand vacation/honeymoon touring the world. I thought he understood that I couldn't take time off, but he'd been so angry when I nixed any honeymoon plans. We were staying in a bed-and-breakfast and had just finished consummating our marriage when Larry sat up on the edge of the bed. His bare back was to me, but I could tell by the way his shoulders slumped, he was not happy.

"I'm sorry, honey," I said. Though we'd made love, it had been rough, like it was fueled by anger and not love. We'd slept together prior to marriage, and though it wasn't spectacular, it wasn't cold like this.

Larry took a deep sigh, then turned on the bed to face me.

"No, I'm the one who's sorry. I understand you have to get back to work. *Beulah* is the number one show in the country right now. You very well can't take time off to go traipse the world. Hopefully, we can get away and have some quality time at a later date," he said.

My smile was instant. I crawled over to wrap my arms around him. "Thank you, my love." Finally, a man who understood my work.

He leaned in and kissed me, then stood and pulled his lounging pants on. "Well, since we're talking about work. Now that I'm your husband, I was thinking that I should manage you," he said as he began pacing the room, his hand under his chin as if he was thinking.

I fell back against the headboard, confused at what he was saying to me. When I didn't reply, he continued, "I think we really need to capitalize on everything you have going on right now. And that's my specialty."

"Your specialty? You're an interior designer," I said.

"But I know about managing. I've given this a lot of thought." He went over to his bag and retrieved a leather notebook. He opened it and began reading some handwritten notes. "I would handle all your day-to-day scheduling. I mean, I'd have to have an assistant to do the actual grunt work, but I would be your gatekeeper. And I would renegotiate your contract so that you could get some time off to enjoy the fruits of your labor."

"Whoa." I held up my hands. "Ruby does a good job as my secretary and keeping my schedule."

"I'm sure she does, but as your husband, I know what best suits you," he replied.

I stared at him in disbelief. I wanted to ask him how he could know me best when he'd known me only just over a year.

But I didn't get a chance because he shocked me even more when he said, "I also think we should go open a joint checking account so I can make sure the financial affairs are in order."

It was my turn to sit up in the bed as that bubbling in my stomach that I'd felt at Clark's wedding returned.

"I'm not letting no man handle my bank account." The words poured out of my mouth before I realized it.

He spun and stared at me. "*No man*? I'm your husband."

"There's no need for you to have anything to do with my money. I manage just fine," I said defiantly.

"What?" he said, angrily tossing the notebook on the bed. He snatched his shirt off the chair and pulled it over his head. "Do you think I'm some kind of thief?"

"No." I took a deep breath as I scooted toward him on the edge of the bed and took his hand. "Let's just enjoy our time together before we head back to LA later today."

He jerked away and stomped toward the door. "I'm going for coffee. Or maybe I'll just go see where I can steal some coffee from!" He was gone before I could say another word.

What the heck just happened? I got an immediate sinking feeling in my stomach. Did I love my husband? Yes. But I wasn't a fool when it came to my money. I made a mental note that first thing Monday morning, I'd be calling my lawyer so I could protect myself and all that I had worked for. The thought that I needed protection from the man I'd said "I do" to less than twelve hours ago made me want to cry.

CHAPTER 44

June 1949

Regret had paid me a visit and set up permanent residence in my gut. My heart was pained at the fact that before we even left Yuma, Arizona, I didn't feel like my marriage with Larry Williams was going to last.

Three days after becoming Mrs. Williams, I knew it even more. And the way he was acting this morning as we sat in my attorney's office erased any sliver of doubt.

"So you want me to do what again?" Larry said, his eyes boring into my attorney, Marvin Manual, as we sat in front of his massive mahogany desk. Both men wore expensive tweed suits.

"Miss McDaniel—"

"*Mrs.* Mrs. Williams," Larry interrupted. "That's her name."

"Mrs. McDaniel-Williams," Marvin said slowly, "would like for you to sign away any claims to her assets."

Larry looked over at me. I'd been avoiding eye contact since we walked into Mr. Manual's office. I think Larry thought we were coming here to sign paperwork to make him my manager. When he'd brought it up again upon our return to Los Angeles, I told him we'd go see the attorney in the morning. I relished the fact that he was in a jovial mood because he was sure we were seeing the attorney to make him my manager, which was never going to happen. Love or no love, I wasn't a complete fool.

"Are you serious?" Larry asked.

I finally found my voice. "If you love me, this shouldn't matter. It's just a formality."

"If you love me, you wouldn't ask me to do this," he spat.

"She didn't ask," Mr. Manual interjected. This was why I loved my attorney. When I'd called him with this yesterday, I'd explained that Larry wasn't going to be happy about it. He said he would make it all his idea. "I suggested this because, as you know, Mrs. McDaniel . . . Williams is worth quite a bit and it is my duty to protect her interests," Mr. Manual continued.

"And as her husband, I worry about her best interest as well," he countered.

Mr. Manual began moving papers around as if searching for something.

"I've done some research. You claim to be this highly successful interior decorator, yet I haven't been able to confirm any major projects that you've done," Mr. Manual said.

Larry was appalled. I was too. I hadn't seen Mr. Manual pulling that rabbit out of the hat. An inquest into his professional business would anger Larry.

"What are you talking about?" Larry yelled. "I just opened a studio in Los Angeles's chic La Cienega district. And I have secured the Beverly Wilshire hotel as a client."

Mr. Manual pulled a piece of paper out of the stack and held it up as he read.

"A contract which you received just this morning after news of your nuptials to Miss McDaniel hit the front pages."

"Wow," Larry said, falling back in his chair.

"Sweetheart, this really isn't that big of a deal. It's just for . . . you know . . . my protection." I patted his hand.

He jerked his hand away from me. "Why would you even marry a man you need protection from?" Suddenly, his demeanor changed and he leaned up. "You know what? I don't need this. Give me your stupid paper," he said, thrusting his hand across the desk toward Mr. Manual.

If he was to be intimidated, Mr. Manual didn't seem fazed. He slid the document across the desk. Larry picked it up, scanned it, stabbed his signature onto the back page, then flung it onto the desk. Without saying a word, he stood and headed toward the door.

"Larry, wait," I said, standing and taking off after him.

"I'll get these filed with the court," Mr. Manual called out after me.

Outside, Larry spun to face me, grabbing me by the arms. "I can't believe you tried to blindside me like that!"

His aggression startled me. When I looked at his hands squeezing my arms, he released his grip and pushed me away.

"It's not like that at all," I finally said.

"Why did you bother to get married?" he asked.

"I don't understand what the big deal is. You say you love me and not my money," I said.

"Nobody wants your money," he spat. He stomped away, then turned back and thrust a finger in my direction. "I wanted you, Hattie. But obviously that wasn't good enough for you." He huffed in exasperation. "I'll take a taxi home."

"Home? We're supposed to be going to Welby's party," I said.

"Who?"

"Welby, from church." I attended the African Methodist Church and Welby was a deacon there. He was having a retirement party that we were scheduled to attend.

Larry scoffed. "First of all, I have better things to do than dine with your church folk. And secondly, what would make you think that I want to spend any time with you after that stunt you just pulled?"

I stood and watched my husband walk away. I shouldn't have been surprised that he bailed on Welby's party. Had I been going to one of my many celebrity friends' parties, Larry would have put aside his anger to accompany me. While we were dating, he would eagerly attend Hollywood premieres and concerts but didn't want to go to parties with less famous friends. He made my friends and family feel unwelcome, so my friends had stopped coming around. He never took me around his friends, so I'd become isolated.

I said a silent prayer for my marriage as I headed to my car to go to the party alone.

• • •

Things remained tense for the next two weeks between Larry and me. I was busy with *The Beulah Show* and he stayed busy with his project at the Beverly Wilshire. He'd barely talked to me until this morning, when I'd reminded him about the NAACP picnic and told him all the celebrities that would be there, including Lena Horne, whom he'd yet to meet.

"Great weather for the picnic," he said, peering out the kitchen window at the beaming sun and ignoring the fact that he had given me the silent treatment for two weeks.

For most of the day, it was as if nothing was wrong. Larry fixed lunch and enthusiastically talked about his Beverly Wilshire project. It felt good to have a stress-free, normal conversation for a change.

Later that afternoon, I dressed for the picnic in some casual knickerbockers and a silk blouse. Larry, who always took longer than me to get dressed, was still in the shower, so I went to work on scripts in my office.

Thirty minutes later, Larry appeared wearing a full, double-breasted suit.

My eyes started at the extra pomade in his hair and ended on his spit-shined oxfords. "Uh, it's a picnic. At a park. Outside," I said.

"And?"

I looked at my husband, debated whether to push this, and ultimately decided to just leave it alone.

"And nothing." I shook my head. "Let's go," I said, standing and grabbing my purse.

I was pleasantly surprised that we both had a nice time at the picnic. There had to be at least three hundred people there, dressed in the finest casual wear. Of course, Larry was overdressed, but it didn't seem to bother him.

We laughed with some of my friends who were spread out at benches throughout the park, watched a heated game of dominoes, then cheered young people on in a potato sack race.

When it was time for us to go, I told Larry, "Honey, hold on. I almost forgot something."

"Ralph, we had a spectacular time," I said, walking over to the cook who was positioned at the barbecue pit.

"Well, that's good," he said.

"I mean, you're an award-winning academic scholar. Who knew you were a master of the pit too?" I laughed. Ralph Bunche was a noted scholar who was up for a Nobel Peace Prize for mediation in Israel, so to see him here, relaxed in a casual tan button-down shirt instead of his usual business suit, was a refreshing sight.

"Thank you, Miss Hattie. I'm glad you enjoyed it. Though I love my students at Howard, I do relish coming home to LA and visiting with my old friends." He waved the long tongs. "And I can't tell you the last time I got to barbecue."

I chuckled and we made more small talk about the Spingarn award he'd just received from the NAACP and how he'd be the first Negro man to win the Nobel Peace Prize if he was actually selected as had been rumored.

"I'm trying to be a first like you," he said, and laughed.

I wanted to tell him how my "firsts" hadn't quite opened the doors that I expected, but I didn't want to tarnish an otherwise enjoyable afternoon.

"Well, it's been a pleasure catching up with you," I said when I noticed the time. "Did you save me the scraps?"

He motioned toward a plate of rib bones behind him. "I sure did. Let me get these boxed up for you."

"Thank you so much," I said. "The dogs are gonna eat good tonight." Ralph used the tongs and began scooping up bones that had been stripped of their meat.

I tapped my foot to the bebop tune Ralph was whistling, so I didn't notice Larry approach me. "What are you doing?" he asked.

I smiled as Ralph dumped another plate of bones into a bag. "I'm taking some bones home."

"You're taking scraps?" Larry asked, his mouth dropping open in horror.

"Yes. For the dogs."

Larry's face was aghast. "What in the hell?" he screamed, startling several people who were sitting nearby. "Here I am with a million-dollar decorating business and you are a radio star wanting to take scraps to dogs? Are you insane?"

I looked around at the people staring at us and was instantly humiliated.

"Can we not do this here?" I whispered, my eyes darting around the park.

Ralph handed me the bag of bones, his eyes firmly on Larry.

"You good, Miss Hattie?" he asked.

"I am," I said, taking the bag, my head lowered in shame. "Thanks a bunch." I pulled the bag close to me and hastily made my exit.

Larry continued ranting as he followed me, despite my efforts to play it cool. "And you did this in front of Ralph Bunche?" he asked incredulously.

"Ralph is among friends and he's enjoying himself." I didn't slow my stride.

"Who in their right mind asks for scraps at a professional event?" he yelled from behind me.

"Plenty of people," I replied, though I didn't stop walking. I just wanted to make it to the car. To get away from judgmental eyes, before I was even more humiliated than I already was.

Larry couldn't care less about who was watching. In fact, if I didn't know better, I'd think he was putting on a show. He stopped and motioned around wildly. "Who? Who would do that? You're the only person around with a doggy bag!" he shouted. "It's vulgar and embarrassing."

What was embarrassing was the way he was acting. I finally stopped and spun toward him. "Larry, you are overreacting," I calmly said.

"And you are pathetic!" he replied.

"Calm down," I said, moving closer to him and lowering my voice. "People are staring." We were on the outer perimeter of the park, but all eyes were still on us.

"Yes. Let them stare." In a dramatic fashion, Larry stretched his arms out and yelled, "Let the world see that Academy Award winner Hattie McDaniel is taking scraps from a picnic, like some common vagabond."

He looked at me in disgust. I was stunned silent, my chest heaving in shame and disbelief.

He shook his head and walked past me, his shoulder bumping me to the point he nearly knocked me over. "I'm leaving." And once again, my husband stormed away, leaving me wondering what in the world had just happened.

CHAPTER 45

October 1949

My life had become a joke. A miserable joke with no laugh track. Standing here in my own house, eavesdropping on people I thought were my friends, confirmed it.

I'd thought allowing Larry to host a party would help ease the tension in our marriage. Things had been awful in our relationship since the NAACP picnic. We operated in silos. Larry did his thing and I did mine. We didn't have dinner together. Didn't make love. Hadn't had a civil conversation. Oh, there had been a whole lot of arguing and fussing, but the love was lost and it had permanently moved out of 2203 South Harvard.

I had hoped this party and Larry having the opportunity to show off in front of everyone would help. And for the past week, it appeared that it had. He'd been happy in the week leading up to tonight's party. And now that the house was filled with nearly a hundred people—mostly my friends, since he had very few—Larry was in the best mood he'd been in since the day we exchanged vows.

Right now I was pressed up against the wall outside my kitchen. I had been going in there to get more ice for the ice bucket when I heard my name. Ethel and a group of her friends were standing by the sink talking about me.

"Did you see the way Hattie was fawning over him?" Ethel said. Ethel and I were friends, though we were more competitive than my friendship with Louise and Lillian. So it shocked me that she would be standing in my house badmouthing me.

"Girl, yes. It's actually quite sad," one of the women replied. I recognized her voice as one of the extras who frequented our movies.

"And after the way he treated her at the picnic . . . couldn't be me," another voice that I didn't recognize said.

"Between all the men she's had, one would think she wouldn't be so desperate," the extra said.

"Because she knows the truth. Those men don't want her—they just want her money," the unidentified woman said.

"You know, Larry was actually after me, but I would have nothing to do with him," Ethel interjected. "Can you believe he redid this entire house? All the linen in the bedrooms is labeled 'Mr. and Mrs.' The bathrooms are all decked out in bright pink." Ethel doubled over laughing. "You see, that's why I didn't want that man in my house. I'm glad she got him."

I swallowed the lump in my throat and turned and walked away. But then I started getting angry with myself. This was my house. I was a strong woman. But you'd never know it by the way I'd been reacting lately—to Larry, to these women badmouthing me in my own house, to life in general. What happened to my fight?

I knew the answer to that. I was tired. No, "tired" was an understatement. I was worn-out. Fighting all my life had taken its toll.

I walked back into the living room to see Larry talking to Ruby Dandridge. I wasn't going to let Ethel and those gossiping biddies ruin my day. I was going to join in the conversation with my husband and Ru and just try to make it through the evening. As I headed over to them, I noticed Ru's body language. Larry's back was to me and Ru was facing me. She seemed tense and her fists were in balls. Ru did that only when she was trying to control her temper. Whatever Larry was saying to her wasn't sitting well with her. Ru and I locked eyes, and she said something to Larry, then walked over to me.

"Ummm, what was that about?" I asked as Larry headed over to talk to someone else.

Ru looked uneasy, then took my arm and pulled me into the hallway.

"Hattie, you know I love you dearly," she said.

"I know that. You, Dorothy, and Vivian are like family to me," I replied.

"Well, as your family"—she inhaled a long, deep breath—"please don't think I'm stepping out of line, but . . ." She paused and looked over her shoulder toward Larry. "I do not like your husband."

I don't like him either, I wanted to say. Instead I just said, "What happened?" I braced myself for her to tell me that Larry had completely disrespected me by coming on to one of her daughters. Ru was open about her relationship with Geneva, so I didn't think Larry would've made a pass at her.

Ru said, "Your husband . . . He's trying to convince me and other staffers that you're all about yourself and that we need to watch our backs. Larry is one insidious piece of work." She balked. "He's really standing in your house, trying to tear down your work and stir up trouble among your *Beulah* castmates. What kind of husband does that?" Disgust blanketed her face.

I stared at Larry as he laughed with the man he was talking to at Clark's wedding, the man he'd yet to introduce me to.

I knew the answer to Ru's question two hours after I said "I do." A husband that needed to go.

• • •

I'd tossed and turned all night thinking about what Ru had said to me. I'd already had trouble sleeping for the past few weeks. My weight had been dropping because of the stress of being married to Larry. My first instinct had been to just go into the guest room that Larry had been staying in since our honeymoon and curse him out, but our last fight had ended with us physically tussling. He had snatched the neckline of a dress he deemed "too homely to be seen in public with him" and pushed me against the wall. I'd had just about enough of him at that point so I'd pounced on him like a tomcat and scratched his pretty little face all up.

But today I just didn't have it in me to fight another man. All I wanted now was to act like this marriage had never happened. These had been the worst four months of my life, and more than anything, I just wanted to wake up from this nightmare.

I decided to try and get my mind off Larry by diving into the mounds of fan mail I'd been getting since starting the radio show. I grabbed a letter opener and sat down at the table.

"What are you doing?" Larry said a few minutes later as he entered the dining room. He was dressed in his usual suit and I couldn't help but think that the only men who I knew wore suits all day, every day, were businessmen and con men.

I didn't reply as Larry walked over, picked up an envelope, read it, then tossed it back onto the table.

"Oh, excuse me, you're getting your head pumped up from all your adoring fans," he said, sneering. "Those good white folks love them some shucking and jiving Beulah."

I wanted to remind him that it was that shucking and jiving Beulah that was keeping him living high on the hog, in those fine suits he loved traipsing around town in. But I didn't have the energy.

He wasn't fazed by my lack of reply. He made his way into the kitchen, humming a Nat King Cole song. I heard the coffee percolator and silently prayed that he'd take his coffee and go sit on the porch or something.

No such luck as minutes later he was back in front of me in the dining room.

"Did you see this?" Larry asked, waving a copy of the *Kansas City Call*, an influential colored newspaper, in my face. He smiled as he sipped his coffee with one hand and flashed the paper with the other.

"Of course I saw it," I said. Why did he think it was sitting on the kitchen counter?

The newspaper had published a list of "Things that must go" and they'd prominently featured my name and photo. And of course, an interview with Walter White. I guessed he had moved from attacking me in film to attacking me in radio.

But more than that, what kind of husband took pleasure in his wife's misery? And the smirk on Larry's face told me he was definitely enjoying every minute of the scathing article.

He stood in front of me, reading the newspaper. "Wow, this is actually embarrassing," Larry said.

"I guess you're going to write another letter to the editor, defending Beulah and arguing how the characters you play reflect reality?" he said once he was done reading.

I sighed, set my letter opener down, and looked at my husband. "I should. But why bother continuing to sing this same song? It's not like anyone is listening."

"Oh, here comes the pity party," Larry said, his eyes rolling upward.

I fought back the tears that threatened to overtake me at Larry's cruelty. I couldn't get love from the public. I couldn't get love from movie producers. And I couldn't get love at home.

"So you're just going to stop talking?" Larry said when I didn't reply.

I hadn't even realized that I'd gone silent. But in that moment, I decided there was nothing more that I wanted to say to my husband.

I picked the letter opener back up and resumed opening the letters. It was a move that must've infuriated Larry because the next thing I knew, he took his hand and knocked all the letters to the floor.

"You hear me talking to you!" he exclaimed.

I stared at the scattered letters, then slowly moved my gaze back up to him.

"Does that make you feel like a man?" I asked.

"I need something to make me feel like a man because you don't," he spat.

Okay, it was obvious he was trying to pick a fight with me. Not today. Not ever again. I was done. I leaned down and started picking up the letters.

"I'm not arguing with you, Larry," I said, placing the letters back onto the table. "You stay angry and I don't have the energy to deal with it."

"Maybe if you learned how to be a wife, I wouldn't have cause to be angry," Larry continued. "You can cook and that's it. You don't know your place. You're awful in bed and you don't make me feel like a man."

I couldn't help it. I burst into laughter. I mean, I doubled over and cracked up laughing. I'm sure I looked like a cackling fool.

"What's so funny?" he asked.

"You." I sat up, caught my breath, then leaned back in my chair, losing my smile as months of sexual frustration boiled over. Larry and I hadn't been intimate since our honeymoon. And it wasn't because of me. He was always "too tired," "too angry," or "too busy" to show me any love. And after a few weeks, that became just fine with me.

"You wouldn't know what to do with a woman's parts if I drew you a map." My mind flashed back to the man he'd laughed and talked with all evening at his party. "Maybe if I had an Adam's apple, it would be more appealing to you," I added.

Larry slammed the coffee cup down on the table at my not-so-subtle innuendo. "How dare you? Half your friends are gays and lesbians. You think I don't know what's going on with you and that Tallulah?"

It was my turn to roll my eyes. It should be no surprise that he would throw my relationship with Tallulah Bankhead in my face. She really was just a good friend, but she was proudly bisexual as well and people assumed because I was tolerant of her lifestyle, that made me bisexual. I wasn't. I simply respected people for what they were and disdained people who tried to be something they were not.

But as I looked at my husband standing there glaring at me, I couldn't help but tell myself, maybe I *should* consider a woman, because anything had to better than this.

CHAPTER 46

January 1950

Oh for four. That was my track record. Or that was where I was headed. Larry had officially moved out and had his own apartment. He'd lit a match to my life, set off an inferno, and simply walked away. And now I was left to sift through the embers.

I'd gotten notice yesterday that I was behind on my mortgage. When I'd gone to the bank, I was mortified to learn that my mortgage check had bounced because all my money was gone. I guess that's how he'd gotten his plush downtown apartment.

I had given Larry access to one of my checking accounts, not the one where I kept the bulk of my money. But Larry had forged my signature and that's how he'd been able to get the money from one of my main accounts. He'd wiped me clean, leaving $113.

Now here I was, standing outside Maxferd Jewelry & Loan. I eased the door to the small shop open and tiptoed inside. The company had been a staple in San Francisco and had recently opened a store in Van Nuys. I had hoped to go incognito, but since discretion was one of their slogans, I walked in with my head held high.

A balding man stood behind the glass counter filled with rings, watches, and other jewelry. On the wall behind him hung rows of musical instruments. In a corner, several mink coats hung on a rack. In another lifetime, I would've been here to see which of those coats were coming home with me. But that part of my life was a closed book now. I found myself wishing that I'd worn my mink instead of this wool coat. I'd paid eighty dollars for my white mink. Maybe I could've gotten at least half of that.

"Good afternoon," the man said. "How may I help you today?"

Thankfully, the man smiled, instantly putting me at ease as he stretched out his hand. "You got some jewelry you'd like me to take a look at?"

I nodded as I set the velvet jewelry sack on the counter and gently loosened the string to reveal the three diamond necklaces, along with a ruby necklace, two brooches, one of which I'd worn to the Academy Awards, and a bracelet.

"Trying to see how much I can get for this," I said. I hesitated as my thumb and index finger on my right hand twirled the wedding band on my left hand before I removed it and set it on the counter.

"Are you selling or pawning?" he asked.

"What's the difference?" I'd never been in a pawnshop.

"Selling gets you a little bit more. Pawning means you'll have a certain amount of time to come back and retrieve the items."

With the way my luck was going, I had only one option. "Selling."

"Okay. Give me just a few minutes," the man said as he took out a magnifying glass and started examining the necklaces.

He must've sensed my uneasiness because he looked up at me and said, "Feel free to look around. We have lots of nice stuff."

I eased away from the counter and glanced at some of the pieces in the display case. I found myself wondering about the stories of the people behind these pieces. Were they like me, done wrong by a man? Had they needed money for a lifesaving operation? To pay for a kid's college? Or had they traded in their prized possessions because it reminded them of some heartache? So many stories.

After a few minutes, the clerk said, "Ma'am, nice jewelry you got here. I can give you three thousand dollars."

"Three thousand?" I said, my mouth agape. "But the necklaces alone are worth that." I'd bought the yellow-gold, ruby, and diamond necklace with my paycheck from my first credited role as Queenie in *Show Boat*.

"That's what I'm paying for," he said. "The others are costume jewelry and aren't worth much."

I picked my wedding ring up off the counter. "This alone has to be worth a thousand dollars."

I couldn't make out the expression in his eyes. Was that pity?

"Ma'am, I'm sorry, but that's not even worth ten dollars."

I shook the ring in his direction, like he needed to take a closer look. "What? That's a diamond. Maybe you need to clean your magnifying glass."

The compassion in his eyes said he was used to comforting people who had been duped into thinking they had real jewelry.

"I'm sorry, ma'am. That's actually glass. And the band is synthetic metal. Basically, it's something you'd get out of a high-end gumball machine."

The one thing Larry had given me was fake?

"Ma'am, do you want the three thousand dollars?"

I nodded as I pushed back tears. I had to put my hands on the counter to steady myself since my knees felt like they were about to give out.

"Y-yes." I didn't have a choice. The money would buy me at least a few more months in my house.

"Th-thank you," I managed to say, before turning to leave. The small shop no longer seemed quaint. It was suffocating and I was desperate to get out.

That's what I did as the clerk shouted, "Ma'am, you forgot your ring!"

I ignored him and raced to my car before I passed out.

• • •

It had been six weeks since Larry moved out, two weeks since I found out my wedding ring—like my marriage—was a sham. Larry still had a few items here. My first instinct had been to burn them, but now I was glad I hadn't. It gave me an excuse to look him in the eye and let him know what I truly thought of him. He had phoned today and said that he was returning to Sugar Hill to retrieve the rest of his belongings.

Larry had the audacity to use his key to enter like he still lived here. I heard him calling me from downstairs.

"Hattie, I'm just here to get the last of my things."

At the sound of his voice, I found energy I hadn't had for the past week and scurried out of bed. I brushed my hair down and cursed myself for not changing out of my housedress, then reminded myself he wasn't worth the effort as I met him in the stairwell. Larry wore a paletot overcoat, matching trousers, a fedora, and a black scarf, looking like he was a member of the Mafia.

"How dare you just walk in here," I said as he walked up the stairs.

"Move, woman. I just came to get my things." He continued up the stairs and brushed past me, the mixture of jasmine and sandalwood from his cologne assaulting my nose.

"You're even more low-down than I thought," I said, following him into the bedroom. "A fake ring, Larry? Really?"

He paused like he didn't know whether he wanted to rub it in my face or play dumb. When he turned around with that stupefied expression, I figured he chose the latter. "That ring is real. I don't know what you're talking about."

"It's not!" I yelled. "I took it to the pawnbroker. Do you know how humiliating it was for me to go to a pawnshop?"

He scoffed. "This from the same woman who takes bone scraps at an NAACP event. Ha!"

"I had to do something since you stole my money."

He had just picked up a box when he spun around to face me. His face contorted into a grotesque sneer. "Stole? I didn't steal anything. I walked into the bank and took what was rightfully mine as your husband. You're lucky I didn't take it all since, by law, I am your husband and entitled to it."

"You forged my signature."

We glared at each other until he smiled and said, "Ooops," before resuming putting his belongings in a box.

"You are evil" was all I could get out.

He stepped so close to me I could smell the mixture of peppermint and scotch on his breath. "I'm the best thing that ever happened to you. I deserve some kind of compensation for putting up with your fat ass."

I could hear the slow heave of my breath as my chest slowly rose, then fell. But I willed the tears back, refusing to give him the satisfaction of seeing me broken.

"Get. The. Hell. Out," I said.

"With pleasure," he said, once again pushing past me as he carried his box of things.

I'd never in my life been so glad to see someone go, and I cursed the day I met Larry Williams.

CHAPTER 47

March 1950

Larry had left me in more dire of a financial strait than I'd ever imagined. He'd taken out lines of credit in my name. And one creditor had even reached out to Procter & Gamble, seeking to be paid. The ultimate humiliation was having P&G execs tell me I needed to get my personal life together.

I just wanted to escape my life. My thinned, frayed emotional threads were ready to snap. I'd been lolling around in bed for days—ignoring my friends' calls and making excuses anytime someone wanted to see me. Depression had set up residency again, and this time, I felt like it was here to stay.

I lay in bed for more than an hour, replaying the movie of my life. The mind is powerful because at the forefront of my thoughts were all my lost loves, tragedies, and failures. Even winning the Oscar was now a faint memory.

After a while, I dragged myself out of bed and over to the phone to call Louise. Her boarder, a young actor named Michael St. John, picked up on the second ring. I'd met Michael through Tallulah and had connected him with Louise. He was staying with her while he attended UCLA and worked to break into show business.

"Hi, Michael," I said when he answered. "Is Louise home?"

"Hey, Miss Hattie," he replied in his usual chipper voice. "No, she's not."

I contemplated my next move. I didn't even know why I was calling

Louise. I think I just needed someone to help me out of this pit of darkness.

"Okay," I said, my voice frail.

"Miss Hattie, is everything okay? You sound kind of strange."

Again I hesitated. Then I said, "I'm okay. Just tired." I paused. "Michael?"

"Yes, ma'am?"

"I just want to wish you luck in your acting career." An eerie feeling was creeping over me and I felt compelled to say that.

"Um, okay. Thank you. But, Miss Hattie, what's going on?"

I sighed. "Nothing. You just take care of yourself, Michael. Tell Tallulah and Louise, thank you for being dear friends."

"Huh? Why can't you tell them?"

I hung up the phone without replying, thought about it, then took the handle off the hook. I trudged back upstairs to my bedroom. My steps were slow, but it was like some external force was guiding me—over to my nightstand, where I grabbed the small bottle of sleeping pills next to the lamp and screwed the top off. I just wanted to go to sleep and escape my life.

I tapped the container until two pills popped out. I swallowed them. Then my pain whispered to me. *Take them all.*

I paused, debated arguing with my pain, decided against it, and poured the entire bottle of pills down my throat. I took the bottle of brandy that was also sitting on my nightstand and chugged as much as I could. I winced as the liquor burned my throat. Then I lay back across my bed. I slowly felt the booze and pills working their magic.

Images of my mother floated above me. She was illuminated and wearing a long, flowing dress. "Time to rest, baby, come on," she said, her warm smile welcoming.

Howard, my first husband, stood behind her. "Told you that career was gon' be the death of you. Come on with me. It's nice here."

I could feel a faint smile spreading across my face. I took slow, deep breaths, closed my eyes, and whispered, "I'm coming."

The sound of banging on my door pulled me back to my bedroom just as I prepared for my peaceful journey.

Part of me wanted to go ask whomever was making that incessant noise to stop. But I decided to go with the happy place and closed my eyes, smiled again, and drifted.

But my journey to utopia was interrupted by a cold slap across the face.

"Miss Hattie, wake up! Get up, get up," the male voice said. I felt him pulling and shaking me. I was angry because he'd interrupted my journey.

My eyes fluttered wide open because the man wouldn't stop yelling. "Michael?" I muttered.

"Yes, it's me, Michael." He was pulling me from the bed, trying to make me stand.

"Wh-what are you doing?"

"I need you to walk, Miss Hattie." He had put one of my arms around his neck, but I was much too heavy for him and, after a few steps, slipped right out of his arms and onto the floor. I forced my eyes all the way open.

"Michael?" His figure came into full view. "Why are you crying?" He had somehow gotten me into the bathroom and doused my face with water.

He said, "Why in the hell would you try something like this?"

Then I remembered the pills. The booze.

"Were you trying to kill yourself?" he cried.

"No," I moaned as the world came back into focus and my mother and Howard drifted away, waving good-bye.

"I just want to go with them," I cried, outstretching my arms.

"Go with who? Who is them?" He slapped me again, but this time not as hard. "No, Miss Hattie! Open your eyes."

I squirmed as I felt a wet towel wiping my face.

"Stopppp, Mich—" I was interrupted by his fingers being thrust down my throat. I squirmed, gagged, then leaned over and threw up.

"Good," Michael said, rubbing my back as I vomited right onto my linoleum floor, just inches away from the commode. "Get it out. It's not your time, Hattie McDaniel," he sobbed. "It's not your time."

After I felt like I had nothing left inside me, I leaned back against the cabinet, spent.

"I'm just tired. I'm just so, so tired," I cried. "I just wanted to rest."

"Well, rest, but not like that." He scooted over to me and held me as he rocked me. "Hattie McDaniel, you're a queen and your work is not done here on earth."

"How did you get to be so wise?" I said, sniffing as the reality of what almost happened set in.

"I was inspired by people like you." He rocked me while I closed my eyes and willed my heart rate to slow down.

Finally, I pulled myself away. "Well, that would be a first. I don't usually inspire anyone. Everybody hates me."

"Stop talking that foolishness." He dabbed my face again with the wet cloth. "You are so inspirational. You've just let the negativity steal your joy." He helped me to my feet and led me to my bed. Then he waited as I pulled back the covers and climbed in.

"It's not your time," he repeated. Michael St. John was a good man. And he was right about my joy. It was gone—snatched away by whites and coloreds who wouldn't just let me live.

I wasn't ready to die, though, so that meant I had to find a way to get my joy back.

Right now, however, I just wanted to sleep.

CHAPTER 48

June 1950

I just wanted to be loved. By my fans. By the public. By my friends. By a man. I was joking when I said maybe a woman would be better. But sitting here at this gathering and watching Tallulah slither all over the actress Patsy Kelly, I found myself questioning whether I was closing off my opportunities for happiness.

If there was anyone on this earth who loved life and exuded happiness, it was Tallulah Bankhead. She refused to live in a box. She didn't care what people thought of her. And she walked in joy.

I wanted some of that.

That's why when she'd invited me to the Sewing Circle gathering, I'd agreed. Tallulah had been devastated when Michael told her what happened. And though I tried to explain that I hadn't actually been suicidal—rather, emotionally drained and not thinking clearly—she'd taken to being by my side every day.

Her company had proven therapeutic. She brought laughter back into my life, and anytime she felt like I was slipping into a dark hole, she would find something for us to do.

Today, that something was a visit to the Sewing Circle, Hollywood's not-so-secret secret: a group of actresses who were all allegedly lovers. They met at one another's houses for lunch, conversation, and possibilities.

Today's gathering was at the art deco Pacific Palisades mansion of Dolores del Río, who had a lavender marriage (that's what we called marriages that appeared normal to the public, but privately the spouses had same-sex lovers).

"Hattie, why are you sitting over here looking like you were forced here at gunpoint?"

I hadn't even noticed Tallulah sashay over to where I was sitting by the window. She was known for her crass and unapologetic behavior, so you usually knew when she entered a room.

When we'd arrived here an hour ago, she'd left me sitting on the sofa while she flirted with Patsy. And I hadn't moved.

"Come on, now. The whole world knows Hattie McDaniel doesn't mince words." Tallulah handed me a glass of scotch.

I glanced around the room as I took the drink. There were about twenty-five women here. Jazz music filled the air, and colored and white women laughed, danced, and chatted.

"I-I don't know, I just feel a little out of my element here." I wasn't bold like Tallulah, who walked into parties and introduced herself by saying, "I'm a lesbian. What do you do?" She made no secret that she'd had dalliances with everyone from Joan Crawford to Billie Holiday. And though she proudly claimed lesbianism, she had no problem getting with a man as well.

I'd enjoyed hanging out with Tallulah, but was it because I truly enjoyed being with a woman, or because I'd had such bad luck being with a man?

"How do you know this is for you?" I finally asked.

Tallulah plopped down in a chair next to me, crossing her long, tanned legs. She pulled a cigarette out of her clutch, lit it, inhaled, leaned back, and released circles of smoke.

"I've tried several varieties of sex," she said. "The conventional position makes me claustrophobic. And the others give me either stiff neck or lockjaw."

That made me laugh. Tallulah had been married once before, to the actor John Emery for four years. She'd said she would never remarry.

"So you do consider yourself a true lesbian?" I had been thinking about my sexuality since Larry left. Maybe that was why none of my marriages worked, because I was a secret lesbian. I quickly dismissed that thought. I loved the hard body of a man, so that couldn't be it.

"I could never become a lesbian for real, because they have no sense of humor!" Tallulah deadpanned. "I'm ambisextrous."

That elicited another laugh.

"Well, I'm unsure what I am," I said. "I just don't know . . ."

Tallulah shrugged as she blew more rings of smoke. "That's the great thing about the Sewing Circle: you don't have to be sure. It's here for Hollywood women who are either bisexual, committed to lesbianism, or just visiting."

I watched the women in the room. Several were smoking as they chatted and laughed. There was an intimacy among them. A touch here, a gentle gesture there. But no one seemed ashamed.

I was shocked when Vivien Leigh walked in with another lady I didn't recognize.

"Is she . . . ?" I leaned in and whispered to Tallulah.

"We don't talk about who is and who isn't here," Tallulah said. But then she leaned in as well. "But no, she's not. She just enjoys our company." Tallulah leaned back and smiled.

"You know I should've been Scarlett O'Hara?" she said as she watched Vivien greet Joan with a hug.

"I did hear that," I replied.

"At the last minute, they decided to go with Vivien."

Tallulah had been a major Broadway star for years. And it was no secret that she'd wanted that role.

Her scowl revealed this was still a sore spot. After a few more minutes, she shook off her thoughts and said, "How are you doing, Hattie? Really?"

I debated whether I should lie, as I'd been doing to everyone around me.

"It's hard," I finally admitted. "It's hard to believe I had another marriage fail."

Tallulah shrugged as if I was overreacting.

"People divorce all the time," she said. "And they bounce back. Look at Dorothy. I heard she was in New York living it up." Dorothy had finally had enough of Harold's philandering ways and filed for divorce a few months ago.

"She is. She's performing at the Cotton Club and really making a name for herself," I said.

"And everyone knows she had an ugly divorce. We are strong women. We aren't going to let anyone—man or woman—break us," Tallulah said.

I smiled. I used to believe that. Now, as the sound of laughter filled the room, I decided—at least for now—I would simply live in the moment.

CHAPTER 49

December 1950

I was losing weight again, but this time, I knew why. I was still stressed about my impending divorce, and my near-death experience had frightened me. Couple that with the grind of rehearsing and appearing on a five-days-a-week radio series and my shooting appearances as maids in three films, and I knew that I was simply suffering from exhaustion.

But today I had to summon all my strength as I was in court again, before Judge Caryl Sheldon.

Louise and Ruby Dandridge were here with me today. They'd been especially worried that Larry would try to intimidate me or get aggressive with me. They didn't need to worry about that since Larry hadn't even bothered to show.

"Miss McDaniel, are you ready to give your testimony?" the judge asked.

I nodded, then stood by my seat next to my attorney. I knew Mr. Manual wanted to say "I told you so" about my marriage, but he'd said only, "This is exactly why I pushed him to sign away claims to your money."

I glanced back at Louise and Ru, who nodded their encouragement.

After being sworn in, I took my seat next to the judge and began replaying my four months of marriage.

"I'm miserable, Your Honor," I said after I'd recounted the humiliating NAACP episode. "Everyone knew that Larry was only interested in using me to advance his own ambitions."

"Did he ask you for money on a regular basis?" Judge Sheldon asked.

"He didn't," I admitted. "He had access to one of my checking accounts and, unbeknownst to me, was making regular withdrawals, and he forged documents to get access to my other accounts. Over the course of our marriage, he only contributed sixty-five dollars to cover household expenses and happily accepted any cash he could get."

I spent twenty minutes rehashing the lows of my union. After I finished, Ru testified on my behalf, backing up everything I'd told the judge and adding how he tried to turn my castmates against me.

When she stepped down, the judge looked over at the other side of the courtroom.

"Since Mr. Williams couldn't see fit to be here today," Judge Sheldon said, "Miss McDaniel, I hereby grant your request for a divorce and grant all your terms." He banged his gavel. "Court is adjourned."

Mr. Manual stood and shook my hand, a wide smile on his face. "Make sure you get these final papers to me and I'll get them filed with the court," he said.

"Of course," I replied, still shocked that my marriage was over just like that.

On the way out of the courtroom, I saw Hedda Hopper. How did she even know about the hearing? And when had she slithered into the back of the courtroom?

Hedda whipped the feathers from her large pillbox hat out of her face and smiled as I approached.

"Hattie, darling. Another divorce is in the books," she said. "I must admit, I thought this one would work."

I didn't bother giving her a smile. I simply said, "Well, it didn't."

"Word around Tinseltown is that this marriage was doomed from the start," she said. "I saw the photos of your nuptials and your smiling husband. My sources tell me that he fussed over that basket of flowers in the photo for over an hour. Most men couldn't care less about flowers."

The way the corner of her mouth went up into a sly smile, I knew what she was implying. The same thing that Ethel was that day in my kitchen.

"Anyway," she continued, when I didn't engage her, "can I get a comment regarding your marriage? It lasted only four months but the streets are talking."

I hesitated, debating how much I should say. I wanted to tell her that what was lacking in my marriage was as much physical as it was emotional.

"Baby, it's cold outside. But I'm only mentioning incompatibility. Of course, I could say a lot more," I finally said.

She lowered her voice, leaned in, and with a whisper said, "Well, I hope you don't think I'm forward with this, but are you seeking warmth from Tallulah Bankhead?"

I froze. That was nothing but Larry starting a rumor.

"And if I were?" I asked. "Would that be an issue?"

I knew it would—that's why my visit to the Sewing Circle could never get out.

"I know how Hollywood is about this," I said before she could make up a lie. "And I'm sure the rumor started from the fact that I count among my close Hollywood friends a number of gays and lesbians. But if you're looking for some salacious tidbit, you're barking up the wrong tree. I am not involved with Tallulah or any other woman. Or man for that matter. Today, I am simply a brokenhearted woman who lost another husband."

Ru scowled at Hedda, then took my arm. "All the more reason why we should be going," Ru said. "Good day, Miss Hopper."

CHAPTER 50

February 1951

I'd crossed to the other side yet I remained confused as ever. I stared across the room, studying Tallulah's naked form, wondering why she'd been blessed with a perfect, thin frame, glowing skin, and long flowing hair. And I . . . had not.

Funny how I'd never had a problem with my hefty frame, my chocolate skin, or my coarse hair. But as I looked from Tallulah to my reflection in the mirror, I realized that the majority of my problems in my life came because of how I looked. If I were thin and white, I'd get decent roles, white people would embrace me, and Negroes wouldn't despise me. Maybe men wouldn't leave me.

Tallulah slipped on her robe and studied me for a minute, then said, "I have no mind to sit around here and sulk over that no-account man."

I pulled my silk lounging robe over myself, taking pains to hide my naked body.

"I wasn't thinking about Larry," I said.

Tallulah sat on the edge of the bed.

"You're thinking about this?" she said, motioning between us.

I nodded, trying to unravel how this had happened. Tallulah had come over to my place last night and I'd cried on her shoulder about my marriage. I was angry with myself for its failure. I was livid because I hadn't listened to my gut in the first place, which had sent warning signs from the first day.

Tallulah had dried my tears, then comforted me in ways I'd never imagined.

It was no surprise that she actually brought some laughter to my life. She did that every time we were together. And when I'd taken her into an embrace to thank her, I'd felt an electric shock shoot through my body. I don't know if the scotch we had been sipping had been some sort of liquid courage, but I did something I'd been thinking about a lot over the last few weeks: I leaned in and kissed Tallulah. She was momentarily taken aback, but when I realized it felt good, I moved in closer and kissed her again.

To her credit, she tried to stop me.

"You're vulnerable right now and . . ." she'd said.

"And I'm in my full mental capacity. I want this. I need this."

Now that I'd had it, I was torn as I replayed what I'd done.

"Don't beat yourself up, darling," Tallulah said. I loved her ability to lighten stressful situations. "One encounter doesn't make you a lesbian. You wanted to try it. You tried it. Now, what's for breakfast?" She stood and pranced out of the room.

Tallulah was right. This was whatever this was. I wasn't going to beat myself up over it. I had enough people doing that to me. I didn't need to do it to myself.

• • •

Tallulah had gotten dressed and was at the table reading the trades while I cooked breakfast. I set a plate of food in front of her on the table.

Tallulah looked up for a moment, then said, "Hattie, darling, you do not look good."

"I wish everyone would quit telling me that. I'm fine. I'm not despondent anymore. I'm not upset about Larry or what happened between us."

Tallulah stood and moved closer to me. She took her hand and lifted my chin as she studied me. "I'm not talking about emotions. Your eyes are gray and hollow. You're not yourself. You don't have your usual old energy and verve."

"Well, if it's time for me to go, it's just time," I said with a chuckle as I pulled my head from her grasp. "I've played everything but the harp."

Tallulah didn't laugh as she returned to her seat. "This is serious, Hattie. You know what? I have an amazing medical specialist, a German-born author named Gayelord Hauser. He's Greta Garbo's diet doctor."

I gave a faint smile. "Are you trying to tell me that I need a diet doctor?"

Tallulah's hands went to her hips like a mother chastising her child. "Oh, I love every ounce of you, darling," she said with a sly grin before turning serious again. "But you aren't well. And Gayelord isn't really a doctor, but he's thoroughly researched diets and written several manuals on nutritional health. He advocates a holistic approach to diet, pushing natural foods, like wheat germ, yogurt, and brewer's yeast. He insists his patients abstain from dead foods and not focus on processed sugars and carbohydrates."

"Umm, sounds delicious," I said, picking up a piece of bacon off her plate and biting into it. "Just what I want, to be nibbling on salads and wheat germ yogurt all the time."

"His diet does include fresh fruit and vegetables," Tallulah said, pulling the bacon from my hand and dropping it on her plate. "But it really does help with overall health. I know he has a high-end protein diet that includes the regular use of the Swiss."

"A laxative?" I balked. "Really, Tallulah?"

"Yes, really. And Gayelord says that the diet has a strong impact on the emotional outlook of his patients and helps them live longer and happier lives," Tallulah said. "You're going to call him," she added like it was a done deal.

"Fine." I resumed fixing my plate. I really was ready to try anything if it would make me feel better, not just emotionally, but help with this fatigue that I couldn't seem to shake.

"Perfect. I'll be in touch with his information. I must really get going." Tallulah stood and grabbed her plate. "I'll take this to go."

She smiled at Ruby, who had just entered. "Hello to the most fabulous personal secretary in the world," she sang.

If Ruby felt any kind of way about Tallulah being here so early, she didn't let on.

"Hi, Miss Tallulah. You have a nice day." Ruby set her purse on the counter. "How are you today, Hattie?"

"Just dragging. Tallulah was telling me about some doctor she wants me to see," I felt compelled to say.

Ruby didn't seem to give Tallulah a second thought as she said, "Well, since you're going to see people, maybe now is the time to go see my minister too."

Ruby had been trying to get me to visit her minister, who delved in Christian Science, which was a religion whose members believed that only God and the mind have ultimate reality and that sin and illness are illusions that can be overcome by prayer and faith.

"And just how would she help me?" I poured a generous helping of syrup over my pancakes.

"I told you her teaching blends biblical doctrines with mental healing and mind power. She encourages her followers to seek oneness with God's eternal presence in hopes that they will find salvation, happiness, and physical well-being."

When Ruby first told me about this, I hadn't given it much thought. After all, I was raised in a strict Baptist household. But this sounded just like the kind of self-help philosophy that was appealing to me.

"Well, I do see the positive effect Christian Science has had on you," I admitted. Ruby was a master at finding the good in people and situations. No matter what obstacles were thrown in her path, she looked at the glass as half-full. Maybe Christian Science could give me some of that insight.

"Yes, it can be uplifting and give you faith that can wield some considerable power over your life," Ruby said. "Anyone can tap into God's energy and make a change for the better."

"Well, let's set that up too," I said, feeling hopeful.

Ruby smiled, then pulled out a notebook and sat down across from me as I continued eating my breakfast. "Since we're setting up appointments and getting things in order, there's something else we have to deal with."

I sighed. I had agreed to see a medical specialist and a minister, what more could I do? "What?" I asked.

"Your finances, Hattie. I know you make a substantial salary on the radio show, but I don't know what's happening to it."

Just the thought of my dwindling finances caused my stomach to rumble.

"You know I help my family, friends, and various charities."

"I understand that. But there are a number of things that need to be done around Sugar Hill. The water heater is leaking. Termites have destroyed the back porch. There are so many things that need fixing. And I've been asking you to take care of them to no avail. And then you got this." She pulled a piece of paper out of her notebook and held it up. "It's from the mortgage company. You're three months behind, Hattie. What's going on?" Her expression was more concerned than disappointed.

I slumped back in my chair. It was bad enough Tallulah knew what Larry had done. I knew my close friends wouldn't judge me, but the fewer people who knew what a fool I'd been, the better. However, I didn't want Ruby thinking I was neglecting my bills either.

That's why I sighed and said, "Larry drained me of a considerable amount of cash. And I just can't keep up with all the things that need to be fixed. It's just so much going on. The divorce, the house upkeep."

Her eyes widened in shock. "I'm so sorry to hear that, Hattie."

"I'm trying to keep it all together. Eddie's person usually helps me around the house, but he's been so busy getting Eddie's house together to sell because you know he's leaving?" I said, referring to my neighbor Eddie Anderson.

"Yeah. I heard about that. He's headed off with the Jack Benny radio show for a tour of the US and Europe."

"That reminds me. I need to do something for him too. Some type of going-away party."

"But why do you have to do something?" Ruby asked.

"Because I just do," I replied. "He and Mamie are my friends and this is a huge deal."

Her expression was incredulous. "And Eddie Anderson is the richest Negro actor in Hollywood. He doesn't need you to do anything."

"Which is exactly why he needs to go out in style." I snapped my fingers, an idea coming to me. "You know what I need to make me feel better? A party!" I said, not allowing her to answer.

Ruby massaged her temples. "Hattie, I don't think that's what you need. Your health, your finances are at a crossroads and a party is not the answer."

"Yes. A party. That's exactly what I need," I said, ignoring her. "I'm gonna throw an extravagant party to say farewell to Eddie and his wife."

"Hattie, you are not in a financial position." She sighed. "I was going to suggest bringing Cliff back on board."

"Yes, that's a good idea too," I said. Cliff Rogers was a CPA who had done some work for me early in my career. "Set it up. Meanwhile, let me get to planning."

Ruby let out a long sigh, but I wasn't deterred. I knew she didn't approve, but I didn't think anyone realized how much my parties gave me joy. I was feeling better already at just the idea of hosting the most lavish shindig Hollywood had seen in years.

CHAPTER 51

February 1951

I began seeing Gayelord Hauser and Carol Malcomb, a Christian Science Truth teacher, who practiced the tenets of Mary Baker Eddy, the founder of Christian Science. I quickly discovered Ruby was right. Christian Science gave me faith that I could wield considerable power over my life. Carol taught me to tap into God's energy and make a change for the better. So, mentally, Christian Science worked wonders. Physically, it had yet to help. I was hoping that this lettuce diet Gayelord had me on would help with that part.

I took to shutting myself away one day a week, every Sunday. I didn't take calls or see anyone. I just made up my mind that once a week, I would just have to sit down with myself.

It had given me a sense of peace, but in this moment, I was enjoying the scene in front of me. My home was once again filled with guests. I'd catered a lavish dinner for Eddie and Mamie, and invited more than a hundred of their friends. There was dancing and impromptu performances by Wonderful Smith and concert pianist and blues singer Monette Moore.

"Hattie, you really didn't have to do this," Eddie said, approaching me with his wife at his side. His gravelly voice always made me smile. Eddie's vocal cords were ruptured when he was a youngster selling newspapers in San Francisco. Apparently, newsboys thought whoever shouted the loudest sold the most papers, and even back then, Eddie was determined to be the best. That raspy voice had become his signature.

"You especially didn't have to do that," Mamie said, pointing to the enormous three-tiered cake that said "Bon Voyage Mamie and Eddie," which I had placed in front of a re-creation of an old-fashioned sailing ship with a powering mast.

"You know I had to send my friends off in style. It's not every day that a Negro gets to go on tour with one of the top white actors in the country."

Mamie squeezed her husband's arm. "Yes, we are excited. We just have to work on my husband's punctuality."

We all laughed because it was well-known that as talented as Eddie was, he was always late because he had a habit of losing track of time. Jack Benny had even started fining him, but it hadn't made a difference. Eddie made a hundred thousand dollars a year, so he just paid the fifty-dollar fine and moved right along.

"Well, go. Mix and mingle," I said. "Enjoy yourself."

Family, friends, Hollywood luminaries, including most of the staff from *Beulah*, my neighbors, they all hung out at my Sugar Hill home until the wee hours of the morning.

"I guess we better get going," Wonderful said when the clock struck two A.M.

"No, stay, have a good time. You've been thrown out of better joints than this," I said.

Wonderful laughed and returned to pour himself a drink. Folks might've been talking about leaving, but no one made a move to go.

My heart was full as I watched all my friends. What no one knew, what I hadn't even told Ruby, Tallulah, or anyone else: this party wasn't just for Eddie and Mamie; it was also a party to say farewell to Sugar Hill as it was time for me to move.

CHAPTER 52

March 1951

My heart pulsed with every pound of the hammer. I fought off tears as I watched the real estate agent batter the Sold sign into my front yard. The gardeners had done an amazing job and the lawn looked lusher than it had in years. The grass was a vibrant green. My rosebushes were in full bloom, looking like something out of a magazine. I hadn't told a soul that I'd contacted an agent to put my house on the market. And even I had been surprised when three days after listing it, she told me we had an offer.

"I heard rumors, but I had to see for myself if it was true."

I looked up to see Bessie staring at me, mouth agape. She was still wearing her housecoat and pink curlers, which was completely out of character. I could only assume she'd seen the sign and come running.

I swallowed the lump in my throat and nodded. "It's time." I looked back at the place I'd called home for many years. "This place is just too big for little ol' me."

"Take in boarders like everyone else," Bessie said. It must've dawned on her that she was outside in curlers because she began slipping the large wire-mesh rollers out and dropping them into her housecoat pocket.

"Believe me, I thought about that. But this place needs a lot of work, and I'm just tired. I moved into the downstairs bedroom. I never go upstairs anymore. Plus, there are just too many memories attached to this house." Images of Larry hitting me so hard I fell onto my piano, of Winston in my bed with another woman, of Ethel and those biddies gossiping about me—all flashed through my head. "I'd just as soon forget. Besides, even if you have a house with eight bedrooms in it, you can only sleep in one of them."

"I'm so sorry, Hattie. We're gonna hate to see you go."

"I hate to leave." Truer words had never been spoken.

We both paused as the Realtor approached us. She was perky and petite, with bleach-blond hair. She was no doubt excited about the hefty commission she was getting for a week's worth of work.

"Miss McDaniel, is it okay if I go get some photos of the basement? I forgot the new owner asked for some more photos," she said.

"Of course," I replied, nodding. "Go right on in."

We watched her bounce back inside. Then Bessie turned to me. "Where are you going?"

"First, I'm going to spend a vacation in isolation, working on my autobiography," I said.

"Oooh, I didn't know you were writing an autobiography."

"Yep. It's gonna be called *Help Yourself*, which is kind of my philosophy of life." I managed a smile.

After chatting with Bessie a little more, I assured her that I would stay in touch and promised to touch base before I actually moved. Only, when moving day came two weeks later, I didn't have the heart to say good-bye to my neighbors. I'd told the movers where everything went, asked Ruby to make sure all went as planned, and left quietly in the night.

• • •

I would always miss my home in Sugar Hill. But this eight-room cottage on Country Club Drive was a nice consolation. I actually enjoyed having a one-story. A small house was what was proper at this stage of my life. It was perfect for me to calm down and possibly gain some serenity.

I stood on the porch and looked out toward Central Avenue as a wave of nostalgia passed over me. I'd come full circle. Central Avenue was a far cry from where it was when I'd first moved here in 1931. The thoroughfare was still bustling, but the nightlife had drifted into a decline. Part of it was because LAPD Police Chief William H. Parker was a puritanical crusader who vehemently opposed race mixing and had started targeting colored nightclubs and juke joints that were also patronized by whites. His goal to stop the races from mixing had been achieved, as many of the clubs shuttered their doors. Between that and Mayor Bowron outlawing liquor on Central Avenue, the area had slowly lost its luster.

I was staying busy giving speeches and focusing on me when I wasn't working. I'd even taken a vacation to Mexico, but no matter how hard I tried, I couldn't recapture the energy that had been my trademark for years. My body felt like it was on a slow decline.

Tallulah had tried to get together again, but I always made excuses. As much as I enjoyed my time with her, that wasn't where my heart lay. And I'd also sworn off men. I'd resigned myself to being single for the rest of my life. No man could love me for the right reasons. So I would make no further efforts at permanent romantic attachments. I was going to die in my bungalow on Country Club Drive, tending to my mementos and Beulah. And that was just fine with me.

CHAPTER 53

May 1951

I was jinxed. That's all I could think as I watched Ethel laugh and dazzle reporters. I'd taken *Beulah* to soaring heights on the radio, yet when it came time to put her on TV, CBS had chosen to go with Ethel Waters.

"I'm so sorry, Hattie. I think the execs just think it will be too hard for you to do the radio show and a TV show."

My agent's words had haunted me for the past four weeks, since he'd broken the news that, yes, Beulah was going to TV, but no, I wouldn't be playing the role.

At the time, I didn't know how to feel. On one hand, I was happy that the radio show was doing so well—more than 20 million listeners a week. At the same time, I didn't understand why then they'd give the TV job to Ethel. I could've managed them both.

I couldn't be mad at Ethel. That's just the way this business worked. But I would be lying if I said it didn't hurt me to my core. Jack Benny did radio and TV. I guess they didn't think a colored woman was capable of that.

The powers that be had requested that I attend this presser today as a united force to promote *Beulah* because the newspapers were rife with gossip that Ethel and I were publicly at odds. I did think she should've shown me some modicum of respect and called me once she was offered the role, but ever since that incident in my kitchen with Larry when I'd overheard her laughing at me, we'd been distant.

Anyway, thanks to the teachings of Mary Baker Eddy I'd learned to focus on the positive. I'd been meeting with Carol regularly for the past few months and it had really helped.

The reporters pummeled a few more questions at us. Harry Levette, the Negro entertainment columnist, stepped up. Harry had been covering me since my early days. If he felt some kind of way about my interviews with Hedda Hopper and Louella Parsons, he didn't show it.

"So, Hattie, tell the truth. Are you really okay with not doing the TV role?" he asked.

I feigned a smile. "Yes, if only I were a twin, I could have added TV to my repertoire," I said. "My sponsors approached me several months ago about doing both shows, but I had a feeling that I couldn't do justice to both roles. So I decided to stick to radio. I was well aware of the intention of my sponsors. And in fairness to them, I think the public should know that they gave me every consideration."

Ethel's lips pursed and I could tell she wasn't happy about that comment, but she'd have to take it up with the top brass. That was the carefully crafted statement I'd been told to give.

Harry continued, "So, do you think Ethel will do Beulah justice?"

I patted Ethel's arm, my fairness on full display for the cameras. "Miss Waters is a fine actress and I feel that Procter and Gamble made a fine choice in selecting her for TV," I said.

Ethel returned the smile—and it was just as fake. That actually saddened me. We were two talented actors in Hollywood, but our possibilities were so limited that competition bred conflict. I could only pray that future actors would find ways to better get along and recognize that if one of us rose, we all rose.

• • •

The Beulah Show was the talk of Hollywood—at least the radio show was. The TV version was not getting the response Procter & Gamble had hoped. While I was getting 20 million listeners a week, the TV version was barely pulling in 5 million. One newspaper had even rated Ethel's TV performance as "a letdown for such a skilled artist." White reviewers said she played Beulah too stiff and uncomfortable, not as the lovable mammy that they had expected. A few critics had even said that the storylines were torturous and the acting rudimentary. They said the show was even more offensive on television than it had been on the radio. I didn't find Beulah offensive, but I'd come to believe colored folks would find any domestic role offensive.

I was headed into the commissary to grab lunch when I spotted Butterfly McQueen standing in the doorway to the studio. After years of being out of work, she'd been tapped to play Oriole, Beulah's sidekick, on the TV version. The radio show was recorded on the sixth floor and the TV show was recorded downstairs.

"Hey, Butterfly," I said. Things had been icy between my former costar and me ever since that day on the set of *Gone with the Wind* when she felt I hadn't stood up for her. Plus, she had told a castmate then that she didn't care for me because I "had no book learning."

"Hi, Hattie. Can I talk to you for a minute?" she said in her high-pitched voice.

"Umph, you want to talk to me? That may be difficult since my lack of book learning might make it hard for me to comprehend what you're saying."

"Look, I'm sorry about that," she said. "After working with Ethel on the TV show, I could worship the ground you walk on."

I don't know why that made me erupt in laughter. "What in the world is going on?" This hadn't been the first time a cast member had complained about Ethel. She was brash and abrasive and it had rubbed lots of folks the wrong way.

"I can't do it, Hattie," Butterfly said, sitting and scooting close to me. "She's just a beast to work for. And it's not just me. Bud finds her so frustrating that he taught his dog to growl whenever he heard her name," she added, referring to Bud Harris, who played Beulah's boyfriend on the TV version.

Freeman Gosden, who played on the *Amos 'n' Andy* radio show, walked up. Butterfly seemed embarrassed that he'd heard her.

"Well, you might not need to worry about working with Ethel much longer," Freeman said. He looked around to see who was within earshot, then leaned in and whispered, "Ethel just quit."

"Quit!" both Butterfly and I exclaimed in unison, then quickly lowered our voices.

"She quit?" I asked again, this time whispering.

He nodded like he'd been officially appointed to bring us the news. "Yep. She said she had pressing commitments elsewhere. Now that she's wrapped the filming, she wants to move on."

Ethel complained that Beulah was filmed in Hollywood, keeping her confined to the West Coast for long periods of time. And she was interested in Broadway shows and doing other pictures, but this was a complete shock.

I loved Hollywood so I couldn't relate. But I knew a lot of folks who had worked in New York who couldn't wait to go back.

"I heard a rumor that the NAACP was targeting our show along with *Amos 'n' Andy*," Butterfly said, her voice dropping an octave. "You think that's why she's leaving?"

Freeman jumped quickly to his program's defense. "*Amos 'n' Andy* shows the Negro in a very good light."

Butterfly stared at him like she was deciding whether to refute that. She must've decided against it because she simply said, "Nevertheless, the NAACP warned that if certain changes were not made, the organization would boycott."

"It's because of *Beulah* that we have the Marian Andersons, Roland Hayeses, and Ralph Bunches of the world," I said, not believing we were still dealing with the same thing all these years later.

Freeman swatted Butterfly's arm and stood erect. He motioned with his head and we both turned to see Ethel walking toward us.

"Five dollars says you are talking about me," she said.

For a second, no one spoke. Finally, Freeman said, "Is it true that you're leaving?"

She folded her arms and nodded confidently.

"Yep. I don't like the racial stereotypes the show perpetuates. And my friend in the army said they refuse to even broadcast the show because it demoralizes their colored members." She looked at me. "Since you took pleasure in telling the media how the sponsors really wanted you, I'm sure you can jump right into the role."

I couldn't make out the expression on her face as she looked at me, shook her head, and said, "Good luck. You're gonna need it," then turned and walked away.

CHAPTER 54

August 1951

The decision to have me play Beulah on both TV and radio was well received by listeners and the viewing public. The plan was to film *Beulah* TV in the summer while radio was in recess until the fall. That way I could keep scripts and characterizations from becoming confused between the two mediums. That worked perfectly for me. And more than anything, I welcomed the chance to challenge the color line in television.

"Hey, Ru, I want you to play Oriole on the TV show," I said to her as we wrapped a writing session for our last radio show of the season.

"What?" she said. "Butterfly plays that part."

"Butterfly *played* that part. During the Waters era. Maybe she can spend her time getting some more book learning," I added sarcastically. Then I chastised myself. I had just been wishing colored actresses could better get along and I was being mean over an old issue.

"Plus, would Procter and Gamble even let you do that?" Ru said.

After Ethel left, the sponsors went back and forth on whether I could do both. I convinced them that I could and they gave me free rein to deliver results for TV like I'd done for radio.

I brought Ernest Whitman from radio on to continue playing Bill. I kept up the grueling schedule for months and everyone commented on it.

"I don't know how you're doing it all," Ru said one day after we'd wrapped taping for the TV show. Her eyes were heavy and she had slumped over from exhaustion. "And you're still doing live performances at local theaters."

"I'll rest when I die," I said, shimmying into some blue pedal pushers. I was headed to a charity softball game sponsored by the Hollywood Junior Chamber of Commerce, where I was slated to be a bat girl. I had hoped I could get a chance to get in the game and maybe even hit a home run. I'd been feeling so tired lately. I welcomed the opportunity to get out and be active.

"How do I look?" I said, modeling for her.

"Those loud red socks are hurting my eyes." Ru laughed.

"Good. That means I'll be seen with all those skinny actresses in their little shorts. You sure you don't want to come?"

"Child, as much as I'd love to come hang with Bob Hope and Gary Cooper, I can't do it," she said, referring to the two men that were coaching the charity teams. "I'm just thankful Geneva is out of town so I can go home and get right in the bed. I don't know how you do it."

"Mind over matter," I said, chuckling as I grabbed my bag and headed out.

The game was more fun than I'd had in a long time. We raised money for needy children. While I didn't get my home run in, I hustled the balls and swung bats, and put on a show singing and dancing while doing it.

"Hattie, I think you were our good luck charm," said Bob, whose team had emerged victorious.

"Thank you," I said with a salute. "I aim to serve."

Just as I dropped my hand, a sharp pain shot through my chest. I doubled over in pain as I heard someone yell, "Call a doctor!"

• • •

My eyes fluttered open as the room came into focus. Was I in the hospital? I glanced over to see a physician lifting my arm and examining underneath.

"What are you doing?" I asked, my voice raspy. I desperately needed some water. The nurse must've had some kind of telepathic powers because she immediately lifted a cup to my mouth. I sipped and felt like a dying man in the desert who'd just been given relief.

The doctor gently set my arm down. "Looking at that boil under your arm. Does it hurt?"

"Yeah, it's been quite painful but I was just hoping it would go away." I shifted in my bed, then looked around the room. "Why am I in the hospital? What happened?"

"You happened. I'm Dr. Stratton, your attending physician." He walked around to the other side of the bed and looked under my arm on that side. After examining it, he lowered my arm and said, "Hattie, you're suffering from exhaustion."

That was understandable. We had filmed six episodes of the TV *Beulah* this month. I was scheduled to start taping radio *Beulah* for the upcoming fall season next week. I'd spoken at four events last week, hosted a party for the newly formed chapter of the Links, Inc., and judged a children's talent show at First AME.

"You're going to have to take it easy," Dr. Stratton said.

"Okay," I said. "Tomorrow I am slated to be the mistress of ceremonies at a Sigma Gamma Rho function at the Columbia Theatre in Hollywood. But I can rest after that."

"That's not happening, Miss McDaniel," Dr. Stratton said sternly. "Can you get someone to take your place?"

I wanted to protest, but my body told me the doctor was right. I could barely move my arm. "Well, I suppose I can get someone to do it, but can't I just go do it, then go home and rest?"

"No. Your situation is not critical, but it's more than serious."

"What does that mean?" I asked him.

He took a deep breath and looked at his paper, then back up at me. "Well, I thought that it might be diabetes when I first started examining you, but Miss McDaniel, I'm sorry to tell you. I think you suffered a heart attack."

CHAPTER 55

November 1951

I was so ready to get out of this bed. Thankfully, I'd been confined to bed at home, but it had been three months, and being restricted to this bed was torture.

Louise had come to my rescue, taking over for me as Beulah on the TV show. She was here now, replaying how she'd just nixed a script where they had Beulah delivering an awful dialect.

"I'm gonna carry on your legacy, making sure they never have Beulah play a stereotypical maid," she said.

"Thank you," I said, grateful that she'd been able to step in.

"And I let everyone know I'm just filling in until you come back."

"What's that?" I pointed to a large bag that Louise had dragged in behind her.

"More 'get well' cards," she said, lifting the bag up onto a chair.

The private nurse that I'd hired tapped on the bedroom door.

"There's a Cliff Rogers here to see you," she said.

"That's my CPA. You can send him in."

Louise leaned down and kissed me on the forehead. "Well, I'll come back later. Don't tackle those letters just yet. Get you some rest," she said.

"No, I'm planning to go do the jitterbug on Central Avenue as soon as you leave," I joked.

"You play around too much."

She exchanged greetings with Cliff on her way out the door. He walked over and squeezed my hand. His concern was genuine. "Afternoon, Hattie. How you feeling?"

"Ready to get out of this bed. Please tell me you have some good news about the loan."

At this point, my finances had been exhausted. I'd stayed in the hospital for two months before I came home and I'd had to borrow fifteen hundred dollars from the City Finance Company. I told them I would get back to work in a few days and I needed the money on a sixty-day note to help pay medical expenses. Those sixty days had come and gone and I had even less money than I'd had when I got the loan.

Cliff shook his head. "They'll give you one more month to start paying back the loan, but that's it."

I turned my attention to look out the window. I didn't know where I was going to get the money from. My ex-husband James had reappeared after he found out I was sick and offered to loan me some money. I'd said no, but I was going to have to break down and accept. I had no other choice.

• • •

I was no longer bedridden, though I couldn't yet return to work. It had taken several months, but I felt myself on the road to recovery. I was on a regular diet and exercise program to keep my heart in proper order.

I felt good about my progress and being alone in my house for a change. I'd given the nurse the day off so she could celebrate New Year's with her family. I was feeling energized so I decided to start taking down the Christmas decorations I had insisted that Ruby put up.

I didn't know what happened in between the time I took the storage box out of the basement and now, but the sun was setting and I looked up to see Wonderful Smith calling my name.

"Hattie, are you okay?" he said, his voice panicked. "The paramedics are on the way."

How did I end up sprawled out on this cold floor?

I got the answer three hours later when Dr. Stratton appeared in my hospital room, an admonishing expression on his face.

"Christmas decorations, Hattie? That's what you were doing?"

"I've been feeling fine, Doc. I don't know what happened."

"It sounds like you had another heart attack," he said matter-of-factly. "But we'll run some tests."

"Another heart attack?"

"Listen to me. I need for you to take it easy. That is not up for discussion," the doctor warned before leaving me with my thoughts.

That's where I'd sat for the next hour, until I looked up and saw James in the doorway. I motioned for him to come in. He looked healthier than the last time I'd seen him, like he'd lost weight and maybe even grown an inch.

"Hi, James, you didn't have to come," I said. I was happy he was here, but I really didn't want anyone's pity.

"I told you, Hattie. Ever since Ruby wrote to tell me what was going on with you, I knew I had to come. I would never let an old friend down in sickness and time of need. I told Ruby we needed to get together and get you up off the floor."

"Well, I appreciate it." I really did. James and I had been friends who messed up by getting married. We had ended on a bad note, so I'd had no idea how he would respond to Ruby's request for help.

James took my hand. "I've been pondering what to do about you for months. You've had a hard spell. If you had come east for a year, as I had suggested, you would not have had so many health problems, but you were making big money and neglecting your health."

I turned my head. I wasn't in the mood to be chastised. James didn't care. He squeezed my hand tighter. "I'm not trying to be harsh, but you know I tell it like it is. If you stay here in Hollywood and don't change climates, I look for you to die inside of a year. A change of climate, food, and water is your only salvation."

In the past, had James said something like that, I would've instantly balked. But I was so tired and feeling so horrible. And the boil under my arm had gotten worse and was painful on top of everything else.

"You know what, James"—I patted his hand—"I really do appreciate that and I just might have to take you up on that when I get out of here."

That seemed to pacify him and he smiled.

The door to the hospital room opened and Dr. Stratton stepped back in. The expression on his face wiped the smiles right off ours.

"What?" was all I could manage to say. His eyes darted to James.

"I'll step outside," James said before easing out the door.

Once he was gone, the doctor headed over to the right side of my bed.

"Give it to me straight, Doc. How bad is my heart?"

His expression was stoic, as if he was trying to suppress any emotions. "Hattie, your tests have come back from that boil under your arm. I'm sorry to tell you, but it's breast cancer."

CHAPTER 56

February 1952

Another dream home was gone. My heart ached as I signed the final paperwork. I'd known my health outlook was bad, but I was determined to get better, and my dream had been to return to my cottage and live out my last days. But the reality was, I could no longer afford to stay there.

Over the last few weeks, when I wasn't in the hospital, I was bedridden at home, wondering why breast cancer had chosen to set up residence in my body. To my knowledge, I had no history of the disease in my family. But such was the tragic life of Hattie McDaniel.

I shook off the pity mindset that often plagued me these days and faced the papers in front of me. I scribbled my name and the date, then handed the papers back to the Realtor.

"I'll get these filed right away. Enjoy your new home," the petite woman said.

She scurried out of the room, and I looked around at the Motion Picture Country Home Hospital, my new living quarters. This was a hospital established for celebrities by the actor Jean Hersholt, who was president of the Motion Picture Relief Fund.

I fluffed the pillow on my trolley—that's what this hospital bed felt like, with its wheels and collapsible sides—and chuckled.

"What's funny?" Louise asked. She and Lillian had been so quiet while the Realtor explained all my paperwork. I almost forgot they were here.

"Do you know I'm the first colored person to move into this place? I'm yet another first." I sighed as a heavy silence filled the room. "Can you open the window, please?" I asked Lillian. "Let's get some air in here."

Lillian didn't say a word as she rose from her chair, brushed down the billowy skirt on her dirndl dress, and headed over to the window to open it. She closed her eyes and inhaled as the breeze swept in.

I leaned back against my pillow and inhaled as well, welcoming the scent of the walnut and orange groves that grew on the hospital grounds.

I had requested to stay in one of the cottages on the forty-eight-acre hospital grounds. Yet, as liberal as this hospital claimed to be, they were not about to give a colored woman one of the coveted cottages. Even if that colored woman had won an Oscar.

I shook away my thoughts and turned to my next task—the reason I'd summoned Cliff, and my executor, John Charles Gross, to my room. It was time to put my affairs in order. I knew it. My friends knew it, and though they didn't want to face it, I knew what I had to do.

I wasn't ready to die, but the thought of death was like a great burden being lifted. And I took comfort in my visitors and the thousands of "get well" cards that poured in.

I'd tried to let Ruby go, since I could no longer afford to pay her. But she'd dismissed me, saying "Some things are more important than money, Hattie. The accounts of friends are settled in the heart." Though I didn't really have any work for her, Ruby visited me often, taking a bus for the thirty-mile journey from Fullerton to Woodland Hills. Her younger sister Frances was often with her and they would sit at my bedside and talk with me. Frances would comb my hair. I loved when she did that.

Clark came regularly, but thoughts of my demise brought memories of Carole and I could tell it was hard on him.

"Hattie, this is ridiculous," Louise said, snapping me from my thoughts. "Must you do this right now?"

"When do you want me to do it? When I'm dead?" I asked.

Those words made her gasp and she clutched her pearls.

"Come on, Louise. We all are gonna leave this earth sometime," I said.

"But it's not your time."

"Uh, look around you." I motioned around the hospital room. "We're in a hospital—the clock is winding down."

The newspapers had reported my going into the Motion Picture Country Home, but they had made no mention of cancer. Thank goodness. The public never knew of my radiation treatments, my heavy sedation, or my doctor's lack of hope for survival.

"So, let's get started with this will," Cliff said. "What do you want to be done with your Oscar?" Cliff asked as he pushed his spectacles up on his wide nose and glanced uneasily in my direction. He sat in a steel-handled chair on the other side of the room, under a painting that looked eerily similar to the Scarlett-and-the-twins scene from *Gone with the Wind*. Every time I looked at the painting, I couldn't help but wonder if I'd been placed in this room on purpose.

Cliff and I had known each other since I got the role of Mammy. There were not many Hollywood professionals I truly trusted to manage my money. I'd been introduced to him by my brother. And if Sam said he could be trusted, I knew he was a good guy.

Cliff brushed down his tweed gray-and-white pin-striped suit. He liked to boast that it looked just like the one Nat King Cole wore when he recorded "Unforgettable" last year. He told me that every time he wore the suit, which was often.

"What did that appraiser say about the Oscar?" I asked. I'd had Cliff take it to an appraiser just to get an idea of its value in order to get an accounting of my estate, but I never had any intention of selling.

"Yeah, we got nowhere with that appraiser. He dismissed it as having no value. And we both know better than that," Cliff said.

I sighed. Why did that not surprise me?

"You think they gave her a different Oscar, one that was worthless, since, you know, she was Negro?" Louise asked.

"I can't imagine Hollywood passing out worthless statues and plaques," Lillian said.

Cliff nodded in agreement. "That was my first thought, but the appraiser said he'd had other winners bring theirs in and he'd told them the same thing."

That was good to know. I didn't know how I would've handled knowing that my monumental moment was tainted by a different, less expensive plaque.

"What am I looking at, Cliff? How bad off am I, really?" Cliff might have been trustworthy, but I was afraid even he hadn't been able to rescue me from my bad decisions.

Cliff's whole body tensed like he didn't want to deliver the news. Finally, he said, "I've valued everything at about $10,337." He paused. "And you owe the IRS $10,438."

The lump in my throat was instant. I'd been working since I was six years old. I'd worked until it was physically impossible. And I was ending my life negative a hundred dollars.

I refused to cry as I turned to John. He had sat quietly in the corner, waiting for me to get to him.

I pointed to his notepad. "Can you get to writing? I want to get this will done today."

Louise huffed her displeasure and plopped into the seat next to my bed.

I ignored her and began. "I want to leave my Oscar to Howard University in Washington, DC." I didn't care what some appraiser said; my Oscar meant something. And that wonderful luncheon the drama department gave me was one of the highlights of my career. I would forever cherish the love those students showed me. And I hoped that it would inspire young people for years to come.

John scribbled furiously as I continued. "The bulk of my estate, for whatever it's worth, will go to my brother Sam, my nephew Edgar, my niece Marion, and my two great-nephews. I also want Sam to take Danny, my Dalmatian." I paused as I thought about my beloved dog. Frisky had died years ago, but Danny was with Sam and he was probably wondering where I was and when I was coming back.

I took a deep breath and went on. "Ruby Berkley Goodwin is to receive my set of demi teacups, and she should have access to the materials needed to complete my autobiography."

I rattled off a listing of a few more mementos—small amounts of cash and personal possessions to friends, $150 to help a young acquaintance complete her education, four dresses from my wardrobe to two friends: a schoolteacher I'd befriended named Estella Fort and Alma Scott, who I also left some serving dishes, figurines, and pots and pans.

I knew that my gifts seemed modest. But they were all I had left. And everything I bequeathed meant something to me. I appreciated the value of even the smallest and most common possessions. I hoped my friends and family would too.

Finally, I said, "And to Larry Williams . . ."

Louise sat up. "Hattie!"

I held up a hand to tell her to calm her nerves. "I don't want to hear any admonishments, but I never got around to filing the final divorce papers, so . . ."

"So Larry would be entitled to her entire estate," Cliff said, his eyes wide with the news that I had shared with no one. It's not that I hadn't wanted to file the papers. I was just always too busy to get it done.

The thought of Larry getting anything from me made me feel even sicker. "Exactly what Cliff said, and not even over my dead body am I about to let that happen."

I turned my attention back to John. ". . . To Larry Williams, I hereby bequeath the grand sum of one dollar."

John stopped writing and looked up at me as Louise and Lillian burst out laughing and Cliff shook his head.

"One dollar?" John asked.

"I didn't stutter."

I motioned to his paper. "And add this. I really, really hope that he doesn't go and spend it all in one place."

John finished writing, then handed me the paper. "Y-you have to sign and date it, Miss McDaniel. That's the only way it will be valid."

I took the paper and, with a shaky but still bold hand, added one final wish: *I desire a white casket and a white shroud; white gardenias in my hair and in my hands, together with a white gardenia blanket and a pillow of red roses. I wish to be buried in the Hollywood Cemetery.*

I inscribed each page with my initials and, at the end, signed my name. Cliff signed as my witness.

As John retrieved the paper, I looked over to see Louise and Lillian with a mist covering their eyes.

"Now, don't you come in here with all of that. I'm just getting my house in order, just in case. You know I'm a fighter. Mix that with my faith and mind power and I'll be fine. Isn't that what you told Hedda Hopper, that I'm going to be back at work soon?"

I gave a sly smile. Louise nodded and dabbed her eyes. I squeezed her hand. My prognosis was grim, but I appreciated my friends feeding the media optimistic outlooks to keep my spirits up. But we both knew the truth. Louise was here last week when Dr. Stratton had informed me that the breast cancer had been festering for two years. It was too advanced. There was nothing they could do.

Dr. Stratton had said it was possible they could treat me and continue giving me radiation, but it probably wouldn't work and I'd find myself even sicker. I nixed that idea immediately. One of the things I'd learned from Christian Science and Mary Baker Eddy's teachings was that traditional medicine should be rejected.

I was going to use meditation, prayer, and utter tenacity to see me through, but my body was racked by cancer, diabetes, and a bad heart, so whatever was meant to be, would be.

"Now that we have the will out of the way," I said, turning back to Cliff, "did you request the royalties for *Beulah*'s reruns?" I asked.

Cliff nodded. "I did. But it could be months before we get a check."

We were interrupted by a light tap on the door, followed by the nurse peeking in.

"Miss McDaniel?"

I smiled at Nurse Marjorie. She had been a godsend to me since my arrival. I wondered if she learned to be a nurse in the military because everything about her appearance suggested it. Her bright white nurse's cap rested on her head like a crown and her white nurse's uniform and white shoes didn't have a speck of dirt on them. Here was someone who inspired confidence.

"Yes, Marjorie?" I said, shifting to get comfortable, which was near impossible with the tubes pasted to my chest, stuck in my arms, and wrapped around my wrists.

"It's time for your visitors to go. The doctor has ordered some more tests," she said.

"Why are we testing when I'm gonna die anyway?"

Louise gasped again.

"This is just a way for you all to bill me some more," I said.

"Miss Hattie, you promised that you wouldn't give me a hard time," Marjorie said, coming over to unhook all the contraptions and help me out of bed.

I let her guide me into the wheelchair. "I did, didn't I? Well, since I'm a woman of my word, let's go."

She wheeled me toward the door.

"Y'all stop watching me like I'm some circus act," I said, motioning for her to push me out. "Act like you ain't never seen a dying woman before."

I laughed on my way out of my hospital room. It wasn't lost on me that I was the only one who found anything funny.

CHAPTER 57

October 1952

I was going to die just as I'd lived. With a smile on my face, even if there was an ache in my heart. I'd learned long ago that misery was a condition of existence and I'd taught myself to seek joy to burn out the pain. And my signature dinner parties were one of my sources of joy.

That's why the concerned stares of my friends situated around my hospital room here on the grounds of the Motion Picture Country Home Hospital didn't bother me one bit. I knew they would give in eventually, even as they sat here glaring at me, judging me.

For a brief moment, the only sound in the room was the faint hum of the machine monitoring my blood pressure.

"Hattie, you can't be serious. You're having a dinner party? Today? Here?"

I thought Louise couldn't believe I'd bring people into this hospital room with this hideous parakeets-and-roses wallpaper. But the aesthetics were not her concern.

"This place can fit, what, ten, maybe twelve people?" Louise said. "Why in the world would you want to entertain here?"

I pointed to Louise's plum-colored bell-sleeve tea-length swing dress. "Well, I thought you'd found out about the party and came ready in your fancy dress." I winked at her, trying to lighten the worry that was written all over her face. "Looking like you raided Lillian's closet."

Lillian, who sat on the other side of the room reading a magazine, chuckled. Louise was not amused.

"Change the subject all you want," Louise huffed. Her plump cheeks puffed in exasperation.

Lillian had no interest in moderating our war of wills. In this case, I was sure she'd take my side. But she burrowed her head more deeply in her *Jet* magazine. The magazine was fairly new and was all the rage in colored Hollywood because it featured national news, entertainment, and fashion for Negroes. It was the only place we could see brown-skinned women like us on the cover. And Lillian hadn't stopped talking about the issue she was reading. It had the actress Suzette Harbin on the cover along with a story on why brown-skinned girls get the best movie roles.

Jet obviously didn't interview me for that article because my brown skin hadn't gotten me any good roles and now it was too late.

I knew Lillian was dreaming of being on the cover like Suzette and Pearl Bailey, who we'd heard would be on next week's cover. But we all knew that wasn't going to happen. Lillian, Louise, and I were "inside" magazine material. We weren't fair-skinned like Lena and Dorothy. We weren't male like Sugar Ray Robinson. We reminded them of their mothers and grandmothers. We reminded them of the parts of their lives they'd rather forget. They were ashamed of us. So we were relegated to our stories only being inside the magazine—if we were covered at all.

Louise's hands went to her hips as she leaned in and studied me. "I know you, Hattie McDaniel. And you're in pain. Look how stiff you are sitting up in that bed."

Oooh, she was right about that. I'd been having sporadic pain in my rib area all morning, and right about now I was wishing I'd taken some of that "Jive," which was what I called the drugs the doctors tried to pump into me every time I complained about aches.

But I was determined to shove the pain away today and focus only on what brought me joy.

"I'm just fine," I said, flashing a smile like I was on camera. "I've invited twenty guests—and since you know my dinner parties are the hottest ticket in town, they'll probably all show up."

"They're the hottest ticket when you're in Sugar Hill, not the hospital," Louise protested.

I fanned away her comment. "The flowers and fruit trays are already here," I said, pointing to the windowsill where I'd had the hospital orderly set the items I'd ordered for my party. "Ruby has ordered some of those tea cakes from Helms Bakery—you know I can't have a party without those tea cakes." I rubbed my stomach, which was growling just thinking about the pastries. "We'll put the food and drink in the lobby across the hall." I hadn't run that idea by the hospital staff, but I felt sure they'd do whatever I requested. They had all been quite lovely. The hospital catered to celebrities, and at least here I qualified.

"The pastries and decorations will be delivered at four and the guests arrive at five," I said.

"Yesterday, you hardly had the energy to move," Louise said.

"Well, I feel better today."

My hand instinctively went to my head, where a red scarf kept my coarse pin curls in place. I was squeezed into a dreadful baby-blue hospital gown that was two sizes too small for my hefty frame. I'd asked Ruby to bring my Christian Dior tulle cocktail dress because I might be dying, but I sure wasn't gonna look like death. I'd had that kind nurse Marjorie pin curl my hair, and in a few hours, I'd remove the pins right before the guests arrived.

"Lillian, say something, please. You know Hattie's stubbornness is going to set her back," Louise said.

I knew that while Lillian had no interest in parties, she wasn't totally against them like Louise. That's why I was sure she'd be supportive.

"Well?" Louise folded her arms across her ample bosom, waiting for Lillian to respond.

Lillian set her magazine on her lap. Her hair was smoothed back into a bun and her light makeup was immaculate. Even still, she took out her compact and dabbed a sponge on her cheeks.

"She's right, Hattie," Lillian finally said, her eyes on her reflection in her compact. "A party is the last thing you need to be worrying about."

I smiled as images of my last party with Eddie danced in my head. I knew how to celebrate. That's why I told my friends, "Well, I think a dinner party is a great idea." I grabbed one of the wrought-iron spindles on my headboard and tried to pull myself up. I shifted under the thin woven blanket, trying to get comfortable.

"As your trusted accountant, I would strongly advise against this," Cliff interjected.

Cliff had broken down my finances yesterday when he'd told me I only had enough in the bank to cover two more weeks in the hospital.

The way this breast cancer was ravaging my body, I suspected I had only a week to live, so that wasn't much of a concern. Plus, Cliff had submitted the paperwork to get my care gratis, since the Motion Picture Country Home Hospital was established in the 1930s for Hollywood stars who ended up destitute.

Destitute.

I'd been in more than seventy films and I was destitute. The thought made me even sicker than any cancer ever could.

"It doesn't matter what you all think," I said. I wanted my friends to remember me as happy, as being myself in my last days. I refused to turn my death into some kind of pity project. "It's too late. The invitations have been mailed. Folks will be here in five hours."

An empty silence filled the room. My friends knew there was no sense in arguing with me.

"Dr. Stratton said you need rest," Lillian said.

"I'll rest in Heaven."

"Not a party," Louise added, ignoring my comment.

This conversation was draining. This was exactly why I'd purposely done all my planning while they weren't here, which had been hard since between these two, Ruby, and Ru, someone had been here almost daily.

"It's done. My feelings won't be hurt if you decide not to stay." Of course, I didn't really mean that.

My exasperated breath put a period on the conversation and none of my friends said anything more.

Ever since I'd learned the news about my cancer, I tried to absorb the fact that my life as I knew it was over. Thirty years ago, I'd bought a small Louis Vuitton trunk with my check from *The Little Colonel*. It was an extravagant purchase, but I wanted to make sure that no hotel clerk ever, ever looked down on me. Now it sat in the closet with all my scarves and the jewelry I hadn't pawned, and the white ermine stole I wore when I got my Academy Award. I planned to wear that this evening as well.

Louise had brought me some photos that I'd taken at my past parties. I'd insisted that she get the photos out of my storage facility so I could display them around my hospital room. Louise had been reluctant, but this was going to be the home I died in.

I desire a white casket and a white shroud; white gardenias in my hair and in my hands, together with a white gardenia blanket and a pillow of red roses. I wish to be buried in the Hollywood Cemetery.

I'd probably read that portion of my will a hundred times. That was my dream.

I looked up at Cliff, who had returned to his notepad, no doubt trying to figure out my finances.

"Have you heard anything back from the Hollywood Memorial Park cemetery?" I asked him.

His non-answer was my answer.

Louise shook her head. "I don't know why you even want to be buried around all those white folks," she huffed.

"If folks like Douglas Fairbanks and Rudolph Valentino can be buried there, why can't Hattie McDaniel?" I asked.

"'Cause they're white," Louise said, touching me gently. "If they don't want you there, why would you wanna have your eternal soul there?"

I jerked my arm away. "When have you ever known me to back down from going somewhere I'm not wanted? I'm not wanted in a lot of places. The cemetery is for Hollywood royalty and I'm Hollywood royalty. A Negro woman never won an Academy Award and I did. This hospital never had a Negro stay here before me. Why can't I be the first Negro woman buried at the Hollywood Memorial Park cemetery?"

Louise sighed. "You need to just go to Rosedale Cemetery with all the other colored folks. Why you even want to fight this battle is beyond me."

I fell back against my pillow. I wasn't about to have this conversation with Louise again. The past 637 times were enough. She and Lillian could stay inside their safe little boxes. Anyone who knew Hattie McDaniel knew there wasn't a box on the planet to confine me. I'd let the world—both coloreds and whites—occasionally rob me of the joy I felt in life. No one was going to rob me of my joy on the brink of death.

"I heard there was a party going on in here today." I smiled as Clark entered the room. Beside him were Dorothy and Ru.

"And you know I love a good party," Dorothy exclaimed. All three came over to my hospital bed and took turns kissing me on the forehead. Their presence meant a lot. Dorothy was in the midst of filming *Tarzan's Peril* and Clark was filming a western called *Lone Star*.

"Clark came to your rescue again," Ru said, smiling in his direction.

"What happened?" I asked.

"That dreadful Hedda Hopper is outside in the waiting area," Dorothy said.

"What?" Louise exclaimed.

"I told her you weren't doing any interviews," Clark said. "Especially . . ." His words trailed off as he exchanged somber glances with Louise.

I'd accepted death was impending. My friends had not.

"Let me go tell that woman she's not wanted here," Cliff said, standing and heading toward the door.

Something—I don't know what—made me stop him. "You know what? Let her in."

Lillian's head spun in my direction. "Hattie!" After a scathing review of Lillian's performance in *The Great Gildersleeve* radio show from *Ebony* magazine a few weeks ago, where they'd called the program the "WORST SHOW" because of its "damaging stereotypes" of Negroes, Lillian had followed my lead and written a rebuttal, defending her role as the character Birdie. It was eloquent, and I agreed with every word she wrote when she reminded *Ebony*'s readers that the show's writers had never written dialect into the script and were particularly careful not to offend Negro viewers. But that didn't do anything but make things worse as more newspapers picked up the story.

After that, we all had vowed to stop doing press. So it was no surprise when my friends looked at me in shock.

"It's all right," I assured them. They really didn't understand: this would be my last interview. I felt it in my bones, and there was no amount of wishful thinking that would change that.

"Marjorie, do you mind getting the lady out there in the hat, because I know she has on one." I chuckled. No one else did. "Tell her to come on in."

Marjorie, who had just finished checking my vitals, nodded before easing back out the door. Moments later, Hedda poked her head in my room. The usual exuberance that danced in her eyes was gone and she seemed genuinely surprised. I didn't know if that surprise was from seeing me on my deathbed or at the fact I'd let her in.

"H . . . hello, Hattie," she said, adjusting the clutch purse that was under her arm.

"Good afternoon, Hedda," I said. "Come on in."

She eased into the room, each step filled with trepidation as six sets of eyes glared at her. "I'm sorry, I . . . I didn't really . . ." she said.

"You didn't really expect to get in?" I asked.

I tilted my head, studying her. This was the same vivacious, bulldog gossip columnist that loved tearing down Hollywood celebrities. Right now she looked like she could truly have a heart.

All my friends glared at Hedda. Cliff spoke when no one else did. "How may we help you, Miss Hopper?"

Hedda's eyes scanned the room like she was painting a mental picture. Her gaze stopped at the windowsill and she took in the trays of fruits and vegetables. Bouquets of fresh flowers lined the baseboard. I'd paid the orderly to pull together the food trays and bring in an assortment of flowers. I'd heard that flowers helped in healing and I had enough in here to heal all ten patients on this floor.

"I heard you were having one of your infamous dinner parties and I . . ." Hedda began.

Lillian balked. "And you just thought you'd crash it trying to get a story?"

"Hattie . . . I'm . . . I'm sorry," she said. "I-I didn't realize you were this sick."

Wow, I must've looked really bad.

"Well, she is," Ru quipped. "And she doesn't need you coming here in search of gossip."

I gave Ru an admonishing look. My friends had gone into protective mode.

"Yes, Miss Hopper, it is true." I sighed. "I am dying, but this evening, I am choosing to live, celebrating with my friends."

"How did you even know?" Lillian snapped. That was a good point. Up until now, my illness had been a well-guarded secret. I imagined the only way she even got in the hospital today was because the nurses knew I was having a party and assumed she was invited.

"Honestly, I just now heard some of your guests talking about your dire condition," Hedda said. A guilty look flashed across Dorothy's and Ru's faces. "I came to the hospital because I just wanted to get your reaction to your request being denied. A request I thought was just a formality and not a real soon-to-be-needed request."

"What request?" Dorothy said.

My brow furrowed as I leaned forward. "What do you mean, my request was denied?"

"The request to be buried in the Hollywood Memorial Park cemetery." She started fumbling through her notes in a small reporter's pad. She dropped the notepad and quickly picked it up as she turned to the page she was looking for. "I got word yesterday that the request was denied. The owner"—she looked down at her notes—"Mr. Jules Roth, said the Hollywood Memorial Park has, quote, 'never been a place for coloreds. And we are not gonna make an exception. No matter how popular the colored woman is.'"

I was silent as I stared at her. An ache was turning somersaults in my heart.

"I-I'm sorry," Hedda said, as she looked around the room at the shock on everyone's faces. "I-I just assumed you knew."

"Hmph," I said, closing my eyes as if I needed darkness for the words to settle in my spirit. I wasn't a crier and I wasn't gonna start now. But still, the expression on my face must've been concerning because this time it was Lillian who placed a hand on my forearm.

"You okay?" she asked.

I nodded, unable to open my eyes, because if I did, tears would come out .

I heard Cliff say, "I'm sorry, Miss Hopper. I really don't think now is a good time for an interview with Miss McDaniel."

"Right. So you probably should be leaving," Louise said. "And, Hattie, I really think we should cancel . . . I mean, reschedule the dinner party," Louise added.

I nodded. This was a dagger in my heart. Life had been so unfair to me over the years, and instead of wallowing in pity, I'd used it as fuel. Sometimes, anyway. But now, this one last denial of one of the things I wanted most, crushed me.

"I'll walk you out," Cliff said to Hedda as if he'd made a unilateral decision to cancel my party. He reached for her arm and she darted away from his grasp.

"Just a brief statement, Hattie, please? You never gave me that exclusive you promised," Hedda said.

"If she would talk to anyone, it wouldn't be you!" Lillian said. "Not after that interview you did several years ago where you distorted Hattie's words on spirituality."

My mind raced back to that horrid interview I'd given to Hedda a few years ago. I'd talked to her about my deep sense of spiritual values. Not only did Hedda miss the subtle link between faith and colored resistance to racism, but she instead chose to focus on when I said, "In my life, God comes first, work second, and men third." She'd launched into a tirade on that being the reason none of my marriages worked.

"I came to Hattie's defense when your people were assailing her over her choice of roles," Hedda replied defensively. "I've written columns about this very thing."

"You make your money preying on people's drama," Ru added.

"Just stop it," I said, my voice weary.

"Hattie, if you're going to do an interview, maybe you should give it to the colored press," Ru said.

I narrowed my eyes at her. "Why? Because they been so much nicer to me? The way I see it, it's a snake in one hand, a crocodile in the other."

I adjusted the blood pressure cuff that was wrapped around my right arm. There had been some colored press that had been fair to me. I could call Charlotta at the *Eagle*. But honestly, I didn't have the energy—and the way I was feeling, the time—to arrange that.

"Hattie, we said we were staying away from the press," Louise said. "Colored and white. Don't mean us no good."

While today had been a good day, the past few days had been filled with fatigue. And now, with Hedda's news, I felt that fatigue setting back in. But I wasn't just tired from my illness. I was tired of fighting. I was tired of the struggles, of smiling when all I wanted to do was cry.

"Hattie, please," Hedda began. "Just something you want people to know. It—"

I held up my hand to stop her. "Feel free to run the story that I'm dying and the Hollywood Cemetery denied my request to be buried there."

"Hattie!" Lillian said.

I kept talking to Hedda. "But I will ask that you let me enjoy my party today and you can run your story on your Monday show."

"Hattie, that's not a good idea," Clark said.

"Oh, she's going to run the story with or without my blessing," I said, eyeing her knowingly. "Better I give her a statement than she make something up."

My friends groaned as the light of an exclusive interview returned to Hedda's eyes.

"I will hold the story, I promise," Hedda said. "And I won't tell people where you are."

"I appreciate that," I replied, sighing, though it wouldn't be hard to guess. "I want you to report how the Hollywood Cemetery didn't think I was good enough for their dirt to be my final resting place. But like every other adversity in my life, I didn't let it define me."

I smiled as I reached for Lillian's, Louise's, and Ru's hands. "Tell the world that I left surrounded by friends, celebrating life. That's what I want my fans to focus on—how I lived, not how I died. Tell the world that I've always rather have played a maid for seven hundred dollars than been one for seven dollars. And finally"—Hedda was scribbling furiously—"tell them that no matter what people think of me, how they feel about the roles I've chosen, I rest well knowing that when I leave this earth, God will look at me and say 'Well done, my good and faithful servant.'"

A smile crept up on my face and I looked around the room at all my friends.

"If y'all don't wipe those tears," I said, releasing their hands. "This ain't that type of party." I shifted again. "Hedda, feel free to stay for the celebration. Just know that everything from this point forward is off the record."

Hedda smiled. "As you wish." She dropped her notepad into her purse. "And for once, I mean that."

Dorothy turned on the small radio that sat on the counter across from my bed. I pushed back the pain and bobbed my head as the jazz music filled the room.

"I've never seen someone have such life in the face of death," Hedda said as Clark took Dorothy's hand and began dancing while Ru and my other friends clapped and danced around them.

"Haven't you heard?" I said, smiling as I watched my friends. "They don't call me the Queen of Sugar Hill for nothing. I go all out or I don't go at all." I motioned toward the radio. "Turn up the music, please. And let the celebration of life begin!"

HEDDA HOPPER'S HOLLYWOOD

October 26, 1952

"Hello, everybody, Hedda Hopper reporting to you from Hollywood, that fabulous place where everyone wants to live but seldom does. Today, I am sad to report the passing of Academy Award–winning actress Hattie McDaniel at age fifty-nine. She slipped into a coma on Friday after hosting one of her infamous dinner parties from her hospital room. She held on until Sunday afternoon, when she quietly departed this life.

"This reporter had the opportunity to visit with the accomplished thespian prior to her death and just after the Hollywood Cemetery denied her request to be buried there. Can you believe the final resting place for movie stars won't let one of the biggest movie stars be buried there because of the color of her skin? Simply tragic.

"But Hattie McDaniel said don't weep for her. Though she was alone when she died, she'd spent the days prior surrounded by family and friends, and in fact, hosted one of her signature dinner parties just days before passing. If you've never been, you missed a treat. Hattie McDaniel knew how to throw a party.

"As she told this reporter—and this reporter only—Miss McDaniel wants you to remember that she would always rather

have played a maid for seven hundred dollars than been one for seven dollars.

"McDaniel's elaborate funeral will take place at her church, People's Independent Church of Christ, and will be followed by a procession to Rosedale Cemetery. Look for a motorcade of 125 limousines, two dozen vans to transport the flowers, and I'm sure a tremendous outpouring of love and affection as more than five thousand fans are expected.

"This reporter finds her courage inspirational. Her bravery during her long illness has given many people strength. It takes a lot to touch my heart and Hattie McDaniel did just that. So, in the words of the first Negro Academy Award winner, leave the tissues at home because there will be no crying at this celebration of life!

"You're listening to Hedda Hopper's Hollywood. *Good day, America!"*

HISTORICAL NOTE

How do you tell the story of a woman whose career spanned decades? Who was a trailblazer in a number of areas? Who experienced more triumphs and tragedies than any one person should ever have to endure? A woman who was fiercely private and an open book? You have to take some liberties.

That's exactly what I did in telling the story of Hattie McDaniel.

What I love about historical fiction is that you take the facts and merge them with your own creativity to tell a complete story. Though this is a work of fiction, know that I took care and spent thousands of hours researching Hattie McDaniel. I wanted to get into her psyche so that in those areas where I had to fill in the blanks of her life, I could truly capture her voice.

However, in order to tell a complete story of a segment of her amazing life, I had to make a few adjustments.

There are some details that were outright fiction, like the fact that Clark Gable was not actually at the 1940 Academy Awards. He had gotten early word that he'd lost for his Best Actor nomination, so he and his wife Carole Lombard decided to skip the festivities. But because I had limited time to tell the story of Clark and Hattie's friendship, I had him attend. And since he was a die-hard supporter of his dear friend, the scenes I wrote are what I imagined them to be had Clark attended. The same thing applies to their visit to the club afterward. We know that cast members went and Hattie was not allowed in, but that's the extent of the facts. So it was up to me to craft how that night played out.

I took those same liberties with Hattie's friend actress Bette Davis, who, along with Hattie, was being honored at an NAACP Unity Awards Ceremony. I wrote how Bette introduced Hattie, but in reality, she did not attend the event.

Because Hattie's life did span decades, I had to compress some time and that meant adjusting the timeline of several key events. For example, July 23–28, 1940, was the American Negro Exposition (Negro Week) at the New York World's Fair. Since Hattie was later honored by First Lady Eleanor Roosevelt, I combined those two events and moved that week to October to go with the flow of the book.

In reality, the premiere for *In This Our Life* took place in May 1942. I moved it to August. The same applied to the premiere of *Beulah*, the TV show. It actually premiered in October of 1950, but for the sake of the story, I had it premiere in 1951.

Regarding Hattie's husbands: When I began the research on her personal life I was stunned at the number of websites, articles, and publications that talked about her second husband, George Lanford. I had visited research libraries and pored over Census documents and there was no record of George. I did find a Nym Lankford and I can only assume that over the years, the erroneous information of her marrying a man named George spread. I was stunned to discover that Nym was married to another woman and again, since few people even knew of that marriage, I had to imagine how that relationship could have played out.

Other changes were made simply to enhance the flow of the story. For example, because there were so many Rubys in Hattie's life (Ruby Berkley Goodwin, Ruby Dandridge, Ruby Dee), I shortened Ruby Dandridge's name to Ru, simply so the reader could better keep track of Hattie's friends.

I also poured a lot of energy into researching colloquialisms of the era. You'll find that Hattie is most often referred to as Miss Hattie. That's because "Ms." didn't become popular until the feminist movement of the 1970s. And one of the biggest decisions was about the use of "Negro," "colored," and "Black." During the 1940s and 1950s, in Hollywood, "Negro" and "colored" were used interchangeably. On the East Coast, W.E.B. Du Bois was making a push to use "Negro." In Hollywood, some people had started using the term "Black." The country's elite hated the term. So keeping true to the historical timeframe, I stuck to "colored" and "Negro."

I loved discovering new things. Like so many other people, I thought the Brooklyn Dodgers were only a baseball team. But there was actually a football team of the same name, and they were playing the New York Giants when Japan bombed Pearl Harbor.

I took other liberties, too. Hattie loved herself some men, but rather than make all of them separate characters, I combined a few of them to create Winston.

Conversations like the one Hattie had with Thomas Griffith in chapter 36 were actually between Hattie and someone else (in that case, Dr. Stanley Bates). But rather than introduce another character, I kept the flow of the story going by attributing some dialogue to different individuals.

I also spent a lot of time poring over the Loren Miller papers at the Huntington Library in California. And while I found amazing details of the facts of the "Sugar Hill" trial, much of what you read in chapter 34 was fictionalized, based on how I perceived the plaintiffs and defendants would have acted. Loren kept meticulous notes about the trial, but in order to capture the emotions and the intensity of the defendants and plaintiffs, I had to rely on my own creativity.

One of my favorite parts was inserting the presidents and founders of the esteemed National Panhellenic Council sororities into the story. There is no record that they actually met Hattie, but as leaders and active members of the NAACP, the presidents of Alpha Kappa Alpha Sorority, Delta Sigma Theta Sorority, Zeta Phi Beta Sorority, and

Sigma Gamma Rho Sorority (of which Hattie was a member) would have attended the national convention in 1943 and could have interacted with the actor, as I describe them doing.

I am proud that the dedication and thoroughness of my research rooted Hattie's story in as much factual information as possible. One way I was able to do so was by relying on the Black press. I devoured the archives of Black newspapers like the *Los Angeles Sentinel*, *Pittsburgh Courier*, *Chicago Defender*, *California Eagle*, *New York Amsterdam News*, *Kansas City Call*, and *Houston Defender* (where I currently work, so you know I had to include it).

I'm looking forward to the discussion that this book will spark. Hattie McDaniel has been in the news again because of the efforts to "cancel" *Gone with the Wind* and the lambasting of Hattie's Mammy character. We look at Hattie's history of playing stereotypical characters through a twenty-first-century lens. I hope this book will help readers gain a better understanding of the life of a woman who was just making the best of the hand she had been dealt.

And always remember her words, which she wrote in 1939 (and are now housed at the *Gone with the Wind* Museum in Marietta, Georgia).

> I find there is something more than just working at my profession in doing the part of "Mammy." There is an opportunity to glorify Negro womanhood. Not the modern, streamlined type of Negro woman, who attends teas and concerts in furs and silks, but the type of Negro of the period that gave us Harriet Tubman, Sojourner Truth, and Charity Hill. The brave, efficient type of womanhood, which, building a race, mothered Booker T. Washington, George Carver, Robert Moton, and Mary McLeod Bethune. So many people have assured me they "could see no one else" as Mammy in *Gone with the Wind* that I am very grateful to Mr. Selznick and his staff for choosing me

> in the part. I trust I shall be able to live the part of Mammy on the screen vividly and warmly and I hope the characterization leaves as warm a spot in the hearts of those who see it as I have in mine for the "Mammys" I know in real life.

Love her character or hate her character, there is no disputing the inspiration that is Hattie McDaniel and the legacy she fought to leave.

AUTHOR'S NOTE

When I was first introduced to Hattie McDaniel in the late 1970s, like many young people of color, I was immediately turned off by her portrayal of Mammy in the "old" movie my grandmother made me watch. Yes, I thought she was extremely talented, but my modern eyes couldn't understand why she had to be such a caricature. My grandmother explained to me then that Hattie was a comedic actress, making the best of the life she'd been dealt. It was a story I knew all too well.

My grandmother cooked and cleaned for white families throughout our small Arkansas town. She reminded me of the life she'd been able to build for her family—a good life, one that allowed her to send six of her eight children to college. She'd done it by working as a maid. One day while watching *Gone with the Wind*, she told me, "I would love to be like Hattie McDaniel and get paid for playing a maid instead of actually being one."

I thought about the difference my grandmother made in our community, all the children she helped, all the lives she changed. The more she described Hattie—as an inadvertent reformer who accomplished more than many who set out to blatantly effect change—the more I felt a connection with the talented actress.

We hear all the time about militant women of the past who changed the world with their aggressive fight for a better future. But there is also a quiet faction of people like Hattie McDaniel and my grandmother, Pearley, who fought the injustices bestowed upon them in other ways. Women who worked *around* Jim Crow laws, who went along to get along while keeping their eyes on a bigger prize. Women who make the best of the life God had given them and used their positions to make quiet change.

I remained fascinated by Hattie's story, which began long before that glamourous night at the Ambassador Hotel, where, as the only Black woman in the room, she stood to accept an Academy Award. As I moved into my career as a journalist and writer (who acted on the side), I shelved my research of Hattie, but she was never far removed from my heart.

Over the past few years, I found myself being drawn to her once again. In fact, she started coming to me at night, telling me she wanted me to tell her story (my mother says I need to stop telling people that before they think I'm crazy), but so goes the life of a writer.

When Hattie's voice became too loud to silence, I once again dove into her story. I became immersed in the life of Hattie McDaniel. While the internet was an invaluable tool in my research, I found that so much of her story had been distorted over the years. So I traveled across the country, visiting research libraries and her Sugar Hill home and the surrounding neighborhood. I did extensive research on Hattie's life, from her humble beginnings to her successful blues career to her relocation to Los Angeles to her history-making fight against restrictive covenants. I spent two years digging through her personal and professional story, continuously pulling back layers to uncover things I didn't know.

Throughout this process, I felt an undeniable connection to Hattie because of her perseverance in spite of criticism from Blacks, who hated her "demeaning" Mammy character. In spite of hatred from whites, who felt Mammy was too sassy. In spite of being pigeonholed into unaccredited maid, servant, and slave roles in more than seventy films. In spite of four failed marriages and never feeling seen. In spite of everything, she forged ahead. This endeared her to me and made me determined to tell her story.

Though I've written many contemporary books, I feel like a debut author and in a sense, I guess I am as I have ventured into the uncharted territory of historical fiction. I learned long ago not to get into the name game when it comes to thanking people, but there are a few people that I simply cannot go without acknowledging.

Of course my husband, Jeffrey Caradine, who for the past two years has had to live with Hattie in our lives. I am forever grateful for the countless discussions, the captivated audience of one as I read passages, and the never-ending encouragement and support.

My agent, Liza Dawson, who pushed me to step out of my comfort zone and blend my journalism and research skills with my fiction writing to create this amazing book. Thank you for seeing what I couldn't.

My editor, Asanté Simons, who passionately believed in this book from the very beginning. Thank you for challenging me and helping me see that yes, some things could be cut out.

There are no words to describe my appreciation of Victoria Christopher Murray and Marie Benedict. There would be no *Queen of Sugar Hill* without you. Thank you both tremendously for helping me navigate this historical fiction journey and for the constant "you can do better" kicks in the behind. And to my writing crew—Victoria, Tiffany Warren, Renee Flagler, and Pat Tucker—thanks for letting me vent, for helping me work through scenes, and just for the never-ending encouragement and feedback.

I have many supportive family members and friends (especially my sister, Tanisha Tate) as well as librarians, booksellers, and book clubs anxiously awaiting this book, so allow me to extend my complete gratitude for your continued support of my career.

And finally, thank you to the readers I'm sharing my passion project with. I hope you'll love Hattie's story as much as I loved writing it. I feel a special connection to this wonderful woman. In fact, one of my best friends commented that she felt Hattie had taken her place because of how much I talked about Hattie like we were old friends. I'd like to think that had we lived in an era together, we would have been.

I believe she would be pleased with my bringing her story to life. I hope you're pleased too.